Lever Templar

A Castellum One Novel

Matt Gianni

LEVER TEMPLAR

A CASTELLUM ONE NOVEL

MATT GIANNI

First Print Edition 2019 Dark Ink Press

www.darkink-press.com

ISBN-13 978-0-9997016-7-6
ISBN 0-9997016-7-3
Cover design by Melissa Volker

Printed in the United States of America

For my parents

"What is history but a fable agreed upon?"

—Napoleon Bonaparte

CHARACTERS, 14ᵗʰ CENTURY – IN ORDER OF APPEARANCE

(Underline denotes historical figure)

Brimley Hastings: English Templar sergeant.

Malcolm of Basingstoke: English Templar knight.

Angus: Scottish Templar squire.

William of Egendon: English Templar knight.

Pietro Bucci: Genoese shipping merchant. Captain of the *Filomena*.

William of Ockham: English Franciscan friar.

Marco Polo: Venetian merchant traveler and author.

Ghazi: Disfigured mamluk warrior. Malcolm's nemesis from Acre.

Henry II de Lusignan: King of Jerusalem and Cyprus (in exile).

Amalric de Lusignan: Prince of Tyre (in exile). Regent of Cyprus.

Francesco Orsini: Cardinal from Rome. Circuitor Consistory leader.

Muhammad III: Sultan of Granada.

Ferdinand IV: King of Castile.

Edward I: King of England.

Boniface VIII: 193rd pope, formerly Benedetto Caetani.

Clement V: 195th pope, formerly Raymond Bertrand de Got.

Philip IV: King of France.

Shayla Kostas: Greek Cypriot apprentice tanner.

Theron Kostas: Greek Cypriot tanner. Templar tack master.

Guillaume de Nogaret: Keeper of the Seal of King Philip IV.

Jacques de Molay: French Templar knight and Grand Master.

Cibalik Darcan: Ambassador to Pope Clement V from Armenia.

CHARACTERS, 14th CENTURY – IN ORDER OF APPEARANCE (CONTINUED)

(<u>Underline</u> denotes historical figure)

<u>Benedict XI</u>: 194th pope, formerly Nicola Boccasini.

<u>Ayme d'Oselier</u>: French Templar knight and Marshal of Cyprus.

<u>Foulques de Villaret</u>: French Hospitaller knight and Grand Master.

<u>Jean de Villa</u>: French Templar sergeant and Draper of Cyprus.

Farah Zayn: Syrian apprentice tanner.

Dabir Zayn: Syrian tanner.

Enzo Fausto: Pisan shipping merchant. Captain of the *Rosabella.*

<u>Landolfo Brancaccio</u>: Cardinal from Naples.

<u>Bartholomew of Gordo</u>: French Templar knight.

<u>Hayton of Corycus</u>: Armenian Cilician monk. Lord of Corycus.

<u>Edward II</u>: King of England.

<u>Hugues de Pairaud</u>: French Templar knight. Visitor of the Temple.

<u>Balian of Ibelin</u>: Prince of Galilee (in exile) and Cypriot nobleman.

<u>An-Nasir Muhammad</u>: Sultan of Egypt and Syria.

<u>Leonardo Patrasso</u>: Cardinal from Alatri.

Rifat Kanaan: Syrian fishmonger and former farmer.

Amira Kanaan: Wife of Rifat.

Yaghoob: Infant son of Rifat and Amira Kannan.

Walid: Syrian fishmonger.

<u>Gentile Portino da Montefiore</u>: Cardinal from Fermo.

Abdullah al-Rasheed: Syrian province Minister of Agriculture.

Malcolm: Infant son of Shayla and Brimley Hastings.

CHARACTERS, 14th CENTURY – IN ORDER OF APPEARANCE (CONTINUED)

(<u>Underline</u> denotes historical figure)

<u>Giovanni da Morrovalle</u>: Cardinal from Morrovalle.

Carlo Petri: Senior Anconian chancery scribe stationed at Acre.

<u>Tankiz an-Nasiri</u>: Viceroy of Sultan an-Nasir Muhammad.

<u>Nicholas III</u>: 188th pope, formerly Giovanni Gaetano Orsini.

<u>Mahmud Ghazan</u>: 7th ruler of the Mongol Ilkhanate.

<u>Oljaitu Khan</u>: 8th ruler of the Mongol Ilkhanate.

<u>Dante Alighieri</u>: Florentine poet, statesman, and political theorist.

CHARACTERS, PRESENT DAY – IN ORDER OF APPEARANCE

Rick Lambert: American agent with Iraqi Ministry of Interior (MOI).

Samir Moozarmi: Iraqi agent with Iraqi MOI.

Zephyros Topolis: Greek priest of the Christian Church of Kanisah.

Danny Dicarpio: Professor of American history.

James Dougherty: Bureau of Intelligence and Research (INR) head.

Ali Kassab: Iraqi chief of the Iraqi MOI Investigations Unit (IU).

Giuseppe Plenducci: Italian priest and Vatican researcher.

Dominic Batista: Spanish cardinal. Vatican Secret Archives prefect.

Mohammed Moozarmi: Iraqi physician and congressman.

Yashira Moozarmi: Iraqi physician.

Maria Anna Belloci: Italian Gendarmerie Corps lieutenant.

Sean and Patrick Duffy: Irish-American twins. US Army sergeants.

Ahmed Makarem: Iranian commander of the Faregh Alethesalan.

Jahangir Nasser Rudahmi: Iranian founder of the Faregh Alethesalan.

Gerald Burggraf: Iran Desk, Central Intelligence Agency (CIA).

Omar Volkan: Turk fisherman and deep-cover CIA transporter.

Farouk: Iranian commander of the Faregh Alethesalan.

Abu: Syrian teen at the Arwad fuel dock.

Mahmood: Syrian harbormaster and customs officer on Arwad.

Raja Kichlu: Sunni imam and curator of the Roza Bal shrine.

PART ONE

Militia Dei

Shipley Preceptory – 1307

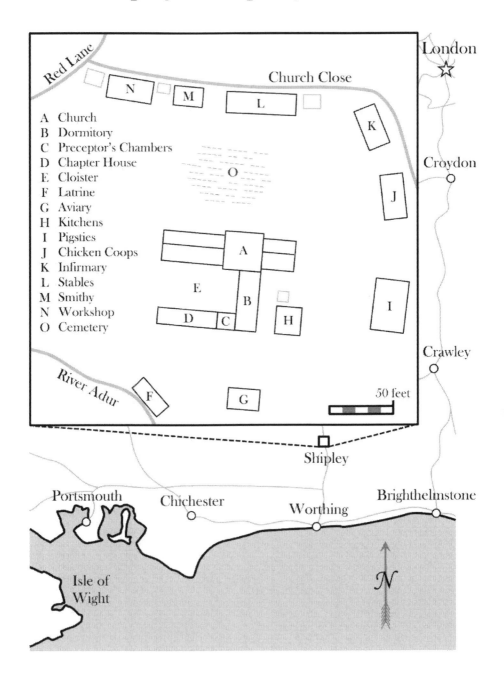

A Church
B Dormitory
C Preceptor's Chambers
D Chapter House
E Cloister
F Latrine
G Aviary
H Kitchens
I Pigsties
J Chicken Coops
K Infirmary
L Stables
M Smithy
N Workshop
O Cemetery

Red Lane

Church Close

London

Croydon

Crawley

River Adur

50 feet

Shipley

Portsmouth   Chichester   Worthing   Brighthelmstone

Isle of
Wight

N

East Kanisah – Present Day

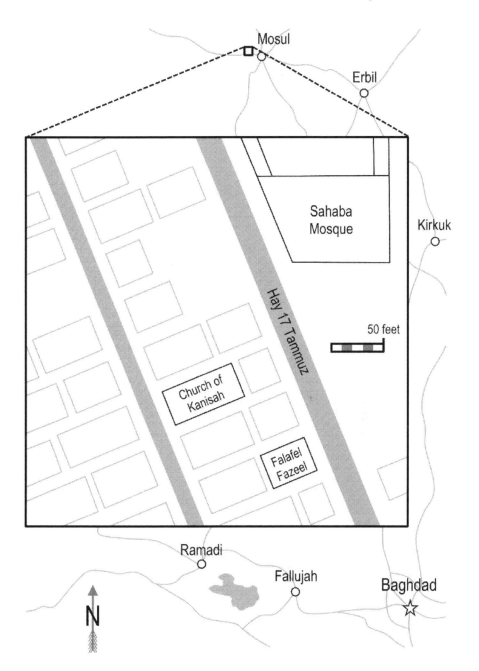

CHAPTER 1

AUGUST 14, 1307

SHIPLEY, ENGLAND

Of the oaths sworn to the order, Brim Hastings knew it was his obedience being tested. His poverty had always been transparent given the enormous communal resources of the order, and his chastity had yet to be seen as a sacrifice, given his mostly cloistered seventeen years of life. But obedience? This he found difficult. Nevertheless, he nervously followed his mentor, Malcolm of Basingstoke, through the narthex of Shipley Church. Angus, the knight's squat and brutish squire, led the way.

The three crept along the darkened north aisle. Brim flinched upon hearing a gasp ahead. Malcolm calmly guided Angus toward the pews to the right with his right hand on the squire's left shoulder. The knight then addressed the figure in front of them. "Continue."

The wide-eyed novice monk with the tonsured head had been relighting candles placed in alcoves along the wall in preparation for the midnight liturgical service of matins. Brim knew this monotonous task well, having used a similar brass candlelighter himself on many nights after being admitted to the London preceptory eight years earlier.

Frustration welled up through the tension as Brim, once again, had to follow orders without having full knowledge of events. The accumulating questions in his mind had been gnawing at him since their hurried ride from London the day before. He surmised something was to be stolen from Shipley. Otherwise, Malcolm would have announced his arrival to Preceptor William of Egendon, who'd likely appreciate hearing of Cyprus from the Preceptor of Kolossi.

What troubled him most, however, was Angus the Scot acting with such drive, as though he knew of their purpose. Why did Malcolm

1

continue to place such trust in a man from a country led by an excommunicate? Despite his years of service with Malcolm on Cyprus, Angus, and others of Scottish descent, should have been expelled from the order after the pope excommunicated Robert the Bruce from the one true faith. Otherwise, how could those in the Order of the Temple of Solomon continue as the elite of Christendom?

Brim felt relief from the summer night's heat as the trio descended the stone steps curving under the north transept. Their flickering shadows, thrown by the large beeswax candle Angus had grabbed from the nave above, projected the illusion of movement onto darkened walls. Dirt he felt underfoot replaced the cleanliness of the nave above.

The smell of mildew intensified as they reached the damp lower level. They turned one last corner and approached an iron door. Angus plunged the candle onto the tine of a wall-mounted candleholder. The knight and the Scot removed their brown woolen riding cloaks tucked into the backs of their belts.

Brim followed their lead, his chest tightening. Donning the cloaks concealed their uniformed mantles—Malcolm's being white, the other two black, and all three displaying the distinctive symbol of their order: the *croix pattée rouge*, or red-footed cross.

Angus angled his head, as if to listen, while inching toward the door. Brim saw the outward-opening door was ajar and heard the sound distracting the middle-aged squire—a repeating pattern of shuffling feet followed by a dull thud. Angus revealed a smile of darkened teeth, held up his right hand, then paused for a moment before drawing his sword. It was a short sword, a favored weapon of the Highland clans.

Trust in Sir Malcolm, Brim told himself, though the words did little to stop his hands from shaking.

After the next thud, the squire pulled the door open just wide enough for his girth and led with his blade. "Hold where you stand."

"What . . . ?" a voice called out.

The clipped question went unanswered as Malcolm and Brim entered the small foyer, Malcolm with a palm on the pommel of his broadsword and Brim with his Roman gladius drawn. The guard flattened himself against the left wall. Against the right wall ten feet away lay an upturned table with a dagger stuck in the center of a cluster of indentations. Two large candles in shielded brass carriers, likely meant for the upturned tabletop, burned on the floor nearby.

Malcolm held out a length of twine he'd pulled from his cloak pocket. "Secure him."

Angus scowled and turned his blade toward the room's only chair. The guard sat.

Brim sheathed his sword, tried to slow his breathing, and tied the guard's wrists to the chair back's lower rail.

The bound man seemed fixated on Malcolm, as many often were. "Who are you?"

The elder knight stood a head taller than the others. His cropped hair, beard, and mustache were all nearly white, but it was his piercing blue eyes that made his look mesmerizing. The motions of others alternated between pauses and jolts, but Malcolm seemed to move with effortless grace, pulling the iron door closed, ignoring the guard's repeated questions, and turning to Brim.

"Retrieve the vault key."

Brim noticed a thin leather strap around the nape of the guard's neck. Pulling it up produced a large key under the guard's chin. Malcolm gestured to Angus to watch the guard and for Brim to join him at the end of the twenty-foot-long foyer, at a vault door made of heavy iron bars.

He knew the chests of coinage would be gone. His work in the London scriptorium keeping the order's ledgers included logging the recent transfer of funds from all English preceptories. But surely Malcolm, a knight of Latin Rule who'd forsaken worldly wealth, was not interested in silver pennies and gold bezants. He could see through the bars before using the key to open the door—the contents of the vault had indeed been depleted. Only a small collection of uniforms, chain mail, and broadswords remained.

Malcolm entered, stood in the middle of the ten-foot-square vault, gestured toward the nearest broadsword, and looked down. "Breach the stone here."

3

The knight backed two steps away. Brim grabbed the sword from the rack and positioned the tip on the one-foot-square center floor tile. After sheepishly glancing once more at his mentor and receiving a nod, he grasped the hilt with both hands and began slamming the tip of the heavy blade into stone. Pieces of tile cracked apart and fell away out of view. He assumed the stone floor had been installed over solid ground. There now appeared to be a cavity beneath. He continued chipping away at the stone tile from the center outward.

"Tend to your charge!"

Brim jumped, nearly dropping the broadsword. Malcolm pointed at Angus. Outside the bars, the thickset Scot had crept closer, trying to gain a better view of activity inside the vault, neglecting his watch over the bound guard.

Angus wore a disgruntled expression but resumed his position near the foyer's entrance. Brim felt a small measure of satisfaction upon realizing the Scot was in a similar state of ignorance as to their mission.

The center tile soon disappeared. Malcolm took the broadsword. "Enough. Retrieve the contents."

On his knees, he felt something smooth two feet below, positioned in the hole diagonally. He had trouble getting a grip on whatever it was.

"By the straps," said his mentor.

Finally, Brim curled fingers under leather strands and pulled out a dark leather satchel. At just under a foot square and about four inches thick, it appeared to be covered with dried grease or animal fat. He'd seen this kind of satchel before during his scriptorium duty—it was one way parchments were prepared for long-term storage.

Brim drew a startled breath after hearing a sharp crack from the foyer. Both he and Malcolm swiveled their heads.

The guard had apparently wiggled out of the twine threads binding his wrists to the chair. His bolting for the door had caused the chair to fall backward onto the stone floor, alerting Angus, who'd again been distracted by activity in the vault. The guard pushed on the heavy door.

Brim held back a scream as Angus plunged his Highland blade deep into the guard's back.

"No!" Malcolm rushed from the vault. "None of our brothers were to be harmed."

Sinking to the floor and rolling onto his side to stare up at the knight, the guard's last word conveyed his astonishment. "Brothers?"

CHAPTER 2
JULY 20, 12:08 P.M. GULF STANDARD TIME (GST)
NORTHERN MOSUL, IRAQ

Rick Lambert had gotten used to his partner rolling his eyes. He knew Samir Moozarmi couldn't understand how he wasn't sick and tired of falafel by now. He looked forward to the fried chickpea wraps at about this time of day, every day. No matter where in Iraq their job took them, a falafel vendor was always just around the corner.

During the last two months, the pair of agents from Iraq's Ministry of Interior Investigations Unit was assigned the case of the Christian priest abductions. This morning, they'd responded to a call from Father Zephyros Topolis of the Christian Church of Kanisah, in the dusty northwestern Mosul suburb of the same name. Topolis claimed men had scoped out the small warehouse he'd turned into a chapel, an insignificant structure compared with the Sahaba Mosque two blocks north and Mosul's Grand Mosque just across the Tigris to the east.

Lambert had gotten to know Topolis during his time in Mosul. The priest had his mobile phone number. This morning had been the first time he'd used it. The agents spent the morning walking the neighborhood, talking to locals. It looked like a false alarm. He couldn't blame Topolis for being jumpy; news of the recent abductions had become known throughout Iraq's small, but close-knit, Christian community.

Despite the pounding in his head, Lambert finally felt hungry, probably because he'd skipped breakfast. He'd accepted hangovers as his price for avoiding sleepless nights being haunted by memories of Fallujah and its aftermath.

A falafel vendor opened a block east on Hay 17 Tammuz, Kanisah's main thoroughfare named for the fasting holiday. Lambert ordered and the food soon arrived.

"Only two today?" Samir asked in Arabic.

"Working out later, don't want to feel bloated," Lambert answered, also fluent in Arabic since his college days.

His partner shook his head, unwrapped three dried chicken kebabs, and joined him at the small table on the vendor's patio. It was Samir's third month serving with him, having replaced his former partner, who'd become their unit chief.

He started on his second wrap, then heard muffled gunfire around the corner. With the ebb and flow of Islamic State activity, it was a common sound in the rougher sections of Mosul.

Samir pushed his chair back and quickly stood, apparently assuming they'd investigate.

"How about we finish lunch?"

Samir looked appalled. "We should check that out."

Lambert turned his head slightly. "Not our mission."

The diminutive Iraqi turned in the direction of the blasts, rubbed a palm across his close-cropped scalp, then turned back. "I thought justice was our mission."

Now it was Lambert's turn to roll his eyes. He'd served with others so motivated. In fact, Samir reminded him of himself after his 1999 commission in the US Army. It now seemed a lifetime ago. "Come on, Mooz, we can't save them all."

"Could be at the church," Samir prompted.

Good point, Lambert thought.

Louder gunfire erupted from the same area, this time fully automatic.

"Okay, let's go."

The pair abandoned their food and bolted around the corner. From two blocks south, Lambert saw a black van parked in front of the church. Two figures in black tactical gear stood between the van and the church entrance aiming what looked like Heckler & Koch HK33 machine guns. His pulse surged as he gestured for Samir to cross over and approach from the left side of the street, opposite the van. With their ministry-

7

issued Beretta 96A1 pistols drawn, the few frightened civilians running in their direction gave a wide berth.

Lambert felt his legs weaken as he crouched behind an old Toyota facing the church twenty yards south. He engaged the gunman nearest him. "Drop the rifle!" he shouted in Arabic.

The surprised figure swung the H&K around and let loose a barrage of 5.56mm, walking the bullet impacts down the street and onto the car.

A rivulet of sweat ran down his back as thoughts of his initial training at Washington State's Fort Lewis came rushing back—specifically the drills emphasizing the difference between concealment and cover. From his squat behind the right rear fender, he took two small steps left to position the engine block between him and the unrelenting stream of lead. At the left rear fender, he'd be able to slip back behind the car if the shooter swung around to the other side of the van for a clear shot down the street.

His jaw tensed as the shattered glass from the Toyota's rear window rained down on and around him. A sudden silence gave way to two sounds near the van, similar in volume but different in timbre. The first was the hollow, high-pitched sound of the empty H&K magazine hitting the street. The second was a deeper-pitched thud.

The shooter dropped his replacement magazine!

Lambert took a deep breath, swung around the left rear fender, and set his sights on the shooter as the man picked up the loaded magazine. His first shot missed, hitting the van just above the rear bumper. His second shot impacted the shooter on his right rib cage, spinning him clockwise. The impact only focused the shooter's attention onto his new location.

Body armor!

The gunman's head jerked right as sounds of pistol fire peppered the van's driver's side window. Samir had engaged the other shooter.

The second figure already had the van started and shouted something unintelligible, prompting the first to dart around and dive into the open sliding door on the right. The van raced north as both agents emptied their magazines in an attempt to flatten the rear tires—tires that seemed to be the run flat type used on armored cars. They replaced magazines just as the van turned a corner.

First-class weapons and armored vans—who the hell are these guys?

The double doors to the church burst open. A young man, also in paramilitary garb, pushed Father Topolis out with a pistol to his head. His face next to that of the elderly Topolis emphasized just how young he was. The young gunman looked intense and moved in quick, jerking movements like a cornered animal. The priest's blood-splattered face displayed a badly broken nose.

Lambert felt rage replace fear. He nevertheless waved his left hand downward in a calming gesture while struggling to appear calm himself. "Take it easy . . . put the gun down and we can talk," he said in Arabic.

"You get back! I kill him!" the gunman said, also in Arabic, and obviously not his native language. "You give car! Or—"

With an apparently unexpected surge of energy, Topolis bent forward, escaping the young man's grip and thrusting his head out of the line of fire before the gunman reactively pulled the trigger. The priest then dropped to his knees.

Both agents, sights already locked on the gunman, returned fire. Samir put his shot at chest center while Lambert, assuming this gunman was armored like the other, put his round in the man's mouth, blowing out the back of his head. The gunman fell backward, and reflex action pulled his semiautomatic's trigger a second time.

Topolis stood. A red spot appeared on the side of his robe. A look of horror appeared on his face. He clutched his stomach, then stumbled back inside the church.

"Father, wait . . ."

"Lambert! Down the street!" Samir pointed north.

A man with a large mark on his left cheek sat on a motorcycle. He held a metal box in his left hand and a mobile phone to his ear with his right. When he saw he was noticed, he dropped the phone into his shirt pocket and pressed buttons on the box.

Two explosions sounded from inside the church. A third tore the body of the dead gunman apart and soaked the sidewalk in blood.

Holy mother of Jesus, Lambert said to himself.

Stunned and temporarily deafened, Lambert watched the man spin the bike around and speed around the same corner as the van.

The two agents turned and approached the entrance to the church from opposite sides of the open double doors. Except for the ringing in Lambert's ears, all was quiet. They spun into the doorway and scanned the nave for more gunmen. He noticed the priest's continued struggle through the smoke toward the altar. His eyes adjusted to the darkness, and he saw three figures in monk's cloaks slumped over the backs of pews to the left. Sprawled out in the center aisle near the entrance lay the remains of two figures, blown apart like the gunman outside, lying in a pool of blood. The smell of burning flesh filled the church. He fought back the urge to vomit.

Lambert moved along the right wall, Samir the left. They cleared spaces between pews on their way forward. By the time they reached the front pew and determined the entire nave was clear, Topolis was behind the altar.

He joined the priest. "Mooz, call an ambulance." Assuming Topolis was taking refuge out of fear, he tried to comfort the priest. "Father, they're gone. An ambulance is on the way. Stay still."

Topolis spoke in a short exhalation. "Help me . . ."

Lambert was about to repeat that help was on the way, but then noticed the priest punching the corner of the wooden altar.

The wood at the corner splintered, and Topolis jabbed his hand into the gap. The priest pulled out an object no larger than a cigarette lighter, wrapped in a rag tied in knots at both ends, and thrust it into his hands. "Richard . . . don't let them find it . . . protect Cyprus . . ." After those words, Topolis collapsed.

Lambert checked for a pulse. He found none, and his chin quivered. With the amount of blood loss, he knew nothing could be done and felt the air crushed from his lungs.

Why didn't the priest just stay still?

The sound of sirens began converging on the church.

Lambert knew he had to swallow the pain and act. He untied the rag, revealing a piece of marble. But not just marble. It was a domino. Three-dot and five-dot squares on one side, one-dot and four-dot squares on the other. Single words were etched into all four edges. Each in capital letters. And each in Latin. He shook his head; how could he be of Italian heritage and even speak Italian, yet have such a hard time with its parent language? It had been a curse during his college days when studying history, for which he received constant but good-humored ridicule from his classmates. He shook his head again and pocketed the stone. As important as it may be, playing with dominoes would have to wait.

The local police entered the church. He and Samir held up their Ministry of Interior IDs. For the next twenty minutes, explanations of events were given and recorded. No forms of identification were found on the remains of the gunmen in black or the armed monks. A closer inspection of the gunmen's remains revealed nylon web gear, secured by miniature padlocks in the back of each. Built into each harness was evidence of directional explosives, in front and in back, designed to kill the wearers and anyone positioned directly ahead or behind. Lambert assumed all charges had been detonated remotely by the blackened-cheek man on the motorcycle. He glanced at the remains of the gunmen in the center aisle and winced, knowing the horrible scene would remain in his memory.

Lambert exchanged contact information with the Mosul precinct officer in charge and agreed to meet again if any other information was desired. He didn't report on the priest's last words or the domino. Since they had possible bearing on the more general case of Christian priest abductions, he wanted more time to work on any potential connections.

The two agents walked back to their unmarked Hyundai SUV, one of many used by the MOI's Investigations Unit. Lambert solemnly shared the priest's last words and the domino with his partner.

Samir rubbed his chin stubble. "What did he mean by that?"

"Not sure. Did you notice the rifles they had? HK33s. Very pricey. And the bullet-proof van?"

Samir nodded. "Yeah, I put four rounds in the driver's side window. None penetrated."

Lambert assumed the four impact points had been in a precise group. A few times during the three months they'd been partners, he joined

Samir at the range. During all his years in the military and intelligence communities, he'd never seen a better pistol marksman.

"So who do you think they were?" Samir asked.

"Don't know, but I think the driver was yelling in Farsi."

"I couldn't hear from across the street." Samir looked back at the domino. "So you don't know the words on these edges?"

Lambert sighed. "No, but I know just who to call."

5:25 P.M. GST
NORTHEASTERN MOSUL

The accusations from southwest Tehran were thrown across the encrypted telephone line in guttural Farsi. "You allow them death too soon."

"Apologies, Excellency," was the reply from Iraq. "Those at the Church of Kanisah were ready for us."

"Bested by Christian monks?"

"They had outside help . . ."

"Uncover more about this church, and the 'outside help' you refer to. It may lead to what we seek—and allow you to redeem yourself."

"Yes, Excellency."

CHAPTER 3

AUGUST 15, 1307

OFF THE COAST OF PORTSMOUTH, ENGLAND

Their lives had been ruled by two loyalties: a vow to their Lord Jesus Christ and a pledge to their brotherhood. The first was eternal. The second now seemed betrayed.

Brim Hastings leaned back against the sterncastle's starboard railing, watching activity aboard ship. Malcolm was still talking to Pietro Bucci, the *Filomena's* short but energetic captain. Two from the crew of twenty-four young Genoese leaned on the rudder stock to hold their westerly heading. In two hours, the single-mast cog would turn south to sail abeam the northwest corner of France. A few others adjusted the halyard, buntlines, and backstays at points along the ship's seventy-foot length and twenty-five-foot beam. The remaining crew moved piles of provisions below, items flung onto the vessel's main deck after he and Malcolm boarded. It seemed their arrival hastened the *Filomena's* departure.

Ahead to the west, the sun neared the waterline. To the east, the Isle of Wight drifted below the horizon. The overcast sky threatened the approach of a summer storm but, for now, provided a welcome change from the heat just hours before.

He breathed in the salty air, listened to the creaking of the hull's oak timbers, and thought of all he'd been through that day. Before they'd departed Shipley preceptory grounds, he and Malcolm acquired fresh mounts from the stable's collective in exchange for the fatigued palfreys taken from London. They walked them ten miles until dawn, then rode to cover the remaining thirty miles, arriving at the Portsmouth docks by early evening. Very little discussion had taken place along the way,

Malcolm making it clear explanations would be forthcoming only after getting under way.

With trepidation about a future unknown to him, Brim instead thought of things he may be leaving behind. Two were paramount: planning improvements at farms owned by the order in southern England with help from Franciscan friar Wil Ockham, and completing the French-to-Latin translation of the fascinating new travelogue from Venetian merchant Marco Polo.

"Brimley!"

Brim shot up from his slouched position and opened his eyes. From the hardened expression on his mentor's face, it wasn't the first time he'd been calling for him. "Yes . . . yes sir."

"My calls for you shall not fall on deaf ears."

"Apologies, sir." Brim noticed the deck was clear of the haphazardly placed provisions.

Malcolm smoothed his furrowed brow, relaxed his stance, and turned his gaze to the coastline. After a long pause, he whispered. "I shall never see England again."

Brim also faced the shore and felt a sudden chill. Had he also just left England forever? He rubbed the wisps of chin hair that had appeared in recent months, waiting for an explanation that never came.

His eyes still focused on the coast, Malcolm straightened and clasped his hands behind his back. "Brimley, you have shown your dedication to the order, and to me. Your trust these last two days has reaffirmed my faith in the principles of our order." The knight turned to face him. "For this, you have my gratitude."

Brim felt bewildered but remained silent. The order's hierarchy and protocol had always precluded such familiarity. What had changed?

Malcolm continued. "Our families have served the order faithfully, and we are both the last of our bloodlines."

"Yes sir." Brim had been proud of their families' connection and service for as long as he could remember. His uncle had been Malcolm's sergeant years before, as well as sergeant for Malcolm's uncle. Such was the case for four generations. In each family, the second son was pledged to the Order of the Temple of Solomon. From one family came knights, from the other their sergeants. Both were honored to serve. And the order honored their tradition.

"For this reason I have kept you with me."

The comment caught Brim completely off guard. His vow to the order was perpetual, as was his place by Malcolm's side. "What of Angus, sir?"

Malcolm shook his head. "Angus was discontent. As seen at Shipley, he lacks the temperament required for monastic life. As we speak, he rides north with fifty silver groats, returning to his clan in the Highlands."

"And what will you have of me?"

"In the days to come, you must choose: disembark at Bordeaux with fifty gold bezants to begin your new life or continue with me to Cyprus."

Brim recoiled. "Sir, you must know I have no desire to leave the order."

"The order shall soon be thrown into chaos, an upheaval our brotherhood will not likely survive."

Brim stiffened. "How can that be?"

"Choose Cyprus, and I will have you study the marshal's ledgers from Paris. All will then be made clear. But choose with care." Malcolm turned and took the stairs to the main deck, leaving Brim alone again on the sterncastle.

Despite years preparing for the rigors of monastic life, Brim had found the transition shocking when accepted at the age of nine, following the death of his mother. Through letters from Cyprus to his overseers in London, Malcolm ensured any time not working or training was spent in prayer and study. That was Latin Rule—a devotion to poverty, chastity, and obedience. Within a few years, Brim had become fluent in Latin, Greek, and Arabic, as well as the English and French spoken within preceptories.

He'd particularly yearned for training with the sword. When younger, he dreamt of defending Christendom in his black mantle beside Malcolm in his white, their embroidered red crosses facing down their enemies. Malcolm corrected such misguided thoughts early by having the monks teach him that war was a hell on earth, devoid of true glory.

Choose Cyprus? That had been his goal as long as he could remember.

A six-month visit to Cyprus had been granted after his promotion to sergeant three years before, a reward for five years of service to the order as a novice monk. Since his return to London, he'd wanted nothing more than to be sent back to serve his mentor.

All the new questions in his mind were agonizing. The brotherhood was twenty thousand strong and growing. The Grand Master and seneschals from Cyprus had traveled to France, planning a return to the Holy Land. How could the order perish? To learn more, he was being asked to follow a man he had no intention of ever leaving.

So much about the knight was locked away by his stoicism. While discussions of individual histories were forbidden, Brim had been able to learn a great deal about his mentor's past during his work in the London scriptorium. The chronicles of the order contained much about the loss of the Holy Land, one of the most poignant being Malcolm's detailed account of the Fall of Acre.

Brim had read it several times. The nightmares that followed filled in details.

On that day sixteen years earlier, his uncle and Malcolm had defended the northernmost tower. To the west was the Mediterranean, to the southeast were double-walled parapets linking eleven other towers. The southernmost tower was also at the shoreline, the entire line of battlements protecting the small triangular city from land attacks. For weeks, Sultan Al-Ashraf Khalil's artillery was unrelenting. Heavy catapults and trebuchets pounded the crenellated walls. More mobile mangonels lobbed rotting animal carcasses and shards of obsidian into the city, the rancid flesh spreading disease, the sharp stones raining down like daggers. When the main assault finally began, the defensive ditch in front of the outer wall filled with the charging bodies of Khalil's youngest slave soldiers, each loaded with baskets of dirt to form bridges of earth, flesh, and bone. Thousands of infantry followed, with ladders and grappling hooks, supported by hundreds of archers.

In front of the main gate, dozens of the strongest mamluks brought in a huge shielded battering ram from the northeast. Upon reaching the gate, arrows, spears, boulders, and scalding oil rained down from the ramparts. The most maniacal soldier at the front of the ram periodically unshielded himself while encouraging his men forward. This earned him screams of "Ghazi! Ghazi!" from the hundreds still behind the ditch and struggling forward, *ghazi* being Arabic for warrior. Malcolm gallantly fought the ladders off the wall to the north but was distracted by the scene below. Every time he heard "Ghazi! Ghazi!" and glanced down, the courageous mamluk energized his fellow combatants with his fearlessness. At last, one of the defenders above timed a cauldron of boiling tar just right. Although he couldn't hear him, Malcolm saw the huge soldier below scream in agony, then dig his face into the ground, trying to scrape off the black searing pitch.

The dead from the main assault's first hour piled at the foot of the wall, lessening the height needed to be scaled by succeeding waves. One of the many heavy bolts from powerful mamluk crossbows penetrated Brim's uncle's chain mail, and he fell upon the hundreds of dead below.

Khalil's forces began rolling over the crenellated walls. The dirt-covered floor of the parapets became coated with a dark mud produced from Christian and Muslim blood. Malcolm, fighting off three of the first swordsmen over the wall, was backed into an elevator chute used for bringing supplies to the north tower by rope and pulley. The platform was roped off only ten feet below, but the impact rendered him unconscious. His next sight, much later, was that of several mamluks staring down at him with hateful eyes. By that time, Acre had fallen.

Malcolm was pulled from the elevator chute and had his hands bound behind him, despite a broken left arm resulting from his fall. Through his pain, he noticed two figures atop the center tower above the main gate. The first was the kneeling Deacon of Acre, who must have been pleading for the lives of his congregation. The second was the fearless mamluk from the battering ram. After the deacon was decapitated and his body kicked off the tower's edge, the disfigured soldier held the holy man's head up for Khalil's entire army to see. The eruption of "Ghazi! Ghazi!" was louder than any sounds from the battle. All seemed to understand—whatever the warrior's name was before, it was now Ghazi.

Malcolm and the few other surviving knights were forced from their towers and herded out the main gate. Ghazi soon appeared. Each knight was led past. Eyes, surrounded by blackened flesh unnaturally contoured by fresh burns, stared at them.

After their final victory, several of Khalil's soldiers began marching the surviving knights to Cairo. Two days into the journey, the men of the detachment continued to celebrate their victory. One of the Muslim guards noticed Malcolm's broken left arm, decided he was in no state to attempt escape, and chained only his right wrist to a tree. This allowed the knight to break out of his shackle by dislocating his right thumb.

Malcolm was unable to free his brethren, who had to convince him to slip away during the night. He reached the coast and negotiated passage to Cyprus on a merchant vessel.

This was the man who filled Brim with awe. This was the man he would faithfully follow. He made his choice—he would stay beside this man for as long as they both lived, their futures entwined.

AUGUST 16, 1307
LONDON, ENGLAND

If the order's relay stables had been any further apart, the horses the courier used would've died from exhaustion or dehydration. Despite the stifling summer heat, he'd cantered the forty miles from Shipley to the London preceptory in less than three hours, faster than he'd ever done before. Being stationed at the Shipley preceptory, he'd ridden the route several times at a more leisurely trot. But the last had been an urgent ride to report the crimes from two nights ago and the traitors' reported departure from Portsmouth.

The entry tower sergeant, apparently not understanding the report of the theft from under the vault, led the courier to the knight on duty because of the murder report. The knight, also not knowing the significance of breaking into the vault's floor, led him to the Preceptor of London.

The preceptor appeared unmoved by the report of the murder, but the theft from beneath the vault sent him into a near panic. The senior knight commanded his sergeant to assemble riders and told his subordinate knight to join him in his chambers.

The courier settled into a corner stool after being told to remain for further questions. They'd have to wake him first.

CHAPTER 4

JULY 21, 1:15 A.M. GST

DOWNTOWN MOSUL

It felt like he'd just fallen asleep when the alarm on his watch sounded. He set it so he'd wake to call Seattle at midday local.

Rick Lambert impatiently reached for the watch atop the nightstand, but instead knocked over an open container of oats, spilling its contents to the floor. He knew he should've placed it against the far wall with all the others. He frowned on the practice while on active duty but, after Fallujah, accepted the offer from his prior company's sergeant to mail bottles of Jack Daniel's Tennessee whiskey to local post offices, concealed in half-emptied containers of Quaker Oats.

He silenced his watch's alarm, then looked up the contact details on his phone: Danny Dicarpio, UW Professor.

He and Danny had been fellow undergraduates in the University of Washington's history department. Lambert enjoyed studying history, but the distractions of football games and frat parties were enough for him to put down the books. Not so for Danny. History was Danny's passion, and he had such a knack for research he often came up with revelations about historical events that intrigued even his most skeptical professors.

Lambert transitioned into an Army career, and Danny continued with graduate school and teaching assistance jobs, finally becoming an associate professor. Beyond teaching duties, the study of history also dominated Danny's private life. Lambert called on his friend from time to time, both for his research skills and for the enjoyment of talking about their old college days together.

Danny answered after one ring. "Dicarpio."

Lambert focused on not slurring his words. "Helping any more Army pukes through college?"

"Rick! It's been over a year, hasn't it? Are you still in Iraq? What's going on?"

Lambert remembered his overly excitable friend tended to ramble if his questions weren't answered immediately. "Closer to two, and yeah, still working for MOI."

"Cool! I found some fascinating source material for the building of the Ziggurat of Ur. Are you anywhere near Nasiriyah?"

"No, Mosul. We're working a case involving abductions of Christian priests."

"Oh yeah," Danny said. "I heard about that on the news . . ."

"Yeah, not exactly a vacation destination right now. Listen, I got something strange from a priest here named Zephyros Topolis. I'd like to ask you about it."

"Shoot."

"It looks like a marble domino, but has one Latin word on each edge."

Danny chuckled. "Still struggling with Latin, are we?"

"I used an internet translator, but it still makes no sense."

"Internet translator . . ."

Lambert ignored Danny's mock disgust. "On one short edge is IUBET, I-U-B-E-T."

"That's 'commands' or 'orders'—as in direction from authority."

"Okay, on a long edge is SORVACORE, S—"

"Sorvacore?" Danny asked, with a much louder voice.

"Yeah, what does it mean?"

"No . . . Sorvacore's a village in Persian folklore. The short story is that Sorvacore was destroyed by some kind of 'ghost legion' of Rome. And that legion was later decimated by sympathetic jinn, or genies, commanded by a Persian warlord whose home village was Sorvacore." Danny sounded nearly out of breath. "What are the other words on this domino?"

"On the other short edge is FERT, F-E-R-T."

"Okay, that's just 'supports' or 'bears'—as in a column supporting a roof. And the word on the other long edge?"

"PRAXIMUS, P-R-A-X-I-M-U-S, a Roman name, right?"

"Not one I'm familiar with. It is clever, though, don't you think?"

"What?"

"Don't you see?" Danny explained. "One way around it reads SORVACORE SUPPORTS PRAXIMUS and the other way around it reads PRAXIMUS COMMANDS SORVACORE. The grammar's not quite correct but clever nonetheless."

Lambert was confused. "Why do you think this was made?"

"Even though it would predate, by centuries, the oldest known traditional domino found in China, I'd have to say for playing a similar game."

"I'm serious," Lambert said, hearing the frustration in his own voice.

"Sorry, me too," Danny said. "What I mean is, if this domino is real, I mean really from the Sorvacore of legend, it was probably a campaign memento." Danny went into professor mode and explained. Where Roman military units traveled, local craftsmen would often create mementoes for their officers, showing how their lands were friends to Rome. They would also sell them to soldiers of the units as keepsakes. Like the Nazi silverware American troops came home with after World War II, they were soldiers' reminders of their time in service. In Roman times, custom dice were common but, if they existed, inscribed dominoes might also be desirable. "Come to think of it, that's pretty clever too . . ."

"How's that?" Lambert asked, again totally lost.

"If the craftsman was sly enough, he'd have a whole *set* of dominoes for sale, prompting each legionnaire to buy one to complete a 'regimental set,' as the Brits might call it." Danny sounded dazzled. "You may have something special there. It might tell us Sorvacore is more than just legend. I need to research more on Sorvacore and find out about this Praximus."

"Thanks. That might help me make sense of what's happening here."

"Okay, I've got contacts in Rome who are the real experts on Roman military units. I'll get with them about it."

Lambert was still amazed by the story of Danny's Roman contacts. When the academic's dream vacation came true a few years prior, he and several other American professors had been granted a one-month research excursion to the Vatican Secret Archives. While other scholars combined their reading with walks around the Vatican and tours of Rome, Danny used every waking hour to absorb as much of the fifty-two linear miles of shelving as possible. His strategy was unique—rather than *seeing* what was there, he spent most of his time in the index room *finding out* what was there for future reference. With his language skills and historical knowledge, he inferred most documents' contents by their titles and dates. He gained so much knowledge during that time that embarrassed Apostolic Library researchers he developed contacts with still called him for help with their own library.

"Email some photos of this domino, would you?" Danny asked.

"Sure. Oh, one more thing: Father Topolis said 'don't let them find it' and 'protect Cyprus' before he died. Do you see any connection between those words and this domino?"

"Not offhand. Sorry to hear the priest died. Were you close?"

"We were getting to know each other," Lambert said with a tinge of sadness, his mind flashing back to Kanisah. "At least now we might be onto the bastards behind these abductions."

"Great. Let me get with my friends in Rome and call you back. You be careful."

Lambert smirked. "Cluck, cluck, mother hen."

CHAPTER 5

AUGUST 22, 1307

OFF THE COAST OF BORDEAUX, AQUITAINE

The Bucci family had been a large stakeholder in the Genoese merchant consortium for many generations. Their massive fleet sailed a continuous loop around Mediterranean ports, through Granada's Strait of Gibraltar, north to other European ports, and back again. On any given day, Portsmouth welcomed one or more Genoese vessels. Although the Genoese usually shipped for the Hospitallers, a rival military order, Brim Hastings had learned that Malcolm's family and the Buccis had known each other for several years. Through letters, the knight had arranged a standing offer of passage to Cyprus aboard any Genoese ship.

By the time they'd sailed from Portsmouth, Brim knew the night guard's death and the theft from the vault would have been discovered. By a process of elimination, their identities would be known as well. By this time, their crimes would have been reported to the order's London preceptory, such thoughts filling Brim's mind with waves of anxiety. Soon, the Grand Master in Paris would be informed. From this point on, they were fugitives.

Over the course of their first week under sail, Brim had studied what Malcolm called the marshal's ledgers. The sums he balanced in the order's London ledgers over the past year were a small subset of the massive transfer of treasure summarized in the ledgers from Paris. In amazement, he read of contracts for at least a hundred ships, to be dispatched from all the major maritime powers of Christendom. Entries transferred huge sums to mercenary groups and guilds of metalsmiths specializing in weapons. Also recorded were vast amounts for supporting efforts from porters, carters, drapers, fullers, grooms, infirmarers, and traveling kitcheners. The focal point for all was Cyprus. Men and material were scheduled to be transported on ships at different times, depending on their origins, to arrive at the island's major ports near the time of the following year's Easter Sunday. The purpose of such a massive undertaking seemed clear—the order's staging of a fighting force on Cyprus for an all-out effort to retake the Holy Land.

During the last three days, the summer storm battering the continent's west coast had intensified, growing swells requiring battening of hatches and stowage of loose items. Brim had translated a Greek study of maritime dynamics in the London scriptorium years before and believed his understanding of ship movements could perhaps counteract his seasickness. He was wrong. His knowledge of how the surging, swaying, and heaving were coupled with the rolling, pitching, and yawing only added to his misery. That focus, combined with his study of the last of the marshal's ledgers, left him nauseated.

Knowing he would not be able to hold down any food himself, he brought a plate of dried beef into their enclave below the main deck, amidships, against the port hull. The space contained two cots hung from deck beams and two footlockers fastened to the keel beam. Built into the hull were a table and two bench seats. Malcolm knelt on one knee, facing a portal, eyes closed in prayer. Brim put the plate on the table and turned to exit. He exhaled in frustration, feeling as though he'd displayed remarkable patience awaiting further explanation from his mentor. After all, the purpose of the order was the protection of Christian pilgrims traveling to the Holy Places. So how could their return to the Levant be anything but righteous?

"Brimley."

He spun around and saw Malcolm rising. "Sir?"

"Your study of the marshal's ledgers is complete?"

His stomach churned. "Yes sir."

"Your thoughts?"

"They summarize the finances behind staging of men and material on Cyprus for retaking the Holy Land as championed by the Grand Master."

Malcolm raised an eyebrow and took a seat on the far bench. "You found nothing odd? Nothing . . . missing?"

He sat across from his mentor. "Missing, sir? These are plans for staging on Cyprus. Plans for transport to the Levant must be elsewhere."

"Must they?" Malcolm paused before continuing. "You know of the order's history on Cyprus?"

"Yes sir." Brim knew of operations on Cyprus from the order's chronicles. The island had been conquered by King Richard on his way to the Holy Land over a hundred years ago. Being such a magnificent strategic base for supplying operations to the mainland, the order convinced the king to sell it for a significant sum. For a short time, they ruled over their own sovereign nation—the Templar Kingdom of Cyprus. But they were forced to abandon their rule due to rebellion. The king absolved them of their future payments and bestowed the island onto the House of Lusignan.

"You may not know of the torment that loss has inflicted on the order's leadership." Malcolm explained how it was considered the greatest loss of power the order had ever experienced. Since that failure, the order's leadership had secretly been searching for a way to regain their kingdom. King Henry II of Lusignan had been ruler of Cyprus for eighteen years. During the last year, however, the Temple Council conspired with his brother, Amalric, Prince of Tyre in exile, and was successful in ousting Henry, exiling him to the Armenian Kingdom of Cilicia. With the resulting political upheaval on Cyprus, these knights were convinced it was time to act. The meetings in London and Paris were the initial planning sessions for their invasion of Cyprus.

"Cyprus is the *final destination*?"

"It is," said the knight.

Their cabin's interior space seemed to collapse. "The Holy See would never allow such a venture!" Despite their wealth and power, the order still answered to the pope. "Christian fighting Christian? How would they get support for such a plan?"

"Give me a lever long enough, and I shall move the world."

"Sir?"

"A principle of Archimedes."

"That of leverage?"

Malcolm nodded. "We have an item in our possession that has been the order's leverage over the church for nearly two hundred years. You've heard of the excavations under the Dome of the Rock during the order's first years in Jerusalem?"

Brim inhaled quickly upon hearing of the forbidden topic. His voice was a whisper. "I have. It's been said several important relics were found below the ruins of the Second Temple."

"Not just relics. *Documents*."

"Of what kind?" asked Brim.

"Documents that redefine Christianity."

"Why had they not been relinquished to the pontiff?"

"At first, fear. They would have been considered heretical. The early leaders in Jerusalem assigned scholars within the order to study them. After much debate, it was decided they would be retained."

"But how is there such leverage if the church has no knowledge of them?"

"They know of one." Malcolm described how, nearly two hundred years ago, a small parchment had been shown to a visiting emissary of the Roman Curia, who'd reported the scroll's existence to the pope. Several representatives later arrived from Rome, demanding the order turn over the document. They were sent away with the explanation that transport was too dangerous without more security. Gradually, a balance of power developed between the Holy See and the Temple Council. As with the Grand Master and select knights of the Temple Council, only the Bishop of Rome and top cardinals of the Roman Curia's *Circuitor Consistory* had knowledge of the scroll and the leverage the order had over the church.

Malcolm removed the small piece of vellum from a foot locker and placed it on the table. "Read, and our return to Cyprus will be explained."

Brim stared at the small scroll with trepidation, feeling as if the writing upon it was about to change his life. "From under the Shipley vault?"

Malcolm nodded. "The Temple Council refers to this as the Praximus Command, as do certain others at Kolossi. The church employs a different moniker."

"Which is?"

"*Vectis Templi.*"

Brim frowned. "Lever of the Temple?"

His mentor smiled.

What little time it took him to scan over the small parchment produced a renewed bout of dry heaves. He clenched his eyes shut and felt his stomach, nearly empty for days, extrude its last drops of bile into his mouth.

Malcolm leaned across the table, placing his right hand on Brim's left shoulder. "This, and more, we shall endure."

AUGUST 26, 1307
PARIS, FRANCE

The guard enjoyed his duty for the order in Paris, but his true allegiance was to the Circuitor Consistory in Poitiers. He wasn't sure how many others shared his position, but followed orders from the one knight in Paris he knew shared his loyalty.

The Paris preceptory had been in turmoil since the theft of some ledgers the month before. The more recent theft in England had them near panic. For hours, the Grand Master and most of the Temple Council deliberated feverously at the Levant Wall, the floor-to-ceiling map of the Holy Land depicting Egypt to the south and Armenia to the north, Cyprus to the west and Syria to the east. Carved out of stone, most major preceptories had one.

He was quietly ordered to ride the two hundred miles south to Poitiers and report the chaos gripping the Paris preceptory. He memorized and repeatedly verbalized the cryptic report before leaving. During his weeklong ride, he'd rehearse the details so they'd remain fresh in his mind: Malcolm of Basingstoke, Praximus, Portsmouth, *Filomena*, Cyprus . . . not knowing the context made it difficult, but he would succeed in delivering the information. Cardinal Francesco Orsini did not accept failure.

CHAPTER 6

JULY 21, 5:24 P.M. GST

DOWNTOWN MOSUL

Rick Lambert had been struggling for answers since the Kanisah attack. Samir worked with the Mosul police but had no luck identifying the bodies of either the monks or the gunmen. Lambert visited other Christian churches in and around Mosul, asking clergy about Kanisah. They all cooperated, hoping he could help stop the abductions. But the more churches he visited, the more he realized answers would not be forthcoming.

The Christian churches of Iraq aligned with either the Eastern Rite or the Armenian Church. They'd operated in isolation during the reign of Saddam Hussein. After Saddam, individual churches had more interaction with one another, mostly within their denominations. Each he visited had contacts at others in the area. Some even called ahead and arranged introductions. But none had any contacts at the Church of Kanisah. After getting the same result several times, Lambert began asking why this might be. The answer became clear—the Eastern Rite churches assumed Kanisah was more aligned with the Armenians and vice versa.

Kanisah was an island unto itself.

He and Samir returned to their hotel after a long day and met in the adjoining restaurant for dinner. Before they could order, his phone buzzed, showing an incoming call from James Dougherty.

"Hello, sir," Lambert said.

Dougherty worked for the US State Department's Bureau of Intelligence and Research, or INR, as the department head for the Office of Near Eastern Affairs. Lambert was one of the twenty-five analysts who made up Dougherty's team when first on loan from the Army. "I read your dispatch on the Kanisah shootings. The Vatican has a researcher en route to Mosul to investigate."

"Sir, it's *not* a Christian-friendly environment here right now."

"Just passing on intel. Let's talk Kanisah when you're done."

"Okay, I'll call back. Thanks."

Samir was staring at him with a 'who the hell was that' look on his face.

"My old boss from State. Sounds like Danny's research raised a few eyebrows at the Vatican. We're going to get a call from Kassab to look after someone from Rome."

"To help with the case or just waste our time?"

"Your guess is as good as mine."

"How's the US State Department involved?" Samir asked.

It was time he let his partner know about his stint with INR and his ongoing relationship with them. He did so over dinner. After all, Mooz had always been open with him.

Samir Moozarmi had been born in Basra, to politically active physician parents opposed to Saddam and the Baath party. Saddam's secret police targeted their political organizations, prompting them to immigrate to San Francisco in the late eighties when Samir was four years old. Later, the three became naturalized US citizens. While a gifted student, Samir felt the need to rebel against his parents' expectations of college and enlisted in the US Army after high school. He served two years as a translator in Basra while loaned into a British Army unit, then enrolled at Stanford University to study mechanical engineering. When Iraq's government began to form after Saddam, his father was contacted by old political associates who sought his help in building a new Iraq. Shortly after his parents moved back, his father was elected to the new Council of Representatives as the member from Basra. After graduation, Samir was accepted as an agent in Iraq's Ministry of Interior and paired with Lambert in the Investigations Unit.

Samir looked as though he didn't approve of his continued involvement with INR. "Do they ever try to interfere with our work for the ministry?"

"No, they just like to keep tabs on me. Besides, they've been a helpful resource for cases over the years."

Samir's frown persisted. "You're sharing ministry case data?"

"Just getting related intel from them once in a while. Come on, Mooz, I'm not a spy . . ." Feeling defensive, Lambert was grateful for his phone's buzz. It was Ali Kassab.

"Chief." Lambert had known Kassab since he'd first come back to Iraq. They were two of the founding agents before his former partner was promoted chief of the MOI Investigations Unit. At that point, Kassab let power go to his head and became increasingly difficult to work for.

"Just read your initial report on Kanisah."

"Samir's still working IDs, and I'm trying to find out more about the church itself."

"Right now, I need something else from you two. The prime minister's office got a call from someone high up in the Vatican. They heard about the shootings and have someone en route now, some researcher . . ." Kassab paused, as if working out a written name's pronunciation before speaking. ". . . Monsignor Giuseppe Plenducci. I need you two to pick him up at Mosul International at 2100 local."

"The Mosul precinct still has the place locked down. Does the guy want to *enter* the church?"

"Just spoke to Mosul precinct's Captain Jaffari. They'll have two officers unchain the front doors. Listen, Lambert, I want you and Samir to look after this guy. Let him see the church, then get him back on his jet and out of Mosul."

Lambert frowned, glanced at Samir, and shook his head. "Chief, we don't have enough security here for this."

Kassab's once nervous tone was now laced with anger. "As I told the prime minister's office! They passed on the concern and the Vatican will accept the risk, so just do it."

"Okay. I don't like it, but alright. Could some patrols cruise the neighborhood?"

"I'll ask Jaffari."

"We'll let you know how it goes."

CHAPTER 7

SEPTEMBER 4, 1307

THE STRAIT OF GIBRALTAR

Captain Pietro Bucci raised the *Filomena's* anchor a mile off the coast just after sunset. Their entry into the Mediterranean, through waters claimed by the Emirate of Granada, began under moonlight intermittently dimmed by scattered clouds. While it was a maneuver he'd performed many times before, he again felt his pulse rising.

Nasrid Sultan Muhammad III, a vassal of King Ferdinand IV of Castile, had been under increasing pressure to raise income by imposing exorbitant tolls for passage through the strait. The maritime republics, having no intention of sharing the wealth of their labors with the emirate on the north shore, simply sailed to the south side of the strait. Things were no longer so simple.

The sultan had taken control of the North African city of Ceuta two years prior. Naval activity from both shores was ramping up in an effort to intercept shipping, forcing those wishing to retain all their cargo to slip through the strait under cover of darkness.

Bucci peered at the dim firelights to the north from the port railing of the sterncastle before scrambling to join Malcolm to starboard. There seemed to be more activity on the coast to the south. He cupped his hands around his mouth, directing his voice toward two young Genoese leveraging the rudder stock. "Five degrees port."

The elder knight glanced north before returning his gaze toward Ceuta, as if judging the relative dangers from both.

Bucci leaned on the starboard railing and tried to appear calm while speaking to the imposing Englishman in their only shared language of Arabic. "I suppose you've had no need for such maneuvers on previous passages?"

"None."

This fact was known to all captains of the maritime republics. Based in the western French port of La Rochelle, the Fleet of the Temple had sailed unchallenged since the time of Eleanor of Aquitaine. Upon entering the Strait of Gibraltar, their mangonel-equipped warships and huge *usciere* horse transports they escorted had always been given a wide berth by the Nasrids. "A condition of privilege, to be sure," said Bucci.

Malcolm's eyes remained on North Africa. "Not privileged. Merited."

"Yes, of course." Bucci cocked his head. "Still, as potent as your warships are, your fleet of twenty is small by our standards. There are even rumors of many Genoese ships sailing with yours in the coming year."

"Are there?" asked Malcolm, turning to Bucci and arching an eyebrow. "You heard this from whom?"

Pietro Bucci heard the authority of the question from the Preceptor of Kolossi and had to remind himself, as captain of the *Filomena*, he was able to speak to anyone aboard *his* ship as an equal. "None in particular. But gossip about massive shipments next year has filtered down to some captains."

"Do your tales tell of such an armada's purpose?"

"Most assume a new campaign for the Holy Land." He paused, then looked at Malcolm curiously. "Others look to the invasion of Rhodes by the Order of the Hospital and ask if the Order of the Temple will soon control a Byzantine island as well."

Malcolm's voice simmered with anger. "If either is ordered by His Holiness, it shall be done."

Bucci instantly regretted his probing into such affairs. He knew what the military orders felt about Genoa's violation of *Fuit Olim*, the papal bull of Boniface VIII prohibiting trade with the Saracens, but not once during their journey had the venerable knight mentioned it. He looked southwest toward the dimming firelights of Ceuta as he changed the subject. "Is the boy feeling any better?"

"Brimley is a boy no longer." Malcolm also shifted his gaze toward Ceuta. "He will be fine."

The boy—the *young man*, he corrected in his thoughts—had overcome his nausea shortly after the summer storm off the coast of Aquitaine two weeks before. But since that time, his demeanor soured. Before the storm, he seemed excited about traveling to Cyprus, eager to help perform chores aboard ship. Now, he was in a near constant state of contemplation, staying belowdecks for days at a time. Bucci wondered what kind of burden the stern knight may have placed on his young subordinate. "We should see no such storms again between here and Limassol."

"We shall not put to port at Limassol," said Malcolm.

Bucci turned to Malcolm, mystified. "You do not return to Kolossi? Why?"

"For the safety of all aboard this ship."

"If not Limassol, where?"

Malcolm looked east. "Larnaca."

POITIERS, FRANCE

He knew he was obsessive about leading the curia in this time of transition, but Francesco Orsini couldn't help himself. If he didn't make the hard decisions, someone less knowledgeable would. He was one of the elder Italian cardinals and often spoken of as leading contender for pope. But, after escaping Rome following the violent clashes between his family and the rival Colonna family two years ago, security had become paramount. The price of that protection was an alliance with the French Crown and their election of Raymond Bertrand de Got, the Archbishop of Bordeaux, as Pope Clement V. The influence of King Philip IV was undeniable. Every cardinal created in the past two years was French. Hoping to appease those offended, plans were being made to move the curia three hundred miles southeast to papal-controlled Avignon. But Orsini knew Philip's influence would persist.

Despite the increasing French influence, Orsini still wielded authority in the curia. He employed his power to deal with news from the Paris preceptory. He and the other four cardinals of the Circuitor Consistory had just learned of the chaos within the Order of the Temple, a maelstrom so great the theft reported to them could only be that of the heretical *Vectis Templi*. He would possess the scroll, or it would be destroyed. In either case, the order's power over the church would soon be severed, freeing them from their Templar yoke. If he could manipulate the French Crown as planned, the accumulated wealth of the order would be his.

CHAPTER 8

JULY 21, 8:42 P.M. GST

SOUTHERN MOSUL

Rick Lambert knew which checkpoints to pass through and where to park. He and Samir had done so before, usually to pick up and escort representatives from the UN or Arab League. The isolated section of tarmac was used as transient parking for the most secure arrivals and departures. It was away from the flow of other aircraft and ground vehicles.

He used the wait time to call Seattle while Samir monitored the ground control frequency.

"Dicarpio."

"Hey, Danny."

"Rick!" Danny sounded excited, as always. "Every time I'm about to call, I think of something else I should look into first. Sorry for not getting back."

"No problem. Hey, you must've made quite an impression calling your Vatican pals."

"What?"

"We're here at Mosul International to pick up a Monsignor Plenducci. Despite the security risks, he wants to see Kanisah."

Danny's voice raised in pitch. "You've got the CDF coming down on you?"

"CDF? This guy's from the Vatican."

"No, Rick, Giuseppe Plenducci is one of the senior inspectors in the Congregation for the Doctrine of the Faith, the oldest of the curia's nine congregations."

Lambert didn't know how to respond. "Okay . . ."

"So . . . the CDF is the nice, new name for what used to be called the 'Holy Inquisition' back in the day."

The words hung in Lambert's mind as a feeling of unease spread through him. "Oh shit."

"Yeah, they're the guys who went after Galileo." Danny described Plenducci as he remembered him from his time at the Vatican Secret Archives. Whenever Apostolic Library researchers had major difficulties acquiring information, Plenducci would be called in. He was the *force recon* of their academic world. Even people he helped were anxious about working with him. His energy level was impressive for a man in his seventies. But his intensity was abrasive, all social graces replaced with an efficiency of speech and motion. Plenducci was all business, 24/7.

"Well, we'll deal with the monsignor as best we can. What did you find out about Praximus and Sorvacore?"

"Nothing new on Sorvacore yet, but I did find out quite a bit about the Praximus family." Danny began with what he'd found from his contacts at the *Archivio Storico Capitolino* in Rome. Also known as the Roman Historical Archives, they were the world's experts on Roman military units. Danny's first hunch, based on the indication that Praximus was so far east as to come into contact with the Persian Sorvacore of legend, was that he pursued slaves from the Servile Wars. This would've put the march between 135 BC and 70 BC. But what he found out about the Praximus family changed his opinion. The records of military service showed them with *Legio III Gallica*, the Third Gallic Legion, which was levied by Julius Caesar around 49 BC. By that time, Rome had more pressing concerns than chasing descendants of escaped slaves.

The Praximus family was of the political elite for several generations before a record of the first family member with a military career, at which point their record in the political arena vanished. In addition, the Third Legion, garrisoned in the province of Syria, would not have been a prestigious post, considering the family's astute political past. Records showed four generations of Praximus men who'd served in the Third Legion between 52 AD and 114 AD. The researchers knew of no other

Praximus family member who served in any Roman legion. Strangely, none of the four attained a rank higher than *pilus prior centurion*, roughly equivalent to a modern army captain, despite their lifetimes of service. "I began to wonder why none were promoted to *tribune*," Danny said. "Perhaps it was related to their family's disappearance from politics generations before."

Next, Danny described the contacts with his colleagues at the Apostolic Library concerning Sorvacore. He'd found they used the same references he did. But when he tried to cross-reference the Praximus information he found, he got defensive reactions. His colleagues, while normally eager to talk, became very guarded. After each claimed to have no information, Danny sought another. Lastly, he reached Cardinal Dominic Batista, Prefect of the Vatican Secret Archives, who asked him to stop his line of inquiry. "I think they know something about the name Praximus they can't disclose."

"Maybe Plenducci can tell us."

"Unlikely. Plenducci will be asking questions, not giving answers."

"Great . . ." Lambert pressed the back of his head against his headrest. "*We're* the ones needing answers."

"I'll keep digging . . . Oh, about your priest with that unique name— Zephyros Topolis. Turns out he was secretly excommunicated back in the seventies."

"Really? Why?"

"They wouldn't say," Danny said. "It seemed the priest I found out from realized he shouldn't have told me. He got quiet soon after. Topolis must have really ruffled some feathers back in the day."

"Thanks, Danny. Plenducci's flight just got here. Talk to you later."

"Okay. Good luck."

Lambert didn't notice the jet touch down but heard the handoff from the control tower to ground control. The white Dassault Falcon 50 business jet soon turned off the taxiway onto the isolated section of tarmac.

"Hope this guy's smart enough to leave his robes in the jet," Samir said.

"Yeah."

The Dassault stopped, the forward door facing them opened, and air stairs extended. A young Mediterranean-looking priest in black stepped out, looked around, then glared at Lambert and Samir standing beside their MOI Hyundai. He walked down the steps and over to the SUV, and asked to see their IDs over the spin-down whine of the turbines. Seemingly satisfied, he trotted back up the stairs. Plenducci appeared after another few seconds.

The priest looked more like a retired prizefighter. Lambert thought he appeared overweight, then decided the extra mass must have been muscle based on the way the man powered down the stairs. He wore blue jeans, a dark blue shirt and a white elastic skullcap, common on the streets of Mosul.

At least the guy won't draw too much attention, Lambert thought.

The elder priest marched to the car with an impatient look on his face, and spoke to Lambert in chopped English. "I am Monsignor Plenducci. We go to the Church of Kanisah now?"

"Monsignor Plenducci, welcome to Mosul. I'm Richard Lambert, and this is Samir Moozarmi. We've been asked to take you there."

Plenducci turned and paced toward the back of the SUV. Samir was barely able to open the door fast enough. With little nighttime traffic, the ride from the airport in southern Mosul to the church just north of the city would take about twenty-five minutes. They left the airport checkpoints, and Plenducci told them his airplane would wait for his return, then asked to see the domino.

Danny must have described it to the Vatican librarians.

Lambert handed the domino, sealed in a clear plastic evidence bag, to Plenducci in the backseat. "We'll need that back."

Plenducci retrieved a penlight from his shirt pocket and examined the stone through the plastic for several minutes. He then wrote in a small notebook for several more minutes. When finished, the priest just stared out the window.

Lambert felt the need to fill the awkward silence. "So, Monsignor, can you tell us what it is about the Church of Kanisah that has the Vatican so interested?"

"We are concerned whenever Christian clergy are harmed," Plenducci said defensively.

"Yes, of course. I just mean . . . there've been many abductions in this case, but it's the first time the Vatican has become involved."

"Yes, I am sure you will solve your case soon."

To avoid saying something he'd regret later, Lambert took a couple minutes to calm down after the deflected question. He then tried a different angle. "So, can you tell us anything about the priest who was killed, Father Zephyros Topolis?"

"No, his parish was isolated during the Saddam Hussein regime," Plenducci answered.

Lambert assumed Plenducci was aware of Topolis's excommunication. With a glance and slight head shake in Samir's direction, he decided they'd wait until arriving at Kanisah to press further. Perhaps getting Plenducci to the scene would prompt him to be more forthcoming.

CHAPTER 9

SEPTEMBER 21, 1307

LARNACA, KINGDOM OF CYPRUS

From his visit three years before, Brim Hastings knew the usual port of arrival for the Kolossi preceptory was Limassol, located just two miles southeast of the compound. Instead, Pietro Bucci had reluctantly diverted forty-five miles east and dropped anchor off Larnaca, allowing his men to row Brim and Malcolm to shore. Along with personal supplies, Brim hauled the three satchels containing the documents from Paris and Shipley.

By the time they'd purchased provisions for the walk along the south coast road, it was late afternoon. The two entered a camp containing about thirty small tents just south of the markets. Brim learned those from the island's south shore typically camped for the night, then either attended the markets or traveled home the next morning. Their camp consisted mostly of others traveling between Larnaca and Limassol. Brim noticed Malcolm greeting several people he knew as they walked. Many seemed surprised by his plain russet jerkin, apparently unaccustomed to seeing the knight out of his uniformed mantle. From their appreciative conversations, it appeared many owed their livelihood to Malcolm and the Kolossi preceptory.

"Brimley Hastings?"

Brim's eyes went wide as he turned to see a young woman with her hands on her hips and a smirk on her face. She wore a leather vest and waist belt over a light tunic, and dark brown plain-weave trousers tucked into leather boots. He thought the attire strange for a female until recognizing her and remembering her family's trade. She was the girl he'd met on his trip to Cyprus three years before. But she was no longer the girl he remembered. She'd grown into a woman. He wondered if she saw the same growth to adulthood in him. Was he the young boy she remembered, or was he now a man in her eyes? To make up for the inch or two height advantage she had over him, he tried standing more erect and tilting his head back. "Shayla Kostas, hello."

Shayla's father, Theron, walked around from behind a wagon and embraced Malcolm in the double hand-to-forearm hold common to comrades-in-arms; Brim remembered hearing the two men had been friends since their time at Acre.

As the evening progressed, Brim learned the former tanner was now a leather craftsman who regularly attended the Larnaca markets for raw materials. His daughter was now his apprentice. With Malcolm's influence, Theron had become the prime supplier and maintainer of Kolossi's horse tack and leather armor components.

At dusk, Brim used his flint block to light a campfire by Theron's wagon. The four discussed their planned travel to Limassol to begin at daybreak.

Darkness fell. Malcolm and Brim set their sleeping rolls beneath Theron's wagon to avoid foot traffic. Theron bid them good night as he and his daughter hopped atop the wagon and prepared sleeping pads out of the hides they'd purchased.

Brim positioned himself so his head protruded from below the side of the wagon, allowing a view of the star-filled sky. He reflected on his awkward attempt at conversation with Shayla earlier, then on the teachings of the London preceptory priests regarding women. They were to be considered inherently wicked, responsible for both the original Fall of Man, and the fall from grace of many men since. The brothers were instructed to consider women a corrupting influence and to avoid contact with them whenever possible.

During his first five years in the order, working as a cloistered novice in the scriptorium, he'd taken the word of the priests as fact. His last three years working as steward and record-keeper of the order's farms in southern England often put him in contact with women who worked the land since, like his father, so many of their men had been conscripted into the army of King Edward I to battle the Scots. They did not seem wicked. Did the priests mean *all* women were corrupt? Were their own mothers? Was Shayla?

The wagon creaked. Shayla's face obscured Brim's view of the stars. Each pair of eyes opened wider, expressing surprise at seeing the other. She smiled, giggled, then disappeared from view.

Brim heard continued snickering from above.

What could she possibly think was humorous? he thought.

He shifted so he was completely under the wagon.

Were women evil? No. Impossible to understand perhaps, but not evil.

POITIERS

From his window nearly forty feet above the courtyard, Cardinal Francesco Orsini looked out over southern Poitiers, across the Clain, and onto the Boivre valley. When the curia arrived at the Palace of Justice two years before, he favored the chamber atop the south tower and claimed it for both his residence and office. The circular room, twenty feet in diameter with brick walls and heavy wooden flooring, was originally used as a mass holding cell by the Count-Dukes of Aquitaine. Orsini had many changes made to the interior space. A hinged frame of translucent linen replaced the window bars. The iron door was retained but the lock reversed so the key could only be inserted from inside the room. Several polished metal mirrors mounted to the walls reflected light from the single window during the day and several candles at night. Between the mirrors hung the favorite paintings from his former residence in Rome, each depicting a biblical scene. A large desk and high back chair were to the right of the window. A cot and standing partition were positioned to the left. In the center of the room was a rectangular table surrounded by half a dozen chairs. At this table, Orsini presided over key meetings with top cardinals.

The view from his tower sanctuary usually relaxed him, but it did little to ease the tension caused by the departing aide to Guillaume de Nogaret, the man soon to become Keeper of the Seal of King Philip IV.

Orsini was told Nogaret had just arrived in Poitiers and required a meeting the next day.

Orsini knew the subject of the meeting. His own proposal had been for the French Crown to begin legal inquiry into the Order of the Temple on the basis of contract disputes. He knew the price of using the resources of the Crown would be steep. Tomorrow, he would offer much of the Temple's lands, not only to the king, but to Nogaret personally, which would make him one of the richest private land owners in France.

LARNACA

What a strange boy Brimley Hastings has become.

Shayla Kostas had patiently listened to him that evening. He described Malcolm's trip to Paris with Grand Master Jacques de Molay as if he was by his mentor's side. He then spoke of de Molay's conversations with the pope about retaking the Holy Land, as though there remained any such desire in anyone outside the church.

She was puzzled. Did Brimley think of himself as somehow important by association? Did he have any thoughts of his own besides his desire to become Malcolm's attending sergeant?

She'd try speaking with him again in the morning, with the hope he'd not become as arrogant as he seemed.

CHAPTER 10

JULY 21, 9:26 P.M. GST

NORTHERN MOSUL

Rick Lambert, Samir, and Plenducci approached the Church of Kanisah. A patrol car from the Mosul precinct passed in the opposite direction. Lambert turned the final corner and saw another parked in front of the west side main entrance. He parked their MOI Hyundai behind it. Two officers already had the front double doors unchained and swung open onto the sidewalk.

Lambert turned off the headlights and shut down the SUV, feeling suddenly uncomfortable with how dark and deserted the street had become this time of night. Despite the scheduled rendezvous, the two officers approaching the vehicle appeared nervous, holding flashlights in their left hands and asking for IDs. Satisfied, they slipped their right hands off their holstered sidearms.

He was glad to see them taking the danger seriously. "Thanks for coming. You'll keep watch out front while we're inside?"

"Sure," the older officer said.

Lambert nodded. "Shout if you see anything."

Plenducci had already marched through the double doors and glowered back impatiently. "Show me where the domino was recovered."

Lambert led Plenducci behind the altar while fighting off a wave of nausea from the lingering smells of burnt flesh and spent ammunition. He pointed at the cracked corner of hollowed-out wood. "Topolis pulled it from this crevice."

Plenducci knelt to examine the damaged altar.

Lambert decided to try another approach with the old Italian. "Monsignor, we would be grateful for any information you could share with us."

Plenducci just nodded.

He pursed his lips and thought about the Vatican librarians' reactions to Danny asking about Praximus. "Can you tell us what the name Praximus may mean to this case?"

"You need not concern yourself with that."

Is he kidding? "Monsignor, we must pursue all leads we uncover during this case."

Plenducci bolted to his feet. "You do not tell me what must be done."

Enough. "You're wrong about that, Monsignor. I'm the agent in charge of this case and I want these abductions to end. I know the Vatican has information about the name Praximus, and I think you're aware that Father Topolis was excommunicated. Why are you withholding information?"

Plenducci surged a step closer, the veins on his brow bulging. "Because I decide what information you receive!"

Something slammed into one of the open front double doors.

"We need help out here!" the younger Mosul officer outside screamed.

Another crash was heard.

Only the front entrance was unchained and was the only way in or out. Samir had his Beretta drawn and was already midway between the altar and the front doors. Lambert pointed at the suddenly disoriented priest while drawing his own weapon and following Samir down the main aisle. "Stay behind us!"

At the double doors, both officers crouched on the sidewalk with their service pistols drawn, anxiously scanning for targets in the darkness to the south. The older officer called for backup on his handheld radio.

The younger officer cried out and fell onto his back, his body rigid. A cylinder the size of a blunt cigar protruded from his shoulder, emitting a crackling sound.

"Stun slugs! Mooz, they're going for Plenducci!" Lambert had seen such shells at an Army demonstration. The cylinder in the officer's shoulder and the crashes heard against the open doors were NMI rounds, wireless Neuro-Muscular Incapacitation projectiles. The self-contained, battery-powered, microprocessor-controlled devices delivered the same bio-effect as a handheld stun gun. Sized for 12-gauge shotguns, the primer and slow-burning ignition produced a quiet, non-lethal muzzle velocity of three hundred feet per second. Once out of the barrel, the outer shell jettisoned and small stabilizing fins deployed to deliver the forward-facing barbed electrodes into the target to close the circuit. The battery then discharged for twenty seconds, causing a total loss of muscular control.

With their flashlights off, their eyes adjusted to the darkness. Lambert, Samir and the older officer ducked behind the south double door. Only one could peek around it.

Lambert quickly dragged the young officer inside, then handed Samir the incapacitated man's flashlight. *If we get trapped inside, we die.* "Shine that while I get in front of their car."

Samir pointed the flashlight around the open door to the south.

Lambert gritted his teeth and lunged across the sidewalk to the front of the patrol car and saw a mirror image of his movement ten yards away; someone with a shotgun rushed out of the alley at the southwest corner of the church to get behind their Hyundai. Two small circles obscuring the gunman's face reflected in Samir's light.

Oh, this just keeps getting better.

The two circles were undoubtedly image intensifier tubes of night vision goggles.

Lambert felt his heart rate surge as he checked around the patrol car's left front fender, down the middle of the street, making sure the gunman wasn't approaching from that side. He then heard running footsteps behind him.

"Wait!" Samir yelled.

Turning, Lambert saw Plenducci bolt into the alley around the northwest corner, away from the gunman.

Samir ran after him, and another stun slug impacted one of the open double doors.

Time seemed to slow for Lambert as he realized the slug must have come from a second gunman near the southwest corner of the church, since the first was hidden behind their SUV. If this second gunman was right-handed, then it meant he'd be exposed while shooting north around the southwest corner.

Lambert steadied himself on the right front fender and shot into the dark corner. After three rounds, he heard a shout. Off to his right, he saw movement behind the SUV. Then all sensory inputs were lost.

He fell backward. Every muscle in his body seemed to lock up at the same time. His legs shot out from under him and he landed flat on his back. No sights or sounds made sense—he just saw stars and heard white noise. It felt like a thirty-minute gym workout condensed into seconds, every muscle obeying the bioelectrical command for maximum exertion.

The charge from the slug's lithium battery depleted, and cognitive thought slowly returned. He processed where he was and what had happened. His body was still too weak to move well, but sights and sounds started making sense again.

The sound of a roaring engine came around a corner to the north—a Mosul patrol car responding to the call for backup.

Lambert sat up. "Mooz . . . Plenducci?" Using the patrol car front bumper for leverage, he struggled to stand.

The approaching pair of headlights illuminated the gunman standing next to their Hyundai, hand over his goggles' intensifier tubes. The older Mosul officer leaned out from behind the church door and shot him through the center of his neck. The officer then scanned a flashlight to the south. The other downed gunmen could be seen at the corner. A second patrol car stopped in the middle of the street, just as distant automatic gunfire was heard from behind the church. Two officers jumped out, crouched behind their open front doors, and scanned for more gunmen.

The young Mosul officer just inside the double doors got to his feet beside his partner and pulled the barbed slug from his shoulder. Both checked up and down the street.

Lambert tore the barbed slug out of his neck. He was about to slam it to the ground until, on second thought, he realized it was evidence and placed it on the hood of the patrol car.

He stumbled to the northwest corner, took a quick peek down the north alley, and saw nothing. "Mooz," he whispered. No response. He then shone the flashlight down the alley. Still nothing.

He felt his muscles tense as two blasts sounded from the southwest corner of the church. He looked down the sidewalk in front of the church. The mangled, smoking bodies of the enemy gunmen lay illuminated by the patrol car's headlights. They'd apparently been fitted with the same explosive harnesses as the gunmen from two days before. Luckily, the Mosul police officers hadn't been close enough to be injured by the detonations.

Lambert returned to the northwest corner. He now shouted for Samir and Plenducci then proceeded down the alley, scanning from side to side with a flashlight in his left hand and his .40 caliber Beretta in his right. At the end of the alley, near the northeast corner, he saw his partner motionless and staggered to him.

"Mooz!"

He checked for a pulse, finding none. Samir's pale body was riddled with multiple bullet wounds, and the amount of blood loss was horrific. He shone the light behind the church. Scattered around the street lay spent 5.56mm cartridge cases. It appeared Samir had run into automatic fire trying to save Plenducci.

Lambert crumpled to both knees beside his partner and found breathing difficult—he was only capable of shallow, rapid inhalations. His felt his body go numb as he gripped his partner's hand for the first and last time.

The Mosul police set up a perimeter and canvassed the area looking for the priest. It soon became clear that Plenducci had been taken.

Procedure required Lambert to immediately report events up his chain of command. This he ignored. Notifying the Moozarmi family of his failure to defend Samir was the only thing that seemed to matter.

10:47 P.M. GST

NORTHEASTERN MOSUL

He could not believe his luck. After hearing from his informers at the Mosul precinct, he had less than two hours to put together the operation to grab the man from Rome called Plenducci at the Church of Kanisah. The plan was simple. The six young recruits of his sacrificial first wave were outfitted with night vision and were to approach the church, stunning as many as possible before being put down. The second wave of six riflemen was to then move in and kill all but the man from the Vatican. When the three vans arrived from side streets, any of his men still alive were to leave with their hostage.

When the radio call had been made about the man thought to be Plenducci running alone around the northwest corner, two of the men with night vision were instead diverted to apprehend him. The lead van intercepted them behind the church. He ripped off the skullcap, examined the elderly man's Italian features, and knew it was Plenducci. Mosul police converged, and his men were ordered to retreat back into the darkness to be picked up by the other two vans on side streets.

On the way back to base, he reflected on the mission with mixed feelings. He'd expected the frontal assault to deplete most of his men and equipment in Iraq. Instead, it only cost him two new recruits, two night vision goggles, two semiautomatic shotguns, a couple dozen stun slugs, and a pair of radios.

What still enraged him were the losses *behind* the church. After he and his driver forced Plenducci into the van, two shots rang out from the northeast corner, dropping both men who'd intercepted the old priest. His squad leader exited the van's sliding door and set the sights of his H&K rifle on the corner. The figure in the alley was visible for only a split second, shooting the man in the head before slipping back out of view. His explosives expert then leapt from the van with his own rifle and moved to the east wall. The figure in the alley dropped this man as well with another impossible headshot, considering he'd been visible for only a blink of an eye.

How could only one man with a pistol have done that?

Livid, he'd picked up his squad leader's rifle and walked north, knowing he had a full magazine of thirty rounds. He cycled the trigger, sending three- to five-round bursts around the corner in a continually decreasing angle. Nearing the point of being able to shoot directly down the alley, he saw the muzzle flash from the pistol as his own rounds tore through the man's body. His rifle jammed just as the man fell. A quick inspection revealed the reason—a bullet impact deformed the top of the magazine, just below the rifle's receiver. At the time of impact, it was inches from his chin. His rage and audacity had saved his life.

Allah favors the bold!

He recognized the young man as the one who'd spotted him directing operations from the motorcycle the day before.

When he and his martyred colleagues arrived at the site used as their Mosul base, he would inform his leadership of their actions.

He had redeemed himself, as Allah willed it.

CHAPTER 11
SEPTEMBER 22, 1307
LARNACA

The camp south of the markets sprang back to life at dawn. People began to wake and pack belongings in preparation for travel. A group of panicked families stumbled in from an adjacent camp to the north. Word spread—armed men searched the camps surrounding the markets. New arrivals had heard talk of stolen documents.

Brim felt a shiver, realizing the port stops made by the *Filomena* along their route could have allowed a dedicated vessel ample time to reach Cyprus before them. He assumed, therefore, these men had arrived in Limassol, found no record of the *Filomena's* arrival, then expanded their search up the coast. He rubbed the back of his neck with a sweaty palm.

Malcolm beckoned the three others closer. The knight gathered the document satchels and explained that he could not allow the approaching men to find them. Theron seemed to understand at once. Brim assumed it was related to his conversation with Malcolm the night before.

Over a dozen men, armed with crossbows and swords, stopped at the camp's center. One man, wearing a sleeveless black jerkin, offered greetings and asked those within earshot to remain calm. Those who rushed away slowed to a walk and looked back.

Malcolm frowned toward this leader, then growled, "Darcan."

The mere mention of the name filled Brim with revulsion. On occasion, the church required armed force to resolve matters. When it was justifiable, the monastic military orders were called upon. When it was not, the church called on Cibalik Darcan.

Darcan was the ambassador to Pope Clement V from the Armenian Kingdom of Cilicia. His corrupt family held a precarious grip on power by making repeated concessions to Mongol forces pushing further west each year. Repeated attempts by the curia at brokering alliances between Christian and Mongol forces had failed. It had, however, fostered contacts between Darcan and every major mercenary group in the Eastern Mediterranean. For access to these groups, Cardinal Francesco Orsini turned to the ambassador. In return, Orsini applied just enough papal influence on Mongol leaders to keep them from overrunning all of Armenia.

Standing next to Darcan was a tall, hooded figure controlling the armed men with simple hand gestures. It was clear the ambassador had hired an established team of mercenaries.

Malcolm handed Brim the three satchels, then ordered him to flee west. Theron told his daughter to do the same.

From camp center, the announcement continued. "Again, good people, we search for stolen documents brought to Cyprus." Darcan held up a sheet of paper. "This warrant permits our search of this encampment. Cooperate with these men, and we will leave you in peace."

Soon after leaving, Brim and Shayla encountered more armed men who'd apparently surrounded the camp and worked their way inward. Dejected, he realized they would not be able to slip out. Returning, he caught sight of Malcolm and Theron approaching camp center with swords drawn.

He'd failed to protect the Praximus Command and the marshal's ledgers. Determined to use the distraction meant for him, Brim emptied the contents of the first satchel into the smoldering remnants of an abandoned cooking fire. If he couldn't escape with the documents, he would destroy them. Before he could stoke the flames back to life, he heard his mentor's voice.

"Ghazi!"

The men at camp center turned in Malcolm's direction, including Darcan. The knight had his broadsword pointed at the huge hooded figure. Men armed with crossbows raised their weapons, then turned to their leader, who slipped the hood off his head.

Brim's blood froze as he looked upon the fearless mamluk warrior who'd haunted his dreams since his reading of Malcolm's account of Acre.

Several women in the camp screamed at the sight of Ghazi's burned and contorted features. Light from nearby campfires cast macabre shadows onto the textures of his face, creating an illusion of motion in his unnaturally contoured flesh. His darkened features displayed an expression of puzzlement.

Brim understood—Ghazi's men would never address their warlord as anything less honorable than "Amir," let alone by name. Yet his name had been called out by someone in camp. Everyone near camp center watched Ghazi march to within eight feet of Malcolm. His blackened features then displayed the shock of revelation. With a lowered scimitar in his right hand, he held up his left as a gesture to his men; they shall not interfere. He then uttered the single word that encapsulated his relationship with the man before him. "Acre . . ."

The great mamluk looked deep into the aged knight's eyes. Malcolm stared back, as if trying to determine how the celebrated warrior from the sultan's army had become the mercenary warlord he now faced. His distraction was apparently the opening the Saracen sought.

In the blink of an eye, the tall Muslim spun right, extending his scimitar and completing the pivot with a crouching lunge. Against any other, Brim knew his mentor would have been out of range, but his opponent used his unusually long reach to extend the arc of his sword tip to a point just above Malcolm's right knee. The maneuver denied the knight the time required to rotate his broadsword downward and block with his blade. Only by jerking the sword's hilt downward was Malcolm able to block the tip of Ghazi's blade with the hilt guard, located less than an inch away from his index finger. After the deflection, Malcolm sprang backward, establishing a guard position.

The men who had the camp surrounded rushed in from all directions, eager to see their warlord battle the knight. The new arrivals were told by others not to interfere as their leader fought a nemesis from Acre. The mercenaries appeared enthralled.

Before Brim could empty the second satchel's contents into the weak fire, two armed men passing by finally noticed him. One slammed the stock of a crossbow into the back of his head while another stomped out the fire's embers. Barely conscious, Brim was dragged to the circle of men at camp center.

The duel continued. Brim heard Darcan ordering men with crossbows to shoot Malcolm. Each time he was ignored, he became more incensed. Finally, he grabbed a crossbow from one of them and aimed it at Malcolm. Brim noticed Theron circumvent the armed men, intercept Darcan and crash his blade down on the crossbow. Darcan released the weapon, jumped back, and drew his own sword. Darcan's orders for shooting his own adversary were also ignored by Ghazi's men, who supported their warlord with shouts of encouragement, forcing the ambassador to square off with Theron.

Brim's head pounded, but his fuzzy vision cleared enough for him to take in the surreal scene around him. One fight raged within a circle of nearly forty men while another took place outside it. He soon understood why. The fight between Theron and Darcan mostly involved shouting; neither man risked getting within range of the other. The fight between Malcolm and Ghazi, however, was a display of two master swordsmen, each with a vastly different style. The powerful mamluk's initial forceful strikes required a sturdy defensive by Malcolm, precluding counterstrikes. The elder knight withstood the onslaught with footwork, keeping the Muslim warrior off balance, forcing him to lunge, turn, and twist during his powerful swings.

After a short time, Ghazi appeared to tire, his strikes lacking their previous strength. With his sword not being deflected as forcibly, Malcolm began delivering short counterstrikes, producing small cuts on Ghazi's arms and shoulders. The wounds began having a cumulative effect on his opponent as blood streaked down his sides, then onto his legs. Still, the huge mamluk tried to end the knight with each swing.

Still on his knees, Brim glanced around at the circle of men. Looks of distress replaced their initial cheerful expressions, their howls of encouragement changing to shouts of concern. The swordsmen raised their blades in preparation but obeyed their leader's order of noninterference. Others handled their crossbows nervously but were not willing to sight in Malcolm and risk taking aim at their warlord or the men on the opposite side of the circle.

The Muslim let his frustrations show. His face displayed the rage Brim imagined from Acre, his strikes growing more erratic. Ghazi pounded Malcolm's horizontally held sword with repeated blows from above, trying to use his height and remaining strength to overwhelm the knight. After the fourth block, Malcolm shifted left, knelt, and held his sword close, away from the downward arc of his opponent's blade. The tip of the mamluk's scimitar buried itself into the ground, and Malcolm drove his blade upward, though Ghazi's midsection.

In an instant, the entire camp fell silent. Malcolm looked up and to his right, staring into the wide eyes of the crouching warlord. The knight rose from his kneeling position, pushing Ghazi to a standing position with his sword, then used the continued momentum to extract his blade as the mamluk fell to the ground on his back. Malcolm stood in the center of the circle, seemingly awaiting the inevitable.

Several seconds passed. A scream of agony from one of Ghazi's crossbowmen broke the silence, as he walked to within two feet of Malcolm and shot a bolt into his chest. The knight remained standing, maintaining the grip on his sword with his right hand and grabbing the protruding quills with his left, prompting screams from more of Ghazi's men. Several impaled Malcolm with more bolts, and the dying knight fell beside his dying nemesis.

Brim's stomach muscles involuntarily contracted, forcing him to bend forward. Tears blurred his vision as he gasped for breath.

Two other mamluk crossbowmen finally adhered to Darcan's demands, each shooting a bolt into Theron's legs. Darcan's slashing blow then produced a mortal wound to Theron's neck and chest, prompting Shayla to run to his side. The Greek tack master fell to his knees and his weeping daughter knelt beside him. Shayla applied pressure, trying to slow the profuse bleeding, but the gash was too large.

She seemed to realize this and pressed her torso against her father's wound and wrapped her arms around him—a final embrace.

Brim broke free of the mamluk holding him and scurried over to Shayla's side, kneeling beside her. He could see no hope for her father as blood coated the entire left side of Theron's cotton tunic. Brim's concern was now for Shayla.

"Search every tent for documents!" Darcan roared. Ghazi's men attended to the body of their fallen warlord. Slowly, a few obeyed their employer, ripping tents from their stakes and searching underneath. Two men told Darcan of the documents they saved from the cooking fire and left to retrieve them. In minutes, the slightly charred documents were on the ground before Darcan.

Brim stayed on his knees beside Shayla, rocking back and forth and clenching his teeth.

Several who'd fled the initial arrival of armed men returned for their belongings. Darcan told the mercenaries to prepare for the march back to Limassol, then pointed his sword at Brim. "Take your wench back to Kolossi. Say unto your brothers their time is coming to an end."

Brim saw Darcan's blade float up, the hilt jerk down, then nothing more.

POITIERS

Francesco Orsini nervously listened to the approach of Guillaume de Nogaret on the stone steps leading to his chamber atop the south tower. On his orders, two curia guards escorted the king's man and his two bodyguards. The first stood in the open doorway and spoke. "Guillaume de Nogaret to see Your Eminence."

Orsini beckoned them inside, and the two curia guards took positions on either side of him. The two royal bodyguards entered the room, looked around cautiously, then parted to make way for Nogaret.

Orsini, wearing a simple red robe, frowned with disgust at the elaborate attire donned by the French lawyer. "Your presence here is inappropriate while outside the grace of the church."

Nogaret chortled. "Your Eminence, my continued excommunication was the condition for Benedict's lifting of that wrongly imposed on His Grace by Boniface."

"Is that so?" asked Orsini, knowing it was. He also knew the Frenchman's hatred of the church was spawned from the burning of his parents during the continued purge of the Cathars years before his clash with Pope Boniface VIII. Both men also knew it was only a matter of time before Pope Clement V restored Nogaret, as Pope Benedict XI had for King Philip IV.

"It is," said Nogaret, while glancing at the curia guards, then his own. "Shall I begin discussing why I am here?"

Orsini pursed his lips, disgusted at himself for allowing the man's sly manipulation, effectively ordering the room cleared. "Leave us."

The last guard closed the heavy iron door behind him, and Nogaret spoke. "His Grace recognizes your authority within the curia. He wants you to know of the secret arrest warrants issued one week ago."

Orsini tensed. "Arrest warrants? For whom?"

"The Poor Fellow-Soldiers of Christ and of the Temple of Solomon," replied Nogaret.

"For whom within the order?"

"All currently in France."

The room fell silent. Orsini saw the pleasure in the Frenchman's eyes as he spoke of what he thought was to come. "Impossible!"

Nogaret shook his head. "Inevitable."

Orsini swallowed hard. "The church will never allow it!"

"In the case of heresy, the Inquisition demands action by *secular* authorities."

"Only for individual suspects found guilty and convicted of unrepentant heresy!"

Nogaret shook a piece of lint from his lace collar as a peacock would from its feathers. "All are guilty and shall be proven such."

"Impossible," repeated Orsini, realizing over five thousand members of the order served in France. The coordination and resources for such mass arrests would have to be extraordinary.

Nogaret seemed to let him ponder the information for a moment longer before speaking again. "It is simply an extension of your own proposal."

"I proposed legal inquiry! Nothing about heresy or mass arrests!" Orsini saw the direction the Frenchman was leading.

"His Grace has sources within the order, as I'm sure you do. Jacques de Molay himself has asked Clement to investigate such heresies."

"No." Orsini shook his index finger. "That was only regarding spurious rumors involving a small number of brothers. Their central discussion concerned the merger of the military orders."

"A merger the Grand Masters of both rejected," said Nogaret, too quickly.

"Ah, there it is. You know of the proposal for command of such a united order falling to the hereditary kings of France, making Philip *Bellator Rex*."

Nogaret perused the artwork adoring the walls.

"And if he cannot gain control in that way—"

"I've been instructed by His Grace to inform you of the secret arrest warrants. I've done so. Do you have any further questions?"

Orsini studied the man's expression and body language. Amazingly, the Frenchman appeared to believe the arrests would actually occur. "If such simultaneous arrests were possible, when would they take place?"

"In three weeks' time, preparations will be complete and the arrests will proceed," said Nogaret.

"What makes you believe I will not warn de Molay?"

"As I've said, this is an extension of *your* proposal."

He considered objecting again, then realized the futility of doing so. Another question formed in his mind. "Why am I being told of this?"

Nogaret nodded, as if finally being asked a question he'd been waiting for. "His Grace asks something of you."

A heaviness materialized in the pit of Orsini's stomach. "Which is?"

"When the arrests commence, you are to ensure Clement does not interfere."

CHAPTER 12
JULY 22, 12:04 P.M. GST
BASRA, IRAQ

The sun's elevation heated the five-acre space to a nearly unbearable temperature considering the formal attire worn by most present. Dust filled the air, despite police stationed around the periphery redirecting the local children who typically used the sandy expanse as a soccer field.

A saddened Rick Lambert knew choosing the Basra War Cemetery—known to locals as the English Cemetery—was not without controversy. Due to security concerns, Samir's body had already been laid to rest at a location known only to family and in accordance with the Islamic tradition of burial taking place as soon as possible. Lambert also understood the choice of location made by Representative Mohammed Moozarmi for the public service. It reflected his son's service with the British Army as translator in Basra while on loan from the US Army. It also emphasized a pressing issue for his Basra Governorate—how and when to allow the Commonwealth War Graves Commission restoration of the cemetery containing the graves of thousands of British servicemen from World Wars I and II to its condition before Saddam's 1991 invasion of Kuwait.

Besides family and friends, the public funeral service attendees included the elder Moozarmi's Iraqi Council of Representatives colleagues from governorates surrounding Basra and their entourages. Lambert positioned himself on the southern tip of the Basra Memorial Wall. Through blurred vision, he recognized council members from Muthanna, Dhi Qar, Najaf, Al-Qadisiyyah, and Maysan. It was a surprisingly large turnout, given the short notice.

Six large white canopy gazebos located in front of the Basra Memorial's central obelisk provided some relief from direct sunlight.

Attendees began filing out from the shade in a slow procession toward the cemetery's south gate, many dabbing at their necks and faces with handkerchiefs, undoubtedly looking forward to entering their air-conditioned vehicles.

Two of the many men Lambert had identified as working security approached his southernmost spot on the wall. They turned left and stopped four paces in front of him. The taller of the two spoke. "Representative Moozarmi would have words."

Lambert nodded. This, he expected. He watched the two security men turn right and continue toward the south gate, then turned his gaze north toward the gazebos.

The powerfully built Mohammed Moozarmi meandered along the west side of the memorial wall behind two more security men, periodically accepting condolences. Nearing the wall's end, he glanced at Lambert, then whispered something to his protection. Both men nodded. The elder Iraqi stopped, turned, and faced Lambert, his protection detail continuing south.

Lambert sighed inwardly. The inevitable moment he'd been dreading had arrived. "Representative Moozarmi, please accept my sincere condolences on the loss of Samir."

Mohammed gestured back to the gazebos. "You do not sit with the others?"

"No sir. I didn't know if . . . if it was appropriate."

Mohammed nodded. "Where is Kassab?"

"Sir, Chief Kassab has been unavoidably detained in Baghdad."

Mohammed pointed to the wall's south tip, then slipped around to the east side, away from the flow of others walking past. Lambert followed. Only when they were alone did the representative speak again. "So, you have been sent to bear my wrath alone?"

Lambert stared at the Iraqi politician's tie and said nothing, instead focusing on the same feeling of guilt he'd experienced years before after Fallujah.

"You will not have it."

Lambert looked into the grieving father's eyes. "Sir?"

"I spoke with Samir before the monsignor arrived. You advised against taking him to Kanisah before more security could be arranged. You and Samir were ordered to escort him there, despite your objections. I know these things."

"I could have stayed with him . . ." Lambert lowered his head. "Perhaps—"

"No," Mohammed argued. "You had been shot."

"By a stun slug."

"You were incapacitated. Had you not been, you would have been killed with Samir." Mohammed shook his head. "No, you will not be burdened by false blame again. Not like you were after Fallujah."

Lambert jerked his head back up.

"Yes . . . I know this also."

Bewildered, he continued staring straight into the eyes of the Iraqi representative from Basra.

"You will continue on with this case?"

"Yes."

"You will call me for any request . . . any asset . . . any resources you require from the government of Iraq?"

"Yes sir."

Mohammed nodded. "Very well. I will have words with Kassab about—"

Lambert was surprised to see Samir's mother, Yashira, appear around the south tip of the wall. Mohammed stepped aside. She strode up to Lambert and raised her veiled eyes to meet his. With a scream, she tore the bandage off his neck and began beating his chest.

Mohammed grasped his grief-stricken wife from behind, pulled her back, and whispered into her ear.

Lambert moved his hand to his neck, then saw blood on his fingers as he pulled it away. In addition to tearing off the bandage, Yashira had torn open the wound from the stun slug barbs.

Looking at the shrouded expression of the woman being awkwardly embraced by her husband, the message in her eyes was clear—*Samir is dead because of you.*

Behind her, Mohammed's eyes beamed a message equally poignant—*avenge our son.*

11:08 P.M. GST
NORTHEASTERN MOSUL

Over the years, he'd witnessed the full spectrum of human willpower. Getting answers from some required little effort. Others presented more of a challenge. He was exhausted and genuinely impressed; he'd rarely seen the strength shown by Plenducci, even in men half his age. It took nearly twenty-four hours to get the information he thought pertinent. The last few hours uncovered no further coherent thoughts from the old priest. Given the man's age, keeping him alive that long had been a challenge.

He knew orders from southwest Tehran would be to act on the information immediately. After reporting in, however, he would need to sleep. But sleep would be difficult, given the outrageous new information racing through his mind.

PART TWO

Pastoralis Praeeminentiae

Kolossi Preceptory – 1307

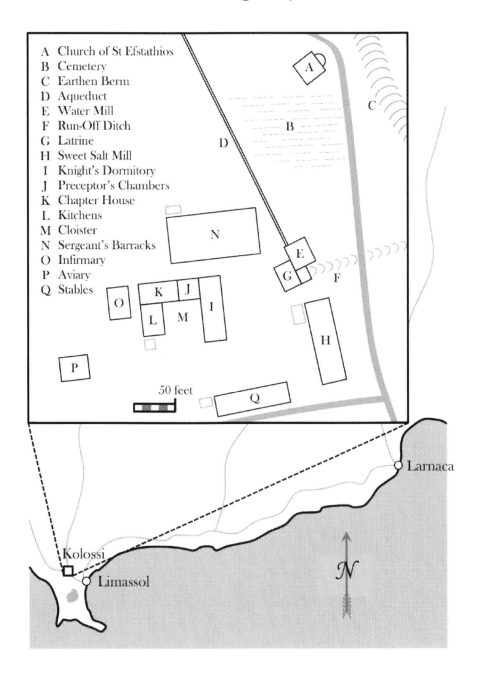

A Church of St Efstathios
B Cemetery
C Earthen Berm
D Aqueduct
E Water Mill
F Run-Off Ditch
G Latrine
H Sweet Salt Mill
I Knight's Dormitory
J Preceptor's Chambers
K Chapter House
L Kitchens
M Cloister
N Sergeant's Barracks
O Infirmary
P Aviary
Q Stables

50 feet

Larnaca

Kolossi

Limassol

N

Kolossi Castle – Present Day

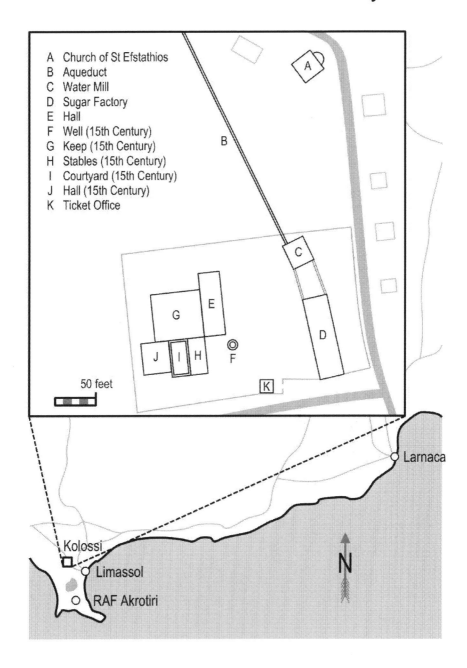

A Church of St Efstathios
B Aqueduct
C Water Mill
D Sugar Factory
E Hall
F Well (15th Century)
G Keep (15th Century)
H Stables (15th Century)
I Courtyard (15th Century)
J Hall (15th Century)
K Ticket Office

50 feet

Larnaca

Kolossi

Limassol

RAF Akrotiri

N

CHAPTER 13

TIME AND LOCATION UNKNOWN

Despite the darkness, Brim Hastings sensed fire. The burning in his throat had been increasing for a duration he found difficult to estimate. He tried swallowing, but his throat would not obey. Upon moving, he sensed pain on his shoulder blades. His back was against something hard. Rolling lessened the pain to one side and increased it on the other, but it confirmed he was not restrained.

Struggling to see through the darkness, he opened his eyes as wide as he could. What little light entered through entangled eyelashes proved his eyes were not open at all, the salty sting indicating they were instead caked shut with sweat.

As his anxiety ramped up, Brim raised his arms from his sides. They seemed heavy. His strength waned, and his hands fell upon his face. He then forced open his eyes with his fingers.

A small arch of stone curved eight feet above, dimly lit by flickering flames of several nearby candles, fallow rather than beeswax, based on their offensive odor. Despite the pain it caused his neck, he turned his head to the left. Several columns supported a series of identical arches. Under each was an empty fabric-covered sleeping pallet. From out of the corner of his left eye, he could see he lay on a pallet of his own. Again ignoring the pain in his neck and turning his head to the right, he saw his was the pallet nearest a heavy wooden door ten feet away.

He suddenly recognized his location—the Kolossi preceptory infirmary. He'd seen it from the doorway three years before and remembered its stark contrast to the infirmary in London. While the space in London sheltered the sick and injured in ample light and cleanliness, this room had been dark, damp, and infested with insects.

From the right of the door came a snore. Brim craned his neck and saw the slumped, aproned infirmarer. He tried calling out but could not force sound from his burning throat. He inhaled as deeply as possible and coughed, intensifying the burn.

The portly brother woke, his head jerking upward.

"Water," whispered Brim.

The infirmarer nodded and lifted a ceramic cup from the floor, then brought it to Brim's mouth. After half the cup's contents filled his mouth, his inability to swallow caused him to cough again, this time sending water into the infirmarer's pockmarked face. He swung his head to the left and heard the cup crash to the floor. He coughed up the remaining water and turned his head back to the right. The infirmarer backed out the doorway, gesturing with both hands for him to wait. He was in no condition to do otherwise.

Rolling to the right edge of the rigid cot, he could see the stool the monk had been sitting on. On the floor next to it, a wide stone water vase beckoned. Funneling his thirst into strength, he pushed himself into a sitting position and looked down. He was fully dressed, from his plain russet tunic to his filthy leather boots. Initially puzzled, he soon realized this was to be expected. While the old knights and those supporting them in London had surrendered to the comforts of nightshirts and slippers, he again travelled overseas—to lands the French brothers termed *Outremer*. In these more inhospitable realms, the order adhered more strictly to Latin Rule, which meant sleeping fully clothed.

Pushing himself off the pallet to a standing position, he felt the strength in his legs betray him. He kept his head from slamming into the stone floor by landing on his forearms but could not protect his knees from impacting the tiles. While crawling the eight-foot distance through shards of the shattered cup, he grabbed the thick-based bottom portion, which looked like it would still hold a mouthful of water.

After rolling his body off the floor and onto the stool, he threw his right arm over the rim of the water vase while keeping a tight grip on the cup bottom and thinking one thought—do not drop the fragment into the vase. Finally being able to swallow, he downed the first few mouthfuls of water rapidly, despite the pain it caused. The burning in his throat subsided, and he began to notice a pain atop his head. He rubbed his left palm over his scalp and was surprised to feel a clean-shaven head, smooth to the touch with the exception of what felt like crude stitches just above his forehead.

Touching the treated wound triggered memories of events from the Larnaca campsite in reverse order: Cibalik Darcan glowering above him, Shayla kneeling by his side, the killing of her father Theron and, most staggering, the deaths of Malcolm and his Acre nemesis, Ghazi. His grip on the cup fragment tightened. The ceramic shattered, and several pieces cut into his right palm before falling to the floor.

Brim stared at his vacated cot through wet eyes and asked himself the pertinent questions. How had he travelled forty-five miles southwest to Kolossi? How long had he been unconscious? Was Shayla still alive?

"Finally awake!"

The surprise of the booming voice from the doorway caused Brim to jerk back against the wall. He realized his position on the stool inside the stone doorjamb had blocked the sound of the man's approach. He tried to stand.

"Stay. Conserve your strength." The tall knight, resplendent in his bright white mantle, walked to the nearest sleeping pallet, turned, and sat. The pockmarked infirmarer followed and stood beside him.

"They say you are Brimley Hastings, sergeant to the Preceptor of Kolossi until he was killed the day before yesterday."

Has it been two days?

Brim felt the urge to ask questions, but his rank limited him to giving answers. "Yes sir."

"And you know who I am?"

"Yes sir."

The knight tilted his head down and raised an eyebrow, clearly wanting a more substantial answer.

"Marshal of Cyprus Sir Ayme d'Oselier." While normally stationed in Nicosia, Brim remembered him touring the Kolossi preceptory three years before. While the Grand Master and Visitor of the Temple traveled to France, d'Oselier would be in command on Cyprus.

The marshal nodded. "I have questions. First, why was the Preceptor of Kolossi back on Cyprus?"

Brim knew trusted Venetian merchants transferred the order's sealed communication packets between Paris and Nicosia at regular intervals. How had the thefts and killing of a guard remained unknown? Were the Venetians late? Or did the information wait for d'Oselier in Nicosia? Whatever the reason, he knew it would eventually arrive and his answers had to agree. "To deliver documents, sir."

"What documents?"

Brim glanced at the infirmarer, then back at d'Oselier.

The marshal seemed to understand the concern and turned to the man beside him. "Leave us."

Alone with d'Oselier, Brim continued. "The ledgers documenting the mobilization on Cyprus."

"Brought to Cyprus for what reason?"

"I do not know, sir." Brim decided to elaborate on what the marshal would soon learn. "They were acquired surreptitiously. A guard was killed at the Shipley preceptory."

D'Oselier frowned. "Killed by whom?"

"Sir Malcolm's squire, Angus."

"Is he on Cyprus also?"

"No sir. I believe he returned to Scotland."

Ayme d'Oselier lowered his head and directed a more intense gaze. "These ledgers—you have read them?"

"Yes sir." Was d'Oselier among the "others at Kolossi" Malcolm had mentioned off the coast of Bordeaux? Until known, the Praximus Command would not be discussed.

"Where are the ledgers now?"

"Taken by Ambassador Cibalik Darcan, sir."

D'Oselier sat back and gave an accepting nod. "That's what the tack master's daughter reported when she arrived this morning."

So Shayla is alive.

The marshal continued. "Darcan came to our gates one week ago, seeking your master. We told him the preceptors from Kolossi, Kyrenia, and Famagusta all traveled with our delegation in France." The marshal stood and put his hands on his hips. "It seems the Armenian knows more about our order's business than we do, does it not?"

Brim assumed the question was hypothetical and remained silent.

D'Oselier crossed his arms. "On whose orders did Sir Malcolm do this?"

"I do not know, sir."

"Is there anything further you can tell me of this?"

Brim thought of his oaths to the order and his mentor. The latter now seemed paramount. "No sir."

"You speak truth?"

"Yes sir."

Clearly frustrated, the marshal began walking toward the door. "We shall see. You will be questioned further. See the draper for a uniform. You are confined to preceptory grounds."

POITIERS

Francesco Orsini reflected on the latest excruciating meeting of the Circuitor Consistory while waiting in the outer chamber for his audience with Pope Clement V. The other four Italian cardinals had been shocked to hear the details of his meeting with Guillaume de Nogaret. They demanded he divulge the Crown's plans for the Order of the Temple to the man he still thought of as merely the Archbishop of Bordeaux. But this was not the time for panic. He had a compromise in mind.

The French cardinal acting as the pontiff's acolyte opened the heavy double doors to Clement's inner sanctum. "Cardinal Francesco Orsini to see Your Holiness."

Clement, seated in a raised chair behind a similarly raised desk, sifted through papers and nodded toward a chair fronting his desk. "Orsini. Come in. Sit down."

Orsini stood briefly in front of the raised desk, at eye level with the shorter pontiff, and gave a nearly undetectable nod. "Your Holiness." As expected, when he took his seat he sat a full two feet below Clement.

"What may I do for you?"

Orsini heard the sarcasm in the pope's weak, high-pitched voice. "Your Holiness, my colleagues and I have a concern—"

"Your colleagues?" Clement leaned forward. "I trust you do not refer to your so-called Circuitor Consistory. I declared that anachronism disbanded."

"Yes, Your Holiness." Orsini offered another almost imperceptible nod before continuing. "There is . . . a concern regarding the rejection of the proposed merger of military orders by their Grand Masters."

Clement raised a finger in protest. "The unification of the orders is an ongoing issue with many details left to be determined."

"Yes, Your Holiness." Orsini fell silent.

Clement eyed him suspiciously. "With that said, what is this concern?"

"The proposed merger put forth by the Dominicans requires a Bellator Rex for command of the unified order, the most likely candidate being King Philip IV."

"What is the issue?"

"If the unification does not take place, might the king take unilateral action to gain control of the Order of the Temple?"

The question seemed to catch the pope off guard. "Certainly not! His Grace understands and accepts that military orders answer only to me. The secular Bellator Rex would lead forces of a unified order in battle and nothing more."

Orsini feigned penitence. "Apologies, Your Holiness. I do not know the king as you do."

Clement again eyed him with suspicion. Both men understood the influence the Crown wielded over the church during their self-imposed exile from Rome, but to imply Philip influenced the pontiff personally was not to be spoken of openly. The last comment by Orsini came dangerously close to doing so. Clement's expression changed to one of puzzlement. "You mention only the Order of the Temple. Your concern does not extend to the Order of the Hospital?"

"No, Your Holiness." Orsini paused for effect, knowing his next words would enrage the weak pontiff. "Foulques de Villaret's annexation of Rhodes nears completion. It will likely become the

Hospitaller's new headquarters, its lack of proximity eliminating their vulnerability to action by the king."

"You did not hear me!" Clement pounded his desk with a fist. "His Grace knows both orders answer to me alone! He would never take such action!"

Orsini again appeared apologetic. "Yes, Your Holiness."

"You may go."

Orsini recognized the immediate dismissal. "Yes, Your Holiness." He stood and backed away, only turning his back on the pontiff to open the double doors. He'd planted the seed of what was to come in Clement's mind. It was all that was required. For now.

CHAPTER 14

NEW YORK TIMES

(Front Page)

VATICAN OFFICIAL ABDUCTED IN IRAQ

MOSUL, JULY 22—Monsignor Giuseppe Plenducci, a senior Vatican researcher, was abducted last night in Mosul, Iraq. Plenducci had traveled to Iraq to assist with the investigation of Christian clergy abductions taking place since early June. A spokesman from the Iraqi Ministry of Interior said measures are being taken to find the missing researcher. (Continued on page 4)

LONDON TIMES

(Front Page)

OUTRAGE IN VATICAN CITY OVER
ABDUCTION OF REPRESENTATIVE

VATICAN CITY, JULY 22—A spokesman for the Press Office of the Holy See expressed his continued displeasure today over the lack of results in the search for their researcher Monsignor Giuseppe Plenducci. Plenducci was abducted the night before in Mosul, Iraq, and is the last in a string of Christian priest abductions occurring in the last two months. (See page 3)

LE NOUVEL OBSERVATEUR

(Page 9)

VANDALS DAMAGE FORTRESS AT LA COUVERTOIRADE

TOULOUSE, JULY 22—Vandalism occurred last night inside the fortress of La Couvertoirade in Aveyron, Midi-Pyrénées, 120 km northeast of Toulouse. Damage was limited to interior walls. Evidence of drilled holes found in several brick fragments suggests use of embedded explosives. Engineers are confirming structural integrity before allowing continued use of the building. The fortress is used by craftsmen for making pottery and weaved products.

JULY 22, 4:46 P.M. GST
EN ROUTE TO BAGHDAD, IRAQ

The case of the Christian priest abductions in Iraq had been a growing yet localized news story for the last couple of months. With the abduction of Plenducci, the case became major news around the world. As usual, the Associated Press latched onto the most sensational aspects, releasing syndicated articles with maximum speed and impact. Fact-checking had not been a priority. The early AP flashes reported the abduction of "Cardinal" Plenducci and contained several other exaggerations, prompting the Vatican to issue a corrective press release. Yet in their continued public stance, Plenducci had been there to help with the investigation and should have been better protected.

Several Iraqi Army units stationed in northern Iraq had been deployed to Mosul to assist police in searching the city and outlying suburbs. A dirty white elastic skullcap, possibly Plenducci's, was found in a vacant lot south of the Sahaba Mosque.

The most significant items, found in the desert northwest of Mosul, were four armored vans, their interiors burned out. The vans matched those reported missing from the Kirkuk Police Department motor pool two months before. The digital photos sent from the scene showed the small impacts on the driver's side window and rear panels caused by the rounds from Lambert and Samir during the first Kanisah attack.

Several MOI agents investigated individual aspects of the case. Those flown to Mosul attempted identifying the dead and developing leads from evidence: the armored vans, the weapons and equipment, the stun slugs, even the empty 5.56mm brass cases. At headquarters, a team scoured the internet for news of any groups taking responsibility for abductions in Iraq. Others met with informers around Baghdad to learn of any underground rumors being circulated.

The ninety-minute flight from Basra to Baghdad aboard MOI's Cessna 208 Caravan gave Rick Lambert more time to grieve. He needed a sounding board before his debriefing with Ali Kassab. He called James Dougherty.

After hearing the full description of the second attack, Dougherty offered one piece of advice—the best way to honor and avenge a fallen comrade was simply to continue working the case in their name.

With a quiver in his voice, Lambert agreed. He took a moment to blow his nose and compose himself, then began discussing details with Dougherty. He would use every advantage available to him, including resources from the US Intelligence Community. But he knew Kassab would balk.

"Plenducci still had the domino on him?" Dougherty asked.

"Yes sir." Lambert chastised himself for not getting it back before they arrived at the church. It would be something his abductors could base their interrogations on, if they didn't know about it already. The group they were up against seemed better informed. He hated being the outsider and expressed his frustrations to Dougherty.

"Okay, but the enemy doesn't know everything. What *don't* they know?"

Lambert thought for a second. "The Vatican has a thing for Praximus, or the connection between Praximus and Sorvacore."

"Yes, but let's start before that," Dougherty said. Their conversation centered on the original case. The abductions of Christian priests began in and around Baghdad. After the initial attacks at some of the larger churches of both Eastern Rite and Armenian denominations, they seemed to move north to the smaller, independent churches. This would make sense if the abductors weren't finding what they wanted from the "mainstream" Christians in Iraq. "The Persians underestimated Kanisah." Dougherty had been referring to the abductors as Persians since Lambert told him about hearing Farsi during the first attack.

Lambert agreed with the assessment but felt the Persians were close to finding what they sought. Topolis must have known something Plenducci wanted to find out about.

Was it the connection between Praximus and Sorvacore?

"We have to assume they're going to get information from Plenducci," Lambert said.

"Agreed. So what does the Vatican know?"

The conversation with Danny came to mind. "They reacted to the name Praximus. That has to be key." He explained to Dougherty what Kassab told him the night before—the Vatican had a decision to make. If they wanted any more involvement with the general abduction case—the search for Plenducci or the research Plenducci was here for—they would have to share their information.

Dougherty described what he expected to hear from Rome. Their public response would be one of outrage; one of their investigators had been abducted after coming to Iraq to help with the case of the Christian priest abductions.

"Help with the case?" Lambert asked, immediately regretting it. "Sorry, sir. It's just that Plenducci only came to find out what Topolis knew."

"Understood. We know that and so do they. That's why they'll have a private response."

"Private response?"

Dougherty explained the internal consensus from the Vatican would be that they'd acted impulsively sending in Plenducci. And considering the opposition most likely knew what Plenducci knew, a bad situation had gotten worse. They'd now want to coordinate efforts with the Iraqi MOI and the US Intelligence Community to find a way forward. To that end, they'd probably already sent a second Vatican representative to Baghdad.

"Here we go again."

"Maybe not. They're going to be desperate this time," Dougherty explained. "You and Kassab need to stick to your guns about making them share information."

"OK, I'm about to touch down at Al-Rasheed. I'll let you know how it goes."

"Good luck."

CHAPTER 15

SEPTEMBER 26, 1307

KOLOSSI

The development of the Kolossi compound since Brim's visit three years before amazed him. Stonemasons had built several chambers off the knight's dormitory and vastly expanded the stables. The sweet salt mill, once a quiet refuge for monks with a skill in culinary arts, had become a bustling center of frantic production, with hundreds of craftsmen striving to produce the maximum amount of exportable material possible.

The preceptory grounds had expanded even more dramatically. Less than three acres only three years before, the compound now sprawled to encompass nearly four times that area. Over two hundred *confrère* mercenary sergeants supplemented Kolossi's thirty-five brother sergeants, all of whom put to work building temporary wooden barracks for up to a thousand more.

The most perplexing new feature of their enlarged domain was the ten-foot-high earthen berm, all-encompassing with the exception of large gates at the four cardinal compass directions to allow horse and wagon access. Several confrère sergeants walked the outer perimeter of the berm's half-mile circumference in regular counter-rotating intervals. It would be a feeble defensive barricade without additional obstructions. Still, because of the added foot patrols, Brim had to wait until nightfall to scurry over the berm near the east gate and sneak through the water mill's runoff ditch used to irrigate the eastern orchards.

Two days ago, after being discharged by the infirmarer, Brim had acquired a lightweight sergeant's tunic and mantle from the draper Jean de Villa and been assigned scribe duty for the marshal. As was the case with nearly all the other eighty-two knights of Kolossi, Ayme d'Oselier could neither read nor write; "quills for priests, swords for knights," was the pervasive notion. Tomorrow, however, he would report to the Turcopolier of Kolossi, relocating from his small alcove adjacent to the chamber of the Preceptor of Kolossi—a space currently occupied by d'Oselier—to the sergeant's barracks. If he was to see Shayla for answers, this seemed to be his last chance.

Leaving the orchard for the road to Limassol, Brim somberly reflected on what he'd learned of the sad events that had taken place before he awoke in the infirmary. Nearly every man in the compound spoke of the young Cypriot girl who'd driven her wagon up to the east gate with the bodies of the Preceptor of Kolossi and her own father, as well as a young sergeant just barely alive. In the morning of the day Brim had regained consciousness, Malcolm of Basingstoke was buried in the preceptory's cemetery, and Theron Kostas was buried in Limassol. So impressed was d'Oselier with Shayla's ordeal, she'd been declared the successor to her father as Tack Master of Kolossi, an unprecedented position for a woman. During Brim's visit to the stables, the grooms confirmed Shayla still used her father's Limassol residence and workshop.

The clear night sky allowed the two-mile walk to Limassol under moonlight. Although Brim had never been to the Kostas house before, the directions from the grooms led him to it quickly. He neither saw nor heard any activity from the residence, but light escaped from cracks between the sideboards of the adjacent workshop. The side door was ajar, and Brim peered inside. Candlelight revealed Shayla slumped over one of her father's worktables, her hands resting on what appeared to be a pair of heavy iron pliers.

He tapped on the door. "Shayla?"

She shot upright and turned to the door, seemingly alarmed by the nighttime intruder with the shaved head. Only after he took a step into the candlelight did she recognize him. "Brimley? What are you doing here?"

He lowered his gaze to the thatched-mat floor. "Apologies for coming uninvited." Looking up, he continued. "Tonight was my last chance to get away. I report to the turcopolier tomorrow to join the battalion of new sergeants. I don't know when I may be able to get away again, and I wanted to see you . . . to learn of Larnaca."

She stepped forward, with anger in bloodshot eyes that had apparently been producing tears before his arrival. "Larnaca? My father and your master are dead! You wish to relive it?"

"No, please . . ."

"If it weren't for those of your order, and others like them, we could openly trade with those of the East, as the maritime republics do, and a lasting peace would result."

Brim felt baffled. "*Openly* trade?"

"I trade with my friend Farah Zayn from Tortosa—oil for sinew."

"By what possible means?" Brim challenged.

"Cypriot and Syrian fishermen often meet and trade on the sea. Years ago, a request was relayed to me for the neatsfoot oil we render from cattle on Cyprus. It had come from a young apprentice tanner working with her father, just as I had been doing with my father. That was Farah. I sent a sample and asked about Asian elephant sinew. She sent a sample in return. We've been trading and writing to each other ever since. Her Greek is outpacing my Arabic . . ."

Brim raised his hands. "Are you saying the order's armor is held together by *Syrian* leather?"

"I am. And what's wrong with that?"

"Did your father know of this?"

She shook her head. "He was as those in your order. He assumed I obtained the strands from Larnaca."

"Then why did you do it?"

"Because they're the best quality! For any given thickness, they're stronger than anything I can find on Cyprus."

Brim shook his head and decided to change the subject. "All at Kolossi speak of your bravery."

"After the Armenian left with the Saracens, many at the camp helped me. We wrapped the bodies of my father and Sir Malcolm, then loaded them on the wagon."

Brim nodded. "You saved me, too."

She looked down and would not meet his gaze. "It took most of two days to reach Kolossi. While delivering saddles the next evening, the east gate guard told me you'd recovered."

"The gate guard? You're not allowed passage to the stables?"

She shook her head again. "Since raising the embankment four months ago, none outside your order has entered the expanded compound. Speculation in Limassol is rampant."

Brim paused. He remembered seeing empty wagons just inside each gate. Their purpose now seemed clear—the transfer of supplies before being brought into the compound.

"What is the 'battalion of new sergeants' you spoke of?"

Again, he was at a loss for words. How had the addition of two hundred French mercenaries into Kolossi gone unnoticed by the civilian population? Perhaps their numbers had built up gradually, a dozen or so from each ship arriving at Limassol? He realized Shayla deserved an answer. "New arrivals since my time here three years ago."

She tilted her head forward and raised her eyebrows, clearly wanting an explanation.

"I will learn more when I join their ranks tomorrow."

"It may be a challenging transition, from serving one knight to serving as one among many."

"Possibly. But no more challenging as advancing from apprentice to tack master." He intended to acknowledge her loss, as she'd done for him, but he saw it reignite her anger.

"Both deaths for nothing but words on parchment!"

His eyes widened. "You know of them?"

"My father told me that night in Larnaca. Weeks before, he also told me Sir Malcolm would return well before the others."

"How could he have known?"

"Some plan for Cyprus, averting some catastrophe on Cyprus, I don't know . . . none of it matters to me now!" She shuffled to another worktable and began stacking pieces of leather scrap.

Brim did not believe her disinterest. She must have had a desire to know what her father died for. He could, however, imagine the intense division of her feelings in regard to the Order of the Temple; it was both the source of her livelihood and the cause of her hardship. He was unsure how to comfort her. "It appears out of our hands now."

After a pause, Shayla spoke again. "I saw you burning the scrolls from one of your three satchels before the Saracens grabbed you. Does the Armenian have enough of the documents to be a danger?"

"I believe so," said Brim, thinking specifically of the Praximus Command. "I'm not sure why Ambassador Darcan let me live after I'd tried to burn them. He'd instead taken pleasure in mocking me. He may have thought we were joined in wedlock. I remember he called you 'my wench.'"

She frowned. "He may have thought me with child."

"With child? Why?"

She stopped stacking the scraps of leather and looked down at her hands, now idle atop the worktable.

"Shayla?"

Only her lips moved. "I hid the other two satchels under my tunic."

OFF THE SOUTHERN COAST OF CRETE

Cibalik Darcan gnawed at dried beef in his cabin aboard the two-masted Venetian *cocha*. He knew of no ship in the Mediterranean that could equal its speed—obviously the main factor leading to the decision by Francesco Orsini to dispatch him in such a vessel. The cardinal expected a swift return, but not the additional three passengers.

For the death of their warlord, the Egyptian mercenaries demanded additional compensation. Despite his promises, the mamluks had designated three of their commanders to travel with him to ensure collection of what they felt they were due. Even with his ecclesiastical escort between Marseille and Poitiers, answering for Saracens in Christian territory would present a challenge. He would consider that problem in due course.

Darcan began a reexamination of the singed scrolls taken from the Larnaca campsite while softly cursing the boy responsible for their burnt edges.

How many such documents had been completely incinerated upon their initial arrival at the camp?

He told himself he was lucky to find what he did, but it did not assuage his anger.

His second perusal of the documents failed to add any clarity to the picture in his mind. The scrolls appeared to be ledgers for staging men and material on Cyprus in accordance with the calls for retaking the Holy Land by Pope Clement V. What Darcan could see of the plans for the coming year appeared logical with one exception—the contracted routes and payment schedules for the preparations on Cyprus did not extend to the delivery of fighting forces to the mainland. Maintaining separate ledgers for operations that must involve the same ships seemed an unnecessary complication.

His ignorance of such planning also puzzled him. When past efforts toward Jerusalem had reached this point, the church made impassioned pleas throughout Christendom for support of the endeavor.

Why have I not yet heard of such appeals? Why are there no reports of oaths from the gentry and nobility of Christendom for taking the cross to Jerusalem?

Although a member of the Armenian Apostolic Church, he thought he understood the minds of those in the Roman Curia. He now had doubts.

CHAPTER 16

JULY 22, 5:38 P.M. GST

SOUTHERN BAGHDAD

An unmarked Chevrolet LUV pickup waited for Rick Lambert on the Al-Rasheed tarmac. The ride north on the Mohamed Al-Qasim Expressway to MOI headquarters took fifteen minutes. Making his way to the second floor, he noticed the increased activity. Once with Kassab, he gave his report on the abduction of Plenducci and killing of Samir. To save time, an audio recording was made in lieu of a written report. Having heard the short version the night before, Kassab listened intently and did not interrupt. After twenty minutes, a thorough report of the last night's events was complete. A transcript would be made for use by others.

Kassab stood. "We'll save questions for later. Right now, I want you to meet our contact from Rome. She got here twenty minutes before you."

She? He was expecting another male academic like Plenducci.

They entered the floor's only conference room. Kassab switched to choppy English and introduced Lieutenant Maria Anna Belloci of the Vatican City Gendarmerie Corps. At six feet, she was almost as tall as Lambert. Next to the 1970's business attire worn by Kassab, her rugged outfit looked even more dramatic: hiking boots, rough khaki trousers, a denim shirt, and a vest with several pockets. A plain blue baseball cap hid all but a few wayward locks of black hair. After introductions, the three sat at the conference table.

Belloci spoke first. "Chief Kassab informed me of last night. I was so sorry to hear of your partner."

Lambert nodded.

"We understand that you and the other officers did everything possible to protect the monsignor. The CDF erred in indulging him, given the situation in Mosul."

He was confused. "You're not from the CDF?"

Maria explained that the organization of authority within Vatican City was often misunderstood. The apparatus most thought of was the Holy See, headed by the pope, who led the Roman Catholic Church via the nine congregations of the Roman Curia. A separate entity was the Vatican City State, headed by a cardinal who served as president. She had a way of describing this without sounding condescending. "My investigation division within the Gendarmerie Corps is concerned with extraterritorial properties and church possessions outside Vatican City."

"The lieutenant's division has been following our abduction case," Kassab boasted.

Lambert ignored him. "But the Roman Catholic Church doesn't have much of a presence in Iraq. The priests abducted before Topolis were either Eastern Rite or Armenian."

"True," Maria answered. "But our concern is the possible *motive* behind the abductions."

Lambert raised an eyebrow. "Which is?"

Maria took a deep breath. "I will need time to explain."

Kassab frowned at Lambert, then turned back to Maria with a smile. "You have our undivided attention, Lieutenant Belloci."

"Thank you. I have been authorized to disclose what is known. Please consider it highly confidential."

The events she described had taken place in the decades following the First Crusade. After the return from Jerusalem in 1124, an emissary gave an account to a small group of cardinals concerning a scroll shown to him by the Knights Templar. Follow-on envoys to Jerusalem confirmed the report. For nearly two centuries, only the pope and the five most influential cardinals of the curia shared knowledge of the scroll's content. The information, and the threat of it becoming known, formed a secret relationship between popes and Templar Grand Masters.

That knowledge, and the relationship it maintained, had come to a violent end in October of 1307 with the sudden persecution of the Templars by King Philip IV of France. Five years later, the five cardinals entrusted with the knowledge of the scroll had inexplicably leapt from one the towers at the Palace of the Popes in Avignon. Their suicides comprised one of the Vatican's most closely guarded secrets.

Lambert had to interrupt. "Five cardinals committed the mortal sin of suicide? And it was able to be covered up?"

Maria nodded. "Their deaths were recorded as accidents and announced at different times." She continued her explanation. After his death in 1314, a sealed epistle from Pope Clement V had been delivered to his most trusted cardinals describing the indentured relationship with the Templars prior to 1307. The only detail of what he referred to as the "heretical scroll" had been that it involved a covert Roman march to the east under the command of one named Praximus. The scroll was assumed lost with the many Templar preceptories destroyed or reallocated after 1307.

Her account suddenly shifted to the twentieth century. "Clement's epistle itself was thought to be lost until the 1960s. It was found during initial canonization research for several important figures of the Avignon Papacy."

"Avignon?" Kassab asked.

Lambert spoke up. "Fourteenth century. Seven popes resided in what would become part of France, instead of Rome."

Maria smiled. "Yes . . . it is wonderful you know that."

Lambert suddenly realized what a stunning woman she was. He shrugged. "History major."

She continued, describing the team assembled in 1966 to research the canonization potentials. The group had been given access to even the most sensitive of the Vatican's Secret Archives. One of the researchers, a young, newly ordained priest named Zephyros Topolis, found one of the canonization candidates to be from the group of cardinals who'd jumped to their deaths in Avignon and quietly removed him from the list. The research also led Topolis to rediscover the posthumous epistle of Pope Clement V inside a ledger from the same time period. The document's mention of Praximus triggered memories of stories from his missionary work in Iran between semesters at the seminary. He remembered hearing the folklore of a Roman ghost legion many times but also recalled a few of the old story-tellers refer to it as the *Praximus* ghost legion.

The young Topolis had become obsessed with solving the mystery of the scroll mentioned in Clement's epistle. He learned all he could about the Templars, then relocated to Iran to research the Sorvacore legend. Despite leaving the Vatican, he continued attempts at using the secret archives as a resource, provoking the prefect's order, severing his contact with former colleagues. Topolis eventually abandoned the church and started his own Nestorian sect, first in Iran, then relocating to Iraq as the Iranian Islamic Revolution took hold. This prompted an administrative excommunication.

The reign of Saddam Hussein had forced Topolis and his followers into isolation, limiting their research opportunities. After Saddam, the Church of Kanisah extended its inquiries outside Iraq.

Two weeks before his death, Topolis had sent the current prefect of the Vatican Secret Archives an impassioned letter describing the abductions of Christian priests in Iraq and the reason behind them. According to Topolis, enemies of the church had obtained additional knowledge of a historical document they'd previously thought protected. In his letter, Topolis warned that they'd learned their assumption was false. Enemies of the church were determined to discover the content of the document and the impact it could have on Christianity. He ended the letter asking to be contacted so he could share details.

Nothing had become of the letter until an American history professor contacted the librarians, describing the death of Topolis and questioning them specifically about the name Praximus. After that, the history of Topolis's research into the posthumous epistle of Pope Clement V was revisited, and Monsignor Plenducci was dispatched to Mosul to investigate and begin negotiations for a complete search of the Church of Kanisah. His abduction prompted the Vatican to involve the

Gendarmerie Corps and ask for joint assistance from the Iraqi Ministry of Interior and the US Intelligence Community.

A moment of quiet reflection followed Maria's report. Kassab broke the silence. "The formal Vatican request came in this morning through the prime minister's office."

Lambert shifted uncomfortably. "Chief, we're going to need more than just orders from the PM this time."

Kassab frowned. "Like what?"

"We don't know what we're up against yet, just that we're oh-and-two against these guys. They outmanned and outgunned us both times. If we're going to have a chance, we'll need specialists. Will the PM authorize US intelligence assets on the ground in Iraq?"

Kassab winced. "That may be a hard sell. The prime minister is bullish on what he calls 'independent development of Iraqi security.'"

Lambert shook his head. "I think we're going to need all the help we can get." While grateful for Maria's candor, something still nagged at him. Despite their increasing detail of particulars, he knew something significant was being left out.

What am I forgetting?

Maria's background of Topolis and Plenducci helped frame the motives of the abductors. The three agreed that most of what Maria disclosed would be kept between them. She admitted her limited knowledge; Plenducci retained his secrets. They proceeded on the assumption that Plenducci had the information being sought by the abductors. The four vans discarded in the desert was both a good and bad indicator—good if it meant the end of the abductions; bad if it meant the abductors got what they wanted out of Plenducci.

Kassab reviewed details of the first attack, pointing out how he didn't think Topolis knew his attackers personally but that he seemed to know of their motivation. The chief turned to Lambert. "What did he say to you? 'Don't let them find it,' or something like that?"

"Cyprus!" Lambert exclaimed. "I knew I missed something. How could I forget that? Topolis also said 'protect Cyprus' before he died. I need to call Danny . . ."

Lambert began looking up Dicarpio on his phone and noticed Maria turn to Kassab. The chief explained—they needed to find out if Danny had mentioned Cyprus to his Vatican contacts when he telephoned them about the domino. If he had, then Plenducci, and probably his abductors, knew of it also. But if he hadn't, then "Cyprus" just might be their one advantage. If they could just find out what it meant.

Lambert regretfully understood how it had been overlooked. They'd been focused on Topolis's words "don't let them find it," originally thinking he referred to the domino he handed over. After Maria's information, they agreed the priest had referred to the Praximus scroll.

He heard ringing over one of eight new encrypted satellite smartphones sent by secure courier to MOI headquarters, courtesy of James Dougherty and the Bureau of Intelligence and Research. A ninth had been sent to Danny's University of Washington office, and a tenth retained by Dougherty. A microprocessor embedded into each of the ten converted voice into scrambled analog noise. The synchronous nature of the matched set of ten devices allowed the noise to be reintegrated into voice on the other end of an unsecured satellite, telephone, or internet connection.

As long as it remained under the radar of the prime minister's office, Ali Kassab approved of the new devices, as well as other equipment from INR that had been arriving during the last two days.

"Hey, Rick!"

Lambert laughed. "Hey, Danny, did Dougherty pre-program my number into your phone?"

"Yeah, your name's on the screen."

"Nice. Welcome to twenty-first-century communication. Let's activate scramblers." He'd sent the procedure earlier via email. After they switched both devices from normal to private mode, Lambert heard the slight electronic flange effect on the ambient noise.

"Sounds like it's working," Danny said.

"It does. Now, I've got a key question for you, buddy. Do you remember if you said anything about Cyprus when you telephoned Rome to research the domino?"

"Cyprus? What does that . . . oh yeah—Topolis said something to you about Cyprus. I forgot all about that. I was focused on Sorvacore and Praximus. I didn't mention it."

"You're sure?"

"Yeah, I totally forgot about it until you mentioned it just now. Why?"

Lambert closed his eyes and allowed himself a deep breath and long exhale. "That's good news. Topolis told me to 'protect Cyprus.' It might just be the one lead we have that Plenducci's abductors don't."

"What did he mean by it?"

"That's what we've got to find out."

"Could it be related to the recent break-ins in France?"

Lambert again felt their adversaries leading. "Break-ins?"

Being his bread and butter, current events relating to archeology and historical preservation were always on Danny's radar. He explained hearing about the break-ins at the fortress of La Couvertoirade, followed by the main tower at the restored ramparts of La Cavalerie, and finally the tower hall at Sainte-Eulalie-de-Cernon. So far, authorities had attributed the damage at each site to simple vandalism. Nevertheless, the European World Heritage office had issued a general warning to the custodians of historic sites in France, urging off-hours security patrols. What Danny found curious about each case was that only the decorative bricks from interior walls had been torn away, leaving the underlying, larger structural bricks unharmed. After learning of the information Maria supplied, the second parallel he found even more interesting—each of the three sites were former Templar preceptories.

"So it wasn't just vandalism. Someone's searching walls of Templar strongholds for the scroll." Lambert found himself getting excited. "But why only France?"

"Not just France. The *south* of France. These guys did their homework." Danny already had a theory. As the persecution of the French Templars had taken place, some escaped to the Mediterranean. Since the masonry at many sites along their route south had been in a constant state of renovation, escapees had opportunities to hide items in gaps behind walls. In modern times, "Templar Treasure" fanatics had swept sites with powerful metal detectors. But no such scan would've detected hidden documents, so in these most recent searches, the interior walls had simply been torn apart for direct inspection—crude but effective.

"But could escaping Templars have smuggled the document out of Europe and hidden it on Cyprus?" Lambert asked impatiently. "They did have a thing for Cyprus." In their undergraduate days, Lambert had studied history from a military perspective; he described history as his pre-mil degree, akin to biology being premed. And no military history curriculum would be complete without study of Templar operations in the Near East.

Danny, on the other hand, studied history from many angles: cultural, political, financial, and martial. "Could be. Hey, if you're going to Cyprus to look around, I want in!"

"What about your job at the UW?"

"I've got grad students to cover for me."

"Let me talk it over here. I'll get back to you." Lambert hung up and turned to see Kassab and Maria staring at him. "I hear Cyprus is nice this time of year . . ."

CHAPTER 17

NOVEMBER 14, 1307

KOLOSSI

The last ten fine-weave burlap bags had just been delivered by weavers who struggled to keep up with demand. In the settling hall, hundreds of clay funnels containing loaves of sweet salt were taken off pots containing their day-old syrup drippings. Knocked out of their funnels, loaves were pulverized with wooden mallets in large stone pestle bowls. The resulting fine crystals were scooped into bags on one side of a scale until the fifty-pound weight on the other floated upward.

While the last ten bags were being filled and stacked next to the forty filled during the previous four days, Brim Hastings toured the mill to ensure there would be no delays to next week's production. The funnels had to be set back atop their pots and refilled with the thick cane slurry from the settling barrels. The barrels needed to be refilled with purified juice from the boiling hall's copper vats. Refilling vats with raw extract from crushed canes and relighting the fires below them was then required. Finally, the newly arrived cane plants had to be loaded into the bedstone for crushing by the water-powered edge-running millstone.

The quota of two thousand pounds per week—never achieved by the whip-wielding sergeant in charge of the four hundred Greek immigrant laborers two months ago—had been increased to twenty-five hundred pounds per week. This goal being met a mere seven weeks after Brim had been put in charge of the sweet salt mill stunned everyone.

After having been shocked to learn that two thirds of the marshal's ledgers, and the Praximus Command, had been hidden from Cibalik Darcan by Shayla, Brim made two decisions: hand over the ledgers to Ayme d'Oselier and leave the Praximus Command hidden at Shayla's workshop. Coupled with the first had been his admission to defying the order of confinement. For this, he was stripped of his sergeant's mantle.

Being informed of Brim's farm management assignments in England, d'Oselier charged him with the seemingly hopeless task of optimizing sweet salt production as further punishment. "Idle hands are the devil's workshop," the marshal had said.

The labor was a welcome diversion. He needed distraction from the staggering revelations of the Praximus Command and death of his mentor. His mind would return to such thoughts when not otherwise occupied.

Could the words inked so deeply into the scroll possibly be true?

He also fixated on the strange physical dimensions: barely ten inches wide and a few more in length. Gone were the ornate top and bottom edge-clamping rods that scrolls of the Roman Empire were known for. Plain semicircular wooden dowel halves above and below took their places, tied tightly at their ends by leather strands. While no loose fibers hung from the lower dowels, the leather filaments binding the ends of the upper dowel halves hung like crude tassels. The left, extending nearly the entire length of the scroll, had Malcolm's preceptor signet ring tied to its end. The right, while appearing much longer, was wrapped in a knot the size of a large prune.

"Brother Brimley?"

Brim tensed. Transfixed by the water from the aqueduct powering the millstone, he'd not heard the young Greek boy's approach over the sound of the flow rushing off the flume. "Yes . . ."

"All bags are ready."

Brim glanced at the overcast sky. "Have the carters installed the bows and bonnets on both wagons?"

"They have."

"Good. Have them load twenty-five bags into each. I'll fetch our escort."

The Venetian cog expecting the latest shipment of sweet salt was scheduled to slip from its Limassol moorings this day. Despite being stripped of his status as sergeant, Brim had permission from the turcopolier to conscript heavily armed confrère sergeants for the protection of the valuable export and, more importantly, the bag of gold florins they'd be delivering back to Kolossi. After begrudging acquiescence from the three destrier-mounted Frenchmen in the lead, the oxen-drawn wagons began their slow drive toward the coast under a light drizzle.

Upon arrival at the Limassol docks, Brim identified the Venetian vessel by her red flag featuring the winged lion of Saint Mark. The four carters settled the two wagons on side-by-side positions at the edge of the wharf. Their three escorts dismounted and tied their war horses to the wagon frames. The Venetian quartermaster arrived and counted the agreed-upon number of fifty bags, then ordered several sailors to stand by for transferring them aboard. The drawstring from one bag was loosened to allow the taste of one pinch, producing a smile on the quartermaster's face as he addressed Brim in Greek. "Your weights, we know, are true."

"You honor my order with your trust." Brim had come to understand their courtesy of forgoing a second weighing upon receipt and knew it was well earned; even before his time at the mill, and prior to their ability to produce the desired amounts, none in the order had ever presented a bag of less than fifty pounds.

The ship's purser met Brim and the three uniformed sergeants at the folded-down rear door of one of the wagons. After receiving a nod from the quartermaster, the purser laid out twenty-five gold florins on the wood surface in a five-by-five square for ease of counting, prompting wide-eyed stares from the armed Frenchmen.

Brim nodded at the purser, slipped the coins into a soft wool bag, and tightened the drawstring. He gestured to the sailors tasked with loading, then to the contents of the wagons. The transfer began and he tucked the wool money bag into a small leather satchel secured to a belt under his tunic. "May God be with you on your voyage."

"May God also be with you," replied the purser before stepping away to speak to the quartermaster.

Brim noticed all three confrère sergeants looking away from the Venetian ship's loading activity. Following their gazes, he noticed the vessel in the adjacent slip to the east flying the white-crossed red flag of the Republic of Pisa. Two sailors on the sterncastle pointed in their direction and laughed. To their credit, all three escorts stood their posts next to the wagons until the last of the precious sweet salt had been lugged aboard the Venetian cog.

Another two seamen joined the pair on the aft railing, and the raucous laughter became louder. The three confrères drifted toward the point on the wharf directly behind the Pisan ship's sterncastle.

Brim turned to the carters. "Stay with the wagons." He then rushed to catch up to the sergeants behind the ship bearing the name *Rosabella*.

"I see Templar heathens still roam free on Cyprus," said one of the sailors, in Greek, prompting howls of laughter from the three others.

Brim understood their words but not what had prompted them. He glanced at the three Frenchmen to his right and saw by their expressions they did not speak Greek. Instead, they simply reacted to the sailors' obvious taunts by resting their palms on the pommels of their broadswords.

Between chuckles, another of the four on the sterncastle pointed at the red-crossed black mantles worn by the three large men below. "Still able to practice your perversions here, are you?"

The bulkiest sergeant, standing between the other two, pointed at the sailor who'd spoken last, turned to Brim, and spoke French with an angry voice. "What does he say?"

"He speaks nonsense, as all inebriated sailors do." Brim recognized them as Greek contract seamen. Even knowing the words, he could neither understand the basis for them nor the motivation behind the men's taunts. In his experience, uniformed mantles of the Temple of Solomon evoked respect, yet they now drew ridicule. Whatever the reason, he knew getting the gold back to Kolossi was paramount and tried to convince the fighting men of his escort that the sailors were intoxicated.

A fifth Greek appeared at the railing and joined his mates in their scorn. "Your heresy is no longer tolerated in France, aye?"

"His words are Greek," said the largest of the Frenchmen, "but they are not slurred with drink." He stepped forward to the very edge of the wharf where a crossbeam rubbed against the stern's large knotted-rope fenders, drew a bladed mace from a loose leather scabbard slung over his shoulder, and looked up.

The sailor above him lay flat on the deck and put his torso under the lowest railing. "What have you there? Some tool of your perversions?" Bolstered by howls from above, the prone seaman's face contorted with laughter as he reached down and began slapping the hull with his palms.

The sergeant crouched below the laughing sailor.

Dread enveloped Brim as he realized what was about to happen. "Wait!"

The sergeant sprang upward while swinging the mace in a circular arc. At its apex, the head of the mace crashed into the stern where the laughing Greek's left hand had been a split second before.

After the sergeant landed back on the wharf and the alarmed sailor scrambled back to his feet, silence ensued. One by one, each wide-eyed seaman peeked over the railing at the weapon embedded in the capital B of the *Rosabella's* nameplate. The sergeant rejoined his two comrades and watched the mace rise and fall with the motion of the ship, apparently satisfied with the peace it seemed to have restored.

Shouts, in what Brim recognized as the Tuscan dialect spoken by those from Pisa, broke the silence. An old man reached the aft railing of the sterncastle and switched to Greek. "What is happening here?" The aged Pisan glanced uneasily from ship to shore.

One of the Greeks pointed down. "Templars."

"Templars?" The Pisan seemed puzzled as he stared at the black mantles of the three sergeants, who returned his gaze with glares much more menacing.

Brim stepped forward. "Your men provoke sergeants of the Temple of Solomon."

Another Greek pointed over the railing.

The elder Pisan leaned over, saw the protruding mace, and frowned. He then squinted at Brim's plain russet tunic. "And you are?"

"Brother Brimley Hastings."

"And they are, as you say, confrères?"

Brim sensed the three sergeants stiffen at hearing the one word they would understand. He also realized they'd heard, as he had, the negative undertone in the way it was voiced—identifying them as temporary employees of the order as opposed to fully ordained members of the brotherhood. "I speak for the order here. May I know your name, sir?"

The Pisan gripped the aft railing. "I am Enzo Fausto, captain of the *Rosabella*."

Brim nodded.

"The Order of the Temple persists here, despite the arrests in France?"

Brim frowned. "Arrests in France?"

The Greek sailors surrounding Fausto snickered at the confusion.

"Return to your duties!" scolded the captain. "Clear room below for provisions." After the five seamen left, Fausto looked back down from the railing and tilted his head. "We are first to bring such news to Limassol?"

"What news, sir?"

Fausto turned to his left, looking west. "Yes . . . we had only two ports of call since leaving Marseille . . ."

Brim cocked his head but remained silent.

"Brother Brimley," said Fausto, turning back to the men below. "You should come aboard. You need to know what has happened in France."

Brim looked for signs of deception on the face of the Pisan captain. He saw none. He then retrieved the cloth money bag from under his tunic, thrust it into the hands of the tallest sergeant, then switched to speaking French. "Escort the wagons back to Kolossi. Deliver these twenty-five florins to the treasurer. I will return by foot after hearing of news from France."

The sergeant, holding more gold than he ever imagined he would, nodded.

"And retrieve your weapon off that ship."

CHAPTER 18

JULY 23, 11:23 A.M. GST

BAGHDAD

Rick Lambert understood that working the case inside Iraq was one thing, but sending Investigations Unit personnel outside the country was sure to get Ali Kassab and the Ministry of Interior IU into trouble with the prime minister. Their charter had no provisions for operations on foreign soil. It had been Maria's idea to put Lambert and anyone else traveling outside Iraq on administrative loan to the Vatican's Gendarmerie Corps Investigations Division. Kassab liked the idea and suggested it to the minister of justice, who quietly pitched it to members of the Council of Representatives Security Committee.

Kassab hung up his office phone. "The Security Committee is going to propose the Gendarmerie Corps assignments to the prime minister in confidence. They feel it should allow us to pursue the case outside Iraq without violating our charter." The chief turned to Lambert and raised an eyebrow. "It seems a certain representative from Basra is following the case."

Lambert saw Maria's confused look. "Samir's dad."

Kassab then flashed an embarrassed smile at Maria. "I hope you will forgive them for proposing your idea as their own."

"Of course. It is better that way," Maria said.

Kassab nodded. "Let us assume PM approval is forthcoming. Put together a list of what you will need for Cyprus."

Maria described the cover identity typically used by her Investigations Division in such cases—researchers from the Congregation for the Doctrine of the Faith. For Maria, it wasn't much of a stretch; personnel were routinely swapped between the Gendarmerie Corps HQ within Vatican City and CDF HQ at the Palace of the Holy Office, just south of St. Peter's Square. While overseas, those with the CDF were allowed much more access than Gendarmerie Corps agents. The Holy Office also had the Dassault Falcon 50 based at Ciampino Airport, the same jet Plenducci had flown to Mosul, allowing undocumented flight with diplomatic immunity.

Lambert had already discussed Danny Dicarpio joining their team; all agreed his expertise would be of immense value. After hearing what had happened in southern France, two other potential team members came to mind—the Duffy twins.

While on US Army duty in Iraq, Lambert had often come into contact with bomb disposal units. For routine disposal of improvised explosive devices, or IEDs, he'd worked with a variety of soldiers. For the more complex, intricate, or specialized jobs, Staff Sergeants Sean and Patrick Duffy were called in.

The Duffy family had emigrated from Ireland to New Jersey prior to the twins' high school years. After graduation in 2001, and the events of 9/11 a few months later, they enlisted in the US Army. After basic training, they were assigned to explosive ordnance disposal school. It turned out to be a job they had a genuine knack for, their accents prompting countless Irish Republican Army jokes—typically some version of "Hey, you guys put this here?" The peak of "The Troubles" in Northern Ireland had been before their time, so they weren't sensitive to it.

On one job Lambert remembered from East Najaf, insurgents had enclosed a booby-trapped IED behind a hastily erected brick wall in the basement of the Great Mosque of Kufa. After setting up signal jammers outside, Pat Duffy used a carbide-tipped masonry bit to create a small hole through the mortar. Sean then guided an articulating gooseneck video scope through the hole to map out how the bomb was wired to the interior brickwork. With a masonry saw, a gap was made large enough to slip a small treaded bomb disposal remote behind the wall to help them find, identify, and unwire components. They dismantled the entire brick enclosure to safely expose a corroded Soviet-era FAB-100 high-explosive bomb. The 100-kilogram shell was defused, driven out to the desert, and detonated with remote charges, drawing cheers from a nearby Marine Corps unit. Left in the basement, the explosion would have toppled the mosque and damaged several adjacent buildings. It had all appeared a typical day's work for the Duffy twins.

If Lambert and others were going to be poking through walls of Templar strongholds on Cyprus, he wanted the Duffy brothers with him. He telephoned the Army Intelligence and Security Command, or INSCOM, and was relieved to learn they were instructors at Fort Campbell, Kentucky, headquarters of the 52nd Ordnance Group.

Maria used her new INR-supplied phone to organize the team's transportation and CDF credentials. While she conversed in Italian, Kassab leaned in close to Lambert and switched to Arabic.

"Despite any other involvement, I want you to remain in charge. You've been on this case from the start and have been in both engagements with the enemy. Whatever team you put together, they answer to you. Agreed?"

"I'll talk to the lieutenant," Lambert answered. "I don't think she'll have any objections."

JULY 24, 10:47 A.M. EASTERN DAYLIGHT TIME (EDT) JOINT BASE ANDREWS, WASHINGTON, DC

Danny Dicarpio took a commercial one-way flight to Washington, DC, met the Duffy brothers, and boarded a Heavy Air Wing C-17 Globemaster III. The twins explained they'd been at the airplane an hour before and loaded eight suitcase-sized containers of equipment from Fort Campbell. The interior of the lightly loaded four-engine cargo jet was nearly as hot as the tarmac outside; the two sergeants, originally in Army Combat Uniforms, soon stripped down to their boxer shorts and tank tops.

In paratroop configuration, the C-17's seats on both sides faced cargo-loading system rails running down the fuselage centerline. Danny took a seat on the left, facing the twins seated on the right. He connected his tablet computer to his new encrypted satellite phone. As the twins stowed their ACUs in racks above their seats and donned headsets,

Danny noticed their Celtic-themed tattoos, and the matching cursive *Disarming Danger* inked into their left deltoids.

He was eager to get them up to speed during the transport's nine-hour repositioning flight to Papa Air Base, Hungary. He began shouting across the fuselage over the noise of the engines. One of the twins pointed to what turned out to be an intercom headset hanging over the seat next to him. He felt himself flush, but soon recovered and began with a lecture on the history of Cyprus. Near the top of their climb, however, he noticed the twins looking like the hungover frat boys he'd sometimes seen sleeping in his undergraduate classes.

The twins donned their ACUs to deal with the drop in cabin temperature at altitude. One of them asked about Major Lambert.

Danny shot him a puzzled look. "You're Sean?"

He shook his head. "Pat."

"Oh . . . I thought you guys knew Rick from Iraq."

"He said on the phone he remembered us from some mosque job in Najaf," Pat said.

Sean shrugged. "To us it was just another bomb to crater the desert with."

"You got that right," Pat said, smiling for a few seconds before turning back to Danny. "Same Richard Lambert from the Fallujah thing?"

"Fallujah thing?" Danny asked.

The brothers glanced at each other, this time without smiles.

Sean broke the awkward silence. "So what's he like?"

"Well . . . Rick was a history major, like me."

Sean chuckled. "History major Major Lambert? That's cute."

Danny realized the twins were losing interest again and changed tactics. He combined an action-based portrayal of Rick—effectively their new commanding officer—with energized accounts of recent events. The death of Topolis, the bravery and sacrifice of Samir, the fate of Plenducci—all were described as if scenes from an action movie.

After thirty minutes, he still had their rapt attention and described their mission on Cyprus as Major Lambert's next harrowing adventure. The remnants of the three key Templar preceptories were mapped out:

Kyrenia to the north, Famagusta to the east, and Kolossi to the south. They planned to sweep through the sites one by one looking for potential hiding spots.

Initially, the twins had expressed disappointment with there being no plans to "blow shit up," but soon regained interest when told they'd be breaching walls and peering into places unseen for more than seven hundred years.

After explaining the plan for Cyprus, Danny asked the twins to explain their specialization. For the remainder of the flight, he got a personalized course on explosive ordnance, interspersed with heated technical arguments too subtle for his understanding, from two of the world's experts.

A C-21A, the military variant of the Learjet 35 business jet, waited on the tarmac of Papa Air Base. The three men loaded the twins' containers in the aft fuselage, then settled into cots just behind the flight deck and slept for most of the five-hour flight to Baghdad.

JULY 25, 9:13 A.M. GST
SOUTHERN BAGHDAD

A ministry van transported Lambert, Maria, and their equipment to Al-Rasheed airport. In a perfect world, Lambert would allow Danny and the twins to rest and recover from jet lag after such a long journey. In this case, he didn't know when the opposition would move their search east, so he wanted to get the team to Cyprus quickly. To eliminate security and customs issues, James Dougherty had arranged permission for their flight to land southwest of Limassol at RAF Akrotiri, one of two United Kingdom Sovereign Base Areas, the other being RAF Dhekelia, just north of Larnaca. The CDF Dassault Falcon 50 Maria had arranged to be flown in from Rome stood by on Al-Rasheed's secure area, its two pilots preparing for the four-hour flight.

The C-21A arrived and was directed by ground control, rolling to a stop twenty yards from the much larger Falcon 50. Brief greetings were made and equipment transferred over the whine of the turbines.

Danny had trouble getting one of the containers up to the aft cargo door. Both Duffy twins rushed over to help, seemingly eager to display their strength to their new female teammate. Lambert noticed Maria smiling, turning, then rolling her eyes—she was apparently used to such behavior from her time in the Italian Army's Alpine Division.

More thorough greetings and introductions were made after takeoff. The five sat in cushioned seats surrounding a conference table. Danny began hooking up his tablet computer to the miniature projector at the table's center.

Maria stared at one of the twins. Lambert followed her gaze and noticed a *Disarming Danger* tattoo.

The Irish-American sergeant also noticed her stare, and slapped his ink. "That's the motto of the 52nd Ordnance Group. Ever thought of getting inked, Lieutenant?"

"You can call me Maria, until you join the *Italian* Army." She slung her right leg onto the table and pulled up the cuff of her khaki trousers.

Lambert was initially impressed to see the hilt of what appeared to be a short Ka-Bar tactical knife protruding from a sheath strapped to her calf. As she shifted the weapon aside, he was surprised to see a tattoo of a shield decorated with a crowned eagle over the name Julia.

The other twin also seemed impressed. "Is Julia your girlfriend?"

She frowned at him. "Pat, is it?"

"No, Sean."

"You are a funny guy, Sean. This is the shield of Alpine Brigade Julia, my unit before being loaned into the Gendarmerie Corps."

Images of their target locations on Cyprus gradually appeared on a small screen mounted on the forward bulkhead. Lambert summarized their plan.

Danny projected additional photos of Cyprus landscapes, and Lambert took a moment to look around the table at his team.

How will we perform, considering we were all thrown together at the last minute?

His thoughtful expression seemed to catch the attention of the twins, prompting him to end his silence. "I saw you two brought along the full explosive ordnance tool kit."

106

"Yes sir. Consider us explosive ordnance super freaks," Pat said.

Lambert chuckled. "Speaking of freaky stuff, besides our new phones, we're all also getting new watches, courtesy of the US Intelligence Community." He slid them across the table and explained their embedded miniature GPS beacons that could be tracked using an application installed on their smartphones or Danny's tablet computer.

They began their descent into Akrotiri. Lambert's phone buzzed with James Dougherty displayed as the caller.

"Hello, sir."

"Lambert. I've got some new developments."

He sensed excitement in Dougherty's voice. "What's up?"

"You know we've been trying to coordinate with the French about the break-ins and possible connection to the abductions?"

"Sure. French Intelligence rejected our conclusions."

"Well, they're onboard now . . ." Dougherty teased, apparently delaying for effect.

"Why? What happened?"

"They caught a live one."

The air left Lambert's lungs. "What?"

Dougherty explained how he'd just gotten off the phone with his overwhelmed counterpart in the DGSI—the *Direction Générale de la Sécurité Intérieure*—the French equivalent to the US Department of Homeland Security. The previous night, a crew broke into the main tower hall at the *Château de Cramirat*, the central manor in Sergeac, a fortified medieval village in Aquitaine. It was located next to an area with late-night pub activity, and witnesses. The young men were in the midst of demolishing interior walls when police arrived. A shoot-out ensued, killing three officers and five of the six perpetrators. The police found explosive harnesses locked onto each of the young men, assumed terrorism, and called in the DGSI.

Lambert's jaw dropped. "Why weren't the charges blown like before?"

"That took a while to figure out." Dougherty explained that, in addition to being near pubs, Cramirat was adjacent to a small museum offering tours of the tower and surrounding manor estate. The retired

French Army sergeant who ran the museum had access to military-grade signal jammers and slyly employed them to eliminate mobile phone disturbances during his tours. The jamming footprint extended to the tower and beyond, preventing any detonation signals from reaching the harness receivers. Bomb squad technicians removed the harnesses from each body, defused the charges, and turned them over to DGSI for further analysis. The young survivor was hospitalized under guard and treated for gunshot wounds to his legs and right shoulder. A Farsi-speaking DGSI lawyer then made him a deal—full disclosure for political asylum and protection in France. After being told of the alternative, he reluctantly agreed.

"The leader of the team is Ahmed Makarem," Dougherty said. "It's the first we've heard of him. But he reports to a radical cleric named Rudahmi. We know plenty about him."

Dougherty gave Lambert the quick story of Jahangir Nasser Rudahmi. Born in Gomrok, the red-light district in southwest Tehran, his parents had served ministers of the Shah, his mother as a housekeeper and his father as a landscape gardener. The elder Rudahmis became active in the politics of local religious leaders and disappeared with several others from their neighborhood when Jahangir was a child. Those who remained suspected a round-up by the Shah's secret police. He'd thereafter been raised in a madrasa and, years later as a thirty-year-old imam, became one of the main student organizers during the 1979 Islamic Revolution. As a reward for his service, and the sacrifice of his parents, he was assigned leadership of a new mosque to be built in Gomrok after government forces demolished the reminders of the suburb's sinful past. The mosque held no public religious services yet received huge amounts of funding from unknown sources. In the same walled compound as the mosque, a madrasa and massive dormitory were built. After receiving promises of support, parents with "too many mouths to feed" from the impoverished villages on the outskirts of Tehran enrolled their young sons in the school.

The Gomrok School provided the Ayatollah with waves of child soldiers for the Iran-Iraq war of the 1980s. Several were caught bringing IED materials across the border during the Iraq War. Rudahmi supporters also reportedly attacked protesters during the 2011 and 2012 demonstrations against the Iranian government. Nevertheless, the mosque and school had no official links to the Islamic Republic of Iran.

Lambert felt an odd combination of fear and exhilaration. "Did the Cramirat survivor know what his crew was looking for?"

"Not exactly, just that it was a very old document most likely hidden inside a wall."

"What about these explosive harnesses?"

"Yes, that's something new." Dougherty described the DGSI report from the survivor. After enrollment in Rudahmi's school, the young boys had been indoctrinated into radical Islam. Eventually, they were trained as both assault troops and suicide bombers. Such hybrid use was a new tactic—before, during, or after being taken out of action, they were human bombs to be remotely detonated by their team leader. With the size of Rudahmi's school and the time it had been operating, there could be hundreds of such fighters.

Lambert was sickened. "Ahmed Makarem is one of the older boys from this school?"

"That's what it looks like. I'll put you in touch with the real expert on Gomrok from the CIA's Iran Desk."

"That'll be great." Lambert thought about how such access would not have been available in the not-so-distant past. The US Intelligence Community, as established by President Ronald Reagan in 1984, had a major flaw at the time—the Director of Central Intelligence oversaw all federated agencies. As a result, the perspective from the DCI was biased—there was the CIA, and then there was everyone else. After the perceived intelligence failures of 9/11, the Intelligence Reform and Terrorism Prevention Act passed in 2004. IRTPA established a Director of National Intelligence, such that each of the sixteen agency directors, including the DCI, reported to the DNI. In the years since, intelligence sharing between the CIA and other agencies had improved.

CHAPTER 19

NOVEMBER 14, 1307

POITIERS

Cardinal Francesco Orsini had been shocked by the magnitude of the arrests the month before, despite having advanced knowledge from Guillaume de Nogaret. On the morning of Friday, October thirteenth, thousands of the king's soldiers apprehended nearly all five thousand members of the Temple of Solomon in France and seized the order's nearly two hundred major French properties in the name of the pope and the church. Those in walled fortifications were detained where they were found. Others, found on farms and mills owned by the order, were taken to prisons throughout France.

Orsini had seen the cunning in the tactics used by Nogaret. Those who knew of the recent rumors of improprieties among the younger members of the order recognized them simply as initiation pranks. The suggestion to investigate such gossip, made by Grand Master Jacques de Molay to Pope Clement V, was an afterthought, made when discussions of more pressing issues were concluded. Nogaret twisted small-scale barracks frivolities into accusations of widespread denials of Christ, idolatry, and sexual perversions.

Clement, under the impression Orsini had predicted the possibility of such action by the king, impulsively tasked him with drafting a response. Several had already been rejected. The impatient pontiff desired an immediate reversal, a proposal sure to be unacceptable to the king. Orsini delicately argued for regaining control of the order in stages, beginning with commanding all the monarchs of Christendom to seize the order's properties on behalf of the church and place its members under house arrest.

The early drafts of what was to become Clement's first papal bull included inputs from each of the other four cardinals of the Circuitor Consistory. For opinions on what Orsini hoped would be the final draft, he sought advice from one of his most trusted colleagues—the political mastermind Landolfo Brancaccio.

The cardinal from Naples, seated across the table from Orsini, read the hastily inked vellum slowly, then set it down. "It differs little from the last revision."

"Clement's rejections have been less forceful. We are close."

Brancaccio pointed at one line on the parchment and frowned. "Here you wish Philip to interpret the order as *house arrest*, meaning he should allow the brothers in prison to return to their posts?"

"That is my hope," said Orsini.

Brancaccio seemed skeptical. "And the extension of the command throughout Christendom?"

Orsini nodded. "It demonstrates to Philip the far-reaching influence of the church and dissuades other rulers from taking similar action unilaterally."

"I see." Brancaccio crossed his arms and arched his eyebrows. "Will Clement see this as exerting enough authority?"

Orsini turned the vellum around, scribbled the words *Pastoralis Praeeminentiae* at the top, then turned it back toward Brancaccio.

The cardinal from Naples nodded. "Pastoral supremacy is indeed what he seeks."

CHAPTER 20

JULY 25, 1:41 P.M. GST

SOVEREIGN BASE AREA (SBA) AKROTIRI, CYPRUS

Maria displayed her Gendarmerie Corps credentials at the motor pool desk, as planned. "You have a Wolf 110 standing by for me?" She felt clever after learning of the UK MOD designation for the militarized Land Rover Defender shortly before landing.

"Yes ma'am," said the wide-eyed RAF corporal. "Got the call from the base commander himself, I did."

She smiled while towering over the young Englishman.

"It's the one in front, fresh out of maintenance, new tires . . . let me fetch the keys."

The corporal turned and began hunting inside a cabinet. Maria turned to Rick and received a nod. She smiled back. For their mission on Cyprus to succeed, she'd have to take on more of a leadership role. But for Cardinal Dominic Batista's mission to succeed, she knew she'd have to guard against getting too attached to the four Americans she'd be working with.

A man wearing a buzz cut and a plain green jumpsuit tossed another set of keys onto the countertop nearest Rick.

"Thanks Corporal, see y'all later tonight," the man said, in an accent Maria had once heard described as an American Southern drawl.

Rick turned, seemingly puzzled by the uniform devoid of identification or rank. "From Texas?"

The man in green first looked at Rick, then glanced at Maria, Danny, and the twins. Turning back to Rick, he held his hands up in a gesture of surrender, silently backed away, then turned and marched toward the exit.

Rick turned to the Briton. "That was weird . . ."

Maria was relieved she wasn't the only one who thought so.

The corporal nodded. "Yes sir. He's one of those blokes from the big western hangar. They practically own the flight line after sunset, they do."

"US Air Force?" Rick asked.

The young man behind the counter just shrugged.

She was intrigued. "What happens in the big western hangar?"

"Ma'am, I can only tell you what they told me when I asked."

"Which is?"

"Don't ask."

2:36 P.M.

LIMASSOL, CYPRUS

The drive from Akrotiri to their hotel took a half hour. They found their hosts from the capital in the lobby, anxiously awaiting their arrival. The team's task, as had been conveyed to Nicosia, was to perform an initial security sweep and develop a draft itinerary for a potential papal visit to Cyprus. The Holy Office agreed to substantiate as confirmation inquiries were made. Being from Rome, Maria posed as team leader. Lambert played security liaison with the Duffys posing as photographers. Danny, who spoke passable Greek, took on the role of cultural attaché.

Once checked in, Maria and Danny left to hold an introductory meeting in the hotel business center's small conference room. For two hours, they'd lay out the desired itinerary for their hosts, giving Lambert the opportunity for an initial bug sweep.

Danny's would be their designated clean room, the only location he'd subject to technical surveillance counter-measures. One of the crates sent by James Dougherty contained the equipment Lambert had been schooled in at the Interagency TSCM Training Facility after joining INR. The initial electromagnetic inspection was important, not only for discovering any pre-set electronic eavesdropping devices but also for establishing the room's baseline EM profile to guard against future installations.

The Duffys stalked him around the room, making comments about "secret agent shit." He explained it as routine procedure. With lights off, he scanned the room for active radio frequency emissions using the combination RF receiver, spectrum scanner and vector signal analyzer—the range of antennas and filters on the device was designed to detect any localized EM signals. With lights on, he repeated the process with the addition of a portable oscilloscope to visualize the asymmetric EM field curls of any passive devices and to profile the clean baseline EM geometry of the room. Nothing he saw prompted the use of either the portable x-ray unit or thermal imager.

Before getting into his own hotel room's bed, Lambert got ahold of Gerald Burggraf at his secure daytime office phone number. Burggraf was Dougherty's counterpart at the Iran Desk of the CIA's Near East Mission Center, and considered the prime knowledge repository of current events in Iran.

"Thanks for the data about the Rudahmi forces in France," Burggraf said.

Lambert felt the gratitude was undeserved. "We only knew about walls being torn out."

"Well, the French intel from the Cramirat survivor filled in a lot of missing pieces, including this Ahmed Makarem character likely being their current Prom King."

Lambert was confused. "Prom King?"

"Sorry, 'Prom King' is our designation for Rudahmi's right-hand man, sort of his field commander, probably one of the oldest surviving boys from Gomrok."

James Dougherty had already conveyed the key points about the Gomrok School. Burggraf explained other known details. Although the small Gomrok Mosque was built shortly after the 1979 Islamic Revolution, the school wasn't built until the mid-1980s, its first students being male orphans from the Iran-Iraq war. By the war's end in 1988, the huge dormitory and surrounding compound was constructed and filled to its capacity of about two hundred boys between the ages of eight and eighteen. Since then, the make-up of the student body remained nearly constant, meaning roughly twenty of the oldest boys left each year to make room for another twenty of the youngest. Those who left referred to themselves as *Faregh Alethesalan*, roughly translated from Farsi as *Alumni*.

Although the estimated six hundred former students would fall into an age range between eighteen and forty-eight, the older half was thought to have died from their contributions around the world as suicide bombers and insurgent fighters. If true, it meant their current Prom King, Ahmed Makarem, would have about three hundred young men to call upon.

Lambert ended the call with Burggraf and tried to fall sleep, but his mind raced with thoughts of these remaining three hundred Faregh Alethesalan.

Could they be as fierce as another group of three hundred who held back thousands at a narrow pass called Thermopylae? Based on the survivor in France making deals for asylum and the others being forced to wear explosive harnesses, there was no comparison. Unless those they faced so far were only the sacrificial first wave, and others more fanatical waited in reserve.

JULY 26, 8:48 A.M. GST

Danny found their cover so effective it became a hindrance. They had access to any areas they wished but were constantly accompanied by their hosts from Nicosia, eager to assist any way they could, leaving them little privacy. He, Rick, and Maria engaged their hosts while the Duffys quietly documented areas they'd try coming back to in private.

Being historically linked to the Roman Catholic Church, the Templar sites they visited were each plausible attractions for a papal tour. To further avoid suspicion, they were intermixed with visits to more prominent religious sites on Cyprus, including the Church of Saint Lazarus in Larnaca and the Saint Charbel Maronite Church in Limassol.

The Duffys took several detailed photographs at each site with matching high-definition digital cameras. At all but the three Templar sites, Danny knew they slyly deleted the picture files, conserving space on the cameras' internal storage cards while keeping up appearances.

He'd learned the twins were skilled photographers, capturing and analyzing detailed images being important skills in their profession. He hoped such skills would bear fruit on Cyprus.

After the long day of sightseeing, the team converged on Danny's hotel room. Rick scanned the room with bug detection equipment and declared it clean.

The second of the Duffy twins arrived a few minutes after everyone else and realized he'd changed into the identical black cargo pants and dark-blue T-shirt as his brother. "Dork. Bring anything else to wear?"

"Shut it, maggot. Go change if you want," said the first.

While bickering, the twins transferred photos from camera storage cards into folders set up on Danny's tablet computer. The miniature projector borrowed from the Falcon's conference table projected each image onto an ivory-white wall. The team reviewed each photo for concealment potential, and Danny filtered them into sub-folders named Probable, Possible, and Improbable. They found no probable hiding locations at the ruins of Kyrenia or Famagusta, but did at Kolossi. This was the team's expectation and the reason for booking the hotel in Limassol, just two miles southeast of Kolossi. Danny eagerly concentrated his review on areas at ground level in the original main hall, the higher levels of the three-story castle keep known to have been added many years after Templar occupation.

"The Professor's going to love the close-ups we took of the east wall," one twin said.

"Yeah, the patterns match the domino photos he showed us during our flight," the other added.

Danny impatiently abandoned his methodical review of the photos in the order taken, instead sliding the scrollbar down, and scanning until he saw a wide-view thumbnail photo followed by several close-ups. He selected and moved them to the "Probable" folder, then opened them all at the same time. At first glance, the wide view showed a wall apparently made of hand-chiseled bricks. The twins pointed out the edges of the photo, where small shapes about one foot apart could be seen. Twenty-eight shapes formed sides of a rectangle eight feet tall and six feet wide. Close-up photos showed the shapes to be small groupings of tiny holes, deep enough to remain visible despite the chiseled surface. Their groupings of between one and six holes resembled faces of dice or half-faces of dominos.

He didn't know what to make of them. "They may just be holes used to pin up a tapestry or something."

"Then why would that part of the wall be roughed up like that?" asked Maria. "All the other walls are smooth."

He had no answer and flushed. "Not sure."

Rick didn't seem to want this to slow things down. "We can start the search at that wall, but let's map out other potential spots before we head out."

For the next twenty minutes, the team reviewed all other photos and planned their covert excursion inside the remnants of Kolossi Castle. Danny checked his University of Washington email as others checked gear. There was another message from the dean, who'd been expressing displeasure with his taking leave with no notice. But this note was different—the subject line read "Office Theft."

Danny read of the break-in at his UW office and felt as if he'd been doused with ice water. It had been left in a state of disarray, evidently after a thorough search. In his rush, he'd not purged his office of materials relating to his current research, including those pertaining to Cyprus.

Since Plenducci knew he was involved, Makarem did also.

I've put the team in danger . . .

When Danny explained this to the others, all seemed to agree—their opposition was either on their way to Cyprus or had already arrived.

CHAPTER 21

NOVEMBER 16, 1307

LIMASSOL, KINGDOM OF CYPRUS

"Jean de Villa confirmed it after we delivered the sweet salt," said Brim nervously.

Shayla crinkled her nose. "The draper?"

"Jean also serves as pigeon keeper for Kolossi." He paced the length of the tack master's workshop. On each pass by the central workbench, he tapped his fingers on the letter he'd written the day before. "Kolossi pigeons sent from Nicosia bore confirmation of the French arrests."

Her eyes opened wider. "I have heard talk of such pigeons."

He understood her confusion. In their capacity of supplying leather goods, Shayla and her father would have had contact with Jean de Villa only in his capacity as a draper. She would be unaware of the extensive avian communication network on Cyprus, set up after the great revolts forced the order to surrender the island to Guy de Lusignan more than a century before.

Brim had been fascinated by the workings of the Kolossi pigeon lofts on his first visit. Each of the four featured a map of Cyprus over its door, onto which a circle was painted to denote the origin of its occupants: Famagusta, Kyrenia, Nicosia, or Kolossi. The Famagusta and Kyrenia lofts each contained several dozen wooden cages housing individual birds yearning to fly home to their mates. The Nicosia loft contained nearly a hundred such cages containing singular messengers, since more communication was needed with the order's complex in the island's capital than with the preceptories in Famagusta on the east coast or Kyrenia to the north. More than a hundred cages in the Kolossi loft contained both mated pairs destined for separation and individuals awaiting the return of their mates. After sending and receiving several messages from each location, a repositioning of birds took place by wagon, along with other supply transfers.

"You believe this letter can help your brothers in France?"

He nodded.

"How?"

"The Praximus Command's theft disturbed the balance of power between the order and the church." He paced more rapidly. "I think those in Poitiers believe the order is no longer in possession of it and are reluctant to oppose the French Crown."

"You wish to restore this balance?"

He thought of Malcolm's words aboard the *Filomena*. "Give me a lever long enough and I shall move the world."

"Archimedes would agree."

He jerked his head toward Shayla.

She crossed her arms. "Do you forget I'm Greek? Or is a woman not meant to know such things?"

His mind flashed back to his first sight of Shayla at the Larnaca campground. He'd seen her no longer as the girl from three years before but as a woman. By her own words, she felt the same. But did she see him no longer as a boy, but as a man? "Yes . . . I mean no, I mean . . ."

She remained silent, raised her eyebrows, and put her hands on her hips.

Brim took a breath. "I know you are Greek. I know your father ensured your education."

She relaxed her stiffened posture.

He resumed pacing. "First, the church needs to know that which they call the 'Lever of the Temple' is still safe."

"First?"

"Yes, that knowledge will serve to get their attention. For the pontiff to assert his authority over King Philip to free my brothers, more is required."

"More?" She frowned for a moment, then seemed to understand. "You propose a trade—your Praximus Command for papal influence."

He nodded.

"But . . . please take no offense . . . why would he listen to one in your position?"

"He would not. But he would hear such a proposal from a preceptor."

"I have yet to hear of a new preceptor being . . . Malcolm's signet ring?" Shayla's eyes grew wide again. "You came here for Malcolm's signet ring, to seal your letter as Preceptor of Kolossi!"

Again he nodded.

"Brimley Hastings, you are playing with fire."

"I see no other way forward."

MARSEILLE, FRANCE

Cibalik Darcan was surprised at the increased activity on the docks. It didn't take long after dropping fenders and tying to bollards to learn of the reason. The port of Marseille was recovering from two weeks of lockdown, followed by two more weeks of slowdowns. The cause of each had been a massive country-wide arrest of the brotherhood of the Temple of Solomon and an intense search of departing vessels for those trying to escape.

He wondered how the arrests related to the ledgers describing the order's martial preparations. If such groundwork had taken place without the knowledge of the church, it would explain much. He looked forward to learning more after arriving in Poitiers, delivering the ledgers, and claiming his reward.

CHAPTER 22

JULY 27, 1:33 A.M. GST

KOLOSSI

Seven centuries before, Rick Lambert recalled, the valley at the mouth of the Kouris River had sustained lush vineyards and plantations. At its center, Kolossi served as a major trading center for sugar, olives, cotton, cereal, and the sweet wine Commandaria, made famous by King Richard I, who declared it "the wine of kings and the king of wines." In contrast, present-day Kolossi was a dusty, sleepy suburb of Limassol. With the moon below the horizon, only faint starlight could be seen. Crickets in dry bushes scattered around the ruins of Kolossi Castle provided the only sounds.

Lambert parked the Akrotiri Land Rover behind the medieval sugar factory two hundred feet east of the main hall, and the team eagerly unloaded equipment. He opened a case from James Dougherty, one of several sent from INR to the MOI office, containing late-model night vision goggles. After donning them, he silently led the way up the path to the main hall entrance.

Although a popular tourist destination, the interior held nothing of value. The simple lock on the main door was only meant to keep the village children out. One of the Duffys easily picked it. The other twin remained outside with a penlight to make his way to the exterior east wall, opposite the interior chiseled wall surrounded by the small hole groupings. Lambert used pieces of two-sided tape, similar to fly paper, to affix cloth sheets to brick window slits. The sheets served as black-out curtains, allowing their battery-powered lantern to illuminate the interior without signaling their presence.

Pointing at the Duffy inside the main hall, Lambert was irritated at still being unable to tell the twins apart. "Pat?"

"No sir, Sean."

"Okay. What else do you need?"

"Nothing, sir. We'll take it from here."

Sean set the double A-framed sawhorse support to the desired height, mounted the twenty-eight-volt battery-powered drill onto the translating carriage, and tightened the carbide-tipped masonry bit into the keyless chuck. The four in the hall donned clear goggles and filter masks, protecting their eyes and lungs from the powdered dust that would soon fill the space. The drill spun up and advanced along the carriage to form an initial hole in the mortar between two bricks near the center of the chiseled east wall surface. When the bit reached its depth limits, Maria handed Sean the first channeled extension rod to be fixed to the base of the bit, reminding Lambert of the large pipe extensions used on oil rigs. Sean repeated the process, the hole extending deeper into the wall. After six extension rods lengthened the reach to over three feet, the drill bit broke through, slamming the tip of the chuck against the interior surface.

Pat announced what he saw outside over Sean's phone. "You're through."

"Shit. No void," Sean said.

"What do you mean?" Danny pleaded.

Sean explained—at no point had the bit advanced without constant pressure and removal of material, indicating a lack of open space between interior and exterior.

The drilling procedure was repeated at the few other potential locations with the same result—no voids were found. Maria walked around the interior, examining other details of the walls. Danny, obviously getting impatient, pointed out other locations as possibilities. The Duffys, drenched in sweat and covered in white powder from taking turns on the heavy drill, wanted the academic to explain his reasons for suspecting the new locations, prompting more frustration.

Lambert felt their plan coming apart and gestured for a team meeting at the center of the cloudy hall. He raised his right hand to indicate he was speaking through his mask. "Remind me—why did we limit our search to the main hall?"

Danny shook his head and made chopping gestures with his hands. "At each site in France, only the interiors in main halls were blown out. So we're assuming the opposition knows something we don't."

"Okay. And how did we choose the locations here at Kolossi?"

Maria answered. "We chose places where bricks looked different, possibly added after initial construction."

Lambert looked around the room, his gaze settling on the soot-stained bricks at the rear of the fireplace. "The bricks in the fireplace look different. Why didn't we consider there?"

Danny shook his head again. "Of course they look different. They're blackened from countless fires."

"Maybe that's what we're supposed to think." Lambert grabbed the lantern and placed it directly below the chimney, illuminating the entire interior of the fireplace. Behind the mantle and the framing bricks supporting it, the interior stood five feet tall, four feet wide, and three feet deep. He could imagine it being used for cooking by inserting a spit or pot rack. He'd learned the top of the chimney was cap sealed in recent years, preventing birds from entering.

Crouching inside the fireplace, Lambert examined the rear wall. Danny and Maria reached in and ran their hands over the bricks on each side wall. Although blackened by fire, all surfaces had been scrubbed clean.

Lambert saw the two-by-two-foot chimney base above him. Both left and right edges of the chimney base extended down and outward at forty-five-degree angles until reaching the four-foot interior width of the fireplace immediately below. The front edge of the chimney base extended similarly until reaching the interior base of the mantle.

The fireplace rear wall differed. It extended straight down from the chimney edge to the floor and used smaller bricks. Lambert grunted abruptly—he realized that if the original two-by-two-foot chimney base extended down and outward to form a four-by-four-foot fireplace interior, then the rear wall could have been installed later to form the current four-by-three-foot interior. "We might have something here."

Pat dragged the sawhorse-mounted drill motor to the front of the fireplace and poked his head in. "Where do you want it?"

Lambert pointed at a mortar intersection between bricks near the center of the back wall. "Dead center."

Pat drilled the initial hole. Lambert could tell the coarse mortar was softer than that in other locations. The masonry bit plunged to its depth limits. Shortly after restarting with the first extension rod, the bit broke through and the drill surged forward on the carriage. The chuck, however, did not slam against the wall as before. Instead, an inch of the extension rod separated the chuck from the wall, indicating the tip of the bit had made contact with another surface. Pat turned to Lambert and smiled. "We've got a void here."

Sean had joined them inside and already had the gooseneck video scope powered up. Pat backed out the drill bit, then dragged out the sawhorse support. Sean fitted the micro camera/illuminator tip into the hole. He inched the sheathing tube in deeper with his left hand, and the four others crowded around the LCD screen atop the device's handle held in his right. The tight interior of the hole through the mortar opened into a cavity six inches in front of another brick surface identical to the other interior walls of the fireplace. Sean moved two levers between the handle and LCD screen with his right thumb to shorten and lengthen what he described as tiny tungsten braids inside the sheathing tube, articulating the tiny camera tip side to side, up, and down, like the head of a snake.

The gap behind what had been found to be a false back wall spanned the four-foot width, extending to the floor. An object on the floor leaned against the original back wall. With Sean working the articulation levers up and down and the sheathing tube in and out, the team studied the object from all possible angles.

Lambert squinted at the LCD screen. It appeared to be two large pieces of stone tile bound together by rope around their midsections. A black tar-like substance protruded outward from between the edges of each tile. "Okay, I give up. What is it?"

Danny shook his head. "I can't tell."

Avoiding serious damage to the site was part of their plan. Lambert knew that historical preservation was Danny's focus. For himself and the others, it was more a matter of eliminating signs of their activity.

Premixed mortar matching the original shading had already been inserted into the previously drilled test holes.

Sean had a suggestion for the fireplace. "Let's cut out a couple bricks and grab it."

"Whatever we do, we need to be quick," Maria said. "Dawn will soon break."

Lambert saw the team turn toward him. "Do it."

Pat transferred the weakening twenty-eight-volt battery pack from the drill motor to a heavy-duty rotary motor. The motor held a large circular dry masonry saw blade. Sean sat on the floor of the fireplace and balanced the blade shield on his knees to keep the blade horizontal. He pressed the saw teeth against a line of mortar above two bricks positioned just above where the top of the tiles had been seen behind the wall. "About here?"

"Looks good," Lambert answered.

Backing off an inch, Sean started the blade spinning and set the teeth on the centerline of the mortar. He tried to advance the blade deeper, but the lowering pitch of the motor made it clear their battery power was depleted. Sean backed off the saw blade a few inches. "I need more cowbell . . ."

Pat reached over, ejected the spent battery pack from the base of the motor, and slapped in their last charged one.

Sean plunged the blade back in and began spewing a jet of course mortar fragments against the right wall of the fireplace. "We're sucking diesel now . . ."

The radius of the saw blade was slightly larger than the thickness of the bricks. To free the top edges of the two bricks, mortar was also removed above two adjacent bricks.

Sean repeated the process on the mortar line under their lower edges until the two bricks were supported in place only by mortar between them and to their sides. Sean backed out the blade, and Pat went to work on the vertical mortar line between them with a hammer and chisel. Soon, the bricks shifted backward.

"Don't let them fall in!" Danny warned.

"We've done this before, Professor," Pat said.

Danny frowned.

Lambert smiled under his mask. He'd noticed the twins calling Danny "Professor" since the three flew into Baghdad together.

Sean slipped a thin, flat bar with a tiny hook on the end into the upper gap. With two quick pulls, the bricks fell into Pat's waiting hands.

Plunging his left arm into the hole, Sean grabbed the pressed-together tiles by their left edges and slid them up so the front tile was visible. The rope, likely several centuries old, fell away with the slightest tug, but the tiles remained stuck together with the black tar between their edges.

Pat tried chipping off the dried tar to wedge the tiles apart while his brother held them in place. Small bits of their edges broke off, but the tiles refused to separate. "We've got to either break the front tile open or tear out more bricks."

Lambert turned to Maria. "We're looking for a scroll. Do you know anything about tiles or tablets?"

"No, but they may just be for containment."

"I agree," Danny said. "I've read of documents being stored this way."

"We need to get moving. The sun is coming," Maria again warned.

Lambert nodded at Pat. "Crack the front tile."

With the point of a heavy chisel two inches from the left edge of the tile, Pat tapped the other end with a hammer. A large section of the front tile cracked off and fell to the floor behind the false back wall, revealing a one-inch strip of dried tar running up the left side of the rear tile. To the right was something else. It looked like the edge of a dark piece of leather. Reaching in with a smaller chisel, Pat cracked off more of the front tile, making the entire rectangular piece of leather visible. He then lifted it off the rear tile.

Lambert caught himself tapping his heel, but stopped before any of the others noticed.

Pat felt the leather, claiming it was as stiff as cardboard. The hole made by the removal of the two bricks was wide enough to extract it, but Lambert feared it might crack as Pat tried to bend and pull it out of the horizontal opening, like an envelope through a mail slot. Pat pulled slowly. The old leather seemed to bend, but emitted no cracking sounds. When completely out, Pat dropped it into an oversized clear plastic envelope held open by Danny.

Lambert saw three straight edges, but the forth appeared roughly cut.

Danny looked entranced. "Did any break off?"

After dropping the tile remnants, Sean had been articulating the camera tip and reviewing what was left behind the wall on the LCD monitor. "Nope. That's all of it. And I don't see anything on the surfaces of those tile fragments."

Lambert looked through the clear plastic at the roughly cut edge that Danny pointed out and asked Maria if she knew anything about the scroll being altered.

She did not. The only known reference was the posthumous epistle of Pope Clement V. As far as she knew, the scroll was whole in 1124 when it had been shown to the papal emissary in Jerusalem.

Lambert made a twirling motion with his right index finger. "Let's patch up these holes and get out of here before someone shows up."

"I'll prep more mortar," Sean said. "Everything else can go."

Danny tried reading the surface of the darkened leather despite insufficient light.

Lambert chucked to himself, then suggested Danny help with packing out equipment. "It's waited seven hundred years. It can wait another half hour until we're back at the hotel . . . Professor."

4:58 A.M.

While crouching south of Kolossi Castle, he felt the shuttered eyepiece of the infrared night vision camera chaffing his eyebrow. For the last three hours, he'd taken photos of the man periodically strolling around the outside of the main hall. Even by the blurred IR thermal image, it was obvious the man was no security guard.

His orders had been to scout out security at Kolossi Castle. Advanced sweeps in several other locations had also been ordered. A repeat of the Cramirat failure would not be tolerated. Decisions about sending in explosives teams would only be made when success was assured.

Parking a half mile east, he'd approached the castle directly until noticing the Land Rover, prompting him to circle around to the south and take a position behind a stone wall eighty feet in front of the main hall. Finally, the man he'd spent hours photographing, as well as three others, came out of the main hall dragging several crates and a dark object encased in what looked like clear plastic. He made sure to get close-ups of the object and the four faces as they walked down the path to the Land Rover. They turned the corner and disappeared behind the old sugar factory, and he set off back to his motorcycle. His position was becoming visible with the rising sun, and Ahmed Makarem would want to see his photos as soon as possible.

CHAPTER 23

NOVEMBER 21, 1307

LIMASSOL

Brim Hastings remained on the Limassol docks, after his morning delivery of sweet salt, to hear more of the arrests in France from new arrivals. He was shocked to learn details of events recently brought to Kolossi by pigeons from Nicosia.

The day after the arrests, King Philip's legal and political mastermind Guillaume de Nogaret had explained the motivation behind the arrests to a collection of canons and university masters at Notre Dame. Brim recognized the charges as those that would provoke widespread revulsion and fear of the order throughout all levels of society. Three days following his actions, Philip sent letters to all rulers of Christendom to explain further, portraying himself as a protector of Christianity. Regent of Cyprus Amalric de Lusignan had the parchment read to Ayme d'Oselier in Nicosia. The marshal had reportedly left Amalric's presence in disgust.

Brim arrived at the tack master's workshop by early afternoon.

"Your letter to papal authorities proposing the trade is away then?" asked Shayla.

"It is. And I don't know how many more communications satchels will be sent to Poitiers." Brim positioned the Praximus Command on the near side of a saddle mounted on a rack next to him. The heavy plumb-sized knot at the end of the top right tassel provided counter-balance on the far side. "I . . . have concerns."

Shayla turned from her sewing of a leather bonnet destined to serve as a helm liner. "Regrets?"

"No. Everything possible must be done to free my brothers unjustly languishing in French prisons. If that means coercing the church into doing what is right, then so be it."

Shayla nodded and returned to her work. "Then what are your concerns?"

"I struggle with the mechanics of how such a transfer could take place."

"I have thought of this also." She swiveled the bonnet on the shaped rounding block. "Are there none at Kolossi you can turn to?"

Brim felt himself grimace involuntarily. "Despite voicing many hints, I have been unable to detect anyone willing to admit to having knowledge of Sir Malcolm's intentions. His plans may have died with him."

She paused. "I'm sorry."

Several moments passed before Brim spoke. "We spoke of Archimedes before. Do you also know of Aristotle?"

She smiled. "My father and I often discussed Aristotle. Plato and Socrates also. Why do you ask?"

"Before leaving London, a Franciscan friar and I often worked out farming logistics using Aristotelian valid inference concepts."

"A Templar and a Franciscan?" asked Shayla, sounding intrigued. "I would not have thought such a meeting of minds was possible."

"Well . . . neither I nor Wil of Ockham are models of monastic obedience."

"Ockham? Where's that?"

"Two miles southeast of London."

"And you both studied Aristotle?"

Brim nodded. "Wil more than I. He's five years my senior and has read far more. When I left, he pursued expansion of Aristotle to create a kind of *Lex Parsimoniae*, proving that among competing theses, that with the fewest assumptions is truth."

Shayla frowned and tilted her head. "So, the simplest answer is correct."

"Well . . ." He thought for a moment. "Yes."

She returned the bonnet to its original position on the rounding block.

Brim continued. "I'm thinking the exchange of the Praximus Command for Clement's support cannot work in general. The pope will not oppose King Philip unless he's certain to acquire the scroll by doing so. Yet if he obtains it first, he's no longer motivated to oppose Philip in the first place."

"I see." After a moment, Shayla turned and gestured to the saddle next to him. "The blacksmith I made that for paid two gold bezants before I started my work and will pay two more now that I've finished."

He was puzzled. "Yes?"

"Half now, half later."

"No," said Brim, shaking his head. "Clement must influence Philip to release all those imprisoned simultaneously."

"I do not refer to those imprisoned."

His confusion returned.

She held up a pair of leather shears and squeezed out two loud snips.

Brim felt the shock of her suggestion and instinctually placed a protective hand on the scroll. "No, Shayla! Do you forget the message herein?"

"By your admission, words inked by some Roman *magistri militum* centuries ago."

"But what if these words are true?"

"And what if your magistrate was a drunken simpleton?"

Brim glared at her, shaking his head.

She met his gaze with a glare of her own. "For nearly all in this world, each day is a struggle for survival. Very few have the luxury of devoting themselves to such lofty ideals."

He continued shaking his head as his eyes drifted downward. He began mumbling. "*Sicut superius et inferius . . .*"

"Yes—as above, so below. Hermes Trismegistus was Greek also. But we live in *this* world! *This* time!"

Brim was reminded of what vastly different lives he and Shayla had led. As a toddler, she'd witnessed the Fall of Acre, narrowly avoiding either death or slavery. Those first years with her father on Cyprus, she had to fight to survive as thousands of refugees from the evacuation of the Levant overwhelmed the island's resources, leading to mass starvation. In contrast, he'd never known want of food, shelter, or clothing. His pursuits in the London scriptorium were more sublime, his work with the order's properties in southern England more exalted.

Malcolm's words from aboard the *Filomena* echoed in his mind: *"The order shall soon be thrown into chaos, an upheaval our brotherhood will not likely survive."* Then Cibalik Darcan's taunts from Larnaca filled his thoughts: *"Say unto your brothers their time is coming to an end."*

Brim strode to the workbench next to Shayla, seized the leather shears, then stomped back to the Praximus Command atop the saddle. He picked it up, scanned the words, then began cutting the old leather with forceful, desperate clips. The scroll split in two, and the heavy knot at the end of the tassel pulled the top half over the opposite side of the saddle, leaving him with only the bottom half in his left hand. Incensed, he grabbed the top half off the woven mat under the saddle stand, gritted his teeth, and slashed the offending leather sinews like Alexander the Great chopping at the Gordian Knot.

Something fell to the floor as the knot broke apart. What he thought was a large, heavy knot was actually a stone tied tightly within leather strands.

But it was not just stone. It was a domino, the likes of which Marco Polo had described seeing in China.

POITIERS

Cardinal Francesco Orsini paced the length of his chambers. Curia guards had announced the arrival of Cibalik Darcan and escorted him up the steps. Orsini could barely contain his excitement as he took a seat behind his desk. He desired the *Vectis Templi* as Damocles desired the removal of the sword above the throne of Dionysius.

After two customary knocks, a guard entered. "Ambassador Cibalik Darcan to see Your Eminence."

"Show him in and leave us."

Darcan strode into the large room with a leather satchel under his arm and a smug look on his face. Orsini realized, although he'd sworn

Darcan to secrecy prior to his departure for Cyprus, he'd given little thought to how he'd deal with him having firsthand knowledge of the heretical scroll.

The ambassador bowed slightly. "Greetings, Your Eminence."

"You may sit." Orsini gestured to a chair fronting his desk. "Have you brought a gift from Cyprus?"

"Indeed, Your Eminence." Darcan removed the contents of his satchel, and Orsini quickly cleared the more mundane parchments from his desktop. Darcan filled the emptied space with the spoils from Larnaca then sat, maintaining his self-satisfied expression.

Orsini scanned the dozen or so soft hides in front of him, then began sorting through them. Some appeared charred, yet all seemed fairly new and well oiled. Each time he projected his frown across his desk, the ambassador expressed more discomfort. Finally, Orsini spoke. "What are these?"

Darcan now showed genuine anxiety. "The scrolls from Malcolm of Basingstoke, recovered from Cyprus, Your Eminence."

"Cease the 'Your Eminence' drivel! I sent you to recover one Roman scroll, and you bring me temple ledgers?"

"But, Your—" Darcan frowned, then continued. "But they describe finances behind a massive mobilization—"

Orsini held up a hand, closed his eyes, then forced onto himself a measure of calm. "How were they obtained?"

Darcan described reaching Limassol, finding no record of the *Filomena* arriving, then patrolling the southern coast for a week until confronting Malcolm at the campground outside Larnaca.

"Malcolm and the Greek Cypriot attacked your landing party, and you did not recognize it as a diversion?"

"I did indeed see it as such. His boy servant, perhaps his squire— later identifying himself as Brimley Hastings—was driven back into camp by my men after trying to escape with the scrolls and the Cypriot's daughter. That's when he tried destroying the parchments by fire. We recovered them after the knight and his accomplice were put down. By that time the travelers who took flight had returned, so I left young Hastings after thoroughly searching the camp."

"Where was the knight prior to you finding him?"

"We heard from many he'd been put to shore the night before, so he hadn't been anywhere else on Cyprus."

Orsini angrily picked at a charred edge of one of the ledgers. "How many scrolls were completely consumed by fire?"

"I . . . I have no way of knowing."

"Leave me," said Orsini, considering the ramifications of the possible destruction of the *Vectis Templi*. "Stay in your usual chambers in Poitiers until I find time to review these ledgers. I will then call on you."

Darcan gestured to the charred leather atop the desk and spoke in a quiet voice. "There is the issue of expenses . . ."

Orsini glowered. "You bring me only shopping lists and expect restitution?"

The ambassador kept his head bowed for several seconds. He then softly explained the death of the warlord Ghazi, and the insistence by his three commanders on accompanying him to France to collect the five hundred bezants they were owed.

"You bring Muslim mercenaries to Poitiers?"

"They wear Western clothing and are sequestered miles away."

Orsini shook his head, crossed himself, then placed both hands on the fire-damaged vellum fragments atop his desk. "I shall send you away with three hundred bezants and inspect what little you've brought me. Take your leave, and deliver your Saracens from these Christian shores."

Darcan did not move.

When Orsini looked up from his desk, he saw Darcan's brow gleaming with sweat. "Did you not hear me?"

Again, the ambassador spoke slowly and softly. "The men I travel with expect deceit on our part. If I do not return with the five hundred bezants promised to them and their men, I can never travel east again. My life may also be in danger."

Orsini locked his eyes onto Darcan's, which were blinking incessantly to clear the sweat seeping into them. He still had plans involving the ambassador's contacts and influence in the East. He leaned back into his high-backed chair and steepled his fingers. "Tomorrow marks the release of Pope Clement's first papal bull. It will require the arrest of the brotherhood and confiscation of their assets throughout Christendom. For this I will advance you two hundred bezants in addition to the three hundred for your previous work. Have the chest containing this gold sent to your mercenaries under papal guard, then send them away."

A look of relief spread across Darcan's face. "What of me?"

"Amalric de Lusignan of Cyprus has been in league with the Order of the Temple since their help with his coup. He will not immediately comply with papal orders. When the time is right, you will accompany a papal envoy to Cyprus and aid him in . . . *convincing* Amalric of his duty to the church."

Darcan nodded. Beads of sweat dripped onto the edge of the desk below his chin.

CHAPTER 24

JULY 27, 6:22 A.M. GST

LIMASSOL

Back at the hotel, Danny Dicarpio excitedly removed the leather from the plastic, placed it on his room's desk, and positioned lamps on both sides. He then used a magnifying glass to examine the writing on the cracked, darkened surface. He felt the looming presence of Rick, Maria, and the twins behind him. "Okay, what little writing I can see so far looks Latin."

"If it is Roman, how did it survive this long?" Maria asked.

"Might be a twelfth-century copy made in Jerusalem," Danny answered. "But still a good question. From what I've read about leather preservation, it's all about oil retention and oxygen exclusion."

"Like the leather from the Corbridge Hoard?" Rick asked. "That's nearly two thousand years old."

Danny appreciated Rick's perspective of military history, referring to the 1964 excavation of the well-sealed second-century Roman armory chest near Hadrian's Wall. "Right. Or the leather shoe found in the Armenian Copper Age dig a few years back. That was radiocarbon dated to about 3500 BC." Danny continued to gently remove the crust off the scroll fragment with a small brush.

"That old? Was it in pieces?" Maria asked.

He shook his head. "It was whole, still stuffed with grass, and so well preserved in ancient sheep dung that researchers could tell the foot size of the owner by the compressions below the heel and toes."

"Sheep dung? Must've smelled lovely," Sean quipped.

After reaching the cleaning limits of the brush, he nervously considered more invasive options to remove particles from the leather's surface. "I think whoever hid it in the fireplace tried to protect it from rain damage and inadvertently vacuum-sealed it between the tiles."

Maria looked skeptical. "A vacuum seal?"

Danny nodded. "Before drying, the surrounding tar could have reacted with the air between the tiles, drawing out the oxygen."

Rick asked the question Danny knew they all wanted to ask. "So, what does it say?"

"It's not quite legible yet," he answered. "I'm going to have to find a way to clean it without damaging it. It's going to take a while."

Rick seemed to get his "quit breathing down my neck" hint. "Okay, I'll bring back some food from downstairs."

Maria stepped toward him. "I will come also."

The twins shifted to the other side of the room, arranging hardcopies of Kolossi photos they'd printed in the hotel's business center.

Appreciating the solitude, Danny examined the leather anew and wrote his best guess as to the correct letters and words on a piece of paper. For whatever length of faded text couldn't be read off the leather to his left, he kept the same amount of space empty on the paper to his right. He planned to come back later and fill in the blanks. His heart ached when, after one pass, he saw the paper to his right contained only a few sparse words and letters. It became clear he'd have to clean the surface of the brittle leather more aggressively to read it.

Restoration and preservation of artwork and historical documents was a skill best left to professionals. This he knew. During his career, Danny had conversed with many such experts at museums and historical conferences around the world. Nearly all told of dry cleaning techniques being preferable to those involving moisture or chemicals. This ruled out his first impulse of using a warm, damp towel. Instead, he ran a credit card across the surface, lightly scraping the dusty grime. It seemed to have an effect. The team relied on him for answers about the document's meaning, so he decided to take the risk and scrape the surface just enough to make it legible.

The hair dryer placed in the bathroom by the hotel had a heat on/off switch. Danny plugged it in by the desk and used it without heat to blow away the grime he delicately removed from the surface. It was a balancing act. He used the edge of the credit card to open the tiny cracks in the leather so the hair dryer could blow away the material anchored within but made sure he did not press hard enough to scrape away any of the embedded ink. Since cracks propagated in all directions, he ran the credit card at many angles. Soon, some of the text became legible, and he wrote down what he could read.

Rick and Maria returned with bags of sandwiches, laying them out on the entry table by the door. "How's it going?" Rick asked.

"This is fascinating. It's a set of Roman marching orders. Orders to apprehend fugitives."

"Marching orders?" Maria repeated incredulously. "That does not sound heretical. Could it be a different document?"

"We have 'Lucius Valerius Praximus' mentioned right near the top."

"Lucius?" Rick asked. "That wasn't a name you mentioned before."

Danny poked at his tablet's screen. "No. That's what's so strange. Lucius served in the senate—the last Praximus family member to do so. His son, Marius, was thought to be the first to serve in the Third Legion around 52 AD."

"Why was Lucius so far from Rome?" Maria asked.

He thought for a moment. "Senators were often given temporary command of legions as a political favor. They could then return to Rome with military leadership experience."

Maria shook her head. "But why a legion so far from Rome?"

"Not sure. The scroll's in the standard Roman army expedition format. The general orders at the top could be unrolled for subordinates while keeping the more detailed and sensitive information at the bottom concealed."

"Who were the fugitives?" Rick asked.

"I'm getting there, damn it. Give me a little more time . . ."

8:06 A.M.

Lambert shifted his impatient attention to the twins, as did Maria. He noticed they had several photos arranged atop Danny's bed. In the center lay the image of the hand-chiseled brick interior east wall section from the Kolossi main hall. Placed around it, fourteen photos each showed two of the twenty-eight tiny drill patterns surrounding the jagged surface. Off to the right, two more photos showed the domino's sides, close-ups he'd sent Danny from Mosul.

"What's all this?" Lambert asked, pointing to the twin nearest him. "Sean, is it?"

"No sir, Pat."

"Okay. We came up empty when you drilled here."

"I know sir, but we just couldn't let this go."

Sean explained further, "We grew up with old stories about how the Irish used coded patterns like this to confuse the English."

"Meaning?" Maria asked.

Pat smiled at her. "Let us show you a little magic trick."

The twins referenced the two photos of the domino they'd laid out on the bed and asked Maria to pick one of the four numbers shown. She picked the photo with the side showing the 3-dot and 5-dot squares and picked the number 3. Then they asked Lambert to pick a 3 symbol on the center photo and draw a straight line to the 5 farthest from it, across the chiseled wall. They repeated the process with the side of the domino showing the 1-dot and 4-dot squares, drawing a straight line between a 1 and the 4 farthest from it.

They then ran the process in reverse. A 5 was selected and a straight line drawn across the photo to the 3 farthest away. Surprisingly, the three lines shared a common intersection in the upper right quadrant of the chiseled wall. A 4 was selected and a straight line drawn to the 1 symbol farthest away—amazingly, the fourth line shared the intersection of the first three. Of the remaining twenty symbols on the periphery of the wall, there was one more 1 and one more 4.

Lambert shifted his gaze from Pat to Sean. "Seriously . . . ?"

Sean nodded and made a straight line between them. Astonishingly, the fifth line shot through the common intersection. Of the remaining eighteen symbols, nine were 2s and nine were 6s—symbols not shown on the domino.

"That would be one hell of a coincidence," Sean said.

Lambert stared at the center photo in shocked silence. Of the twenty-eight symbols on the periphery of the chiseled wall, ten were shown on the faces of the domino. Connecting them as most-distant pairs produced five lines sharing a single, precise intersection.

Pat broke the silence. "That's no damn coincidence."

"So what was carved onto that point of the wall before being chiseled off?" Lambert asked.

Sean shrugged. "Maybe the Professor over there can tell us."

Lambert turned and saw Danny still seated at the desk with the scroll fragment. Instead of being hunched over as he'd been since their return from Kolossi, he sat ramrod straight and motionless, staring down intently with fingers clenched around the side edges of the desk.

CHAPTER 25

DECEMBER 30, 1307

KOLOSSI

"Yet another from Nicosia." Brim Hastings watched the carrier pigeon enter the Kolossi loft from the landing board through the trap door made of hinged wooden dowels. The red paint of the stamped tin bangle affixed to the bird's tibia identified it as having flown from their complex in the capital city.

Jean de Villa seemed perturbed. "That makes an even dozen over the last three hours."

After news of the persecutions in France, the number of messages relayed by the order's avian network had increased tenfold. Being the only other literate brother currently at Kolossi, Brim had been reassigned from the sweet salt mill to the pigeon lofts, assisting an overwhelmed Jean. In an attempt to streamline communications, the marshal had ordered the coastal preceptories—Famagusta, Kyrenia, and Kolossi—to launch birds bound only for inland Nicosia. After confirming a piece of information from one preceptory, Nicosia relayed it to the other two.

The tiny notes pulled from the bangles of the first six messengers summarized *Pastoralis Praeeminentiae*. Jean copied them into Kolossi's communications ledger. A delay in earlier arrivals had prompted Jean to dash to the preceptor's chambers, reporting what had been learned to the turcopolier of Cyprus, Bartholomew of Gordo.

Brim was about to suggest another trip there as the knight entered the main aviary. "What more from Nicosia?"

"Five more logged, and one more just arrived, sir," said Jean.

After dipping its beak into a water dish several times, the new pigeon fluttered onto the shelf supporting the cage containing its mate. Brim gently removed the bangle, then placed the bird in its cage.

Jean continued. "Message seven contained the marshal's position on how such a papal bull is possible."

Bartholomew raised an eyebrow. "Which is?"

"King Philip pressured His Holiness into issuing the orders."

The turcopolier nodded. "Quite possible. The Grand Master warned of this. Since the curia fled Rome, taking refuge under Philip's wing, the Crown's influence has only grown. What more?"

Jean pointed to the next four log entries. "Messages eight through eleven order a halt to dormitory construction and call for the building of new defensive measures, beginning with erecting a palisade atop the earthen berm."

The knight turned to Brim, pointing at the paper now unfolded in his hand. "And the latest?"

Brim read the tiny text verbatim. "Amalric requesting clarification. Half the men from Nicosia en route to Kolossi."

Bartholomew glanced at the black uniform of Jean de Villa, then frowned at the plain russet tunic worn by Brim. "You are reinstated as Sergeant of the Temple. You will help direct work on defenses as specified in the messages until the marshal arrives."

"Yes sir." Brim handed the last piece of paper from Nicosia to Jean and noticed a slight tremor in his hand before watching the turcopolier leave the aviary. Was there a connection between the order's plans for Cyprus and their persecution in France? Most thought the Crown's seizures had been motivated simply by greed and a lust for power.

Considering the four- to five-week information transit time between Poitiers and Cyprus, the papal bull must have been released within a week of his writing the back-dated letter offering the Praximus Command in exchange for papal influence in the release of his brethren. Brim imagined the ships delivering each message crossing paths somewhere between Sicily and Corsica. He was unsure if *Pastoralis Praeeminentiae* rendered the exchange impossible but decided to retrieve the scroll's top half from the tack master's workshop and conceal somewhere within the Kolossi compound. With all the masonry work taking place, he could think of many potential hidey-holes.

POITIERS

After five weeks, Cibalik Darcan felt both relief and apprehension when finally summoned back into an audience with Cardinal Francesco Orsini.

He was relieved to still have a role, now as more of an outsider than ever, in an environment where ever more papal issues came under jurisdiction of French cardinals, French magistrates, and French bureaucrats.

But he was worried his role would be anything but pleasant. Since the release of *Pastoralis Praeeminentiae*, many within the Holy See had been monitoring responses from rulers of Christendom. All replies promised action would be taken with due diligence and in accordance with papal orders but continued on in length requesting multiple clarifications. Compliance with the papal bull was anything but ensured, making many men anxious.

Following two papal guards to Orsini's chambers atop the stone steps, he heard the first's familiar introduction: "Ambassador Cibalik Darcan to see Your Eminence."

"Show him in and leave us," Orsini replied.

He bowed, gave his customary greeting, and was again directed into the chair fronting the cardinal's desk. On the otherwise empty desktop he saw a folded letter with an opened seal.

"You recognize the broken wax?"

He leaned in, examined it, and nodded. "Order of the Temple."

"Read," commanded Orsini.

Unfolding the letter, he instinctively focused on the bottom, his eyes growing wide. "Impossible . . ."

"Quite." The cardinal paused. "Although it is dated one week before his death, I see no way it could have been delivered to me, considering your testimony from Larnaca."

Darcan knew "delivered to me" meant "intercepted" since he'd known for several weeks Orsini had been diverting communications from the military orders to his office before returning them to regular channels. "Your Eminence, the Preceptor of Kolossi was put ashore the night before his death. This was confirmed by many."

The cardinal nodded. "It was in the latest communications satchel from Kolossi."

While that would confirm the origin, Darcan glanced at the date atop the paper, then back up at the cardinal. "The latest?"

"The latest," confirmed Orsini, seemingly pleased he'd recognized the temporal disconnect. "Based on that date, I should have received it in one of the earlier satchels."

Darcan understood but had nothing to contribute. He remained silent.

"Read it in its entirety."

He scoured each line of Latin slowly, periodically scanning back to the date at the top. "He writes of 'persecutions in France'? Am I to believe Malcolm of Basingstoke had prior knowledge of the mass arrests by King Philip?"

"Only if you are a fool," Orsini replied.

Darcan again looked down at the letter, ignoring the insult. "This 'Praximus Command' he offers is the Roman scroll you seek?"

"It is. But fire consumed it outside Larnaca, yes?"

He heard the cardinal's accusatory tone and knew he must defend himself. "I brought you all documents found at the camp. I have no knowledge of what fueled the fires before my arrival."

Orsini squinted. "Tell me again of Malcolm's boy. Tell me of his reaction when your men rescued the ledgers from the fire."

"Brimley Hastings," Darcan confirmed. "He appeared utterly dejected."

"And then?"

Darcan closed his eyes, recalling events. "Those who'd fled during the attack by Malcolm and the Cypriot slowly returned. We had the right to search the camp and to defend ourselves but would have had to answer for any further, unprovoked deaths. I left the young Hastings and his wench after thoroughly searching the camp."

Orsini leaned forward on his desk. "His wench?"

"The daughter of the Cypriot with Malcolm," said Darcan. "The way they tried protecting each other, I assumed the unborn child she carried was his."

"Child she carried? You fool! The boy would have traveled to Cyprus with his master. Otherwise, he would have been posted at Kolossi. And any family associated with the order would never openly display a pregnant girl out of wedlock. She'd been hiding the scroll in front of your face!"

He blinked several times, replaying events from the campground again in his mind until his teeth clenched and his brow creased.

"You have seen this boy." Orsini pointed a boney finger across his desk. "You will accompany your countryman Hayton of Corycus to Cyprus in the spring. He travels there to ensure Amalric complies with *Pastoralis Praeeminentiae*. You will aid him, but your primary objective will be recovery of the Roman scroll from the boy, Brimley Hastings."

Darcan nodded, meeting Orsini's frown with one of his own.

"Until then, you shall travel to England and learn all you can about this boy who challenges the church." The cardinal tapped a finger on the letter atop his desk. "He is responsible for this bribery attempt."

"Yes, Your Eminence."

Orsini learned back and waved his right hand with mock frivolity, dismissing him. "You should have no problems accessing the brotherhood there, considering young Edward's such dutiful response to his church . . ."

He rose and bowed while backing toward the door. "Yes, Your Eminence." He knew the reason for the cardinal's parting sarcasm. In the written response to *Pastoralis Praeeminentiae*, young King Edward II of England had promised matters concerning the affair of the temple would be expedited in the quickest and best way. It had since been reported that only light inquiries had been made and that the brotherhood continued conducting business in England as usual.

Darcan expected more hesitation on the part of Christian monarchs following events taking place just one week prior. Before cardinals sent by Pope Clement V, confessions of guilt had been retracted by Grand Master Jacques de Molay, Visitor of the Temple Hugues de Pairaud, and sixty others. Rumors of the pope considering the suspension of the French Inquisition to collect evidence to date ensued, inviting potential conflict with the Crown on the basis of heresy cases requiring secular authority.

For Cibalik Darcan, it was a time to tread carefully.

CHAPTER 26

JULY 27, 8:46 A.M. GST

LIMASSOL

As the others examined photos from Kolossi, Danny Dicarpio wrote each Latin word from the scroll fragment onto the piece of paper. He then made an English translation on a second sheet. It allowed him to take in the words and think in English instead of Latin, but it did little to lessen the shock. Deep in thought, he lost track of time until a familiar voice snapped him back to reality.

"You okay over there?" Rick asked.

Danny slowly turned his head. "Unbelievable . . ."

He knew it was his uncharacteristically terse response that prompted the others to join him behind the desk. He shifted the paper with the English translation toward them. The four gathered around it and read:

THIRD GALLIC LEGION

FIRST COHORT

FIRST AND SECOND CENTURIA

COMMAND TRIBUNE

LUCIUS VALERIUS PRAXIMUS

COMMAND EFFECTIVE 14 AUGUST, 786

LIMIT DISCLOSURE OF EXPEDITION PURPOSE

LIMIT DISCLOSURE OF LEGION IDENTITY

APPREHEND FUGITIVES

FLEEING JUDEA EASTWARD

RETURN FUGITIVES

TO MUNICIPAL AUTHORITY OF JUDEA

RETURN FUGITIVES

BEFORE OR DURING SUMMER 788

LIMIT DISCLOSURE OF FUGITIVE IDENTITIES

FUGITIVES POSSIBLY SPLIT

INTO TWO GROUPS

FIRST GROUP

APPROXIMATELY 20 FUGITIVES

LED BY DIDYMOUS JUDAS TOMAS OF GALILEE

SECOND GROUP

The leather was roughly cut just below the last line. It seemed clear the bottom of the scroll had been removed to hide the identity of the second group.

"You sure you got those years right?" Sean asked.

Danny frowned. A moment later he realized the misunderstanding. He'd written the years in the original AUC convention, or *Ab Urbe Condita*, meaning "from the foundation of the city." For anyone who studied Roman history, switching between conventions by adding or subtracting 753 was automatic, but he saw how it could be confusing to others and quickly crossed out the 786 and 788, replacing them with 33 AD and 35 AD.

Pat pointed to the second line from the bottom. "Didymous Judas Tomas?"

"Didymous means Twin," Danny hinted.

Maria snapped her head toward him. "Thomas the Twin?"

"No . . ." It seemed Rick also realized what he was getting at.

Danny nodded. "At the time, 'Didymous Judas Tomas of Galilee' is how Roman authorities would have referenced Thomas the Apostle."

"Whoa, Professor," Sean said. "As in *Doubting* Thomas?"

"Correct."

"You think this is true?" Maria asked.

"We can date a piece of the leather later with radiocarbon testing to within plus or minus fifty years, but it's definitely pre-Renaissance. And it fits," he explained. "The accepted history tells us Thomas ventured east to preach the gospel, traveling outside the Roman Empire, perhaps as far as India. The Indian Nasrani Christians are also known as Saint Thomas Christians."

"*Traveled*, yes," Rick said. "This indicates he and his followers were on the run. Why?"

He shrugged. "Maybe it's explained in the missing lower section. We know temple elders viewed the apostles as troublemakers, and Roman authorities had to appease those rabbis or risk them calling for unrest in their Jewish communities."

"Maybe it has more to do with the second group," Maria suggested. "Did another apostle lead them?"

Danny nodded. "Could be. A few more are thought to have traveled east: Matthew, Bartholomew, Simon . . . hey, I think I can estimate the size of the second group."

Rick frowned. "How the hell?"

Danny explained. During and after the Servile Wars, Roman military units typically used a four-to-one force ratio for subduing, recapturing and transporting groups of slaves back into captivity. If the same 4:1 ratio was used, then the 160 soldiers—80 from each centuria—would correspond to 40 fugitives in total, or 20 in each group.

All five fought exhaustion as they discussed the scroll fragment, none having slept for well over twenty-four hours. They planned to meet with more representatives from Nicosia in the lobby at 3:00 p.m. so Rick suggested they all try to get some sleep and meet back in Danny's room at 2:45.

Before taking the Kolossi photos off the bed, Sean showed Danny the intersections of the lines connecting the domino symbols. He found it interesting but was still deep in thought about the scroll fragment.

"I need to get my backpack from the trunk," Maria said. "Anyone need anything else from the Land Rover?"

Pat tossed her the spare key. "Not me."

9:02 A.M.

Leaving her backpack was a good idea. She needed an excuse to slip away for her call to Rome. Despite her affections for the Americans, Cardinal Dominic Batista had a decision to make.

Their borrowed Land Rover occupied a dark and silent section of the concrete parking garage. Maria entered, and a lone pigeon fled its perch on the pipe above her head, flapping its wings loudly on its way to its next roost. Her right hand instinctively shifted to her Gendarmerie Corps standard-issue Glock 17 holstered in the small of her back.

Stupid little girl. Afraid of birds now, are we?

She approached the SUV and heard other sounds on the ground, at the other end of the parking garage, coming from behind one of the concrete support columns.

More birds. Where's a stray cat when you need one?

She neared the vehicle and pushed the button on the key holder to unlock the trunk. The expected beep was followed by a crash on the wall behind the vehicle. Bits of material fell to the ground. She spun around, drew her 9mm semiautomatic, and scanned the parking garage.

A popping sound came from the shadows to her right followed by another crash, this time on the support column by her head. Through her distress, she sensed the passage of time slow and her awareness sharpen. Shards of what looked like plastic rained down on her. Shifting back to get behind the Land Rover, she saw movement in another shadow to her left. For a split second after hearing the popping sound, she thought she saw another bird, this one darting straight toward her.

She lined up the Glock's front sight before her senses were shocked into darkness and white noise. Her momentum from shifting backward continued. Her legs involuntarily shot out straight, causing her feet to slip forward. Her rigid body slammed back onto the concrete surface next to the support column, and her abdominals and back muscles fought over which way to bend her spine. During the battle being waged by every fiber of her muscular system, she searched for any other sensory inputs beyond the stars in her vision and crackling noise in her ears. Her right index finger, in front of the trigger guard, pulled so hard it nearly broke a bone. Despite her internal pleas, all mental commands to her body were overridden by the invasive signal forcing continued maximum muscle exertion.

The moment the assault on her nervous system ended, her entire body went completely limp. Someone ripped the Glock from her right hand and thrust a hypodermic needle into her left arm.

The few slowly returning sensory inputs soon gave way to darkness.

CHAPTER 27

MAY 28, 1308

NICOSIA, KINGDOM OF CYPRUS

"Can no one imbue d'Oselier with reason?" Amalric, regent of Cyprus, scowled at each of the two men seated in front of his desk.

"The marshal continues to be a man set in ways," replied Lord Hayton of Corycus.

It took nearly all the restraint Cibalik Darcan possessed to maintain his subservient role and stay silent. In the three weeks since returning to Cyprus, Darcan had watched Amalric and Hayton task the most influential men of the island with convincing the top remaining commander of the order to comply with *Pastoralis Praeeminentiae*. The suggestion by Balian of Ibelin, prince of Galilee in exile, of giving up their arms and accepting light confinement in the palace of the Archbishop of Nicosia had been met with a counterproposal of liberal house arrest. Similar invitations from canons of both Nicosia and Famagusta prompted Ayme d'Oselier to recommend that a dedicated galley deliver messages and for them to await a papal response.

"Forced compliance will cost the lives of many." Amalric shook his head. "A burden I do not wish placed on the soldiers of Cyprus."

"A sentiment they share, I'm sure." Hayton paused. "There may be another way . . ."

"Speak of it."

"All efforts thus far have been to convince d'Oselier to *comply* with the papal bull."

"Rightly so. His Holiness has made it clear the Order of the—"

Hayton raised a hand, prompting silence from Amalric.

The seemingly insubordinate act was further evidence of why Cardinal Orsini's decision to send the man had been so cunning. Hayton served as an ordained prior before becoming ruler of the city of Corycus on the southern coast of Armenian Cilicia, thus ideally positioned to act as a bridge between monk and monarch. In addition, he was the very man sent as envoy to Pope Clement V by Amalric the year before to promote the legitimacy of his rule on Cyprus.

"Ayme d'Oselier travels south to Kolossi. Let me follow and present *Pastoralis Praeeminentiae* to him and his priests."

Amalric's frown pinched his brow. "He has been told of the papal orders by many."

"Yes . . . told," repeated Hayton. "But never shown. Let me present the actual parchment to him and his high priests. Let it inspire him to act in the best interests of all involved. Let the decision to comply be his own."

"You feel this will persuade?"

"Combined with a demonstration of force by Cypriot soldiers, yes."

The Regent of Cyprus paused for a moment before speaking. "Proceed."

KOLOSSI

The wooden palisade atop the earthen berm surrounding the grounds had been completed just three days ago. Three weeks prior, the work had been accelerated by word of an envoy from Poitiers arriving in Nicosia, delivering another copy of *Pastoralis Praeeminentiae* to Amalric. Towers along the half-mile circumference were being erected for posting watchmen.

When not called upon to assist Jean de Villa in the pigeon lofts, Brim hauled building materials to the rising towers with the other sergeants. After hours of moving logs atop their shoulders, Brim and the other young sergeant he was paired with welcomed the arrival of water. A few of the Greek boys who'd worked the sweet salt mill before its shutdown had been retained to carry baskets of bread and buckets of water to work crews.

"Hastings!"

Brim turned to see the giant French sergeant from the *Rosabella* incident marching toward him. The confrère had been put in charge of supplying the tower builders.

"More rope reels just arrived at the south gate. You two, cease your dawdling and deliver them to the southeast tower."

"Very well." Brim had learned of the edict from Amalric forbidding financial dealings with the order. Nothing had been delivered to Kolossi for over a week. Instead, out-of-uniform sergeants drove wagon teams to Limassol for supplies. One or two extra gold bezants at points of sale quickly assuaged suspicions of dealing with the order.

The two sergeants left the northeast tower rubbing their bruised shoulders. Brim noticed a pigeon streak past. The messages from Nicosia had been arriving more frequently during the last two days, their contents more forlorn. A couple of minutes later, another bird overflew them. Soon after, a high-speed procession filled the sky.

Brim pointed in the direction of the south gate. "Carry on." He then dashed toward the pigeon lofts.

He entered the main aviary of the Kolossi loft and saw Jean de Villa hunched over the communications ledger, writing with fervor. Sweat pebbled Jean's forehead as he glanced back and forth between the small piece of paper he held and the communications ledger. He looked up at Brim, then pointed toward two birds already perched atop the shelf supporting cages of their mates. "Fetch the notes from those two. We must document messages in the correct sequence."

Brim cupped the nearest bird in his palm, turned it onto its back, and gently removed the bangle from its tibia. Every few seconds, he heard more clicks from the hinged wooden dowels striking the bottom of the trap door frame as more pigeons entered the aviary from the landing board. "The latest?"

Jean shook his head. "The marshal's presentation to Amalric was poorly received yesterday. This morning he departed for Kolossi with nearly all the remaining brethren from Nicosia."

"He will expect the watchtowers to be complete when he arrives," said Brim as he removed the note from the bangle.

Jean finished the log entry and turned to Brim. "What say you?"

May God grant mercy . . . Brim looked to Jean. "The brothers who stayed north have been surrounded by Amalric's troops."

More clicks from the trap door prompted Jean to reach for the note. "Tend to the others."

Four more birds fluttered onto the shelf supporting their cages, and at least a dozen more tried edging their beaks into the water dish atop the entry shelf. Twisting his wrist to expose the underside of the next bird in his hand, Brim was surprised to see that the messenger carried no message. Losing a bangle in flight was possible but very rare. He scanned the next few birds, again finding nothing affixed to their legs. "These carry no word."

Jean de Villa got up from his chair fronting the communications ledger and strode over to the entry shelf. He perused the bird's legs for any hint of red paint from a Nicosia bangle, instead finding a pigeon with a red breast gash consistent with a slice from an arrowhead.

Brim inspected the flock beside Jean. "This one's missing a leg."

The pigeon keeper had the bird with the gash cupped in his hands, inspecting the depth of the slice. "Bastards . . ."

Brim turned to Jean. "Does this mean . . . ?"

Jean nodded slowly. "Our complex in Nicosia has been overrun." He turned an ashen face to Brim. "And we're next."

CHAPTER 28

JULY 27, 1:34 P.M. GST

LIMASSOL

He rarely had dreams. At least those he could remember upon waking. He assumed this was the result of his normally ordered life in academia. He woke early, drove to campus, taught classes, did research from his office, drove home to other personal research projects, then went to bed early to start it all again the next day.

Removed from that structured life, everything had changed.

Each time he'd drifted off to sleep since the team left his room hours before, Danny Dicarpio was jarred awake by one strange dream or another related to the scroll fragment hidden at Kolossi. Some had been scary, others ridiculous, but none of them made any sense. With the curtains pulled closed, he found himself staring through the darkness at the rotating ceiling fan, thinking about the background supplied by Maria, and asking himself questions. He distilled them down to three and convinced himself he could work out the most likely answer to each.

One: Why was the top scroll fragment even in Cyprus?

It had been reportedly seen in Jerusalem but probably withdrawn with other treasures and relics after the Battle of Hattin. If it had been moved to the island as Christian knights lost control of the Levant, it wouldn't have been there long, since the Templars lost control of Cyprus soon after. By the end of the Third Crusade, the scroll would have been kept safe at a Templar preceptory somewhere in Europe. The epistle of Pope Clement V proves the Templars had been in possession of the scroll during their 1307 persecution in France by King Philip IV. Most likely answer: the scroll had been brought to Cyprus by a group of Templars who were on the run.

Two: Who cut the scroll in half?

It was no coincidence the scroll had been cut at the exact spot needed to separate the descriptions of the two groups of fugitives. Those who'd escaped to Cyprus would've eventually heard of the forced confessions and executions of their monastic brotherhood by French authorities while the pope did nothing to stop them. It was possible they'd attempted to coax a more protective role out of Pope Clement V—take a stand against King Philip IV in exchange for the scroll. The "half now and half on delivery" would seem to apply in such a case. Most likely answer: the scroll had been halved by the fleeing Templars trying to make a deal for papal protection.

Three: Where was the bottom half?

Assuming the papal protection deal theory was correct, the false fireplace wall at Kolossi could've been revealed after papal authorities accepted the arrangement, precluding the need for the escaped Templars to show themselves and risk being lured into a trap. The hidden location of the bottom half of the scroll could then have been revealed after the release of Templars in France. Such an arrangement would've allowed those in possession of the scroll halves to control the deal from anywhere in the world. Most likely answer: no idea. He ground his teeth in consternation, knowing the bottom half of the scroll could be hidden anywhere.

For such a plan to be put into motion, the free Templars would have needed a way to pass messages to each other for coordination. With their network taken over by French authorities and rival monastic orders, they would have needed to leave a trail only their brethren could follow. Only in such a way could the location of the bottom half have been secretly perpetuated.

Why couldn't this be like a pirate movie, where "X marks the spot" on a map?

He closed his eyes. A wave of doubt rolled over his thoughts like an angry tide washing over sand messages. He was the historical expert on the team, yet all he'd come up with were highly dubious theories leading them nowhere.

Why couldn't he be more like the twins, always optimistic and pushing forward? It seemed they could keep turning over rocks until they found something without ever feeling dejected. Like the way they found the possible link between the domino and the patterns on the east wall. While certainly interesting, it would only be useful if whatever had been carved onto the wall hadn't been chiseled off.

About that—what could have been so offensive that it prompted removal?

The original structures at Kolossi had been built by the Frankish military early in the thirteenth century and used by the Templars until their persecution. Being devout Christians, they would not have carved graven images. The Hospitallers, who'd taken command of the castle through the fifteenth century, would not have been offended by Christian motifs. The Venetians, who'd ruled until the Ottoman takeover, would also not have taken offense.

The Ottomans, though Sunni Muslims, had not been known for defacing architecture in areas they conquered—signs of the Christian Kingdom of Cyprus still remain at Kolossi.

Yet, there must have been something offensive to them about the east wall.

Offensive Templars . . .

Templar offensives.

Danny jumped out of bed, rushed to his desk, and clicked his tablet out of hibernation mode. The screen flashing to life assaulted his eyes, which had grown accustomed to the darkness. His tablet was still connected to the projector; as the bulb came back to life, the far wall began to glow with the image from his screen. He grabbed the Kolossi photos from the nightstand and threw open the curtains, further flooding the room in light.

While squinting at the twins' hardcopies, he pulled up his cloud-based server, on which he kept a vast amount of historical research. He filtered down through subfolders and shook his head—he'd been so focused on the scroll fragment, he hadn't seen the chiseled east wall for what it was.

He located the digital photo from a rare manuscript describing the interior of the Paris preceptory, a structure destroyed shortly after the French Revolution. It contained a drawing of the meeting room used by senior knights for planning military offenses in the Holy Land. Their attention would have been focused at the center of the image—the Levant Wall.

It had not been their religion that offended the Ottomans on Cyprus; it had been what they did in the name of their religion. The Levant Wall, with Templar crosses chiseled into each occupied territory, would have been a reminder of their conquests in the Holy Land and the severe dominion they held over Cyprus. Despite abandoning their reign late in the twelfth century, the order had guarded its Cyprus preceptories until its demise more than a hundred years later. In that context, it was not surprising that such engravings had been obliterated.

In the preceptories that still existed in Europe and the Near East, there remained no intact Levant Wall specimens, nor had there been for centuries. He felt fortunate to have come across the drawing of the Paris Levant Wall during his studies—and luckier still to have remembered he had it available in his archives. He wondered if the version that had been chiseled off the Kolossi east wall was as exacting as the version in the Paris preceptory. To find out, he opened the photo showing the entire chiseled portion of the Kolossi east wall and began zooming around the periphery. Not all the contours were made by a blunt tool. In certain areas, he saw finer carvings.

Using the Paris preceptory drawing as a guide, he began searching for specific coastlines. Zooming and panning near the bottom left corner, some finer details between the deep gouges could be compared with the shape of the Nile Delta. Scanning the top and right edges revealed other details matching the coasts of the Armenian principalities and the Kingdom of Jerusalem. Along the left edge, intermittent features matched the outline of Cyprus.

Setting the transparency of the Paris Levant Wall photo to fifty percent, he overlaid the image onto the photo of the Kolossi east wall and lined up the coastlines as best he could. Using a drawing tool, he created five lines, fixing their ends at the symbols on the periphery to recreate the intersection the twins had discovered. The intersection neared the shoreline of Tortosa, as shown in the photo of the Paris Levant Wall drawing. He tried shifting the drawing over so the intersection would make landfall, but then the coastlines didn't quite line up.

He felt the cartography of the Paris Levant Wall drawing he referenced could be in error. Knowing the scale, he reversed the process. He grouped the intersecting lines and Kolossi photo together, set transparency to fifty percent, then lined up over the coastlines of a web-based map of the eastern Mediterranean. Again, the intersection just failed to make landfall.

A knock made him jump. He went to the door hearing Rick Lambert's voice. "Danny?"

He opened the door and looked at his wrist before realizing his watch lay on the nightstand. "What time is it?"

"Just after two. I saw the light under the door as I was walking by. I'm on my way downstairs for coffee."

"Let me show you something first."

Danny explained what he found, complaining how either the inaccuracy of the Kolossi Levant Wall or the placement of the symbols themselves around the periphery was to blame for the lines' intersection not making landfall. He switched between the Paris Levant Wall image, showing the intersection off the coast of crusader-controlled Tortosa, and the online map showing the intersection in the same place, just southwest of modern-day Tartus.

He spoke of the Cathedral of Our Lady of Tortosa—now functioning as the National Museum of Tartus—as being a possible hiding place for the bottom of the scroll. He noticed Rick staring at the map projected on the wall and grinning like the Cheshire Cat. He reminded himself Rick could definitely keep up with him in one historical subject matter area—military history. "What?" he asked.

"It's not Our Lady of Tortosa."

"That's the closest Templar stronghold."

"No, it's not," Rick replied. "What's the last piece of the Levant lost?"

"Easy: Acre. But it's far south and—"

"No, I mean the very last outpost."

"What is it you're . . . Oh!" Danny felt a rush and began zooming into the area of the online map at the intersection of the five lines. With each click, the empty blue sea two miles off the coast grew, first into a dot, then a small circle, then finally a defined shape with a label—Arwad Island.

In a final effort to reclaim a foothold in the Levant, Templars had used the island, known then as Ruad, as a staging area for an amphibious assault on Tortosa in 1300. The coordinated land attack by Mongol forces had not arrived in time, compelling the Christians to retreat. The island had supported a garrison until finally besieged and captured by mamluk forces in 1303. The tiny island, renamed Arwad, measured no more than a half mile across in any direction. It eventually became home to a modest fishing community with its main structure, now called the Citadel of Arwad, transformed into a popular tourist attraction.

Danny switched the online image from map mode to satellite mode, showing the town of Arwad filling the tiny island. "I can't believe I forgot about the Fall of Ruad."

"Glad I could help out for once," replied Rick, tapping on the outline of the fortress projected on the wall. "That's where we'll need to look next."

He tensed. "You know Arwad is Syrian territory, right?"

"We're not invading Damascus. It's just a sleepy fishing village. Still, we'll need help. I'll call Dougherty."

A knock on the door prompted both men to check their watches—2:43 p.m. The Duffys entered, bickering about something as usual. Danny began showing them the results of their discovery while Rick called James Dougherty on his sat phone.

Danny had been told Dougherty offered to be a conduit for the team, not just to the State Department's Bureau of Intelligence and Research but to the US Intelligence Community in general, which meant taking secure phone calls day or night. After Rick explained the recent discoveries, Dougherty would most likely have options for getting them to Arwad.

Rick got off the phone at 2:55 p.m. "Where's Maria?"

Danny hung up his hotel room phone. "No answer at her room. The twins are checking downstairs."

Pat entered. "She's not with the Nicosia guides waiting in the lobby."

Rick called the lobby for messages. "Someone left me a message. They didn't leave a name."

Danny waited for an explanation.

"It said to expect a call to my hotel room at 4:00 p.m."

Sean finally entered the room from the parking garage and laid out several items on the entry table. "We have a problem, sir. I don't think Maria made it to the Land Rover earlier."

All four men stared at the objects. Danny thought back to Rick's description of the Plenducci abduction and felt the alarm he knew the others felt also. He knew the plastic fragments and tiny circuit board shards on the table before him were remnants of stun slugs.

CHAPTER 29

JUNE 1, 1308

KOLOSSI

"This one also describes the planned seizures," said Brim, pointing at an entry in the Kolossi communications ledger.

"The same details?" asked Jean de Villa.

Brim nodded. "By secular authorities on behalf of the church."

Shortly after Ayme d'Oselier had arrived at Kolossi three days prior, negotiations for a visit by papal envoy Lord Hayton of Corycus began. Hayton's offer of presenting *Pastoralis Praeeminentiae* directly to d'Oselier had stimulated many preparatory activities in and around the compound. Brim and Jean had been given the task of creating a summary of the papal bull based on interviewing the marshal about what he'd been told and a review of messages from Nicosia. The pair had already presented their synopsis to the marshal and his priests but decided to take a final look through the logbook before the event began at high sun.

The two sergeants left the pigeon lofts with their summation and made their way to the courtyard behind the closed south gate. When d'Oselier appeared, yet again resplendent in his bright white mantle, they took their places in the procession behind him, the turcopolier, and two high priests.

Brim assumed several confrère sergeants manned the watchtowers along the palisade. Those who weren't in them stood below what appeared to be a hastily erected, elevated walkway made of wagons, barrels, and planks just inside the south wall. He was surprised to see all wore full battle gear, including hauberks and plate-metal helms. The motivation behind the assembly puzzled him, until the south gate swung open revealing rows of Cypriot soldiers.

One of the high priests raised a crucifix loosely chained around his neck and strode out the gate to a table positioned under an open-walled fabric pavilion. Upon reaching the table, he recited the Lord's Prayer.

Two chaplain brothers marched out next, each flying the *croix pattée rouge*. The confrères took this as their cue to climb atop the walkway, making themselves visible and causing an audible stir among the lightly armored soldiers of Cyprus. The standard bearers positioned each red-footed cross on opposing sides of the fabric shelter.

What Brim saw next shocked him. Two sergeant brothers each flew *Le Gonfanon Baussant*—the order's black-and-white battle flag. To his knowledge, such flags had only been flown in the Holy Land. The sergeant brothers marched the battle flags toward the sides of the pavilion, and the confrères atop the walkway slammed the tips of their broadswords against the planking in time with their footfalls. The Cypriot soldiers Brim could see from his vantage point looked nervously from side to side.

With all flags positioned and silence returned, the marshal and turcopolier strode toward the sheltered table. The second high priest, Jean, and Brim followed. At the same time, a figure in a plain monk's robe approached between two others. Brim presumed he was the papal envoy, Lord Hayton. A man on Hayton's right wore the decorative robes of the Cathedral of Nicosia. To Hayton's left strode Ambassador Cibalik Darcan. All arrived at the table simultaneously.

"Greetings. I am Brother Hayton."

"Welcome to Kolossi. I am Brother Ayme."

Each man clearly knew of the other such that no titles were needed.

Hayton nodded over his left shoulder. "Cibalik Darcan, ambassador to His Holiness from Armenian Cilicia."

D'Oselier seemed to ignore the introduction and gestured to his left. "Bartholomew of Gordo, turcopolier of Cyprus."

Hayton nodded toward the turcopolier, then returned his gaze toward the marshal. "You know the purpose of my visit?"

The marshal's voice was resolute. "I do."

"Allow me to present the word of His Holiness, Pope Clement V."

The priest from Nicosia removed Lord Hayton's copy of *Pastoralis Praeeminentiae* from a large leather satchel and unrolled in on the table. The two priests of the order inspected the pressed wax on the top edge and nodded, signifying the broken seal's authenticity. One priest read the Latin text verbatim, pausing after each sentence to allow the other to translate into French. After every few sentences, d'Oselier turned to Jean and Brim, who signaled the words matched their summary. Whenever Brim glanced at Darcan, he saw the ambassador looking back at him with angry eyes.

Hayton broke the unnerving stillness after the reading. "May I know of Kolossi's complement?"

"Eighty-three brother knights and thirty-five brother sergeants," said d'Oselier.

All three men facing the marshal looked above the palisade. "I see many beyond those numbers," said Hayton, obviously puzzled.

"Over two hundred confrère sergeants and several dozen domestics are employed by the order. The words of His Holiness apply to none other than those of the brotherhood."

Hayton frowned and glanced again above the palisade. "They are not of the Temple of Solomon?"

"They are not." The marshal turned to Jean. "The Draper of Cyprus can provide the ledger documenting their contracts."

Hayton turned around. Darcan and the priest from Nicosia huddled close and spoke in hushed tones. The priest nodded several times before Hayton turned back around to face the marshal. "We are in agreement. Only brother knights and brother sergeants are subject to *Pastoralis Praeeminentiae*. Upon implementation, the contracts of all others are severed, and they must leave Kolossi."

D'Oselier nodded.

"If I may ask . . ." Hayton gestured toward the palisade. "What was their purpose here?"

The marshal waved a hand toward the papal bull. "It matters no longer."

Hayton pursed his lips but did not force the issue.

D'Oselier opened his palms. "What of us?"

"You and your brothers will be escorted to accommodations in Khirokitia."

The marshal paused for several seconds. "We will adjourn to organize our response."

Darcan looked at Hayton, who nodded. The ambassador then glanced at Brim before turning to d'Oselier. "There is no reason for delay."

D'Oselier turned to Darcan with a frown, as if observing an unruly child.

Hayton whispered into Darcan's ear before turning back to the marshal. "Very well."

Darcan shook his head and gritted his teeth as Hayton turned to face him.

Before turning to follow the procession back inside the Kolossi compound, Brim met Darcan's angry glare once more.

News of the impending surrender spread through Kolossi quickly. Although it was the worst time for dereliction of duty, Brim knew Darcan would eventually find his way to Shayla. Kolossi was lost, but she could be saved.

He changed into his plain russet tunic. His eyes darted back and forth as he made his way to the east wall. The water mill's runoff ditch had been sealed with an iron grill under the palisade. He unbolted the east gate, opened it a few inches, and peeked outside to verify all activity was still focused to the south. He then slipped into the ditch, scurried to the eastern orchards, and began what he assumed would be his final journey from Kolossi to Limassol.

LIMASSOL

"Where is the workshop of the Tack Master of Kolossi?" Cibalik Darcan had the man bent backward over one of his casks.

"Two doors south," said the cooper in a pained voice.

Following hours of searching Kolossi during Hayton's preparation for the march of the brotherhood to Khirokitia, the boy had not been found. At knifepoint, a groom had divulged the approximate location of the tack master's workshop. In haste, Darcan's men had broken into the barrel builder's workplace by mistake.

Dashing to the correct location, he and his men quickly searched the residence and workshop, finding no one. In the fireplace, small logs burned beneath a cooking pot hanging from a rack by chains.

He recognized the boy as clever even before being sent to England to research him. While most in the London preceptory had kept silent, one monk from the scriptorium directed him to a Franciscan billeted in a Winchester friary fifty miles southwest. The reputation of Wil Ockham as one of the brightest young minds in England had made his summary of the boy all the more astonishing—in terms of raw intellect, Brimley Hastings had few equals.

The recollection filled Darcan with even more loathing. He ran outside and looked down the deserted road. "I will find you!" He turned to look in the opposite direction. "I will find you!"

One of his mercenary commanders joined him. After a pause, the man spoke. "How shall we proceed?"

Darcan pointed at the workshop. "Reduce it to ashes."

CHAPTER 30

TIME AND LOCATION UNKNOWN

Maria's lifelong love of cross-country skiing was one of the reasons she'd requested a post with the *Alpini* mountain infantry division after receiving her commission in the Italian Army. To improve her stamina during patrols in the Italian Alps, she'd adopted the philosophy of an American distance runner from a generation before—*No one can endure more pain than I.* The radical self-motivating mantra of Steve Prefontaine hadn't always worked, but it did improve her endurance to the point where only a few of the strongest male skiers in her unit could keep up with her if she decided to push it.

Lorenzo, another lieutenant in Alpine Brigade Julia, was one of her few male friends. He was smart enough not to make a pass at her, as most of the other young officers had. They skied one of their favorite routes between garrisons deep in the Julian Alps, Sako TRG-42 blot-action sniper rifles slung behind them.

She soon realized she was dreaming. Part of her wanted to continue gliding above the snow next to Lorenzo, their arms and legs in perfect synchronicity. But another part of her noticed problems with technique, causing her to fall behind. Her right arm could no longer plant the pole she used to push off with. And her right side felt colder than her left.

Lorenzo continued to extend his lead, seemingly oblivious to her problems.

Per favore! Lorenzo! . . .

Maria slowly opened her eyes and a wall of dark gray replaced the sunny alpine landscape. She lay with her right side on cool concrete. She felt a chill unrelated to the temperature when she realized her right wrist was handcuffed to one end of a four-foot chain, the other end padlocked to a drain pipe running from ceiling to floor. As she sat up, she noticed how much her head hurt.

By the dim light of the single bulb hanging from the ceiling, she scanned what appeared to be a small windowless storeroom. The single metal door was to her right, empty shelves on the wall to her left, and several large crates across from her. The only loose object within reach was an empty bucket near the center of the room.

Her sports bra was visible through her open and torn shirt. She had a fuzzy memory of being stunned and drugged in the parking garage and was unsure if her spasms had ripped the shirt or if it had been torn during a search by her captors. Her holstered Glock, sheathed Ka-Bar, phone, and watch were all missing.

Standing made her feel lightheaded. She tucked her shirt into her khaki trousers, covering herself as best she could, and approached the door as close as the chain allowed. It was still a full three feet beyond her reach. The chain tightened and the padlock slammed against the drain pipe with a loud clang, accentuating her headache.

The reverberating sound of the pipe faded but was replaced by the bang of a sliding bolt on the other side of the metal door.

Making a split-second decision to feign weakness until she could better appraise her situation—not a difficult act under the circumstances—she retreated back to lying on the floor by the pipe and waited for the door to open. The two teenage boys who entered wore expressions of excitement and anger. The first barked a high-pitched order in what sounded like Farsi. The second, slightly taller boy carried a stun gun.

The first boy switched to broken English. "Your name!"

Maria created a communication gap by speaking only Italian. *"Non farmi male . . ."*

The boys glanced at each other and laughed. The first tore her shirt open and retreated a step while the second cycled the stun gun to create a crackling arc between the front electrodes.

She noticed both of them staring at her sports bra. She was initially perplexed until realizing this was probably the only way they'd had contact with women—as their captives.

The first boy lunged at her again and squeezed her left breast.

Pathetic, she thought. She then forced herself to begin crying. *"No. Per favore . . ."*

The taller boy said something, prompting the first to frown, stand, then take the stun gun. The second boy then approached her and pressed her breasts together with both hands.

Any sympathy she'd had for their youth, stolen childhoods, and misguided lives was instead channeled into rage. But again, she forced herself to whimper and play victim. *"No. Ti prego . . ."*

She hoped one of them had a key to the handcuffs. If they got within reach at the same time, she'd find out. But it would not be simple. She'd have to subdue one boy and hold him with her legs as the other came at her. With her hands freed, she could possibly wrestle the stun gun away while avoiding the electrodes. If neither boy had the key, at least she'd have the satisfaction of snapping their necks.

Maria was under the impression the excited boys had been the only two in the adjacent room, until two men strolled in. When they saw the taller boy on top of her, they started laughing.

So much for the escape plan.

A door burst open in the adjacent room. The two boys froze. The two men gestured to the boys to follow them out.

She heard heated orders being given.

The two boys sheepishly reentered the storeroom followed by the new arrival.

Is this the Prom King?

He looked at her open shirt, turned, and frowned at the boys, prompting them to lower their heads. As he turned right, Maria was sickened to see the man's molars through a grotesque hole in his left cheek.

"Non farmi male, signore . . ."

"English please, Lieutenant Belloci," he said. "Please excuse the interruption. I am only here to collect my men for a meeting with your friends. We will talk later."

3:22 P.M.
SOUTHERN LIMASSOL

After hurriedly dismissing their Nicosia guides with an excuse about Maria being in an important conference call to Rome, Rick Lambert dashed back to Danny's room and the four men opened their GPS tracker applications. Danny used his tablet computer for the higher screen resolution, the others following along on their smartphones. The map opened into a full-screen window zoomed into their Limassol hotel's location, the setting used the day before to verify all the watch beacons transmitted. A blue blob formed over their hotel. Four surrounding labels displayed their names, indicating the blob was actually four overlapping dots. Only Maria's beacon was missing.

Lambert watched Danny select the *8-Hour History* option on the *Breadcrumb Trail* dropdown menu. A dashed line appeared over a street route from the center four dots to a blue arrow on the northern periphery of the map pointing further north. Danny then zoomed the scale of the map out and the fifth blue dot, complete with its "Maria" label, became visible four miles north. Zooming in showed her watch beacon in an unlabeled structure across the street from what was tagged as the Pano Polemidia Mosque. Right-clicking and selecting *History Detail* showed Maria's signal had been inactive for more than five hours.

The twins quickly voiced their desire to immediately arm themselves to the fullest and storm the building.

Danny shook his head.

"What's wrong, Professor?" Sean asked. "You think you can *calculate* her away from these assholes?"

Pat seemed to agree with his brother. "Screw that. Let's go."

Lambert prepared to interject but then saw Danny pointing at his tablet.

After panning and zooming to get the closest view of her beacon's location, Danny voiced his thoughts without looking up from his screen. "Since they had the hotel staked out before, it's likely we're still being watched. If we all charge north, we'll tip our hand about the tracking.

They may simply kill her." He looked to Lambert apologetically. "Assuming she's not already dead."

Fearing the same, Lambert tried to focus on the problem. He checked his watch—3:34. "We do nothing until I take their call." His train of thought was at risk of being derailed by the painful memories of recent losses. He'd lost men under his command before, but that was war. After his assignment to the State Department's Bureau of Intelligence and Research, he'd thought such experiences were behind him. While his assignments in INR and the Iraqi Ministry of Interior had occasionally put him and others in dangerous situations, they seldom found themselves under attack. All that had changed less than two weeks ago. Topolis, Plenducci, Samir—their deaths made him feel powerless.

Was lack of leadership and poor judgment to blame?

Has Maria also lost her life because of such ineptitude?

He took a deep breath and tried to reset his mind. "Danny, try to get a precise address for that location."

"I'm on it."

He turned to the Duffys—two bundles of energy craving release. "Guys, move your equipment in here and get ready to mount a rescue mission in case we can find a way."

"Yes sir," they said, nearly simultaneously.

"Remember, this is the only clean room. Assume all other locations are compromised."

The twins left for their crates.

Lambert called James Dougherty and learned a Cyprus-based intelligence asset had been located for their ingress to Arwad, but was out to sea for several more hours and would not be available for their current crisis. He promised to inquire with his counterparts in MI6 about assets available from either RAF Akrotiri or RAF Dhekelia but expressed doubt about finding any help in time to deal with the incoming telephone call—most likely from Ahmed Makarem himself— now just minutes away. For now, they were on their own.

For the last few minutes of their call, Dougherty described the most likely exchange scenarios their opposition would try to play out. All of them ended with Maria being killed and the rest of the team being ambushed after giving up the scroll fragment. He emphasized that point one last time—the only thing keeping them alive was their possession of the document and their opposition's reluctance to risk its damage or destruction. "I wish I could be more helpful."

"Thank you, sir. I'm off to take their call. Here's Danny. He can take down the info about the Arwad contact."

The call came through at exactly 4:00 p.m.

"Lambert."

"Greetings, Major Lambert." The caller's high-pitched voice had a Persian accent.

He decided to confirm he spoke with the Prom King. "Hello, Mister Makarem."

The line went silent for several seconds.

Lambert pressed his room's telephone receiver harder against his ear.

"I see our carelessness at Cramirat has born you fruit. Very well. It is of no consequence."

"What is it you want?"

The Persian chuckled. "Is that not obvious? The scroll you found at Kolossi for the woman's life."

"Where?"

"You will give a mobile number. I will direct you and your team around the city to ensure your Land Rover is not being followed. That is how it works in your Hollywood movies, yes?"

"When?"

"At the end of this call, all will be put into motion. Keep in mind you will be under constant observation."

Lambert gave the number to a prepaid mobile phone he'd purchased on Cyprus. "We'll need some time to—"

"Incorrect! You will gather the scroll and that bickering odd couple who brought it out of Kolossi!" Makarem seemed to regain his composure during a moment of silence. "You will all arrive downstairs at your Land Rover no more than three minutes after we end this call. Failure to comply kills the woman."

Bickering odd couple? He had no immediate response.

Makarem seemed to understand his confusion. "Yes, those who will be tracking you have detailed photos from Kolossi. You will keep all the Land Rover's windows open and remain visible at all times. Failure to comply kills the woman."

Lambert felt his heartbeat quicken. "How do we know she's still alive? And how do we know we'll be able to leave safely once we hand over the scroll?"

The Persian took on a softer tone. "We have no use for more death. Once we have the scroll, all can leave in peace." His timbre reverted back to its original high-pitched shrill. "But the alternative is death. Death to the woman and death to any of you who attempt to leave the hotel any other way."

Leave in peace, my ass. Lambert mentally searched for obvious holes in Makarem's process or any opportunity to deviate from the plan but came up empty. It seemed the Persian had experience with this.

The line went silent for a moment before Makarem spoke again. "Do you have any procedural questions before we begin our little tour of Limassol?"

We'll have to come up with something on the road. "No."

"Very well. You will answer your mobile phone in the Land Rover exactly three minutes from now. Failure to comply kills the woman." The line clicked dead.

Lambert jumped up and ran out of the room while looking at his watch, his mind racing.

4:08:40.

He dashed down the hall and couldn't help but reflect on his impressions of the Prom King. Makarem seemed intelligent but a slave to his emotions. The outburst after his attempt to stall for time was interesting—that kind of imbalance might be useful later. And what of his referring to the twins as the "bickering odd couple"? Sure they bickered, but *odd couple*? And what about Danny? All this based on photos from Kolossi?

Kolossi!

He barged back into Danny's room, thanked God for the realization, and checked his watch.

4:09:07.

"How'd it go?" Danny asked.

"We have less than three minutes to get to the Land Rover or Maria's dead. Danny, grab the fragment. They've got to see it with us as they guide us through the city."

Each twin began to ask questions.

Lambert held up his hands and then pointed at them. "Here's the thing—Makarem thinks there's only one of you."

The Duffys looked at each other, frowning as if offended.

"They have surveillance photos from Kolossi. You two dressed the same and were never outside together. They have photos of you both but don't know you're twins."

At this, both frowns turned to smiles. "Idiots," one of them mumbled.

Lambert glanced at his watch.

4:09:44.

"One of you comes with us. The other rescues Maria."

"I'll get her," one said.

"No. You go with them, I'll get her," the other replied.

He impatiently whirled his index finger. "Decide now, guys."

The twins began a round of rock-paper-scissors.

Lambert then checked his Beretta, wiggled it into the Safariland deep concealment holster inside his right-side waist band, and covered it with his shirt.

"Rick . . ." Danny pointed at his hotel room's easy chair.

Lambert saw white stuffing bulging out of a rectangular hole in the leather seat cushion. "What's that about?"

"After James Dougherty gave me the Arwad contact info, he had a great idea, and the more we talked—"

"Tell me on the way," he said after noticing the twins looking his way. He turned to them. "Which of you is with us?"

The twin with a smile on his face pointed to the other. "Pat . . ."

He pointed at Sean. "Okay, text Danny with your progress. I'll be on the line with Makarem during our drive."

Pat checked his sidearm. "Have fun storming the castle, wanker."

"You know it, loser," Sean replied.

4:10:38.

Lambert inhaled deeply. "One minute. Let's go." He led Danny and Pat down the hall and took the two flights of stairs to the parking garage. "Danny, you're in front. Monitor where we're going with online maps. Don't let me turn into any dead ends. Give me thumbs-up or thumbs-down."

Pat seemed to already know his job—identify trailing cars.

Lambert looked through the door to the parking garage. The space appeared deserted. They made their way toward the Land Rover. He visually scanned the overhead pipes and ducts.

Where was it?

As they neared the vehicle, he saw it—a tiny remote camera, pointed at the Land Rover, zip-tied on an overhead pipe ten yards away.

The three settled into the SUV. Lambert put his index finger to his lips, waved his other hand around the interior, and tapped his ear, indicating their opposition had plenty of time to install discrete listening devices inside the vehicle. He didn't communicate the possibility of another installation—an explosive with a remote detonator. Such an explosion would destroy the scroll fragment, so they should be safe as long as it remained in their possession.

He started the Land Rover's engine. His first worry concerned the tiny camera on the overhead pipe. The hunch about the unknown twin was solid but still just a theory.

Were they expecting only three men to enter the Land Rover?

Lambert's mobile phone buzzed. He checked his watch.

4:11:40.

Time to find out.

He crossed his fingers as he pushed the Talk and Speaker buttons on the cheap mobile phone, then placed it in the cup holder by his knee. "Hello?"

"Get on Spyrou Kyprianou Avenue eastbound," Makarem replied.

So far, so good.

CHAPTER 31

JUNE 3, 1308

TORTOSA, PROVINCE OF SYRIA

Brim Hastings knew that Tortosa—as well as the rest of the Levant—was ruled from Cairo by Sultan An-Nasir Muhammad. The land reverting back to its ancient name of Syria did not stop him from imagining he traveled the County of Tripoli before the loss of the Holy Land to the Mamluk Sultanate. "We haven't a half hour of sunlight left."

"I know this!" Shayla's tone indicated she did not appreciate his prodding. "It should be close."

They'd walked half a mile inland, east of the Cathedral of Our Lady of Tortosa. According to notes passed between fishermen on behalf of the two young women, it was the correct neighborhood. Brim asked the few on the street at dusk for directions to the workshop of Dabir and Farah Zayn. None he questioned knew.

The streets became deserted as dusk gave way to darkness, replacing their anxiety with fear. It was not, however, the panic they'd felt two days before.

Had it not been for the commotion at the shop of Shayla's neighbor, the cooper, they would have had no warning of Darcan's approach. Having had only enough time to retrieve the bottom half of the Praximus Command and two water skins before fleeing a quarter mile away, they watched the smoke rise from Shayla's home, put to the torch by Darcan's men. At the Limassol waterfront, they took one of the twenty-foot sailboats, quietly obtained weeks before for the brotherhood to fish for themselves after Amalric's edict forbidding financial dealings with the order, and spent the next day sailing sixty miles to Cape Greco on the island's east coast, twelve miles south of Famagusta. Shayla refilled the water skins from a stream handling the runoff from Paralimni Lake while Brim bought bread and dried meat with the last of the silver deniers from his leather pouch. At first light they began the hundred-mile crossing on the Etesian winds to Tortosa with the hope of receiving sanctuary from Dabir and Farah Zayn. While Brim sailed, Shayla had wept for the loss of her father and their Limassol home.

Brim knocked on doors of several dwellings showing signs of activity within. Again, none recognized the names of Dabir or Farah Zayn. He then came upon what appeared to be a potter's shop, with stacks of ceramic items littering the area. Light emanated from cracks in a front door that looked as if it had been built from discarded wood scraps. Brim knocked on what appeared to be the sturdiest part.

The collection of wood planks swung open a few inches, partially revealing a plump bearded man who could not have been more than five feet tall. After his eyes darted between the two, he spoke Arabic in a high-pitched squeal. "Who are you? Why are you out so late?"

"Peace be upon you," said Brim. "We seek the workshop of Dabir Zayn. Can you direct us?"

The man grabbed the edge of the door with chubby fingers made gray by wet clay and forced it open a few more inches. His eyes widened. "Zayn? The horse tack maker?"

Brim could barely contain his excitement. "Yes, Dabir Zayn, maker of horse tack. Where may we find him?"

A frown rolled over the potter's eyes as he began shaking his head. "Zayn is dead . . ."

"Dead?" Brim felt Shayla's left arm wrap around his right. "How?"

"The Sweats. Over a month ago."

"And his daughter?"

"They died together."

Brim understood. When those in a household contracted the sweating sickness, they were typically quarantined together. Water would have been left with them, but all consumed would have been lost to perspiration as they died of dehydration.

"Why are you out after curfew?"

"Curfew?"

"The night patrols continue their search for Mongol spies . . ." The potter's eyelids pinched tighter. "You are from inland? Safita, perhaps?"

Before Brim could answer, he heard shouts from the north.

"You must go," said the potter before closing his rickety door.

Brim whispered into Shayla's ear. "Back to the boat. We must sail to Ruad now."

She nodded several times in rapid succession.

They began retracing their steps. Trudging back toward the coast on the road south of the cathedral, they saw torches a quarter-mile west and moving closer. Brim assumed the men carrying the torches made up one of the night patrols the potter had mentioned. Realizing the men would be unable to see far past their own light, he took Shayla's hand and led her around the back of the cathedral, intending to continue west from the other side of the structure, until he saw more flames moving toward them from an eighth-mile north.

Brim suppressed his panic and looked around. He guessed an ongoing conversion from a Christian house of worship to a mosque was the reason for the materials strewn around and against the east wall, away from the main entrance on the west side. Trusting these men would also be partially blinded by their own torches, he pulled Shayla behind one of the wooden pews leaning against the brick wall. Six men moved past and met with the patrol from the west at the southeast corner. From twenty feet away, Brim could hear their conversation.

"A young man and woman were seen slinking about."

"Where?"

"Just east."

"Take your men southeast. We will search northeast."

Brim heard footsteps shuffling away and waited for silence before slipping his head out from behind the pew to look for any lingering torches. Sensing no activity in the darkness, he again took Shayla's hand and led her around the southeast corner of Our Lady of Tortosa and along the south wall. They continued toward the shore on roads they'd traversed eastbound with such high hopes just hours before.

After twenty minutes of careful navigation, they rounded the deserted open market structure lining the beach and saw activity around their sailboat.

Before leaving the boat and wading to shore, they'd lowered the stone anchor off the stern thirty feet from shore, just behind the tiny breaking waves, and tied the bowline around a boulder up the beach. Four small figures had apparently heaved on the bowline to beach the boat and were now hunched over its sides.

As Brim got closer, he realized they were children. "You there!"

Four boys looked up for a moment before reaching back into the boat, grabbing their supplies, then sprinting north up the beach.

Brim gave chase. "Drop what you carry!"

All four boys were fast. The two who carried the bread and meat led, the two others falling behind due to the weight and awkwardness of the oars they lugged. Brim came within ten feet of the closest pair. They dropped the heavy wood and sprinted ahead. He almost tripped over the oars but continued the chase with Shayla close behind, until spotting several torches further up the beach. The boys must have seen the flames also, since they turned and dashed inland.

Brim came to a stop and wiped the sweat from his eyes.

Shayla caught up to him. There was a tremble in her voice. "We must go."

It looked to him like the men carrying the torches progressed toward them. "Yes."

They each hauled an oar back to the boat. Brim weighed anchor, heaved the craft around, positioned the oars in their locks, and rowed past the small breakers. They raised sail and followed the coastline south by moonlight until the Isle of Ruad came into view offshore. They sailed around the west side so, after they beached the craft, it would not be seen by anyone leaving the mainland at daybreak.

Unlike the protective cove of northern Tortosa, the west coast of Ruad was exposed to the forceful land breeze whistling over the island from the east, propelled by the cooling landmass farther inland. The wind nearly overpowered the full keel's leverage for sailing upwind, threatening to blow them out to sea. He lost count of the number of tacks it took to begin making progress toward shore. Eventually, their zigzag course brought them crashing onto a rocky beach, prompting Brim to drop sail and jump out, bowline in hand, to secure the craft to the nearest boulder.

Exhausted, both knelt on the beach for a moment, trying to recover.

"What is that odor?" shouted Shayla, over the sound of the wind.

"I cannot tell." Brim could smell it also—a pungent scent of rot. He scanned inland as best he could, the wind from the east blowing sand in his face. In the moonlight, he saw remnants of what looked like corral fences, but the only true shelter appeared to be the order's old garrison atop the island's slight summit an eighth-mile inland. He pointed to it and turned to Shayla. "To the garrison."

They crossed the beach and began the slog up the incline. It felt strange, the slippery ground depressing underfoot. The smell of rot intensified.

Upon reaching the island's pinnacle, they found the garrison's condition as if the fall to the mamluk siege had taken place not five years before but yesterday. The western gate was smashed inward and remnants of the heavy portcullis littered the area.

They slogged through the interior halls, moonlight illuminating the floor in intervals through narrow arrow slits. Turning a corner, they finally found a place into which the wind did not funnel. They sat together and leaned against a wall for a moment of rest but soon succumbed to sleep.

POITIERS

The latest word from Cyprus infuriated Cardinal Francesco Orsini. The efforts of Hayton of Corycus to obtain compliance with *Pastoralis Praeeminentiae* without bloodshed were of course admirable, but reports of delays and endless negotiations had brought the wrath of the archbishop of Bordeaux, now Pope Clement V.

"Why does His Holiness task you so?" asked Cardinal Leonardo Patrasso.

Orsini grunted. "His blame for the ineffectual execution of *Pastoralis Praeeminentiae* falls to me."

At nearly eighty years of age, Patrasso—the uncle of the late Pope Boniface VIII—was one of the oldest of the Roman Curia. Like Orsini, he'd been created cardinal by Boniface and participated in the conclaves of both Benedict XI and Clement V. The growing French influence on their Church of Rome sickened both Patrasso and Orsini, as it did the other three members of the Circuitor Consistory. "Why does he not engage one of his many new French cardinals?"

He eyed the old cardinal, unsure if Patrasso knew of his meeting with Guillaume de Nogaret prior to the mass arrests. "For one reason, this instrument will further challenge the French Crown."

"Oh, we cannot have that . . ." replied Patrasso.

Orsini had been ordered to draft Clement's second papal bull and considered working with Cardinal Landolfo Brancaccio in private, as he had with *Pastoralis Praeeminentiae*. He soon dismissed the idea. With Brancaccio, the second bull, meant to show the church's authority in a new light, would have instead been a more detailed, forceful version of the first.

He knew the old cardinal from Alatri, a small town thirty miles east of Rome, could be the answer. Advanced age had loosened Patrasso's thoughts in recent years, but the elder cardinal was still capable of intermittent flashes of clarity, often proposing simple and elegant solutions to problems as if from the mind of a child. "This command must serve several needs."

Patrasso, in one of his increasingly rare states of lucidity, tilted his head. "Which are?"

"It must provide a structure for collecting depositions from throughout Christendom."

"And?"

"It must specify all depositions are to be delivered to the pope," said Orsini. "The fate of the order must be seen to rest with the church and none other."

"By ecumenical council?"

Orsini nodded. "In two years' time."

"I see. What are the problems you envision?"

Orsini shuffled in his seat. "You know the lack of compliance with *Pastoralis Praeeminentiae* by rulers of Christendom."

"Oh yes—asking monarchs to arrest friends, allies, and members of their courts. Why would they not jump at the chance?"

The continued sarcasm was not lost on Orsini. He patted on a blank piece of parchment. "This one must be different."

"Yes, it must!" Cardinal Leonardo Patrasso's voice was resolute. "We need to show that the brotherhood will be treated fairly. We need to show that acting on behalf of the church will ultimately benefit the brotherhood. We need to show the church *granting forgiveness*!"

Orsini inked *Faciens Misericordiam* on the top of the vellum. "Go on . . ."

CHAPTER 32

JULY 27, 4:27 P.M. GST

EASTERN LIMASSOL

Rick Lambert had gotten used to driving on Cyprus—in the left lane from the right seat. He, Pat, and Danny spent fifteen minutes in traffic on Highway B8 northbound, then turned east onto Spyrou Kyprianou Avenue. Each had a job to do. Pat scanned behind the Land Rover, trying to spot any tails, while Lambert looked for suspicious activity to their front. Riding shotgun, Danny used his tablet to switch between online maps and the GPS tracker application to monitor their position.

The text message from Sean, arriving on Danny's phone, gave Lambert hope:

Hot-wired van. On my way north.

Makarem's shrill voice had not been heard over Lambert's phone's speaker for several minutes, until the order to turn off Kyprianou. "In two miles, you will turn left onto Stavrou Stylianidi."

They were nowhere near Maria's GPS beacon, an indication of Dougherty's ambush prediction. To make matters worse, the lack of visible surveillance suggested electronic tracking.

Danny scanned the online map and gave Stylianidi a thumbs-up. They entered the Mesa Geitonia suburb of Limassol during rush hour. Everyone seemed eager to get home and out of the heat.

Another text message blinked on Danny's phone:

I'm here. Going in.

4:48 P.M.
NORTHERN LIMASSOL

Sean Duffy ditched the van three blocks south and strolled north toward Pano Polemidia's minaret. His bulletproof tactical vest, worn under his T-shirt and khaki vest, was both irritable and reassuring. The building containing Maria's beacon, across the street from the mosque to the west, soon came into view.

He reached the southeast corner of what looked like an abandoned union hall and knelt down to retie a shoelace while surveying the area.

The chains on the main double doors of the hall facing the mosque were covered in dust. The only people nearby were at the north side of the mosque—one old codger trimming hedges and two others engaged in conversation. A metal side door could be seen down the hall's deserted south alley.

Sean approached the side door, took a deep breath, and let it out slowly.

Positively identify targets, he thought. However many rugger buggers were behind that door, Maria was also.

He tugged on the door's handle with his left hand while reaching under his khaki vest for the shoulder-holstered Colt M1911 with his right. The door didn't budge, so he continued walking to the southwest corner.

After a quick scan of the area, he backtracked east while pulling an eyeglass case from one of his vest pockets. From the case came four "lollipop sticks"—flexible strands of C-4 demolition material designed for insertion into small access points. He returned to the side door and fed the strands through the rusty keyhole, pinching the end of each into the front of the next to make one continuous length. As he'd guessed, only three fit into the locking mechanism's interior volume. He pressed the end of the fourth strand against the door's exterior.

From another vest pocket came a wireless spark detonator the size of a matchbox. He inserted the two protruding electrodes into the gray material, extended the six-inch telescoping antenna, then continued walking east. After one last look around, he removed a miniature transmitter from the same pocket and lifted a button's cover cap.

It's go time, he thought.

He pressed the button. The metallic crunch sounded like an air-conditioning unit falling to the street from an upper floor window. Perhaps a common occurrence in the more ramshackle urban centers of Limassol, Sean hoped. He rushed to the door seconds after the detonation with his .45 ACP drawn and again tugged on the metal door's handle. With the inner workings of the lock destroyed, the unsecured dead bolt angled out of the frame and the heavy door swung open.

Sean scanned the interior of the large room over his pistol sights—it was indeed a dilapidated meeting hall of some kind. His eyes adjusted to the dim and dusty interior. He could see the double doors to the right and an open door to a back room to his left. Ahead, several large suitcases lined the base of a small stage against the north wall. On the cases sat several HK33 assault rifles and some goofy looking uniforms. He froze for a moment to take in any sounds but heard nothing.

Where's the bloody beacon? Did Maria leave?

"Bollocks," he mumbled. He turned to check the drawer of a standing desk next to the door when a shuffle came from a back room.

"In here," Maria said, stepping partially into view.

"Hell yeah!" Sean approached the back room and saw she was at the extent of the range allowed by a chain attached to handcuffs on her right wrist. He entered and stopped short. Two boys lay near the left wall, their necks at unnatural angles. "What the . . . ?"

Maria shrugged. "I told them I had a headache."

"Jesus . . ."

"Can you get these off?" she asked, jingling the handcuffs.

Of all the items Sean had thought to stuff into his vest pockets back at the hotel, keys to handcuffs never came to mind. He looked around for something to pick the lock with and winced—he saw nothing in the sparse room that would help.

4:54 P.M.
EASTERN LIMASSOL

Stavrou Stylianidi curved west for half a mile.

Makarem's voice crackled over the mobile phone's speaker. "You will turn left onto Archiepiskopou Makariou."

Lambert scoffed, involuntarily, then felt the need to follow up. "How are you picking these streets?"

The Persian gave no response.

Danny gave the street a thumbs-up.

In less than a mile, Makarem voiced the expected command. "Turn left onto Spyrou Kyprianou Avenue." A counterclockwise pattern had been established.

As if on cue, Pat snapped his fingers and pointed behind their vehicle, indicating he'd identified a tail. Seconds later, Lambert noticed a black four-door sedan ahead with two men watching him from the back seat.

He gripped the steering wheel with sweating palms and again turned left onto Stavrou Stylianidi after Makarem gave the order to do so.

Within a minute, Makarem changed their route. "Turn right onto Vothilaka."

Lambert knew Danny now had the online map view zoomed and panned for their loop. In an answer to his gesturing for information, Danny gave a thumbs-down—a dead end.

In a hundred yards, they'd have to make the turn.

He tried to sound agitated. "Umm . . . that turn will be tough with this traffic . . ."

"Turn right onto Vothilaka!" Makarem repeated.

He isn't buying it. We need to be more convincing.

The lead sedan made the turn between oncoming traffic. Lambert jerked the wheel to the right just enough for his driver's side mirror to collide with that of the next oncoming car.

Danny, head down with the online map, did not disappoint, yelping in surprise.

Sounding even more flustered was not difficult. "Damn! Did you see that guy?"

They passed the assigned turn, and the trailing car kept on them.

Is Makarem in the lead car, the tail, or at the presumed ambush site?

"Uh . . . we had an accident trying to move over. Is there another way around?"

His cheap mobile phone went silent. He found himself anxiously glancing down at it. Finally, it came back to life with Makarem's voice. "Turn left on Archiepiskopou Makarious."

The three men glanced at one another with relieved expressions. They'd bought themselves time—hopefully another full circuit around the established route.

Whatever Sean's going to do, he needs to do it now.

5:04 P.M.
NORTHERN LIMASSOL

"We need a little trick of the trade," Sean said, while producing what appeared to be a miniature grenade from a vest pocket.

Maria couldn't hide her surprise as he told her to hold it, keeping the safety lever against its perforated cylindrical body. She did so very carefully.

He slid a pin out of the top and stuck it into the handcuff's keyhole. "The pin's chamfered tip works for this."

The steel cuff opened and fell from her wrist to the floor. Sean tried to angle the pin back into the grenade but explained that her tightening grip had bent the safety lever, shifting the pin holes out of alignment.

She heard footsteps. Male voices called out.

Sean leaned toward her and whispered, "Change of plans."

She loosened her grip, and Sean grabbed the top of the cylinder, slipping the grenade out of her hands with a tug. The safety lever flew off with a ping and landed on one of the empty shelves on the back wall.

Sean threw the grenade out the storeroom door, knelt down, put his hands over his ears, then looked up at Maria, seemingly inviting her to do the same. As she did, he closed his eyes and pressed his forehead to the floor. Maria followed his example just in time.

She saw the indirect light entering the storeroom from the open door through her closed eyelids and couldn't imagine the intensity of the flash in the open hall. She felt the concussive power of the blast's high gradient pressure wave in her covered ears and deep in her sinuses.

She tentatively opened her eyes and saw Sean already standing. He helped her to her feet. She feared the carnage they'd see in the main hall as they shuffled out of the storeroom, still somewhat dazed. The men who'd held her hostage spoke Farsi. The men she'd heard entering the side door had called out in Greek—probably just concerned citizens checking out the explosion. She hadn't had time to tell Sean before he threw the grenade.

Making their way out, she was relieved to see motion from three men sprawled out in the middle of the main hall. With their hands over their ears and their eyes squeezed shut, they were obviously in pain, but she could see no blood. Apparently, the grenade had been a kind of flash-bang—a less-than-lethal device used to debilitate targets without causing permanent injury.

Sean headed toward a side door to their right.

To their left, Maria saw rifles atop suitcases. Next to the rifles were several Cypriot National Guard uniforms. She followed Sean toward a side door and noticed an old standing desk next to it. She checked the front drawer and felt blessed—in it were her holstered Glock 17, sheathed Ka-Bar, phone, and watch.

She also noticed a rectangular piece of stone. Upon closer examination, she recognized it as the domino from Danny's photos.

Sean secured his pistol in a shoulder holster as they approached the van. He held out his phone. It had an active text message stream. "I know three guys who'd like to hear from you."

Maria began composing a message. She looked forward to giving the domino to Rick, but it would not begin to make up for her duplicity toward him and the other three Americans. She knew she'd be reevaluating her loyalties, despite Cardinal Dominic Batista's wishes.

5:12 P.M.
EASTERN LIMASSOL

As expected, the instructions from Makarem again took them around the established circuit. Pat never lost sight of the trailing car. The lead car soon returned to its place.

"Turn right onto Vothilaka," Makarem repeated. "You will have no more difficulties."

Still a quarter mile away, the lead sedan slowed.

The oncoming traffic ceased. Lambert assumed Makarem's men had blocked the street.

Nearing the turn, a text message flashed across Danny's phone:

Maria here. Sean and I are safe.

Lambert broke his own rule of silence. "All right!"

Time to end this.

He'd seen Orthodoxias Street on his left the last time around the circuit, a block south of Vothilaka. The lead car passed it. With no time to check with Danny, he spun the wheel left and accelerated.

Orthodoxias turned out to be even tighter than it looked. Lambert had to swerve to miss two garbage cans on his left and a parked scooter to his right. The trailing car kept with them, dodging the garbage cans but clipping the scooter and sending it slamming against a brick wall.

He heard shouts from pedestrians and prayed none would step out into their path as he turned left onto Falirou Street. He imagined their pursuers were not as concerned.

With the listening devices most likely installed in the Land Rover now a secondary concern, Pat gave a running commentary of how the trailing car kept up with them. Lambert appreciated the updates, until Pat's voice raised in pitch. "Machine gun out the sunroof! Heads down!"

Neither car had much room to maneuver between the brick walls as automatic fire began. With both cars' constant jostling, accurate fire would be impossible. After a few seconds, however, quantity made up for accuracy and he heard impacts at the rear of the vehicle.

The rear window shattered. The intruding bullet impacted the dash, accompanied by a spurt of blood.

"Christ on a bike!" Pat howled.

Lambert jerked his head around. Pat knelt on the rear seat, facing backward, his head tucked below the seat back. His elbows rested on the top of the seat with his Kimber SIS aimed at the roof, his right forearm bloody.

The incoming fire ceased. Pat looked over the seat back and reported the gunman changing out a magazine, then used the seat back to steady his two-handed grip. "You want some? You got it!"

Lambert was not prepared for the mind-numbing assault on his eardrums. Danny pressed his palms to his ears as Pat settled into a rhythmic pace, sending a well-aimed jacketed hollow point every three seconds. The spent ejected brass cases bounced off the Land Rover's side window. After Pat's fifth shot, Lambert saw the gunman slump forward.

Pat sent his last three rounds, then changed out the single-stack magazine. "Bullet-proof windshield . . ."

Another gunman emerged from the sunroof.

"Forget this," Danny said.

Lambert didn't fully understand what he saw next. Danny held the plastic folder containing the leather fragment out the side window.

Does he think they won't risk shooting at it?

"Hang on." He made a quick right on Nikis Street, then another right at the first available alley. Before he could check for their tail car, he noticed Danny no longer held the plastic folder.

"Danny? Where is it?"

"Gone," Danny answered, wagging his thumb through the open window.

Lambert hit the brakes. "Everybody out!"

The alley was barely wide enough to open the Land Rover's doors. The three men ran down the remaining half block of alleyway to the next street and turned the corner to the left. At the corner, Lambert took quick, pensive glances south, back down the alley.

Pat seemed to understand. "You think it's rigged, sir?"

"Yeah."

Danny looked to Pat. "Rigged?"

"A remote car bomb."

"Oh my God . . ."

The men waited a few seconds.

He took another glance down the alley. "Maybe not." He turned back and pressed the back of his head against the bricks. "They would've blown it by now. Sorry, guys. Anyway, Danny, you should not have thrown the—"

The stream of glass fragments and shards of metal shot out of the alley as if from a canon. The pressure wave diminished as it expanded around the corner of the building that shielded them. Still, it nearly brought him to his knees. Windows across the street shattered inward. Flaming parts of the vehicle still rained down from above long after the sound of the blast weakened.

Rick Lambert felt lucky to be alive.

5:27 P.M.

Makarem kept the transmitter's button pressed down long after hearing the blast. With eyes closed and face upturned, he savored the feeling of Allah's will being done through his actions. Just seconds before, he'd ordered his driver to stop after seeing the plastic folder tossed out the window of their quarry's vehicle.

His adversaries were both cowards and fools. And now they faced Allah as such.

He opened the door to reenter the sedan. He could see smoke rising over the two- and three-story brick buildings two blocks west and ordered a slow pass of the alley after turning onto Nikis Street.

At the source of the rising smoke lay an object that no longer resembled an automobile. Jagged black strips were bent up and outward, lining a crater at the center of the alley like petals of a charred metal sunflower. He could tell any bits of organic matter not vaporized by the explosion would have been thrown far clear of the blast area.

Makarem shook his head. His replacement explosives man had used far too much Semtex. He sorely missed his explosives expert killed in Kanisah—that man could determine the exact amount for any given vehicle type to keep it, and the bodies within, just barely intact and identifiable.

Makarem glanced at his driver before turning his attention to the leather in the plastic folder. "We go now."

The afternoon sun, intermittently shining through gaps between buildings, precluded his examination of the leather, instead producing flicker vertigo.

They turned onto the wider Spyrou Kyprianou Avenue. He now examined the leather, curious about how much the dark-brown surface shone. The markings he initially thought were words now seemed to be something else, something he could not make out. He removed the leather from the plastic folder and was surprised at its suppleness. He brought it closer to his eyes, scanned the surface, and saw only creases.

Turning the leather over only deepened his puzzlement; the other side was colored light brown and appeared new. His brow pinched together in confusion. The only words on the lightly tanned side were near the bottom edge.

And they were in English.

INSPECTED BY NUMBER 29

LA-Z-BOY

Makarem stared at the words on the material in his ever-tightening grip, the sides of the leather rolling back in his shaking hands. He forced his jaw to unclench in preparation to scream an order at his driver, then reconsidered. He would instead use the time en route to their base to calm himself and think.

The woman will still have her uses.

5:39 P.M.

Lambert still felt the concussive effects of the car bomb. He hurriedly led Pat and Danny in a zigzag pattern through several alleys and side streets. After ten minutes, they reached part of the suburb relatively unaffected by the explosion. A few street vendors glanced at the black smoke slowly rising a mile west into an otherwise clear summer sky.

They entered the Mesa Geitonia Tavern and claimed a table against the back wall. Lambert broke the silence. "You guys okay?"

Pat already had a bandana wrapped around the gunshot wound through his right forearm. "Just a scratch. I'll live."

"My ears are still ringing," Danny said, a bit too loudly.

He frowned at his college friend. "Danny, you should not have tossed our decoy."

"I wouldn't have if I knew it meant being blown up." Danny's voice was tremulous. "Why didn't you tell me about the car bomb?"

"I wasn't sure about it," answered Lambert. "Besides, I didn't want to upset you."

A waiter approached with three glasses of iced tea.

When the three were alone again, Lambert turned to Pat. "Sounds like Sean kept the real scroll fragment safe."

Pat had chugged his iced tea in a series of rapid gulps and was wiping his mouth with the back of his hand. "Yes sir. He's a rale Bulgarian, but he gets the job done."

Lambert chuckled, then pointed to Danny's smartphone. "Tell Sean and Maria we need a pick-up."

Danny texted their location as the Mesa Geitonia Tavern.

The reply from Maria arrived seconds later.

En route. ETA 10 minutes.

"So, where to now?" Danny asked. "Obviously not back to the hotel."

"You tell us," Lambert replied.

"What?"

"Didn't Dougherty give you a contact for getting us to Arwad?"

Danny smiled. "Oh yeah . . ."

PART THREE

Vox in Excelso

Isle of Ruad – 1308

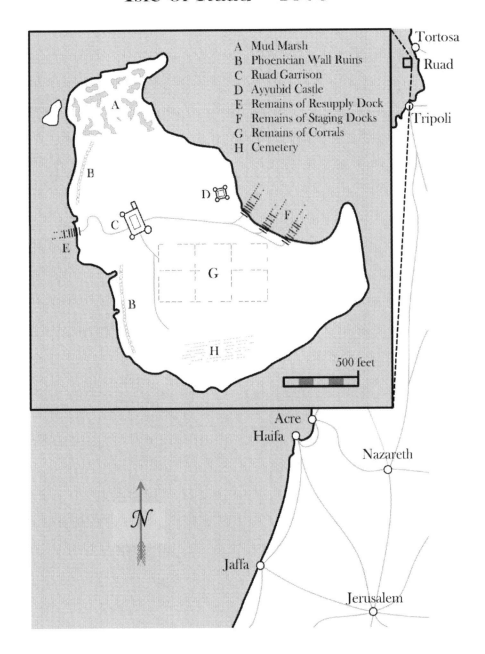

A Mud Marsh
B Phoenician Wall Ruins
C Ruad Garrison
D Ayyubid Castle
E Remains of Resupply Dock
F Remains of Staging Docks
G Remains of Corrals
H Cemetery

500 feet

Tortosa
Ruad
Tripoli

Acre
Haifa
Nazareth
Jaffa
Jerusalem

N

Arwad Island – Present Day

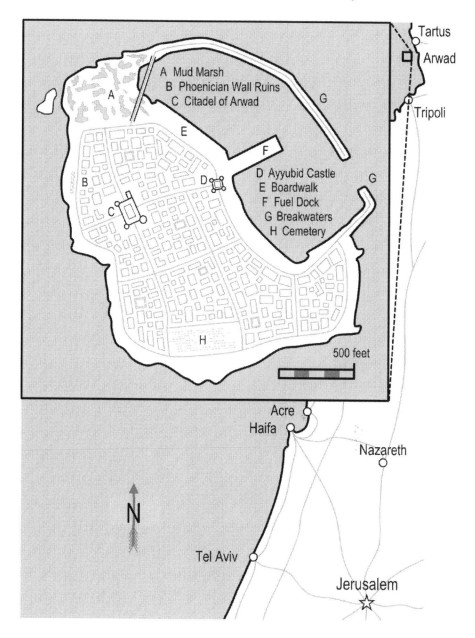

A Mud Marsh
B Phoenician Wall Ruins
C Citadel of Arwad

D Ayyubid Castle
E Boardwalk
F Fuel Dock
G Breakwaters
H Cemetery

Tartus
Arwad
Tripoli

Acre
Haifa
Nazareth
Tel Aviv
Jerusalem

500 feet

N

CHAPTER 33

JUNE 5, 1308

ISLE OF RUAD, PROVINCE OF SYRIA

"Has the pain lessened?" Shayla could tell by his lethargy that Brim still suffered a stomachache from eating nothing but wild leeks for two days.

"Perhaps slightly." He'd returned to the courtyard from the east parapet with sweat dotting his forehead, seemingly grateful for the shade the interior west wall provided. Although their second night in the abandoned garrison had come with softer winds, the same relentless heat of their first day pounded their second.

"And the winds?" she asked.

"The same—from the west."

Much of their first day on Ruad had been spent sleeping off exhaustion caused by their sea crossing and escape from Tortosa. When they awoke, the sun had already swept west of its zenith. With the remaining daylight they split up to search their new surroundings: She embarked on a trek around the fifty-acre island while Brim stayed behind to discover what remained of the once-crowded garrison.

The stench and slippery ground experienced off the beach their first night on Ruad was explained by an abundance of fish entrails and droppings from birds feeding on them. Wild saltwort shrubs were the dominant flora farther inland, their growth of five years nearly obscuring remnants of massive horse corrals south of the garrison. The other major man-made objects were the Ayyubid castle ruins to the east and remnants of the Phoenician wall to the west.

When she returned to the garrison to view the island from the parapet, she was amazed at how Ruad's purpose suddenly became clear. War horses would have been unloaded at the western resupply dock, to recover from the ill effects of sea travel from Cyprus. They would then have made the two-mile transit from the eastern staging docks to the mainland, ready for battle.

She found Brim's report of the garrison itself more macabre. It appeared no one had set foot in the structure since its sacking five years earlier. No discernable trails in the corridors were evident, only layers of rushes and dust deposited by years of winds. In chambers having served as the order's final rallying point lay scraps of uniforms over hauberks, the skeletons within picked clean years before. Upon hearing this, she realized the saltwort had most likely obscured similar sights outside the garrison.

Their plan for this day had been to judge the morning winds and decide whether to sail north toward Antioch or south toward Tripoli. She argued for simply returning to a different part of Cyprus, but Brim tried to explain how it was nearly impossible—something about seasonal winds favoring only eastward travel.

She knew Brim could easily pass for a Greek Cypriot, so they should be able to blend into a region of the Syrian province not under the martial law they'd experienced in Tortosa. If only he could release himself from the stubbornness instilled in him by his order—such stubbornness being the catalyst for yet another argument between them.

"I'm in need of your flint block again." She'd been frying extracted meat from crabs she found in a mud marsh on the northwest corner of the island.

Brim shook his head and placed the block by a torn-apart helm she'd mounted atop three small bricks. "I still do not believe it to be right."

"It is what God has provided in this place." With sparks from the flint block, dry rushes smoldered under the flattened metal helm.

"The order's priests taught from the Book of Leviticus."

Prompted by her breath, a flame soon appeared between the bricks, and she began feeding in twigs. She nodded. "As you said—no fins, no scales . . . no food."

Seeming to ignore her sarcasm, he nodded forcefully to emphasize the point. "All that have not fins and scales in the seas shall be an abomination unto you." He doubled over.

His stomachache persists, she thought.

200

He appeared to be feeling the initial effects of starvation, probably for the first time in his cloistered life. His signs of physical and mental anguish brought back childhood memories of being a hungry refugee from Acre. She had no desire to vicariously relive the experience.

Brimley Hastings seemed highly intelligent and extremely disciplined, but she found the strict adherence to his order's Latin Rule infuriating. To survive, they would need more flexibility than such a code allowed. He would need to see the world anew, from his own perspective, unencumbered by the presumptions of his order.

She hoped it was not too late.

KOLOSSI

Cibalik Darcan felt incarcerated by the preceptory's walls, as if a new recruit of the order. Lord Hayton had given him the chance to check on his hunch about the boy Hastings escaping to the tack master's Limassol workshop four days prior, as long as he and his men returned before sunset. The next day, Hayton began the march of the ordained members of the order to Khirokitia with most of Amalric's soldiers, leaving him in charge of the remainder.

The inventory of Kolossi's arms and various food supplies only took two days. An impressive total of 120,000 bezants was found. Based on reports from the Limassol docks of freed confrère sergeants offering exorbitant sums for passage back to France, he assumed much more of the Kolossi treasury had been distributed to them. What remained was loaded into wagons and sent under guard to Amalric in Nicosia.

For the last two days, Darcan and an occupation force of two dozen soldiers of Cyprus waited for Hayton to return from Khirokitia. To distract his mind from the desire to hunt down the boy, he pored over scrolls found in the chambers of the Preceptor of Kolossi, which he knew had been used by the marshal, Ayme d'Oselier. The ledgers were the same type as those collected from the Larnaca campsite and delivered to Orsini; each described a facet of staging men or material on Cyprus, yet none involved transfers to the Syrian littoral.

He recalled how Orsini had not seemed to know of such preparations—puzzling, given the shared desire by the church to retake Jerusalem.

What began as a fanatical notion in his mind soon gained traction. The Order of the Hospital had escaped the influence of King Philip IV by their invasion of Rhodes. It made sense for the Order of the Temple to act similarly. Considering their knowledge of Cyprus, their possession of the island more than one hundred years before, and the political instability they'd created between the exiled King Henry II and his brother Amalric, it became clear—their goal had been control of Cyprus.

Cibalik Darcan shook his head in amazement at how close all on Cyprus had come to reliving the dark dominion once heaped upon their ancestors.

RUAD

The shadow of the west parapet extended farther into the courtyard as afternoon progressed into early evening. Brim watched Shayla eat her second batch off the steel surface, then load meat from two more crabs onto the hot torn-open helm. The light breeze swirling within the courtyard walls periodically delivered smoke onto Brim's face, bringing with it the scent of the shellfish.

"How much more can you eat?"

"I've had my fill."

He glanced at her, noting her attention directed solely at flipping each strand of meat with a twig. Despite his explanations, she'd repeatedly pestered him to partake. It now appeared she would appeal to his other senses. He again thought of the order's warnings regarding women.

A minute passed as he stared at the crab meat atop the metal.

He wiped a drop of saliva from the corner of his mouth. "Some propose the Book of Genesis as more universal."

"Genesis?"

He nodded. "Every moving thing that liveth shall be meat for you."

"And those say what of Leviticus?"

He glanced at her again, looking for signs of sarcasm. He saw none. "They theorize such laws apply only to the ancient tribes of Israel."

She turned to him. "Then why does your order align with Leviticus?"

"Discipline." He remembered well the lesson from years before. "Compliance with Leviticus satisfies Genesis, unlike the reverse."

She frowned. "In England, did you have shortages of food acceptable to Leviticus?"

He scoffed. "The kitcheners knew such disruptions would never be tolerated."

She nodded twice and returned to turning the darkening meat. "Then no discipline was required."

He was about to explain further but instead considered her argument. He soon understood her point.

"I say Genesis came first . . ." She stabbed a piece of crab with the end of the twig and held it out to him.

He blinked twice, nodded, and accepted her offering. He took in the scent, then placed the morsel in his mouth. Slow, tentative jaw movements soon became vigorous chewing. He turned to face Shayla and she made room for him closer to the fire pit.

In a minute he'd devoured all atop the makeshift skillet, making room for meat from the last two crabs Shayla had brought up from the mud marsh.

Finally eating something of nourishment—as opposed to the barely edible leeks he'd found near the garrison's outer walls—seemed to reenergize his body and reawaken his senses. He appraised their situation anew.

His near-term goal remained—conceal the bottom half of the Praximus Command somewhere inside the garrison. But it was unclear how he could use the document to free his brethren now that he and Shayla had been forced to flee east.

In frustration, he turned his head skyward and noticed the black smoke from the burning saltwort twigs rising above the garrison. He leapt to his feet and ran toward the courtyard door nearest stairs leading to the east parapet.

Before reaching the opening, he called back. "Shayla! The smoke! Snuff out the fire!"

Upon reaching the east battlement, he slid his hands up two stone merlons and peeked through the crenellation between. The shadow of the long, jagged external wall had crept farther east down the slope, draping the shrub field nearest the garrison in darkness. Boats he'd seen leaving Tortosa that morning now returned.

Brim looked over his left shoulder, surprised to see only a slight discoloration rising from the courtyard. He realized the blackened sky he'd seen just minutes before was only evident directly under the smoke plume. Relieved, he returned his gaze to the east.

Then he saw it.

Camouflaged by its sandy color, a boat had beached on Ruad's east shore, by the remnants of the southernmost staging dock. Without the dark-blue Mediterranean as a backdrop, he knew he'd been lucky to have seen it at all. Leaning into the crenellation, he strained his eyes, focusing on the spot less than a quarter mile away.

Two figures moved near the boat. The first stood behind a table nearly obscured by vegetation. The second seemed to be shifting between the boat and the table. Judging by the copious amount of fish innards littering the island, Brim assumed the two were fishermen cleaning their catch before returning to the Tortosa markets.

He shifted to the parapet's southeast corner for a better view. What he saw next made him roll to his left and put his back against the nearest merlon—both figures stood erect, staring up at the garrison.

Had they seen the smoke?

When he looked again, neither were anywhere near the boat. Eventually, he spotted their heads bobbing in and out of view behind shrubs as they crept up the path to the garrison.

On the threshold of the Holy Land about to face Saracens with nothing more than an eating knife tucked into my belt.

Brim ran down the stairs and positioned himself in front of the garrison's east gate. He would not add to his shame by showing fear.

Shayla watched from just inside the garrison.

The pair came into view around the last corner arm in arm. Stunned, Brim realized one was a woman. A pregnant woman.

They halted their approach twenty feet from the gate and the slight man waved. "Peace be upon you," he said in Arabic.

Brim nodded. "Peace be upon you as well."

"From the beach we noticed you on the fortress walkway." He gestured toward his boat and smiled. "We thought you may have been children in need of a scolding for coming to see if the ghost stories were true."

"We are not children."

The man nodded. "I now see."

An awkward silence ensued.

Brim cocked his head. "Ghost stories?"

"The ghosts of the Frankish dead who ravished these lands for so many years and met their ends here." He chortled.

The woman to his right remained still.

The dark-skinned man shrugged. "At least that's what those from these lands tell me."

Another period of silence followed.

Finally, the man gestured to himself with both hands. "I am Rifat Kanaan." He then extended his right hand. "And this is my wife, Amira."

Brim touched his own chest. "Brimley." He gestured to Shayla, who was now standing to his left. "Shayla."

The man named Rifat nodded. "From where have you come?"

"Cyprus."

The Saracen's dark eyes widened. "Long trip." He pointed to the water skin at Brim's side.

The empty skin weighed so little he'd forgotten it hung from his shoulder. He crushed the leather in his hand and shook the opening toward the ground.

The man named Rifat took his own large water skin from his shoulder, and held it out as he approached.

Brim accepted the offer, tilting the skin to his mouth for a taste before handing it to Shayla.

The Saracen nodded his head of close-cropped black hair, seemingly impressed with Brim's chivalry.

Shayla took several gulps before handing it back to Brim, who also drank deep.

Brim extended the skin—still heavy with fresh water—back toward the Muslim.

Amazingly, the man named Rifat held up his right hand, then gestured to Brim's empty skin. "I should take the other."

How can this be? Why would a godless Saracen show compassion toward those he doesn't even know? Why would this enemy of Christ help those he knows are not even from these lands?

CHAPTER 34

JULY 28, 1:24 A.M. GST

8000 FEET OVER THE EASTERN MEDITERRANEAN

Still angered by the decoy, Ahmed Makarem had returned with his team to the rented meeting hall, used as their base of operations, to find a police scene. According to bystanders, two boys had been found dead and three men, responding from the Pano Polemidia Mosque across the street, were injured by some kind of firework inside the building.

How the Italian woman accomplished this, he did not know. But her escape may have served him as well as an interrogation, her movement possibly leading him to the scroll he sought.

Using an electronic tablet, Makarem monitored the UHF signal from the tiny subcutaneous GPS beacon implanted below the woman's cerebellum. Despite its crude accuracy and weak signal, it showed her heading east by water. He'd ordered the repositioning of his team using the Russian-built Mi-8 transport helicopter standing by at Larnaca.

New orders from Gomrok called for regrouping in Lebanon. He welcomed the resupply, but not the reinforcement. The members of his current team were roughly the same age and had trained together. They'd taken losses, but those who remained were tight-knit. The newcomers would undoubtedly be from a younger class. He would need to watch them closely until they proved themselves.

Thinking of ways to integrate the reinforcements, he again caught himself nervously picking at the dead skin of his left cheek. He knew if he didn't stop, it would never heal.

Turning his attention back to the UHF signal, he pondered the possibilities.

Why head east? Did she not find her prize at Kolossi? Who helps her?

Under the whine of the twin turboshafts, his mind again began to wander as his eyes followed the tracking blip on the tablet screen. Such implants had been used with his own forces before GPS beacons were integrated into their harnesses. Developing the method of successful insertion had not come without cost. Several of his young men were accidently killed—or suffered debilitating brain damage and thus killed due to their resulting uselessness—due to the initial trials of beacon implantation. But the implant location had its advantages—it was just far enough from the upper spine to avoid detection by irritating nearby muscles and joints, and the mark at the insertion point was usually hidden by hair.

They passed over the signal, and its representation on the screen made it appear the woman sat inside the helicopter with him. Intrigued, Makarem peered out the bubble window and tried to spot the boat directly below. Despite the calm moonlit waters of the Mediterranean, he could not. It was of no consequence. He'd be waiting for her on shore.

3:31 A.M.
FIFTEEN NAUTICAL MILES WEST OF ARWAD ISLAND, SYRIA

Despite the stench, those below had been lulled into slumber by the drone of the twin diesel engines pushing the thirty-eight-foot fishing trawler through the calm waters of the eastern Mediterranean. Each needed sleep.

Nine hours before, the team had reunited in eastern Limassol and quietly slipped into the territory known as the Turkish Republic of Northern Cyprus. The relatively new country, officially recognized only by Turkey, had formed in 1979 after a failed Greek military coup threatened to absorb the entire island as a Greek possession. The UN Buffer Zone, its border with the southwestern two-thirds of the island, had been only lightly guarded since the Annan Plan attempts at reunification began in 2004, neither Greek nor Turkish Cypriots wishing to appear the aggressors.

Upon their arrival in the eastern port city of Famagusta, Lambert had quickly identified the boat by the flags of both Northern Cyprus and Syria displayed on its stern. A short interchange with its Turkish captain—scripted by James Dougherty and taxing Danny's basic Turkish language skills—verified all parties.

Briefed on their situation beforehand, Omar Volkan had insisted they get underway immediately to make the six-hour eastern crossing under cover of night and arrive at Arwad before daybreak.

Those below were roused from their five-hour nap by a buzzer normally used for waking fishing crews. Lambert checked his GPS—they'd be in Arwad harbor in less than an hour.

Danny and the twins started organizing supplies.

Lambert began ascending the steps to the pilothouse.

"Major?"

He turned to see Maria at the foot of the stairs. "Good morning, I think." He checked his watch. "And please call me Rick."

"Okay . . . Rick. I want to say again how grateful I am for what you all have done for me."

"That's what teams are for, right?" He turned to continue up the steps.

"But I'm supposed to . . ." She glanced back at the others before climbing the steps, closing the gap between them. "I'm supposed to be on *Dominic Batista's* team."

"Meaning?"

"He wants the scroll."

Lambert nodded. "I'm sure arrangements will be—"

"No . . . he ordered me to take it after its discovery." Maria looked down.

Several seconds passed. "Did Cardinal Batista not want the bottom half?"

"I tried contacting him in the parking garage when I was attacked."

A wave of heat seemed to flow through him. "So . . . you put the team in danger."

Maria looked into his eyes. "Yes. And I will never do so again."

The pain of deceit drove twice as deep, coming from the woman who stirred emotions within him that he'd not felt in a long time. "And Batista?"

"He can . . . how do you say? . . . kiss my ass."

Lambert knew he'd typically find humor in that. But not today.

"I will never betray again," she pleaded. "Not after what you all have done for me, and not after what you have endured after Fallujah."

He stared at her in silence.

"Sean told me, just before we picked up the three of you. He said it was well known in Army circles—you led your men well, but became a scapegoat for military intelligence failures."

"Sean talks too much."

"I am glad for it. He said many of higher rank should have been blamed but, being the ranking officer on the ground, you became . . . 'fall guy' is what he said."

"It was a long time ago." Lambert felt an intense urge to escape the situation before saying something he'd most likely regret later. "Look, I need to go see the captain."

She slowly backed down the steps. "Okay . . . Rick."

He entered the pilothouse still fuming. The Turkish captain handed him a thermal imaging monocular and gave a quick nod. His meaning was clear—make yourself useful.

Arwad hid just below the horizon, about to come into view ahead. Rather than simply looking forward toward their destination, Lambert used the infrared device to scan for ships on the horizon in all directions. His second time around focused above the water, scanning for airborne threats.

Volkan seemed mildly impressed. "You have done this thing before?"

"Not by water."

The large screen in front of Volkan overlaid a radar feed onto a GPS moving map. It automatically adjusted to a smaller scale as the boat approached its input destination, adding definition to Arwad's coastline. The two men noted the screen updates and peered ahead in silence.

Lambert did not ask questions. Volkan was an asset of some other agency within the US Intelligence Community, most likely CIA. Dougherty had brokered his cooperation through his chain of command. An INR asset would probably be called upon to return the favor someday.

He knew none of that mattered to the big Turkish Cypriot. He probably just wanted to get this over with and get them back out of Syrian territory.

Volkan looked over from the navigation screens and, in clear but clipped English, explained how it would be done. "We anchor in harbor. After dawn we refuel one tank only. You all slip away. I anchor in harbor and wait. When you call, I refuel other tank. You all come aboard. Then we leave. This is good?"

Lambert nodded. "Will anyone be watching arrivals and departures at the fuel dock?"

Volkan shook his head. "Harbormaster is also customs officer for island. He sits in office and smokes cigarettes all day. If you look like fishermen, no one will care about you."

The dim lights of Arwad Island and the mainland city of Tartus slowly came into view. Their further conversation indicated Volkan had knowledge of their mission in general terms—safeguarding an artifact for the Vatican and searching for another on Arwad. Dougherty clearly trusted the man—or at least his sponsoring agency. They would have to trust him also—the top half of the scroll would stay with him on the boat as they disembarked.

CHAPTER 35

MAY 28, 1309

RUAD

The smell of hummus filled the darkening courtyard as a dozen chatted around a central cooking fire. Shayla and Amira entered the enclosure, each carrying a stack of flatbread from one of the brick ovens located in the enormous kitchen—one of several chambers restored to the working order of the garrison's past.

"Has it truly been a year?" asked Rifat, as eight-month-old Yaghoob wiggled in his arms.

Brim Hastings was continually stunned by how fast the passage of time flew on Ruad. He nodded. "Nearly."

The Syrian raised a ceramic water cup. "What progress we've made in that time."

He shrugged.

"This is true. When you began cutting your fingers on my nets, I'd wondered how the Cypriot farmer could have had such soft hands."

Brim flinched at his memory of taking over for Amira as her pregnancy advanced the year before. "A different labor, harvesting the sea."

Rifat chuckled, gesturing west. "True. But your farming abilities are proven."

"Only by the efforts of all." Brim swung his hand in a wide arc, receiving appreciative nods from all but seventeen-year-old Walid, who had his gaze fixed on Shayla yet again.

"Perhaps for the new planting." Rifat again pointed west. "But I refer to your crescent terraces on the western slope and their first crop of spring wheat."

Shortly after arrival, Brim had realized the island's soil was unusually rich, due to its accumulation of fish waste and bird droppings. He wanted to acquire seeds of various crops for test plots, but their short-term survival precluded the opportunity.

He often thought of his time with Shayla during those first few months on Ruad. Not of their hardships but rather how their feelings for each other had grown: their first kiss, their first expressions of love for each other, and their first experiences with passions and intimacies neither had known before.

Soon after, they accepted an invitation to live with the Kanaans in a poor neighborhood of northern Tortosa. But neither they nor the Kanaans had known domestic bliss. They quickly learned of the pecking order on the mainland—families in Tortosa not linked to the Mamluk Sultanate of Cairo were suspected of prior collaboration with Frankish forces during their occupation. Those, like the Kanaans, driven to the coast from inland regions by the blights of wheat rust spreading west were treated worse—seen as contributing to the burden of coastal overpopulation, they came to expect routine street interrogations by roving mamluk patrols.

After a harsh encounter with sultanate forces near summer's end, Brim and Shayla decided to move back to Ruad, finally engaging in experimental planting when not on the water. A month later, during one his morning meets to deliver water skins and collect Brim for a day of working the nets, Rifat commented on their quality of life on Ruad—it appeared to exceed that of everyone he knew on the mainland. By September, the couple from the Bekaa Valley also made the garrison their home, Rifat having easier access to fishing and Amira grateful for Shayla's support during her final phase of pregnancy. Over the next eight months, two other fishing families made Ruad their home. Their time spent on the mainland became limited to the final few hours of daylight at the Tortosa fish markets, and they were glad for it.

As the Etesian winds had wound down for the year, Syrians returned to the same western waters as Cypriot fishermen. News of the persecutions and political chaos on Cyprus spread, as Amalric continued losing control to forces loyal to exiled King Henry II. While the suffering of the brethren often occupied Brim's thoughts, such information further compelled him to remain on Ruad with Shayla, their struggle for survival only partially distracting him from feelings of uselessness.

Brim refocused on Rifat. "The crescent terraces only tested the trapping of rain."

Amira gave her husband a flatbread trencher, made from spring wheat from those very test plots, topped with two generous scoops of hummus. Rifat held it up. "And what bounty your design has produced. With terraces now encircling the island, not a drop of fresh runoff will reach the sea."

Brim considered the terraced rings around Ruad's circumference, beginning twenty yards from shore, climbing inland in three level steps, each three yards wide. Their near completion would not have been possible without the two mules purchased with dinars collected from fishing and excess spring wheat. The beasts also had a future task—if they were to plant spring wheat again, in the quantity planned, the rotating handstone grinding atop its quernstone would need to be replaced by a much larger mule-driven millstone atop a similarly sized bedstone. But that was a construction project for next year. "We have yet to plow the north arcs and remove rocks that will surely be uncovered."

Rifat shook his head. "That section has been assigned to Walid. I will speak to him. If he does not respond, I will consult his father."

"Good." Brim, and everyone else on the island, knew the overgrown boy would rather daydream of joining the sultanate's auxiliary guard than do his chores.

"I'm more concerned with our seed stock."

Brim nodded. All on Ruad looked forward to planting Egyptian peas and had been collecting seeds from the Tortosa markets for months. "I've been calculating area coverage with optimal plant spacing. We have seed stock for three-quarter's coverage."

"I thought as much."

"Let us all enjoy tonight's feast. Starting tomorrow, we must persist on bread and fish until our seed stock is sufficient."

Rifat groaned but then nodded in agreement.

Brim knew the plan would not be popular. The tiny island community had become accustomed to eating well. Six months prior, they'd begun mashing a fraction of their Egyptian peas into a simple paste to smear atop flatbread. Now, using ingredients acquired from the Tortosa markets, Shayla and Amira enhanced their hummus recipes with ground sesame seeds, juice from crushed lemons, finely minced garlic cloves, olive oil, ground cumin, and sea salt, all topped with more olive oil and paprika.

To celebrate monthly anniversaries of their first days' survival, Shayla had even begun mixing in bits of grilled crab from the mud marsh and frying the shellfish-infused hummus into cakes. Not knowing how a crab could be prepared as *halal*, Brim was reluctant to share the delicious treat with the others—even Rifat and Amira—for fear of offending their Muslim beliefs. He became accustomed to keeping this secret, and to Shayla's teasing him about how they were the "Adam and Eve" of Ruad, the crabs being their forbidden fruit.

In addition to the increasing hummus portions, the small flatbread disks had grown into wide, puffy trenchers over those same six months, further depleting their stores of spring wheat. While such food intake had perhaps been justified in fueling the long workdays fishing and preparing the new terraces, it now had to be scaled back.

Brim stood, about to ask for the attention of others, but noticed Shayla and Walid. She ladled hummus from a chained iron pot hanging from a tripod over the cooking fire while Amira passed trenchers. Between dips, Walid said something that prompted her to wave her upturned palms at him in a pleading gesture.

Before Brim could cover the fifteen feet between them, Walid's father placed a hand on his son's shoulder from behind, causing him to spin around in surprise, bumping Amira's arm and sending flatbread flying.

Positioning himself between Shayla and the two towering figures before him, he saw Walid's father gently pull his son back while whispering into his ear. Despite the hush caused by the commotion,

Brim could not hear the words. Turning his head over his shoulder, he asked Shayla, "What did he do?"

Shayla shook her head. "Nothing."

Turning further to face her, he asked again.

"He just . . ." She looked to the ground and whispered so only Brim could hear. "I usually only have to refuse walking the island with him, but . . ."

"But this night?"

"He . . . he asked me to go sailing with him by moonlight."

Brim turned to face Walid. The large Muslim two years his junior glowered at him.

His father again whispered something into Walid's ear.

"No!" The son turned. "This is not right."

Brim forced himself to remain calm. "What troubles you?"

Walid spun back around to face him. "You treat Shayla as a slave!"

"That is untrue." Shayla stepped out from behind Brim. "I do only what I think is right."

"No . . ." Walid turned to address those around the circle. "She lets him order her about. We have all seen this."

Brim knew he'd be amused if he wasn't so angry. He'd never seen Shayla agree with a suggestion without first thinking for herself.

Walid pointed a finger in their direction. "They are not even married!"

Brim heard a collective groan from around the circle.

"This is not right." Walid continued. "It is unnatural for her to not take a husband."

Brim knew neither Walid nor the others could know anything about the vows of marriage he'd self-administered between himself and Shayla shortly before being joined on Ruad by Rifat and Amira. The paradox had not been lost on him—his ordained standing, while allowing him to act as marriage officiant in lands bereft of Christian priests, was also meant to preclude a marriage of his own. Yet he'd been unsure of his status in the view of the church and in the eyes of God— for the former, he now cared little; from the latter, he prayed for acceptance.

From the circle's periphery, Rifat spoke. "Listen to your father, Walid. Their relationship is a private matter. Let them keep it as such."

"None of you understand!" Walid balled his fists and began stomping toward the courtyard's east gate, turning just before the threshold and pointing at Brim. "I know more about the Cypriot. The Sultanate Guard will hear of this!" With that, he left.

Light chatter soon returned.

Rifat beckoned for Brim to join him by the well head on the south end of the courtyard. "Don't mind the boy's bluster," Rifat said as Brim joined him. "His father told me he's just been accepted into the auxiliary guard."

"Had that not been his desire?"

"It was, but he'll be stationed in Safita. His father feels he'll miss the island terribly. Perhaps his outburst makes leaving easier for him?"

Brim turned to look at Shayla. "Well, he had no reason to embarrass her as he did."

"True," agreed Rifat. "On that subject, however . . . as your friend, I should perhaps tell you that others also ask of the state of your relationship, albeit in more hushed tones."

Brim turned to face him. "A private matter, as you said. People should mind themselves."

"True," repeated Rifat, seeming to avoid eye contact by gazing toward the west wall.

Brim returned his gaze to Shayla.

"But was there not also such talk by Christians on Cyprus?"

Brim turned his head toward him quicker than before.

"I only ask . . . ." Rifat raised his hands in a plea for peace. "I do not speak of religion but only that most propose some union between men and women, and, when a man and a woman disregard this, people ponder why."

After crossing his arms, Brim tilted his head and raised an eyebrow.

"None asked such questions on Cyprus?"

Someday in the future, he hoped he'd be able to tell Rifat about his and Shayla's past. But not this day. "None."

CHAPTER 36

JULY 28, 4:43 A.M. GST

BEKAA VALLEY, LEBANON

Ahmed Makarem knew the brash leader of the Faregh Alethesalan unit ordered to reinforce his depleted group of eight—the mere thought of Farouk filled him with hatred. Before Makarem had left the Gomrok School to become operational at the age of seventeen, Farouk had been an overgrown fourteen-year-old bully the older students had to violently suppress on a frequent basis. On one such occasion Farouk produced a dagger and, despite aiming for his temple, instead thrust it into his cheek before twisting the blade.

He had no time for such struggles today. Farouk and his eighteen young men would submit to his authority as ordered. No insubordination would be tolerated.

His helicopter landed at a previously deserted camp forty-five miles northeast of Beirut. Inside each of Farouk's three additional Mi-8s lay crates filled with weapons, ammunition, and Syrian Army uniforms they'd use operating across the border to the north. Farouk brought another piece of equipment from Gomrok—a touchscreen tablet controller to replace the clunky metal box he'd used to transmit detonation signals to explosive harnesses.

Despite the degraded signal reception in the Bekaa Valley, the track of the woman's GPS beacon had continued toward Tartus but came to a stop two miles off the coast. He checked the time history—despite constant updates, her track did not extend to Tartus Harbor. Perhaps the woman anchored offshore while others used a motorized inflatable to reach the beach.

Puzzled, he set the tablet down on an empty fuel drum and turned to Farouk. "Have your men don the Syrian uniforms and form into squads."

Farouk seemed to have sensed the uncertainly regarding the tracking. "Perhaps we should discuss."

Makarem's brow crinkled as he drew his SIG Sauer PC-9 ZOAF, aiming at Farouk's forehead. He saw the surprised expression a split second before Farouk's head jerked back into a cloud of red mist. The men in camp turned toward the gunshot in time to see Farouk's lifeless body fall backward onto the sand.

He scanned the eyes around him. "Do any others wish to question orders from Gomrok?"

The young men froze in place.

"Good. Don your uniforms and form armed squads by your helicopters."

After gesturing to three of his older team to supervise the new additions, he returned to monitoring the woman's GPS signal. He still saw no advance toward Tartus. With the break from fixating on the signal, however, he noticed the right-hand scroll bar—the resolution was zoomed out two decrements from maximum. He silently chastised himself, adjusted the scale of the map once, and noticed the tiny land mass under the last data point. He brought the tablet closer to his face, zoomed to maximum, and was rewarded with an identification label above the island—Arwad.

Of course Makarem knew the history of Arwad. All self-respecting Muslims did. Known as Ruad over seven hundred years before, it was where the last of the non-believers had been driven from the lands of Islam. But why had this female infidel gone there?

Perhaps that found at Kolossi led her there, with the prize still hidden on Arwad?

"Senior men, to me." Makarem had always used a flat operational command structure—a king surrounded by pawns. Now, he felt he must acknowledge rank. He did this by referring to his original older group of eight as 'senior.' After explaining to them the ad hoc mission he planned for Arwad, Makarem assigned one to each of Farouk's three helicopters, joining a pilot and squad of six juniors.

The remaining five seniors would fly with him and his pilot in the lead ship. He planned to contact Gomrok for additional details after liftoff, then use the remainder of their thirty-minute flight northwest to study the new tablet controller.

5:37 A.M.

ARWAD

Despite it being past dawn, Volkan suggested waiting for more activity at the fuel dock before idling over. Lambert felt the captain did a nice job making his passengers appear to be the crew of a fishing trawler. With the clothes, greasy cap, and engine oil smeared on her face, even Maria appeared to be a fisherman if one did not look too close. If anyone looked out-of-place, it was Danny—no matter what they tried, the academic just did not look the part.

Waiting for the sleepy islanders to wake, and create more of a crowd at the waterfront to cover their arrival, the team reviewed their plans for the Citadel of Arwad. Unlike Kolossi, Lambert decided they'd just take the tour. It was, after all, a popular tourist attraction. With most of the twins' equipment left in Limassol, they couldn't do much more than look around anyway.

Lambert heard the thumping of rotor blades over the harbor. From the main deck, he counted four helicopters and looked for Syrian markings. He saw none. "Is this normal?"

Volkan shook his head, turning toward the stairs to the pilothouse. "Not for Arwad."

After the initial high-speed pass, the helicopters slowed and separated, apparently setting up for a more methodical search.

The Turkish captain returned from the pilothouse with a frequency scanner. "My boat is clean. They tracked one of you. Who had contact with enemy?"

Maria shyly raised her hand.

"Show me your clothes." The Turk followed Maria belowdecks to scan the clothes she wore before changing into the fishing garb. Lambert, Danny, and the twins followed.

After finding no frequency emissions from her clothes, Volkan began scanning Maria herself. She raised her arms.

One of the helicopters overflew the boat. Being closest to the stairs, Danny scurried up to the main deck. He soon returned. "They're all still crisscrossing the harbor."

Volkan nodded and spoke slowly as if deep in thought. "They look for out-of-place boats." The Turk scanned the back of Maria's neck. "Speaking of out-of-place . . ." The frequency-amplitude display on the scanner finally responded. "We have low-level signal broadcasting in UHF band. A GPS beacon." After a few more sweeps of the device to better pinpoint the location, Volkan put down the scanner and pulled a tiny folding knife from his pocket.

Both twins took a step forward. One spoke up. "What the hell?"

Volkan frowned at the young men. "Relax. I only shave hair at top of neck."

"Do it." Maria's sad eyes turned to Lambert. "I am so sorry."

He shook his head. "Not your fault."

"At least I now know the cause of my headaches."

Volkan shaved a stamp-sized patch of skin below the back of her skull, pointed to a red puncture mark the size of a freckle, and turned to Lambert. "Here is where device entered."

"Can we get it out?" Danny asked.

Volkan felt around the area. "Not without surgical tools. It is too deep. But we must silence transmitter." Without another word, he made his way past the group and up the stairs.

Lambert knelt beside her and put a hand on her forearm. "Does it hurt?"

"Just the same dull throbbing. I never get headaches. I should have known something was wrong. I thought it was from the injection they gave me. I feel like such a Judas goat."

Despite the situation, he couldn't help but smile at her reference to the animal trained to lead others of its kind to slaughter. He gently squeezed her forearm. "You don't look like a goat to me."

She smiled sarcastically. "You say the sweetest things."

The captain returned. On the table next to Maria's chair he placed a roll of insulated wire, a box of brass tacks, and a twelve-volt marine battery. Cutting two five-foot lengths of wire and stripping the ends, he wound the bare copper around the one-inch-long tacks just below their domed heads and attached the other end of one wire to the battery's positive terminal.

"Can we just shield the signal somehow?" Lambert asked.

"With what?" Volkan asked. "No, we must overload antenna."

Lambert cocked his head. "How will you avoid shocking her brain?"

Volkan knelt down behind Maria. "Pins will limit travel of arc."

"How's that?"

"Their tips will point at each other under the skin," replied the Turk.

"You want to stick those in her head? Forget it!"

The captain frowned. "We must. Or they will find us and kill us."

"Let him do it," Maria said.

Lambert didn't back down. "I'm not going to stand here and watch you get lobotomized!"

Volkan stood, toe to toe with him.

Maria intervened. "Rick, this is not Fallujah."

All in the small enclosure went quiet. Even Volkan, who did not understand the reference, was silenced by the suppressed reactions from the others.

"This is not your responsibility," she continued. "It is also not your decision. It is mine. And it must be done."

Lambert slowly shook his head but took a relinquishing step backward, prompting Volkan to kneel back down behind Maria. In the ensuing silence, he realized the sound of the helicopters had quieted. He turned to one of the twins, still unable to tell them apart. "Sean?"

Sean nodded.

"Go above and see what's happening."

When he turned back, Volkan had the first brass tack pushed into the original hole from the beacon's insertion. Maria's jaw clenched tight.

Sean stuck his head back into the stairwell from the main deck. "Those chumps are trying to land on the boardwalk north of the refueling dock. They don't have enough room."

Volkan kept his eyes on Maria's neck while he gently pushed on the skin with his thumb. "Next will be new puncture. It will hurt more."

"Do it," she said before tucking her chin.

The Turk inserted the tack just below the bottom rim of her skull. She squeezed her eyes shut, her white-knuckled hands clenching the sides of her chair.

"I felt no contact with first pin. With second I feel something solid one inch under skin."

Lambert watched, impressed with Maria's silent endurance. He turned to Volkan. "How many times have you done this?"

"One time."

"Successfully?"

"I do not know yet."

Before Lambert could respond, the captain pressed the wire's free end to the battery's negative terminal, closing the circuit. With the battery's ability to provide over a thousand cold-cranking amps to a marine engine starter, the muscles of Maria's back, shoulders, and lower neck contracted, jerking her head backward. After two seconds, Volkan pulled the wire away from the terminal. Maria slumped into the chair, unconscious.

6:11 A.M.

While en route from the Bekaa Valley, Ahmed Makarem had been nearly overwhelmed by new information received from Gomrok. Since it appeared their end game neared, almost all other Faregh Alethesalan forces would converge on Arwad.

Those arriving by air would bring a massive amount of manpower and equipment to the Citadel. While similar in objective to their recent missions in France, the magnitude of their operation had increased tenfold. The structure that had dominated the island for nearly eight hundred years would be methodically reduced until they found the scroll.

Those arriving by water would blockade the tiny island and lock down the harbor. No one would approach or leave Arwad until they accomplished their mission.

Upon being given his latest orders, Makarem felt an overwhelming sense of duty. His minor undertaking, begun a few months ago in Iraq, would ramp up into the largest operation Gomrok had ever taken part in. And he had the honor of leading ground operations.

He would not fail.

But, to succeed, he had to guard against his prideful mind becoming distracted.

The woman's signal clearly originated from Arwad, but he could not improve on the quarter-mile precision while airborne. The boat from Cyprus must be in the harbor, but their initial passes had failed to identify any likely candidates from the nearly one hundred vessels anchored between the breakwaters and the old stone boardwalk.

They must take control of the waterfront. Makarem knew from past experience that, when on land, the tracking precision should improve to a two-hundred-foot radius. That should at least provide a ground track direction.

As ordered, all four helicopters approached single-file, descending to land on the boardwalk running south to north. From his position in the back of the line, he could see why the front pilot hesitated—there appeared to be ample room from afar but, from a hover directly above, the tall masts of the boats against the boardwalk looked much closer to the brick buildings across from them. If the seventy-foot diameter of the Mi-8 main rotors could fit, it would be tight.

Makarem considered trying to land on nearby roofs but was concerned about the structures' ability to support the aircraft weight.

Something on his tablet computer caught his eye. In place of the moving map and pulsating icon at the center of the screen, a red box had appeared, surrounding words in bold text—NO SIGNAL.

This made no sense. He knew the miniature battery in the woman's beacon should last at least a week. He also knew she had not vanished. He needed to act.

Control of the waterfront is needed now.

Over his headset, Makarem ordered the senior in the front ship to land on the boardwalk regardless of damage to the helicopter. He visualized his man pointing a 9mm ZOAF at the head of the front ship's pilot and gestured to his own pilot to offset over the water to the east for a better view of the landing attempt.

The front helicopter descended and rotor blades began clipping the top of the nearest mast, shredding pieces of wood and rope. Each revolution reduced the height of the mast a fraction of an inch as the tips of the angled rotor blades began bending upward. The pilot still maintained control as he shifted left.

While wood and rope continually flew off the ever-shortening mast on the right, sparks appeared on a building's brick wall to the left, proving the distance between them was indeed less than seventy feet. The tips of the rotor blades bent further upward but the rate of descent remained constant. Makarem imagined the pilot compensating for reduced rotor lift with increased collective pitch.

The last ten feet of the descent was the most violent, as blade tips chopped into a brick ledge extending further out above the third floor. Finally, no amount of collective angle of attack could make up for the reduction in lifting area caused by the grotesque bending of the blade tips. The crippled Mi-8 plunged to the surface, roughly bouncing on its main tires, flattening both and bending their support structure. The craft wobbled from side to side. The differential pitch of the rotor arc could be seen as the pilot retained control by counteracting with cyclic pitch to keep the aircraft from rolling onto its side and shredding its rotor blades.

The amazing display of airmanship had Makarem entranced. He realized it had only been the gradual nature of the blades' deformation that kept their spans intact and their gearing engaged long enough to retain both collective and cyclic pitch control.

One of the blades finally wedged itself to a stop against the remnants of the wooden mast it had destroyed. The teens from the mangled craft piled out and headed toward several other boats on the seawall. They would soon tear down their masts to make safe landing zones for the three other Mi-8s.

Still amazed by the first landing, he made a mental note to identify the pilot of that front ship. When they returned to Gomrok in triumph, he would make sure to reward that man above all others.

CHAPTER 37

MAY 12, 1310

RUAD

Brim shook the framed bolting cloth, watching the last of the filtered flour drop into the collection box below. "I could use two more scoops."

"One moment." Rifat had become adept at timing his approach, between the ambling mules, to the circular trough below the periphery of the underlying bedstone. "Using both animals is an improvement."

Brim nodded. He and Rifat had eagerly risen before dawn for the final test of their mule-powered gristmill using the last of the prior year's spring wheat. Using a single mule resulted in frequent stoppages but using both created a kind of perpetual motion—the pull of one prodded on any slowdowns by the other. Not having to continually urge an animal onward freed up more time to monitor the process, collect flour, and refill the inverted-pyramid funnel with raw wheat kernels as it rotated with the millstone above its center hole.

Rifat matched the pace of the two animals, then stepped outside their circular path with a large scoop of flour. "The sharper surface dressings work well. No sign of trapped grain separating the stones."

"Good. No heat damage?"

"None."

Brim inverted the bolting cloth frame. Extraneous bran and germ fell away. "The stalks appear two weeks from reaping."

"Agreed," said Rifat with a smile. "And what a reaping it will be. Since the inland blights worsened, we've been able to sell all test flour at the markets for premium prices. Those who've partaken say it's the finest flour they've ever baked with and are clamoring for more."

Brim shook an index finger. "Let us not celebrate. Our last crop would not have succeeded with any less rainfall." Their Egyptian peas had been sowed around the expanded terraced annulus in June and reaped in November of the previous year. He realized there had been barely enough rain for the density of the planting. A below-average amount of rainfall would have either ruined or severely stunted the crop. Instead, their success allowed them to stockpile half the peas in the garrison's sublevel storerooms and sell the other half at the markets, using the proceeds to buy many much-needed supplies. Their prosperity also allowed them to invite others into the island community, which now numbered thirty.

"But with the restored water cistern, we'll be able to focus even more rainwater onto the wheat," protested Rifat.

Brim reflected on the cleaning and retiling he'd done in the subterranean cistern, accessed by the well head at the south end of the courtyard. "Water should be sufficient, but there is much left to do. Wheat rust is becoming more difficult to detect."

Rifat swung his arm around. "The young ones walk the wheat every day. I showed them the blight from the lower east terrace before the eradication there, so they know what to look for."

"We'll need many more linen bags than we've stored."

"Every day, before returning from the markets, we buy all the weavers have. We will continue to collect more, even as the wheat is being reaped and milled. Please do not worry so much, my friend . . ."

Brim sighed and looked out to sea from their leveled shelf on the western slope. He again realized he'd been driving himself and others as if back at the Kolossi sweet salt mill, striving to fill the nearly impossible production quotas dictated by the marshal, Ayme d'Oselier.

He again reflected on news conveyed by Cypriots who fished the same waters. While those of the order were still detained, no trials had yet taken place, due to the continued protective negotiations by the ministers of Amalric of Lusignan. But forces loyal to exiled King Henry II had still been gaining power, and the political situation was as unstable as ever. If Henry regained Cyprus, he would do so with the memory of the order's support of Amalric's usurpation.

Brim heard voices from the direction of the garrison. He turned to look up the slight rise, initially pleased that some had awoken for a day of fishing. Then he noticed three figures on the west parapet frantically waving their arms, each yelling one word: "Boats!" Since they obviously referred to something more urgent than the typical procession of fishing craft from Tortosa, he halted the mules, slammed the locking dowel into the notch between millstone and bedstone, and scampered up the slope with Rifat.

Shayla met him at the garrison's west gate and led him into the courtyard. "Four boats from the mainland, roughly ten men in each, headed for the repaired staging dock."

Amira had similar words for Rifat as the two couples dashed across the courtyard and up the stairs to the east parapet.

Upon reaching the upper walkway, Brim saw nearly all thirty inhabitants of the island gawking and pointing between merlons. He looked over the head of a young girl who had her hands cupped around the edge of a crenellation and had pulled herself up to view the sea. Shading his eyes, he could see the periodic flash of metal reflecting the flat angles of morning light as those below threw out rope fenders and prepared to tie to cleats.

Brim stepped back, looked down the line of fishing and farming families manning the crenellated wall, and felt a chill flow through him. "No . . . no!"

Those closest turned to him with a puzzled look.

He spoke above all other voices. "Everyone . . . standing here projects a defensive posture. We all must exit the east gate and line the edges of the path to the docks in a welcoming gesture."

The adults nodded their understanding with fear in their eyes before ushering their children toward the stairs.

"Our island crops are now visible from mainland shores. Curious visitors were inevitable." Brim turned to Shayla. "Do you and Amira have this morning's flatbread and hummus ready?"

She nodded.

"Good, but today we go hungry. Deliver bread in baskets outside the east gate—the hummus cauldrons and their tripods also. Get the teens to help."

Her smile told him of her approval. "Our hospitality shall impress."

Brim smiled back. "And have them fill every water skin and bring them out."

Shayla rushed off with Amira, leaving Brim and Rifat alone on the parapet.

"All know I was not born of these lands," said Brim. "You should speak for our island. Can you do this?"

"I can." Rifat returned to looking down onto the docks from the edge of a merlon. "But we may have a problem. I think I see . . . yes, I see Walid."

Brim had not expected to hear the name. A few weeks after the boy's outburst the year before, his family had decided to move back to the mainland to escape the continued social awkwardness.

Brim joined Rifat at the east wall and peered toward the repaired staging dock. About twenty in Sultanate Guard uniforms organized themselves into formation on shore. All carried scimitars in scabbards. Some also wielded crossbows. Two on the dock helped an older man disembark. The man wore a formal robe, sculpted white beard, and elaborate turban, indicating he held some high office. Brim hoped the force assembled was only tasked with this man's protection.

Further back, a younger-looking squad in auxiliary guard uniforms straightened their tunics and checked weapons. Near the back, still and staring up to the garrison, stood Walid.

THREE MILES EAST OF PARIS

Francesco Orsini, to the left of the flatbed wagon's driver, gestured toward the two old mares ahead of them. "Can these beasts not quicken?" By the shocked look in the driver's eyes at what he'd been willing to pay for the emergent transportation, Orsini knew he could have purchased such animals outright.

To the right of the driver sat Gentile Portino da Montefiore, a cardinal from Fermo and also a member of the Circuitor Consistory. Although five years younger than Orsini, he was considerably frailer and had been gripping the bouncing bench seat and clenching his teeth since departing their lodgings in Paris. "Must we ravage ourselves so?"

Orsini glanced right and frowned. "We must determine the truth of these reports."

After the curia's move from Poitiers to Avignon the year before, several cardinals had been tasked by Pope Clement V to take part in the papal commission's first session in Paris to consider the fate of the Order of the Temple. The November meetings produced no results since none of the brotherhood in the custody of King Philip IV were allowed to testify. After delegates from the pope had negotiated access to select knights of the order, the papal commission's second session had convened in February.

Since March, many had taken the stand to retract their confessions and state the charges against the order were false. The hopes from the Roman Curia that such mass retractions would lead to a general release of the order by the Crown soon faded with reports of escalating tortures and denial of further testimonies.

The most shocking report had come after dawn—several shackled knights had been loaded onto wagons and taken east under heavy guard to reportedly burn at stakes.

Orsini pointed at a covered carriage with royal seals, surrounded by foot soldiers and being pulled around the northeast corner of the Convent of Saint-Antoine. Dozens followed; half seemed to be pleading, the other half shouting. He turned to his own driver. "Stop this wagon here."

The lead soldier gestured them farther off to the side. "Make way for the king's men!"

Orsini stood. "Stop in the name of Pope Clement V!"

A hush fell over the crowd.

The lead soldier looked over his shoulder. The royal carriage slowed.

A familiar face appeared out the left window. "In the name of the pope?" asked Guillaume de Nogaret. The minister angled his head upward. "Put me beside them."

Orsini waited until Nogaret's carriage came to a complete stop to his left before speaking. "Are the reports true?"

"Cardinal Orsini, it is so fine to see you." Nogaret's smile morphed into a frown as he looked over the flatbed wagon in mock disgust.

Orsini continued his stare until Nogaret's eyes again met his.

"Reports?" Nogaret tilted his head while straightening his lace collar with his palms. "I know of no reports requiring papal involvement. We are here on secular business."

"The business of burning members of an order reporting to the pope?"

"The business of carrying out sentences of relapsed heretics . . . but in this case, yes, they are members of such an order."

Orsini was about to protest further but became distracted by the townspeople returning to their original state of unrest. He understood the knights here were from the Paris preceptory, and many surrounding them were members of their extended families.

The three men in the open wagon followed the collective gaze of those around them to find smoke billowing from behind the convent.

Orsini turned back to Nogaret. "How many are so charged?"

Nogaret ducked inside his carriage, assumedly to converse with a scribe, then reappeared. "Fifty-four relapsed heretics today . . ."

Orsini instinctively crossed himself.

"Your papal commissions produce nothing but confusion," said Nogaret angrily, as if offended by his making the sign of the cross. "His Grace ensures a return to clarity."

Cardinal Montefiore pointed to the corner around which Nogaret's carriage had turned. "You are not to witness sentences being carried out?"

The minister's nose crinkled. He spoke louder so he'd be heard above the escalating shouts around him. "Such events do not agree with my senses. I therefore bid you good day." Nogaret pounded on the side of the wagon above his head and his driver prodded the pair of Percherons back into motion.

The crowd scurried back around the northeast corner of Saint-Antoine.

Orsini gestured for his driver to follow. None of the three were prepared for the horrific sight awaiting them.

An array of stakes rose from the field to the southeast. Through the flames and smoke, Orsini could only see the tops of each stake on the periphery—eight on the north edge and eight to the west. If Nogaret's count was correct, only ten in the grid had been left vacant.

Because a week of sunshine had left the field grass bone dry, and the stakes had been positioned much too close to one another, the entire field became a collective inferno in seconds. Several of the king's soldiers, assumedly assigned the task of igniting materials at the base of the more central stakes, barely escaped the out-of-control conflagration, needing assistance from their comrades-in-arms to pat out their flaming tunics. Some, Orsini guessed, had become too overwhelmed by smoke to exit the maze of heat.

Wind seemed drawn into the center of the blaze, then upward. Flaming materials erupted from the top and rained down over a large area. Buckets of water, carried from the nearby Seine by desperate townspeople hoping to save knights, were instead used to douse new fires on convent grounds.

Cardinal Montefiore had to shout into Orsini's ear to be heard above the hellish cacophony. "The king has abandoned all that is holy!"

Orsini nodded in agreement and thought back to the words of Nogaret. The king had indeed made things clear—nothing but the order's continued admission of guilt would be tolerated.

RUAD

Abdullah looked up the eastern slope, between his guards who led the way, and saw dozens of all ages forming lines on both sides of the trail outside the old Frankish fortress. They marched between the two groups. All but his guard commander peeled off to his side, leaving him face-to-face with a slender man with outspread hands.

The man gave a respectful nod and spoke Arabic with the accent of one from the inland valley. "Greetings, sir. My name is Rifat Kanaan."

"I am Abdullah al-Rasheed, Minister of Agriculture for the Syrian province."

"Welcome," said Rifat, before pointing further up the path. "May we offer you and your men food and drink?"

Abdullah was unprepared for such a lavish welcome. He could see four large caldrons near the fortress gate and had noticed the smell of spiced hummus while still halfway down the eastern slope. Having launched at first light, he knew his guards would be eager to partake. "You speak for those here?"

Kanaan nodded. "I can, sir."

"Very well," said Abdullah. "I thank you for your offer. I have questions for you while the others eat."

With those words, women passed water skins among the guards. Older children each took a large square of flatbread from baskets and filed past the cauldrons for two ladle scoops of hot hummus. After delivering to the nearest guard, each teen gestured for their charge to follow them further up the path and through the east gate.

Kanaan led him into the fortress courtyard, and Abdullah saw several thatched mats had been placed in a circular pattern. He and Kanaan seated themselves near the center. Others began sitting around them.

Abdullah drank deeply from a water skin but gently refused the hummus-covered trencher brought to him by a smiling child. He then turned to Kanaan. "How is it you all have come to inhabit this island?"

"Most of us were inland farmers driven to the coast by crop blights. We turned to fishing and found this location convenient, between our fishing waters and the mainland markets."

"Yes, the markets." Abdullah motioned back toward the east gate. "Even before seeing the crops encircling this island, I've read reports from the markets regarding your wheat."

The farmer nodded. "After the crop of Egyptian peas, we decided all terraces would be reused for spring wheat."

"I see. Much has been said of your exceptional flour." Impressed with the generosity and hospitality shown to him and his men, Abdullah decided to broach the reason for his visit gently. "Less has been said about strange practices taking place here . . . practices which are probably nothing more than idle gossip . . ."

A worried expression appeared on Kanaan's face as his head tilted. "Strange practices, sir?"

Abdullah noticed several of the island's inhabitants straining to hear while quietly talking among themselves. Another slightly built young man seated to his left glanced his way several times with an unusually intelligent look in his eyes. The talk around the circle died down to whispers. "There have been rumors of inhabitants consuming boiled crabs in a manner not consistent with Islamic dietary law."

"No sir—we feed the crabs to our mules to prevent mange."

He raised his eyebrows. "Crabs prevent mange?"

Kanaan nodded. "I can take you to the corral and show you their coats."

"Perhaps later. I know nothing of such a remedy but will ask the mainland breeders of this when I return."

Talk around the circle began to rise to its previous volume before Abdullah's next comment again rendered silence.

"There has also been talk of couples not honoring the custom of wedlock."

Kanaan again looked surprised. "There are only wholesome family units here, sir."

"Even those without children?"

"Yes sir."

Abdullah glanced at those surrounding him, then turned back to the farmer. "What of the Cypriot known in the markets as *Breemlay*?"

The slim man with the intelligent gaze stood and presented himself next to the farmer Kanaan. "I am Brimley, sir."

Abdullah glanced at the captain of his guards seated to his right, who turned to one of the young auxiliary guards, assumedly the boy who'd previously called this island home. A quick nod was transferred from boy to captain. Abdullah then looked up at the wiry young man from the West. "Do you have a wife?"

The Cypriot waved someone over from the east gate. A young female with a belly bump soon stood by his side opposite Kanaan. "This is Shayla, sir."

Abdullah slowly stood and politely nodded at the young woman with Greek features. "I see you are with child."

The woman held her stomach. "Yes sir."

He then looked back to the man who, according to all the reports he'd been able to acquire, was the true leader of this island community. "You wed on Cyprus?"

"We . . . have been together several years, but we first met as children on Cyprus."

"A common-law marriage, as it is known in the West?"

Kanaan raised his right index finger. "We plan to invite a *mufti* from the mainland to perform a ceremony."

Abdullah noticed the Cypriot couple staring at the farmer-turned-fisherman.

"A surprise planned for our second-year harvest celebration," continued Kanaan. "We all praise the God of Abraham, after all."

The Cypriot common-law spouses gradually shifted their gazes back to him. Amused by Kanaan's attempt at interfaith theology, Abdullah chuckled and raised his hands in mock surrender. He'd put the Cypriot at ease before learning what he came here for.

Silence descended over the courtyard as all eyes turned to him.

"His Grace, Sultan an-Nasir Muhammed, took back his rightful place in Cairo two months ago. This he has done after a year-long tour of these lands, during which time he has learned much. He understands men of Syria share fishing waters with those from Cyprus and wishes a return to tolerance with those outside Islam. It is the sultan's wish that Cypriots find the Prophet Muhammad in their own time, as they have found the Prophet Jesus."

Abdullah focused on the young Cypriot, checking for any signs of his taking offense with the reference to Jesus as merely the penultimate Islamic prophet. He saw none. "*Breemlay*, may we walk this island and talk?"

The Cypriot nodded and gestured toward the west gate.

The two men, separated in age by at least forty years, strolled out of the fortress, down past a gristmill, toward rows of spring wheat just up the slope from the burnt ruins of a large dock. During their walk, Brimley spoke of his and Shayla's sea crossing on the Etesian winds two years before, hearing of Farah and Dabir Zayn's deaths, and their short time living on the mainland with Rifat and Amira Kanaan before being driven to island life by roving bands of undisciplined Sultanate Guards.

He took no offense to such descriptions, since it had been a time prior to an-Nasir Muhammad returning law and order to the Syrian province. Instead, Abdullah became captivated by the words of the young Cypriot. Though he spoke Arabic with the same Syrian accent as the others—considered unrefined by many in Cairo—his command of vocabulary while describing history, culture, and agricultural innovation was impressive. There was clearly more to this young man than a life spent farming.

"When a discovery of this island's status was ordered, I volunteered to lead the investigation."

"As Minister of Agriculture?"

"As the only official willing to take the time to do so," said Abdullah, shrugging. "But as the one charged with the agricultural sustainability of the province, I became intrigued by stories of the island from those at the markets." He turned to see the terraces, thick with wheat, bending around both north and south shores. "I see the tales of your wheat being immune from blight are true."

"No sir," said Brimley. "We keep a constant watch for signs of wheat rust. We found a few afflicted stalks near the east shore not long ago. We cleared and burnt, making the gap in the terraces you and your men passed through earlier."

Abdullah did not try to hide his look of confusion. "We pull the afflicted stalks from inland plots also, but did you say only a *few* stalks? We passed through a gap twenty feet wide."

"Yes sir. All stalks within ten feet of those seen as afflicted are removed."

"Why waste so much of the planting?"

"Wheat rust spreads to stalks well ahead of those showing outward signs."

Abdullah paused for a long moment. "If what you say is true, then our efforts to save as much of the crops as possible may have instead *perpetuated* the blight."

The young Brimley looked as though he did not know what to say.

"I wish to replicate your methods on the mainland." Abdullah was convinced of the Cypriot's knowledge and potential, and looked at the younger man intently to gauge the reaction against what he said next. "I want you to help me as Deputy Minister of Agriculture."

The Cypriot's eyes went wide with surprise. "Thank you, sir. A most generous offer. I must, however, decline on account of my child to come—and the island's harvest."

"I shall ensure you have all the support you need on both fronts."

"I'm sorry, sir. I must remain on our island."

In his own nest a beetle is a sultan, Abdullah thought. "Your island?" He realized the time for diplomacy had passed. The mainland crop blights were far worse than was generally known, and sacrifices were required. Despite his initial fond feelings toward the young man, he had a duty to consider the greater good of the Syrian province. He stared intently into the young man's eyes. "This island was besieged and conquered eight years ago by sultanate naval forces. Driving this community off the sultan's land would be entirely justifiable."

The Cypriot remained silent.

He softened his tone. "Help me. In return, I shall ensure this island, *your* island, remains the experimental garden it is, free from taxes and sultanate oversight."

The young Brimley looked up the slope to the fortress.

Abdullah continued his stare. "You will help me?"

CHAPTER 38
JULY 28, 11:38 P.M. EDT
WOODLAWN, MARYLAND

James Dougherty had finally fallen asleep in his own bed. He spent the night before taking cat naps on his office couch while organizing the team's egress from Cyprus.

His secure sat phone buzzed on the nightstand to his left. Except for his chain of command at the State Department's INR, very few people knew the number. He reached for the small lighted screen in the otherwise black room. "Dougherty."

"James, Gerry Burggraf."

Dougherty was impressed with Burggraf's follow-through after arranging for the team's clandestine transport from Northern Cyprus. "Gerry. I heard from my team. Looks like your man got them out clean. Thanks again."

"I heard. Volkan says they're anchored in Arwad harbor. But there's something else."

Dougherty frowned, focusing into darkness. "What's that?"

"My night watch is getting strange signal chatter out of Syria, and your team may be involved."

"What kind?"

"Conflicting messages actually," answered the CIA man. "Their naval communications indicate they're moving in for some kind of conflict with either pirates or rebels, but intercepts from Damascus indicate uncertainty about their navy's command structure."

"A military coup?"

"That's what Damascus can't figure out. If it's a coup, they're wondering why their navy would communicate at all before ground forces attempt taking control of the capital." Burggraf made an audible sigh over the line. "It's almost like half their navy's gone rogue."

"Why do you think our team's involved?"

"Because one of their two Petya-class frigates is racing toward Arwad at thirty knots."

7:56 A.M. GST
ARWAD

After the forced landings of the four Mi-8s, Syrian Army imposters roamed the boardwalk and fuel dock in force. Rick Lambert feared a more thorough search of the harbor would soon begin.

Although her breathing and heartbeat remained strong, Maria was still unconscious from the electrical jolt that burned out the implanted beacon. Danny and the twins did not want to leave her but accepted Rick's argument—to stay together would doom them all when the inevitable boat-by-boat search began.

Volkan described the Arwad safe house—an apartment above a fishing tackle shop fifty yards west of the boardwalk's northernmost end. Since the length of the boardwalk was being patrolled, they'd have to come ashore even further north.

Eight sets of scuba gear sat belowdecks, ostensibly for spear fishing. Lambert and the twins each had diving experience, and gave Danny a crash course.

The four men slowly made their way to the north tip of the island, making sure to remain several feet underwater. They swam under the access bridge to the north breakwater, adjacent to what Volkan described as a mud marsh. In reality, it was a series of rocky sandbars that led to a narrow beach fronting several run-down apartment buildings. The four men navigated through the small channels between sandbars, tossing aside the pesky crabs whose habitat they invaded, until arriving at the beach. They anchored their buoyancy control devices, fins, tanks, and harnesses to the bottom of a channel using their weight belts, then made their way up the beach barefoot.

Entering an alley, Lambert and the twins removed holstered handguns and sat phones from the one-gallon Ziploc bags they carried. Danny removed his phone and tablet computer from his.

Lambert led the way inland and became somewhat bothered by the dilapidated brick structures lining the cramped alleyways. He whimsically imagined Arwad as a *tropical* island. Strange, since he'd always thought of Arwad as a barren rock, devoid of topsoil and incapable of supporting vegetation.

They found the fishing tackle shop two streets inland, just west of the boardwalk, as Volkan had described. Lambert led them up the outside stairs on the north side and used the key given to him. The interior looked normal enough—a small kitchen adjacent to a larger living area in front of a hallway leading to two bedrooms.

Only after entering the bedrooms did things appear out of the ordinary. The large closets, multiple dresser drawers, and huge armoires were full of clothes befitting the region and at least a hundred pairs of shoes in nearly all adult sizes. He realized it was not just a safe house but a major gateway for covert ingress to Syria by intelligence assets.

Danny tried on a brown *thawb*—an ankle-length tunic common to the region. "So now what?"

"One way or another we're going to have to check out the fortress," Lambert answered.

Seat and Pat Duffy tried on shoes. "It's only a few blocks south," one of them said. He pointed to a ladder on the balcony. "From the roof, we could see what's going on."

The other twin spoke. "We could see the boardwalk too."

Lambert nodded and poked at his phone. "I'll join you after checking in with Volkan and Dougherty." He waited to connect and looked at each twin twice. At some point he knew he'd have to find a way to tell them apart.

9:26 A.M.
ARWAD HARBOR

Omar Volkan split his attention between Maria, who lay on a large cot folded out from the inner hull, and activity on the boardwalk. It didn't take long to see changes in both.

Maria began to moan, not quite regaining consciousness but showing signs of pain by the strain on her face. Immediately after overloading the beacon, Volkan had noticed an odor of burning flesh, assumedly from electrical burns to tissue in contact with the device. He had a morphine stick standing by.

The situation on the waterfront worsened. About half of the men from the helicopters had secured both the boardwalk and fuel dock. Volkan watched the men commandeer the four inflatable runabouts used by the harbormaster's office. Each craft, manned by one of the uniformed gunmen and two others pressed into service, fanned out to begin searching vessels.

From the main deck, Volkan received the update from the safe house, then heard Maria call out. He rushed down the stairwell.

She sat up and rubbed the back of her neck.

He anticipated her first question. "They are at safe house. They flee before harbor search."

"The signal?"

"Device is burned out."

A look of relief swept over Maria's face until she touched her neck again, her grimace returning.

"There is morphine for pain," he offered.

"I will be okay. What harbor search?"

As if on cue, shouting in Arabic could be heard off the starboard bow.

"False soldiers forcing Arwad officials to search boats," he said.

"Captain, they know my face . . ."

Volkan thought for a moment. "They will see only what is to be seen."

Maria frowned as he looked at her and slowly spoke two Arabic words. He explained these would be the only words she would utter when they pulled back the sheet that was to completely cover her. He and Maria repeated the words back and forth to make sure she could pronounce them correctly.

He knew he puzzled her again by stripping down to his boxer shorts. "Take off clothes."

The shouting was very close, prompting Volkan to bolt up the stairs. He recognized the three men in the runabout at the starboard railing. The first was one of the Syrian Army imposters he saw on the waterfront, a pistol leveled in his right hand and a radio in his left. Another was Abu, an acne-scarred teen he knew from the fuel dock, who secured the small boat to a railing post. The man whose voice he'd heard was the Arwad harbormaster.

9:42 A.M.

The man on the boat wearing only a pair of boxer shorts raised his hands to shield his eyes from the sun, as if he'd just come out from darkness belowdecks, and bellowed in Arabic.

"Mahmood! My friend! How are you? What is happening?"

Confused, he turned to Abu, who leaned toward him and whispered, "Omar Volkan, fisherman from Northern Cyprus."

Mahmood looked back up to the captain, ignoring his questions. "Who else is aboard?"

"Just my wife. She so rarely gets to leave Cyprus. How is your—"

"We must board and search your vessel," he said. "Stand back."

Abu finished tying up the boat. He and the boy climbed aboard.

The captain seemed offended at his failure to ask for permission but said nothing.

Their drill had just been performed on three other boats—he and Abu searched the vessels while the uniformed man stayed in the runabout and kept radio contact with shore in case of resistance. Abu leveled an HK33, a weapon he had previously slung over his shoulder and was clearly not comfortable with. The boy marched up the stairs to search the pilothouse while Mahmood searched the small engine room.

They met back at the stairwell to the crew quarters, and began descending the steps.

Volkan continued to act violated. "Please leave my wife in peace."

The possible prelude to resistance prompted Abu to swing the rifle in Volkan's direction.

Mahmood entered the crew quarters with his Lebedev 9mm drawn, followed by Volkan. Abu remained at the foot of the stairs and kept his rifle on the captain. Mahmood scanned the crew quarters. The only occupant lay on the cot at the forward port side of the enclosure.

The more he stared at the form under the thin sheet, the more suspicious he became. He crept forward along the starboard interior, keeping his pistol aimed at the sheet, watching the slight up-down movement of breathing. Standing beside the cot, he was surprised at the size of the figure under the sheet. From the position of the head and feet, he could see the cot was barely long enough. Knowing few women were so tall, he took a step back. "Who is this?"

"She is my wife. Please leave her in peace," Volkan repeated, desperation in his voice.

"You think I am a fool?" Mahmood screamed. With the Lebedev aimed directly at the head of the tall figure under the fabric, he lunged and partially ripped off the sheet.

A woman looked back at him with terror in her dark, teary eyes. Her arms were folded over full breasts. Her features appeared vaguely Mediterranean: Greek, Turkish, or perhaps even Italian. Then she whimpered the words, "Please . . . no . . .," in perfect Arabic.

With his mouth and eyes wide open in surprise, Mahmood stepped back. He tried to avert his eyes by looking down and was further shocked at the sight of the gun in his hand, pointing at the woman. He redirected the barrel downward as the woman pulled the sheet up to her neck. He now understood why the captain had been surprised at their approach and wore boxer shorts—it appeared they'd interrupted him making love to his wife.

He turned to Volkan. The captain had his eyes closed and seemed to be quietly praying for his wife's safety.

Praying for her protection from me, he thought.

He turned to Abu, who faced the woman with a look of shock on his face, the HK33 hanging loosely from his arms in front of him.

When he and Abu made eye contact, and the teen turned away, his shame was complete.

He turned to Volkan. "Captain!" he pleaded. "Omar, my friend . . . please forgive me!"

Volkan kept his eyes closed and continued softly voicing prayers.

"We will leave your wife in peace!" Mahmood confirmed, then gestured for Abu to quickly climb the stairs. "Forgive me, my friend!"

9:54 A.M.

Maria Anna Belloci listened to the two men rush up the stairs, across the deck, and over the railing to get back into the runabout, as if they could not depart fast enough. She heard rapid-fire Arabic and hoped the man named Mahmood gave an angry and convincing report to the Syrian Army imposter about how only a local fisherman and his wife were aboard. She then heard an outboard motor, propelling their continued conversation away.

Volkan stared at the ceiling and slowly exhaled.

She lifted her Glock 17, previously hidden between her right thigh and the far edge of the cot. "Captain," she said, shaking her head. "You sure know how to show a lady a good time."

CHAPTER 39

JULY 2, 1311

KHIROKITIA, KINGDOM OF CYPRUS

Cibalik Darcan could see the order's Tower of Khirokitia before even entering the picturesque village surrounding it. Unable to coax more speed out of the aging mare he'd ridden from Nicosia twenty-five miles to the north, he instead tried to calm himself as he and his four armed escorts passed the last orchard of olive trees. He'd been waiting for this day, finally having obtained written permission by the ministers of King Henry II to interrogate the marshal, Ayme d'Oselier.

Despite leaving Nicosia before dawn, he began to feel the summer morning warmth upon reaching the outskirts of Khirokitia. After three years on Cyprus, he was used to the climate.

Ordered to stay on the island and financed by Cardinal Orsini, his first two years' efforts had produced little. By order of Amalric de Lusignan, Regent of Cyprus, only those reporting directly to the Roman Catholic Church had been permitted to interrogate the imprisoned brotherhood. This ensured strict adherence to the prosecuting procedures outlined in the papal bull *Faciens Misericordiam*, for use as evidence during the upcoming ecumenical Council of Vienne, called for by the follow-on *Regnans in Caelis*. Darcan's inability to inquire about the location of Sergeant Hastings, and the existence of a previously unknown heretical scroll, had been infuriating. Then, during the summer of 1310, his fortunes had changed.

Amalric's body was found stuffed beneath the stairs of his home, and Cyprus descended even deeper into chaos. Hayton of Corycus, Amalric's envoy to Pope Clement V, quietly returned to Cilician Armenia. King Henry II returned from exile via aid from the Hospitallers, who imprisoned Amalric's co-conspirators. Letters from pope to king emphasized the importance of maintaining the procedures of *Faciens Misericordiam*, despite temptations for harsher treatment as retribution for the order's support of Amalric. Letters from Cardinal Orsini to Darcan—as well as to King Henry's new ministers urging them to support the ambassador—had also become more frequent. The reason was not lost on Darcan—he was Orsini's final back-channel contact on Cyprus with any authority to discover information on the boy and the scroll.

For the last six months Darcan had been given individual access to knights of increasing rank as they moved from Khirokitia to Yermasoyia, a small village on the northeastern outskirts of Limassol. Only a few knew Brimley Hastings, and none claimed knowledge of a heretical scroll. His frustration at such lack of progress eased after the letter arrived the day before—the written permission to interrogate the last remaining prisoner in the Tower of Khirokitia.

He and his four Cypriot bodyguards arrived at the north gate to the order's complex and came face-to-face with two armed guards he recognized as turcopoles—Christian converts of mixed Greek, Turkish, or Syrian parentage. Initially puzzled, he soon recognized them as descendants of the surviving turcopole auxiliaries who had followed the military orders out of the Levant after the Fall of Acre. Branded betrayers of Islam by those in the East, they had nowhere else to go.

He removed the letter from a satchel and held it up. "Ambassador Cibalik Darcan to question Ayme d'Oselier by permission of King Henry II of Cyprus."

One of the turcopoles fully opened the unlocked gate and relayed the message to others within wearing similar uniforms, one of whom began marching toward the tower.

Darcan and his protection detail dismounted and prepared to enter the grounds before four more turcopoles joined the initial pair at the gate. He was tempted to challenge the gesture but decided to allow them their protocol. Within minutes, the turcopoles gave way to two figures wearing the distinctive robes of chaplains from the Order of the Temple—the two high priests he remembered from the Kolossi surrender negotiations three years before. He again raised the letter authorizing his presence and prepared to repeat his introductions and intentions but didn't get the chance.

The first priest spoke. "You may enter. The marshal will see you now."

The marshal will see me now? Since when does a prisoner decide when to see his interrogator?

He noted at least a dozen more turcopoles on the grounds before he, the four Cypriot guards, and two priests approached the tower's north entrance. He felt perhaps his information about Khirokitia was incorrect. "What other knights are confined here?"

The chaplains looked at each other, then to him with furrowed brows, as if the question offended. "None," said the first priest.

"Sergeants?"

"None," said the second, as he opened the tower door outward—unlocked, as the north gate had been—and gestured for him to enter.

"The marshal will see you now," the first priest repeated. "The chambers of Sir Ayme encompass the uppermost level."

Both chaplains positioned themselves between him and his four escorts. Their meaning seemed clear—the interrogation would be private.

Climbing the steps of the tower, he reflected on what he'd seen: the large number of turcopoles in lieu of Cypriot guards, the unlocked gate and tower door, and finally the continued presence of the two chaplains. He realized the safeguards in place ensured no unauthorized *entrance* into their complex. Even more shocking was the only possible explanation for the chaplains—assisting the marshal with outside communications. The two priests did not *neglect* to review his authorization because they recognized him from Kolossi. They had no need. They *expected* him.

He reached the single door at the fourth floor of the tower. His nervousness reminded him of climbing the steps to Orsini's office. This irritated him. He reminded himself *he* was the interrogator, and *he* would be in charge. Not knowing how many more armed turcopoles waited behind the door, he knocked.

"Enter," came the booming reply.

The entire fourth floor was indeed one large room occupied by the marshal. Several candles on the long center table added to the natural light slipping in from multiple arrow slits. The sparse accommodations were typical for a monastic military order. To Darcan's left stood a large scroll shelf. To his right stood an armoire, sleeping cot, vestment stand, and weapons rack. Noticeably absent from the stand and rack were articles of chain mail and implements of combat.

"Ambassador Darcan, you may sit." D'Oselier, wearing the distinctive white mantle of knighthood, stood behind a desk near the chamber's back wall. He pointed to a chair fronting the desk.

Darcan approached and noticed several vellum maps of Cyprus and the Levant atop the center table. Several more covered the desk in front of d'Oselier, who was now seated.

Does the man still believe he'll be leading a military campaign?

"You look troubled, Ambassador."

He sat. "I do not understand the method of confinement here."

"Confinement?" D'Oselier's brow creased. "I remain at Khirokitia by order of His Holiness. What need is there for confinement?"

"I see." He was suddenly unsure how to begin.

"Have you questions for me?"

He sat up straight. "What can you tell me about Brimley Hastings?"

"Sergeant Hastings?" D'Oselier appeared thoughtful. "It has been said he served Kolossi with distinction, first with our avian communication network and later in the sweet salt mill."

"And his whereabouts now?"

The marshal shrugged. "I assume Yermasoyia."

"He is not there."

"Then perhaps he sailed west with the other—"

"No." Darcan spoke more forcefully than he intended.

D'Oselier raised an eyebrow and waited for an explanation.

"Hastings is not confrère. He is fully ordained."

"True . . ."

"Besides, the docks of Limassol had been scoured, and inquiries were made. Hastings had not boarded any of the ships taking confrère sergeants west."

The marshal paused. "Do you know why I'd agreed to this interview?"

Interview? This was meant to be an interrogation.

"Ambassador?"

"Hayton of Corycus is no longer on Cyprus, and after the surrender of Kolossi—"

"Incorrect," said d'Oselier. "Your knowledge of Sergeant Hastings does not surprise. You and your Muslim mercenaries hunt him as you had his mentor, Malcolm of Basingstoke."

Darcan waved back to the stairs. "Your order also employs Saracens."

"Our turcopoles are converts. Your mercenaries are *enemies* of Christendom. I want to know why you led them in killing the Preceptor of Kolossi outside Larnaca."

"Self-defense. We were attacked at the encampment and—"

"You and your three dozen armed men on the defensive against the preceptor and tack master? Do you see me as a fool?"

"It was an attempted diversion for the boy Hastings to escape with the scrolls."

"Scrolls you have stolen, from both Larnaca and Kolossi."

"Not all," hissed Darcan. "Not the *Vectis Templi*."

"The . . ." D'Oselier thought for a moment. "The Lever of the Temple? Of what nonsense do you speak?"

He stared at the marshal in silence, looking for any sign of deception but seeing none. It had taken him three years to learn as much as he had about the heretical scroll. Numerous requests to Cardinal Orsini for more information had resulted in several envoys being sent to Cyprus, each with a small morsel of information. Either d'Oselier excelled at concealing duplicity, or knowledge of the *Vectis Templi* had been shared with even fewer than he'd been led to believe. Whichever the case, the prospect of his three-year path leading nowhere filled him with dread. "The scroll from the excavation of Solomon's Temple two hundred years ago."

"Ah yes," said d'Oselier. "All in Christendom know we possess Solomon's treasure . . ."

"Not the treasure, you old fool! The scroll!"

The taunting grin on the marshal's face vanished, and he sprang to a standing position, his eyes blazing.

Darcan stood and continued. "The theft of which by those within your order has led to your persecution. Have you knowledge of knights in France burning by the dozens?"

"Knights of God who've given their lives so their order shall live! Do you think King Philip's attempt at silencing the truth just one month after the papal bull *Alma Mater* postponed the Council of Vienne has gone unseen by His Holiness? Philip's covetous plans unravel as we speak."

He leaned forward. "It has also uncovered your plans for Cyprus."

"Here we prepare for the recovery of the Levant by orders of His Holiness."

"You prepare an invasion of Cyprus, not the Holy Land."

"You dare question our purpose and resolve? You are dismissed. Leave my sight."

"I have other questions."

The marshal dashed around his desk and grabbed Darcan's left arm and back collar with surprising speed. "I shall show you the meaning of *dismissed*!"

D'Oselier yanked open his chamber door and forcibly led him down the steps. Each attempt to pry off the clamped grip resulted in a blow to his side.

Through the pain, a thought that had been developing for the last year thrust itself to the forefront of his mind. "How many of your order flee to the Levant?"

The marshal increased both the force of his grip and his pace down the steps. "We do not sail east to flee but to conquer in the name of God!"

Having no official access to the Syrian province, Darcan knew investigating such a possibility would have to be done via back-channel communications with the Mamluk Sultanate, arranged by Cardinal Orsini. His immediate concern, however, was getting free of the marshal's grasp so he'd be seen by his Cypriot escorts as leaving the keep with dignity.

At ground level, ten feet from the tower door, he twisted his left arm downward and furiously pried at the marshal's grip with his right hand. D'Oselier yanked his arm back upward and delivered three quick jabs to his tenderized ribs. The marshal then grasped the back of his belt and kicked open the door.

D'Oselier lifted his belt with his right hand and yanked him forward with his left.

Darcan landed face-first six feet in front of the keep.

"Tell Cardinal Orsini to send only true Christians—no others so tainted as yourself."

RUAD

His small boat approached the repaired staging dock, and Brim Hastings felt the heat from the rising sun on his back. He reflected on the last time a sultanate official visited the island. The shock and fear resulting from Abdullah al-Rasheed's surprise visit over a year ago still resonated in his mind. For that reason he'd dispatched the first craft at dawn to announce his visit and traveled with only minimal Sultanate Guard protection.

His duties as Abdullah's deputy had kept him and Shayla inland for most of the year. The couple were eager to visit their former island home.

Starting up the path to the garrison, he noticed the terraced annulus had recently been plowed and planted, harvested spring wheat stalks making way for Egyptian pea sprouts. The two were surprised to see nearly one hundred inhabitants forming lines on both sides of the trail just outside the garrison's east gate. Brim caught the scent of spiced hummus before he saw the four large cauldrons hanging from their iron tripods.

They meandered through the ranks, crossing from side to side, embracing those they knew and meeting those they didn't. At the end of the path, and in front of the cauldrons, stood Rifat and Amira Kanaan.

Rifat offered the same formal nod Brim remembered from his meeting with Abdullah. "Minister."

Brim chuckled and gripped Rifat by the shoulders. "Such formality. And from my best friend. Here I am only Brimley."

Kanaan shook his head. "I say you are much more than *only* Brimley."

The two embraced.

Rifat turned to Shayla, who had just finished hugging Amira. He tickled the stomach of the wide-eyed nine-month-old wrapped in a sling around his mother's shoulder. "And who is this addition?"

"This is little Malcolm," said Shayla.

"You speak of addition." Brim waved his hand backward. "There must be a hundred here now."

"Just over," said Rifat, nodding.

Young girls Brim did not recognize brought them hummus-covered trenchers. The two couples then entered the garrison and sat on thatched mats near the center of the courtyard. Others took places around them. Brim noticed many looking at him with fascinated expressions. As soon as he'd make eye contact, they'd turn away.

He leaned toward Rifat and whispered. "They look at me strangely."

A guttural chortle came from Rifat. "The new ones have heard tales of how you transformed this wasteland into a garden."

"We," corrected Brim.

"You had the vision," said Rifat. "When your guard arrived with news of your visit, the new ones became excited to meet the Cypriot *Breemlay*."

Brim laughed at Rifat's attempt at pronouncing his name with an Egyptian accent. "Shayla, little Malcolm, and I must return to the mainland tonight, but we've been eager to visit."

Rifat frowned for a moment, then nodded. "Has there been progress with the inland crop blights?"

"Yes, but it has been slow. There is still reluctance to sacrificing crops near afflicted stalks, but it has been the only proven way to stop the propagation."

"Many of the new ones here are from the inland valley. A few others had fled Cyprus."

Brim's eyes met Shayla's before he turned back to Rifat. "Cyprus?"

"You have not heard?" asked Rifat. "They say Amalric was murdered last summer, and it plunged the island into lawlessness. Only with the return of King Henry II in the fall had order been restored, but at a terrible price—hundreds loyal to Amalric were executed."

Brim shared another glance with Shayla. Considering the brethren's support of Amalric's usurpation five years earlier, he feared they may have already been put to death. Still, he would complete the second, more important task that drove him back to Ruad. He would verify that the concealed lower half of the Praximus Command remained undisturbed.

CHAPTER 40

JULY 28, 9:56 A.M. GST

ARWAD

Ahmed Makarem ordered Faregh Alethesalan forces from the first two Mi-8s to secure the waterfront while he took those from the last two inland to secure the fortress.

The additional airborne forces arrived shortly thereafter. Makarem rushed to the parapet's northeast corner and counted six helicopters—not medium-sized Mi-8 troop transports but rather huge Mi-26 heavy cargo transports. He'd been told earlier they were staged at a second Bekaa Valley camp awaiting a destination. Hanging below four of the six were cargo nets holding crates of construction equipment—what he knew he'd be using as *destruction* equipment.

The objects hanging below the remaining two Mi-26s captivated him. At first glance, they appeared to be typical tracked excavators. But thick rods extending from cylindrical enclosures replaced the expected buckets at the end of each boom arm. The massive aircraft neared, and he finally identified the machines underneath as articulating jackhammers.

The prearranged drops proceeded quickly within the expected visibility-limiting storm of dust and sand. One treaded jackhammer was placed inside the rectangular fortress's courtyard, the other positioned outside the west wall. The other four Mi-26s set and released their packed cargo nets and a dozen teen riflemen from each descended ropes thrown out side doors. When on the ground, the boys formed perimeters around their cargo nets, assumedly their final order from Gomrok before submitting to local command.

The deafening storm of the giant rotors precluded Makarem or his seniors from communicating with the new arrivals. Waiting for the Mi-

26 departures toward the east, he took in the big picture from the unobstructed vantage point atop the parapet. Looking north, many patrol boats flying Syrian Navy flags could be seen. Half circled the island clockwise, the other half counterclockwise.

He followed the line of patrol boats clockwise, gradually turning northeast. A large dark shape caught his eye. He jerked his head right.

In the Marfa al-Tahoun ferry lanes between the gap in the breakwaters and the mainland, one of Syria's two Project 159 shallow-water frigates appeared. At 270 feet long and 950 tons standard displacement, it was an imposing sight. Its two 76mm radar-directed gun turrets were directed toward Tartus, a clear signal to the mainland: Arwad is closed.

Makarem knew the Faregh Alethesalan had infiltrated many Middle East countries' armed forces but was unaware their influence could commandeer warships. For the second time that day, he found himself amazed at Gomrok's resourcefulness.

But how had they kept the Russian naval base north of Tartus quiet?

However it had been accomplished, his ground forces were completely isolated and protected from forces outside the island.

For now.

He knew this would escalate into a major event. Very soon, the world's attention would be focused on Arwad.

We must use every minute to the fullest.

10:36 A.M.

Rick Lambert was relieved that Volkan, and a now-conscious Maria, had somehow been able to clear themselves of suspicion during the harbor search.

He also heard from James Dougherty about the strange signal traffic and naval activity out of Syria. Both men recognized it as an Alumni escalation. The evidence from the view off the safe house roof was irrefutable.

Earlier, several locals had made their way to the waterfront to investigate the newly arrived Mi-8 helicopters. When the larger Mi-26 transports began their drops inland, even larger crowds formed around the fortress.

His plan called for Sean and Danny to slip past the Phoenician wall ruins to the west and approach the fortress from the south. He and Pat crept through narrow alleyways to the north.

Lambert heard a new, sporadic thrashing sound—it seemed the tracked jackhammers they'd seen flown in earlier were now operational.

The two pairs of men kept in contact using an open line on the twins' sat phones. "Maria has a 'wanted' poster," Pat said into his phone, gesturing toward one of many photocopies of Maria's face tacked to a wall and annotated with her physical description.

"Yeah, there's a butt-load on the south side," came Sean's reply over Pat's phone.

Pat ripped one off a telephone pole and seemed to struggle with the caption.

Lambert glanced down. "Wanted, rebel, enemy of Syria, reward for information." While nearly as fluent in the spoken language from his service in Iraq, it appeared Pat didn't have the same expertise in written Arabic.

He and Pat drifted through the crowd at the north side of the complex. A full-scale dismantling and excavation had begun. The boom arms of the two tracked jackhammers articulated over the crenellated west wing and pounded holes in the parapet. Inside, smaller jackhammers could be heard at work on interior walls. Locals pushed a steady stream of brick-filled wheelbarrows down side streets, returning them empty.

Lambert turned to face an elderly man near the front and feigned ignorance. "Why are they doing this?" he asked in Arabic.

"The young soldiers say they have orders from Damascus."

"Why should Damascus order this?"

The old man shrugged. "The soldiers don't know. Some say to remove the Christian icon. Others say to keep it from being used by rebels. I only know this—they pay my son well." He gestured toward a table between the young soldiers guarding the northern periphery. A line of locals were being given cash from a young soldier seated behind it and then filing into the fortress's north gate.

Sean and Danny apparently saw the same on the southern side. "You guys have wankers on wheelbarrows working the north side?" came Sean's voice.

Pat replied into his phone. "Yeah, and a lot of kid soldiers. We're not sneaking in there from here either."

Lambert found himself staring at a boy reaching into a burlap feed sack and feeding a donkey oats by hand. He wondered why this image seemed so mesmerizing. Then he thought of all the half-full Quaker Oats containers—and empty Jack Daniel's whiskey bottles—left in his Mosul hotel room. He'd wondered for days why he felt more invigorated despite less sleep. Only then did he realize he hadn't had a drink in a week.

Pat turned to him. "Major?"

He looked down at his own sweat-stained thawb, then at the dirty skullcap worn by Pat. A smile formed on his face.

"What is it, sir?"

Lambert turned to the recruiting table. "We should take them up on their job offer."

4:28 A.M. EDT
FOGGY BOTTOM, WASHINGTON, DC

James Dougherty assumed Gerald Burggraf would also be in early, and that it would be the beginning of a long day.

Traffic delays over Dougherty's earlier-than-usual commute from his home in Maryland were non-existent. He found his predawn arrival at the State Department headquarters complex in the Foggy Bottom neighborhood of DC surreal. Absent were the typical hordes of suited government workers and flocks of George Washington University students on scooters.

The two men had a complementary relationship not uncommon between mid-level managers in the intelligence community. At the Bureau of Intelligence and Research, Dougherty's reporting structure led to the Assistant Secretary of State. As such, he often contacted ambassadors and diplomats. Burggraf's chain of command led to the

Director of Central Intelligence, his contacts being station chiefs, agent handlers, and others in the covert world. For help with politics, Burggraf called Dougherty; for help with espionage, Dougherty called Burggraf.

Both men desired a plausible excuse to raise the flag about Arwad without compromising their on-site assets. Their "discovery" came in the form of a Lebanese freighter captain asking about the naval traffic around Tartus over a common shipping frequency.

He received the latest set of National Reconnaissance Office Eastern Mediterranean satellite images in an encrypted email, then picked up the secure call from Burggraf.

"Notice the Petya-class frigate in the ferry lanes between Arwad and Tartus?"

"Yeah, it's kind of hard to miss," Dougherty answered.

"It's one of only two Syria has in service. What's it doing there?"

"My guess would be sending a message to the mainland—Arwad is closed."

Burggraf blew a faint whistle. "If it is Alumni controlled, then they're really pulling out all the stops on this one. I wonder how long the Russian naval facility at Tartus will stay quiet."

Dougherty was also concerned about that. "Russia's mostly stayed on the sidelines with Syria and its rebels for this long, since both sides have been careful not to 'wake the bear.' Maybe the bear's sitting this one out too."

"You still think this is all about that document you say the Vatican's after?"

Dougherty had conveyed the history of the case, from the Christian priest abductions in Iraq to the clues that led his team to Cyprus and Arwad. Only due to communications security did he leave out the discovery of the scroll's top half. "I do. It seems the Alumni believe it to be as explosive as the Vatican fears it is."

"I added Arwad operations to my 3D-Sum, so we'll see—"

"Your what?" Dougherty asked.

"Sorry, agency-speak for the Deputy Director's Daily Summary from the Near East Mission Center. We'll see it elevated further."

"Likely so."

"I'll send the next NRO photo set when I get it," Burggraf said. "But I've been thinking about a way to get an even closer set of live eyes over target . . ."

CHAPTER 41

AUGUST 7, 1311

AVIGNON, KINGDOM OF ARLES

"Raise the left edge slightly," said Cardinal Francesco Orsini.

The novice monk rotated the frame of the painting with a nervous jerk.

"Fool! I said *slightly*. Lower half of what you raised."

Orsini knew he'd unjustly chastised with the boy, but didn't care. He'd been expecting the report from Cibalik Darcan's interrogation of Ayme d'Oselier for over a week. Each day without news from Khirokitia ratcheted up his level of frustration. He'd continue to cloak his anxiety by redecorating his already lavish chambers. Since Poitiers, he'd added to his collection: miniature frescoes by Duccio, paintings by Cimabue and his student Giotto, and many more, most surrounded by elaborate frames with gold leaf ornamentation.

The Roman Curia had been in Avignon for over a year. The Italian cardinals had argued for a return to Rome, despite the violence perpetrated by factions loyal to the Colonna family. Their French colleagues, having allegiance to King Philip IV, had wished to remain in Poitiers. Avignon was the compromise. Seemingly part of France, the papal state of Avignon was actually a protectorate of Robert, King of Naples. Since the relocation, however, Philip's influence in the city had grown. The king's control nearing the level it had been in Poitiers boiled Orsini's blood.

A papal guard appeared in the open doorway. "Your Eminence?"

"Come."

The guard held a small leather satchel. "Your Eminence ordered any communication from Cyprus be delivered here immediately."

"Bring it to me," said Orsini as he strode behind his desk and pointed a boney finger at the young monk. "You may leave."

The guard placed the satchel on the desk, bowed, and turned to leave.

"You will stay."

Orsini sorted through the mundane administrative letters from Nicosia until he found the report from Ambassador Darcan. After scanning over the communication, he looked up to see the guard gawking at the artwork around him. He ordered the guard to summon the other four members of the Circuitor Consistory.

The temperamental Cardinal Giovanni da Morrovalle arrived first. Having been created cardinal by Pope Boniface VIII less than nine years before, he was the most recent addition to the group. Orsini understood the basis for Morrovalle's seemingly perpetual anger—the harsh decades spent climbing the ranks of the Franciscan Order.

"Francesco, what is so urgent?"

"Patience, my friend. The others draw near."

"Consistory issues? We risk meeting during working hours?"

"This cannot wait."

A few minutes later, Cardinals Landolfo Brancaccio and Gentile Portino da Montefiore arrived together and saw Morrovalle sitting at the small conference table across from Orsini.

"We meet during daylight hours?" asked Brancaccio.

Orsini waved the two cardinals to seats at the table's sides. "As I told Giovanni, this cannot wait."

The nearly senile Cardinal Leonardo Patrasso arrived last. For weeks, he'd been doing his best to prepare a surrogate for travel to Lucca on his behalf, a security precaution becoming more common among cardinals having duties on the chaotic Italian Peninsula. He stopped to admire one of Orsini's latest acquisitions—a painting of Michael and Gabriel with wings spread wide, wearing the *loros* of Byzantine imperial guards.

"The archangels don't need you, Leonardo, but we do. Please close the door."

Patrasso did so and sat next to Morrovalle.

"We finally have word from Ambassador Darcan," began Orsini. "But what he reports is unfortunate."

"Was he able to interrogate the marshal?" asked Brancaccio.

"He was." Orsini frowned. "But he's convinced Ayme d'Oselier knows nothing of the *Vectis Templi.*"

"Impossible!" blurted Morrovalle.

"I'm not so sure," countered Orsini. "I feared this possibility."

Cardinal Montefiore scoffed. "D'Oselier is the highest-ranking knight not imprisoned in France."

Orsini nodded. "This I understand. But, as marshal, his mission is making preparations for retaking the Levant. Darcan writes of this— from his Tower of Khirokitia he continues making plans as if all in his order will be released."

"Your point, Francesco?" asked Morrovalle.

"There is no reason for him to know more. I suspect only the Grand Master, the Visitor of the Temple, and their high priests know of that heretical scroll."

"Jacques de Molay, Hugues de Pairaud, and their closest chaplains are all in Philip's dungeons," said Brancaccio. "Despite our continued efforts, we have no access to them."

"What of the boy claiming to possess the scroll?" asked Montefiore.

Orsini moved the report from Darcan aside to reveal an underlying letter—the nearly four-year-old proposal of trading the *Vectis Templi* for papal influence in freeing the Order of the Temple, sealed by the signet ring of the Preceptor of Kolossi. "Sergeant Brimley Hastings is the reason I called you here," said Orsini. "He continues to elude Darcan's men on Cyprus, but the ambassador presents an interesting proposition."

"Which is?" asked Morrovalle.

"The ambassador believes Hastings has fled east of Cyprus."

"Into the Mamluk Sultanate? That's insane," said Montefiore.

Cardinal Patrasso, who'd seemingly fallen into a trance shortly after the meeting began, sat up straight with fear in his eyes at the mention of Christendom's greatest enemy. "All was lost at the Horns of Hattin!"

Montefiore put a comforting hand on the older man's forearm. "All is well, Leonardo."

"Is it so insane?" asked Orsini. "The boy spent much of his young life learning the Saracens' language and customs from those who'd lived amongst them. He would have no problems blending in and may have thought he'd be safer there than Cyprus. And he'd be correct."

"And Darcan's proposition?" asked Morrovalle.

"He intends to pursue."

"Will you now tell us *that* is not insane?" asked Montefiore.

"You know I have no great respect for Cibalik Darcan," began Orsini. "Supporting the mercenaries protecting the Armenian Kingdom of Cilicia from the Mongols has been a considerable drain on our treasury. But if the chase must continue east, Darcan may be the ideal huntsman."

"How so?" asked Morrovalle.

"Two reasons. As an Armenian official, he should be allowed safe access to sultanate officials, ostensibly for discussing their shared defense from Mongol forces."

"His post as papal ambassador?" asked Montefiore.

"Would not be divulged," answered Orsini.

Brancaccio shook his head. "His Holiness would never—"

"Darcan's travel east will be as an Armenian official," said Orsini. "His Holiness has no need to be informed of such affairs."

Montefiore put his hands behind his head. "Again you have us playing with fire, Francesco. If His Holiness—"

"You said two reasons," said Morrovalle.

"The second involves resolve," said Orsini. "From Darcan's more recent reports, it seems the boy's ability to elude has instilled in the ambassador a tenacity bordering on madness. It is now his life's mission—he will hunt Brimley Hastings to the ends of this earth."

ACRE, PROVINCE OF SYRIA

Brim's year of service as Abdullah al-Rasheed's deputy had allowed him to learn of the continued influence of the maritime republics on the

Levantine coast. What was seen as a violation of papal decree by many in the West was seen by others as simply a continuation of trade. Not being considered Franks, the mariners from the Italian Peninsula were tolerated by those in the Mamluk Sultanate. Some even welcomed them as contributors to the rebuilding of coastal cities still devastated by the forced expulsion of Christians years before.

He'd learned of their continued presence in the remnants of Tortosa, Tripoli, Beirut, Sidon, Tyre, Acre, Haifa, Atlit, Caesara, Arsut, Jaffa, and Ascalon. In these port cities, ships still displayed the flags of the major maritime powers of Venice, Genoa, and Pisa. Less frequently, the banners of the minor city-states of Amalfi and Ragusa were flown.

One of the local Levantine chanceries of the maritime republics would be the origin of Brim's next letter to Cardinal Orsini offering the Praximus Command for papal influence leading to the freedom of the order's brethren. Four years prior, sending the first offer from Kolossi had two advantages: a direct communication conduit to the curia in Poitiers and secure preceptory grounds impervious to attacks by anything but an army. The surrender of Kolossi had taken place before any response could be received, and both advantages had been lost with his and Shayla's escape from Cyprus.

Motivated by news of the return of King Henry II to the throne of Cyprus, Brim had redoubled his efforts to discover a way of again communicating his offer to Orsini. He'd found what he thought may be the solution in the remnants of Acre—a small remaining chancery still serving Ancona. The small city-state of Ancona, on the east coast of the Italian Peninsula just south of its mighty rival Venice, had the advantage of being both a maritime republic and a papal state. A direct conduit to the relocated Roman Curia in Avignon was therefore available.

The four armed Sultanate Guards—Brim's minimum security detail as negotiated with Abdullah al-Rasheed—insisted on securing any structure before he entered. He'd suspected they'd been given a stern warning from Abdullah about keeping him safe. Three of the four entered the small Ancona chancery, a rebuilt structure on Acre's waterfront surrounded by abandoned buildings. A moment later one of the three appeared at the doorway and nodded.

Brim entered the house of letters to find three wide-eyed scribes standing behind their desks. He'd still not become accustomed to the effect the robes of sultanate ministers and their protection detail had on people. "I am Minister *Breemlay*, here to see Carlo Petri," he said in Arabic, using the accent of the Egyptian ruling class.

The center scribe gestured to a door on the back wall. "He works in his back office. I will fetch him."

The senior Anconian dispatch scribe Brim had met the week before soon appeared. "Minister *Breemlay*! How good it is to see you again. How may we help you?"

Brim nodded. "Signore Petri, it is good to see you also. May we speak privately?"

Petri waved his three junior scribes toward the door leading to his office. Two of Brim's Sultanate Guards automatically followed them through the door to ensure his meeting with Petri would indeed be private. The remaining two exited the main entrance to guard the front, leaving the two principal men to take seats at the center desk.

Carlo Petri looked eager to speak but held his tongue until Brim began.

"On my last visit, you described the logistics of secure communication with the West, specifically Avignon."

"Yes, I recall."

"You said a sealed letter could be transferred under guard from this chancery to your Ancona headquarters, then direct to the Papal Palace."

"Indeed."

"And what of secure replies to a confidential location other than Acre?"

Petri nodded. "We can have the response from Avignon rerouted from Ancona to any of the maritime republic chanceries along the coast."

"Any?" Brim cocked his head. "What of your rivalries?"

"In the West, we indeed have rivals. But nearly a dozen years have passed since Genoa won their war with Venice. Besides, those of us stationed here have found our survival is better served by working together. Our dispatch contacts in the West help with this. We wish to be seen by your sultan in a favorable light. Many communications from other republics to Acre are channeled through this house."

"Via instructions contained in outer sealed satchels?"

"Yes," Petri said, looking surprised. "You know of such methods?"

"The workings of the West's scriptoriums are not unfamiliar to me." Brim reached into his robe and removed the sealed letter he'd written days before and slid it toward Petri. "I would like the secure response to this routed to a chancery in Tortosa for my confidential receipt."

Petri looked at both the instructions for delivery direct to Cardinal Francesco Orsini and the wax seal of the Preceptor of Kolossi with a puzzled look.

"I only ask you to have this delivered to Avignon, with the reply logistics in place as discussed," said Brim, seeing the scribe's confusion. "The rest is my responsibility."

Slowly, Carlo Petri began to nod. "This I can do."

"When could it reach Avignon?"

"Perhaps six weeks."

"And the cost?"

"For such a service we would typically ask for . . . five gold dinars?"

Brim stacked fifteen gold dinars in front of Petri. "I want it in Avignon in four weeks."

CHAPTER 42

JULY 28, 3:22 P.M. GST

ARWAD

The interior of the fortress was in deafening chaos. Locals given wheelbarrows were directed to load piles of rubble by figures in uniforms wearing goggles and surgical masks. Because of the intense noise, only visible gestures using hands and rifle muzzles were used. Visibility was limited to twenty feet due to pulverized stone and fumes from portable pneumatic power generators. The inner walls were being dismantled by jackhammers wielded by teen soldiers who'd stripped down to their undergarments due to the heat.

With full loads of brick and mortar fragments, locals were further directed outside the fortress periphery. Four men new to Arwad also pushed wheelbarrows, following others to the dumping site—a vacant lot to the south. Each trip inside the fortress, the four looked for clues of something hidden until being directed otherwise. On each trip south, they shared findings.

"These kids are balls-to-the-wall for this scroll," Pat said. "Looks like they haven't found squat yet."

Like everyone else from the fortress, each man was caked in white as dust and sweat formed a milky film on exposed skin. Sean cleaned around his eyes with a rag. "I passed by one of the walls with a fireplace. They had it in tatters and came up empty there too."

Danny shook his head. "It won't be in a fireplace."

"How do you know?" Lambert asked.

"Not sure—just a feeling." Danny was visibly frustrated.

Lambert could tell the work had taken its toll on the academic more than the other more physically fit men. But he knew something else bothered his friend. The historic structure that had taken years to build was being dismantled in a matter of hours. Lacking modern steel rebar, the fortress that stood for nearly eight hundred years was no match for the juggernaut of jackhammers being unleashed upon it. Even the immense outer walls in sections having had their structural arched roofs partially collapsed were now able to be knocked down by the monstrous tracked beasts.

He attempted speaking in a more calming voice over the chattering noise at the fortress a block north. "You know we can't stop this destruction."

Danny nodded. "I know. That's not it. I mean, yes, it's a piece of history being lost forever . . ."

"What else can we do, man?" Pat asked.

"I'm not sure, but I know their brute-force approach is stupid. I should be able to figure this out, if I can just think like a Templar."

"Like a knight?" Sean asked.

"Knights, monks, squires, priests . . . whatever group hid the scroll's top half on Cyprus and left the Levant Wall clue planned on hiding the bottom half here. In their world, symbols meant everything. I just have to figure it out, then find it," explained the historian, shaking his head. "I was playing with the idea of the top half being associated with fire and the bottom half having something to do with water. Flames rise, water settles, that kind of thing. But we're already on an island, so that doesn't help."

Pat grimaced. "Don't mention water. I ran out an hour ago."

Lambert handed him a half-full plastic water bottle. "I snuck this from an unguarded crate outside the south gate. I don't think our new employers trust the Arwad water supply."

"What's that?" Danny asked.

"I grabbed the bottle from a crate when no guards were looking."

"No, you mentioned a water supply?"

Lambert nodded. "I saw a water tower by the south shore. There must be a freshwater pipeline from the mainland."

"And in the crusader era?" Danny asked, before immediately answering himself. "The fortress must have had an independent freshwater supply in case of a siege. There must be an underground freshwater cistern!"

"Like a well?" Pat asked.

"It would look like one on the surface," Danny replied.

"Yeah, I saw it," Sean confirmed. "It's in the south end of the courtyard, beside that tracked jackhammer monster. I saw it through one of the interior walls that thing knocked down."

Danny looked at Lambert with renewed energy. "That's got to be it!"

Pat took a gulp from the water bottle. "Looks like we're working the late shift."

3:43 P.M.

Before the four exhausted but reenergized men returned to the fortress, Lambert called Maria and Volkan to let them know of their plan. "You're feeling better, then?"

"Yes. It is more of a dull throbbing now," Maria answered.

"Okay. We're going to get you taken care of when this is all over."

"I will be fine. I want you to be . . . you *four* to be careful."

"We will be," Lambert promised, hoping her initial focus on him alone was an indication she shared at least some of the feelings for him that he'd been feeling for her. "Can you ask Volkan to do one more thing?"

"What is it?"

"When we call for it, can you get him to reposition the boat along the bridge to the north breakwater? If we find the bottom of the scroll, we'll try to leave this party gracefully, but they have quite a few eyes on us."

"No problem," Maria said. "They have lost interest in the harbor. There are only a few guards by the helicopters on the boardwalk. All others went inland, probably to the fortress."

"Great. Thanks. I'll call when we're on our way."

8:05 A.M. EDT
INR HEADQUARTERS

The set of "live eyes" Gerald Burggraf had discussed with James Dougherty earlier that morning belonged to a Lockheed Martin RQ-170 Sentinel stealth drone. Originally based at the Tonopah Test Range in Nevada, several of the remotely piloted vehicles were flown by the US Air Force out of Incirlik Air Base in Turkey.

Dougherty appreciated Burggraf keeping him in the loop.

"They're making final preparations for the recon drone out of Incirlik," Burggraf confirmed. "I'll send the link to the secure video feed."

"Thanks," Dougherty answered. "Damascus claims it's not a coup attempt or an escalation by their rebels."

"What do they think it is then?"

"The Syrian ambassador to the UN is claiming it's an external terrorist attack. They say they have intelligence suggesting missiles on the seized frigate are being outfitted with chemical warheads."

Burggraf paused. "Nothing about Iranian fundamentalists?"

"No. They're claiming remnants of Al-Qaeda or young Islamic State radicals."

"Idiots. Damascus only knows they're not in control. They're going to play on terrorism fears until someone's stupid enough to take on that Petya-class frigate."

"And it might work," said Dougherty.

"Seems my boss agrees—he just kicked this up to the Director's Daily Report. But who would authorize attacking that ship?"

"Not sure, but there's a perfect bureaucratic storm forming over Arwad," Dougherty explained, before laying out what he'd heard from his UN contacts.

Ambassadors from the five countries making up the Security Council held private deliberations. Regarding operations to recover a religious artifact, and their Alumni opposition, current US intelligence was shared with MI6, since the UK had already become involved logistically given the use of Akrotiri on Cyprus. The current status on Arwad was also shared with the DGSI, since the French intelligence agency already had information from their Alumni captive from the Cramirat break-in. Russia would be on board with any action to protect its only Mediterranean naval resupply facility at Tartus, the loss of which would periodically force their Mediterranean fleet back to Black Sea bases via the Bosphorus. Finally, Russia could usually be counted on to convince China—the remaining member of the Security Council—to cooperate.

"Activating a peacekeeping force will never fly with the UN General Assembly, especially on such short notice," Burggraf said.

"They're not going to let it get that far."

Burggraf scoffed. "Don't ask for permission now; ask for forgiveness later?"

"Something like that. It sounds like they're sending an investigative team to Arwad to gather further data."

"*Investigative team*?"

"A group of Italian UN blue helmets are training for disaster relief on the *Iwo Jima* in the Med. I heard they'll probably get the assignment." The *USS Iwo Jima* was a Wasp-Class Amphibious Assault Ship, designated LHD-7 for Landing Helicopter Deck 7.

"There's going to be diplomatic hell to pay when this is over," Burggraf said.

"Probably so."

"The drone should be on station within the hour, but sunset on Arwad is in another five."

"Things could be in full swing by then," Dougherty said. "The team may welcome the cover of night."

CHAPTER 43

SEPTEMBER 11, 1312

TORTOSA

Brim had reduced the frequency of his visits to once every two months but still feared his continued checks may prompt questions about his interest in the West. He entered the Genoese chancery for the seventh time in nine months. A dozen scribes—more accustomed to working with sultanate officials than their Anconian equivalents in Acre—labored behind desks, oblivious to his arrival despite his Sultanate Guard entourage.

One of the senior clerks he'd spoken with months before wished a customer farewell, then waved toward the front door. "Minister *Breemlay*?"

Brim nodded, approached the large desk, and sat after the scribe gestured to a chair.

"How may we help you, Minister?"

"As before, I come to receive an expected dispatch, addressed to Brimley of Cyprus and delivered to this house."

The Genoese frowned. "I can remember no such package arriving, but let me check our racks to be sure. Point of origin?"

"Ancona."

"One moment." The man with ink-stained fingers disappeared behind a curtain.

While waiting, Brim recalled the first time he'd been in this structure; November of the previous year was the earliest he'd expected to hear back from Cardinal Orsini. With other officials continuing his farming reforms inland, he obtained Abdullah's permission to patrol the coast, ostensibly for guarding against diseased agricultural imports. During an inspection tour of Acre two months later, he paid Carlo Petri to track the delivery from the summer before, only to learn of delivery confirmations to Ancona in late August and Avignon in mid-September. As recently as two months ago, he obtained confirmation that no response from Avignon had been received in Ancona, from either sea or overland routes.

The senior scribe reappeared from behind the curtain, shaking his head. "Apologies, Minister. We have no such dispatch."

"Thank you for checking." Brim stood, left the chancery for the street, and watched the four guards of his protection detail take their usual positions around him.

He decided to stroll north along the Tortosa wharf to think.

Over two and a half years, his relationship with Abdullah al-Rasheed had grown from mutual, professional admiration to genuine friendship. Abdullah also stayed in Tortosa, attending court of the sultan's new Damascus-based viceroy of the Syrian province, Tankiz an-Nasiri, who'd been touring the coastal cities of his new domain. Brim yearned to hear Abdullah's advice on his problem, but knew he could never divulge his history with the order. Abdullah had been a child during the invasion of Egypt by King Louis IX of France, as warrior monks from military orders killed Muslims by the thousands before they themselves were crushed at the Battle of Al Mansurah.

He continued north, noting yet another ship flying the red-crossed white flag of the Republic of Genoa. From his robe's pocket, he removed the domino previously hidden in the knot of the Praximus Command's tassel. It was the key to unlocking what he'd arranged, but it now seemed useless. Frustrated, he wound his arm back, preparing to throw it into the sea, but became distracted by a familiar voice shouting commands on the main deck of the Genoese cog. He approached the stern and read the nameplate—*Filomena*.

ACRE

"Take your positions to the north," said Cibalik Darcan, while facing two of his mercenaries. His band of nearly forty former mamluk soldiers used on Cyprus had been cut down to the most elite eight for the mission to Acre. Included in this team were Ghazi's original three commanders and their five most trusted men, each of whom was kin by either blood or marriage.

He pointed to two others. "You remain here." He and the four remaining began their march north, up the waterfront, to the Ancona chancery for the second time in two days. On this day, however, answers *would* be forthcoming.

Over a year before, Cardinal Orsini had begun back-channel negotiations for Darcan's team to infiltrate the Mamluk Sultanate in search of Brimley Hastings. After Orsini received the communication from Ancona, it took little time to discover that their sole remaining chancery in the Levant stood among the ruins of Acre.

Darcan understood his role. As an emissary from the Armenian Kingdom of Cilicia, the desire for contact with the sultanate, ostensibly for discussions regarding joint defense from the Mongols, was plausible. Yet, with the Mongol conversion to Islam taking hold, alliances with the West were considered less likely.

After a year of painstaking negotiations and arduous travel, they'd arrived at the Anconian chancery on Acre's waterfront only to be told of the confidentiality of their business dealings by their senior scribe.

After the last of the customers they'd watched enter the structure left, Darcan and his three commanders entered. The last man stood guard outside.

"Mi scusi?" said one of the junior scribes, apparently alarmed by the sight of four armed men.

They'd prearranged their actions. Darcan and two of his commanders kept the three young Anconians seated at sword-point while the third rushed through the back door, known from their visit the day before to be the way to Carlo Petri's office.

The third mercenary marched the senior scribe into the main workplace. Within minutes, all three junior scribes had been tied securely to their chairs with lengths of twine appearing from a haversack Darcan carried over his shoulder. Petri was then tied to a chair across from the junior scribe in the center.

"Let us continue our business from yesterday," said Darcan.

Petri's eyes went wide with fear. "You spoke of a letter from Ancona, not from Acre."

"This letter's origin was Acre," countered Darcan. "I saw your recognition at the mention of Cardinal Orsini."

Petri shook his head. "No . . . I was . . . just surprised at the thought of a letter from Acre to Avignon."

"Avignon?" He raised his eyebrows. "With all your bluster of confidentiality, I had no chance to even speak of Avignon . . ."

The senior scribe glanced at the younger scribe across from him, then back to Darcan. "No . . . but where else would one send a letter to a cardinal?"

He let out a quiet chortle, strode slowly behind the chair across from Petri, and reached around to place a dagger on the skin covering the center scribe's larynx.

"No . . . please . . ." begged Petri.

"Shhh . . ." Darcan pulled the center scribe's head back by the hair and looked at Petri with a frown. "You will start by telling me who sent the letter from here to Ancona, for final delivery to Avignon. You will then tell me where Orsini's response is to be forwarded after arriving in Ancona."

A surprised expression supplemented Petri's look of fear.

"Yes . . . we know you money-mongers all work together here . . ."

TORTOSA

He was at least three hours behind schedule. The loading of cargo and supplies should have been complete by midafternoon, easily allowing departure from Tortosa's harbor before dusk. He now knew it would be a challenge to beat the sun's western fall and get under sail before nightfall.

He'd noticed the young man in official sultanate robes walk the length of the southern pier, seemingly inspecting the port-side loading. The last thing he needed was more sultanate harassment. He knew his luck hadn't changed when the official locked eyes with him, then spoke to a member of his crew.

The sailor scurried up the nearest gangplank. "Captain, a sultanate minister wishes to speak to you."

"Very well." He gestured for the slightly built man to come aboard. "Continue with the on-loading."

The official left his bodyguards and strode up the center gangplank.

He greeted the minister in Arabic. "Welcome aboard. I am Captain Pietro Bucci."

The young official stared at him for an awkwardly long time. "The same Captain Pietro Bucci who smuggles Christian icons to the West?"

"No . . . no sir . . ."

The minister walked to the main deck hatch and peered below before quickly turning back. "The same Captain Pietro Bucci who uses false bottoms in barrels of pickled pigs' feet to smuggle Christian relics from these lands?"

"But . . ." Bucci wanted to object but instead stood bewildered by the man's knowledge of his most trusted smuggling technique—pickled pork never failed to repulse Muslim customs officials.

A smile broke out on the minister's face as he turned his palms up and winked.

Bucci focused on the odd man in front of him, finally looking past the short oiled beard and elaborate turban. "Brimley Hastings?"

Brim performed an exaggerated bow.

"But . . . how?"

"My wife and I fled Cyprus as the order was being persecuted."

"Wife?"

"Yes, the daughter of Kolossi's tack master."

"Ah, Kolossi . . . we heard of Sir Malcolm's death on our return trip. My condolences."

Brim nodded somberly. "He left this world as he would have wanted, sword in hand."

"But . . ." He pointed at the sultanate robes.

"I've played a part in treating the inland crop blights."

"You're Minister *Breemlay*? The one they call the Cypriot?"

Brim repeated his bow with even more embellishment.

"Amazing . . . it is unfortunate others of your order have not been so blessed."

Brim frowned. "The persecutions continue, then?"

"You've not heard of papal bulls from spring's Council of Vienne?"

"No, tell me."

"As you may know, my family in Genoa has strong ties with the Colonna family in Rome, so we keep informed of Roman Curia activities in Avignon. In fact, if it weren't for the Orsini family, the curia could safely return to Rome, but now—"

"Pietro," said Brim. "The papal bulls?"

"Ah, yes." Bucci collected his thoughts. "In March came *Vox in Excelso*, abolishing the Order of the Temple. Then in May came *Ad Providam*, transferring assets to the Hospitallers."

CHAPTER 44
JULY 28, 5:12 P.M. GST
ARWAD

The four men new to Arwad returned to the fortress with renewed enthusiasm. Despite their best efforts, it took two more trips hauling debris under close supervision before a pair of them was finally able to slip through openings in the inner wall unseen.

With Danny beside him, Sean Duffy found the inner courtyard to be the eye of the storm, the only activity being the manipulation of the jackhammer excavator by an operator enclosed in a chain-link cab. The boom arm of the huge machine extended over the west inner wall and pounded away at the walk above the arched ceilings.

Access to the cistern stood fifteen feet southeast of the tracked jackhammer, behind the operator's left shoulder. Because of the noise and the operator's attention to his task, the approach of the two men went undetected before they crouched down to the southeast of the four-foot-diameter well head.

"Let's take a look," Sean said, just loud enough to be heard over the ambient noise. He hopped onto the sunbaked cover boards that formed a square frame atop the three-foot-high circular brickwork and peered down. A black void returned his stare. He slipped a penlight from the vest worn under his light-brown thawb and shone it downward. Again he saw only darkness. Sitting back down behind the well head, he tied a brick fragment to the end of a length of twine retrieved from another vest pocket.

The Professor joined him after examining the exterior bricks around the circumference, sounding impatient. "So what's down there?"

"Couldn't see squat." With the knot secure, Sean scanned over the cover boards for a moment, then tossed in the brick. He counted out each arm span while sliding the brick down the shaft. The tension from the hanging brick waned. "Okay, touchdown twenty-three feet below the cover boards. So, twenty feet below ground level." He retrieved and examined the brick while kneeling. "Bone dry at the bottom. We're about forty feet above sea level, so that makes sense. What now, Professor?"

"I was hoping to find something on—"

Sean noticed Danny distracted by movement. He flicked up his thawb with his left hand and drew his M1911 from the tuck-away holster in the small of his back with his right. In his red-dot front sight crouched his brother, sneaking south along the east wall, followed by Major Lambert.

After confirming the jackhammer operator was still focused on the west wall, Sean waved them over. "Wanker! I almost gave you a .45-caliber headache!"

Pat frowned. "Put that relic away before you hurt yourself."

Danny informed the major of the well depth, and admitted he couldn't find any clues around the well's outer wall. "Let's take the cover boards off."

Guessing he'd be rappelling into the cistern sooner or later, Sean tied a length of rope into a Swiss Seat harness while the others removed the wood atop the well head. The planks of the rickety, rectangular frame, each connected to neighbors by flimsy L-brackets, were easily twisted apart and piled beside them.

Having been under the wood for years, the top slates were covered with insects burrowing into a thin layer of dirt and dried weeds for renewed shelter from the sun. After pulling the clumpy material off the nearest large stone, Danny took off his right sandal and began scrubbing the top surface with its sole. A smooth surface appeared, with the exception of five half-inch diameter circles—dirt-filled holes drilled into the stone. It appeared to be the same *five* symbol from the Roman domino and the edge of the Kolossi Levant Wall, only ten times larger.

"Help me clean the other stone tops," the academic pleaded. He waved the others around the well head's circumference as he glanced at the jackhammer's cab.

In minutes, they'd cleaned the entire top surface of the well head, revealing twelve curved cover slates, each twelve inches long and twelve inches wide. A numerical symbol was drilled into each.

"Connect the numbers from each side of the domino like before?" the major asked.

"Yes!" Danny confirmed.

"I've got another *five* over here, and a *four* next to it," Pat said.

"Here's the *one*. The *three* is to the south, another *five* to the north," Lambert said.

The men fell silent for a moment, drawing lines in the air with their fingers.

"I see it!" Danny said. Sean did also. Lines connecting the symbols on each side of the Roman domino formed a large south-pointing arrow on top of the well head.

Sean began to wiggle out of the Swiss Seat. "The south wall of the fortress then, Professor?"

"No. We found the top half *inside* the Kolossi fireplace. I think the bottom half is *inside* the Ruad cistern."

"Down the shaft's south inner wall, per the arrowhead?" the major guessed.

Danny nodded.

Sean pulled the Swiss Seat back up around his hips and retightened it. "How far down?"

"Maybe three fathoms, since the arrow points to a three."

"Fathoms?" Sean asked, with a frown.

Pat chuckled. "You've been demoted to the navy!"

Major Lambert seemed to ignore him. "Eighteen feet."

"From the slate or from the ground?" Sean was already doing the arithmetic.

All eyes turned to Danny. "I don't know. Check both."

Sean nodded. "Okay, so either two or five feet up from the bottom."

The major seemed to think for a moment, checking his math. "Right."

Sean piled the four cover boards on top of each other across the top of the well head. He then tied another length of rope around them, slid it through the front loop of his Swiss Seat, and sat on one of the top slates. He handed his brother the slack rope between his harness and the boards. "Make yourself useful for once. Lower me down below the boards."

The boards creaked as they began supporting a load for the first time in years. Pat slowly let go of the rope, then stuck his head in. "Bottoms up, Sailor . . ."

"Screw you, doofus!"

Before descending the last few feet, Sean held his position with his left hand and scanned the bottom using a penlight held in his right. Seeing no snakes or scorpions on the floor of the cistern, he touched down and stood. Having kept his southern orientation while descending, he looked over his shoulder and saw how the space opened into the cistern to the north, under the courtyard. He then removed the hammer and chisel from the burlap bag he tied around his waist and began checking the bricks on the southern wall.

The small amount of slack in the rope slapped his face. He grabbed it while looking up, saw Major Lambert facing west over the shaft, and heard him yell in Arabic about the lack of water.

So the jackhammer operator finally noticed them. But why shake the rope?

Then he understood.

He slid the rope out of his Swiss Seat as the major yanked it out of the hole. Above him, Lambert continued to complain about the lack of water in the well as he shook the end against his hand to show it was dry.

Sean positioned himself on his back with his feet high against the shaft's circular west wall, his .45 ACP pointed upward.

After a short pause, Lambert echoed instructions—obviously for his benefit—to leave the courtyard and seek water elsewhere. With a quick look down the well, and an almost imperceptible nod, the major disappeared.

Why nod? Did the operator notice the changes made to the well head?

Sean focused on controlling his breathing.

The operator's face obscured the light coming in from the west side of the circular periphery.

Their eyes met.

Sean's index finger shifted from the slide to the trigger.

9:32 A.M. EDT

INR HEADQUARTERS

James Dougherty saw the secure video feeds from the RQ-170 becoming the hottest show in town. Intelligence planners appealed for views of the island fortress while Pentagon leadership insisted on tracking naval activity.

As the crisis developed, both he and Gerald Burggraf became focal centers within their agencies. Although more of their time became occupied reporting events to their chains of command, they made a point to continue coordinating their actions.

"I heard from a planner with the Sixth Fleet," Burggraf reported over a secure connection. "The *Iwo Jima* is now three hundred miles southwest of Arwad. They're close enough for their CH-46 Sea Knights to transport the Italian blue helmets, then return to the ship."

"They're going to have to wait," Dougherty said. "News of the Security Council deliberations on sending in an investigation team just leaked. Many are insisting on no UN involvement until open discussions are held."

"I heard. That's what's prompted the DCI to include this on the DNI's Daily Summary," Burggraf said, referring to the Director of Central Intelligence and, his boss, the Director of National Intelligence.

"What does Damascus say?"

"Nothing new, but they'll take help from the Devil himself if they can get it. They still claim those in control of the frigate have armed missiles with chemical warheads."

"Do they want someone to sink their own warship for them?" Burggraf asked.

"That's what it sounds like. The ambassador from Jordan suggested a compromise—he wants another effort by the Syrians to reestablish contact with the frigate before the investigation team is considered."

"They tried that with the helicopter overflights," Burggraf said. "The Petya turned them away with warning flares."

"This time, they're planning an approach by the Tartus harbormaster flying the Syrian flag off one of their port authority tugs."

CHAPTER 45

SEPTEMBER 16, 1312

WESTERN TORTOSA

For several days after meeting with Pietro Bucci, Brim mined as much information as possible from the maritime republic chanceries on the Tortosa waterfront. The Genoese captain had given an accurate report regarding the papal bulls. Plans for the order's abolition—obviously known well ahead of time in Avignon—explained the lack of response from Cardinal Orsini. After mentally searching for any possibility of leveraging the Praximus Command to free his brethren, Brim realized all was most likely lost.

He reflected on his recent conversations with Shayla as he strode to his weekly meeting with Abdullah. All ties to the West seemed cut, their future now in Syria. They would make the best life possible for themselves and their son.

The smell of fresh pita bread and spiced hummus permeated the neighborhood. While in Tortosa, Viceroy Tankiz an-Nasiri occupied the structure previously known as the Cathedral of Our Lady of Tortosa, still in the process of being converted into a mosque. For Abdullah's temporary office, he used the warehouse of the adjacent bakery responsible for the local scents.

He'd arrived early and succumbed to the fragrant temptation, pulling a silver dirham from an inside pocket. He found the pita delicious, but the hummus was inferior to Shayla's.

Entering the warehouse as he ate, Brim noticed a large group of Sultanate Guards standing in a circle talking. He and his four-guard detail approached. He recognized Abdullah's six guards but pondered the presence of the others, two of whom were playing Mancala in the circle's center.

Before he could inquire, the door to the warehouse back room opened and Abdullah gently led a frail man out by the arm. The guards unknown to Brim immediately abandoned their game to flank the elderly man. One offered his arm and took over for Abdullah.

The guards slowly led the delicate man through the warehouse. Abdullah gestured Brim into his makeshift office.

"Peace be upon you."

Abdullah waved to a chair fronting his desk. "And also upon you."

"The Minister of the Interior?"

The Egyptian nodded. "The poor man's eyesight fails him, forcing him to step down."

Brim nodded slowly.

"Viceroy Tankiz has asked me to take over that post."

"A promotion? Congratulations, sir."

"I thank you."

Brim tilted his head. "What of the Ministry of Agriculture?"

Abdullah paused. "His Excellency has heard of the Cypriot *Breemlay* and asks if he shall take over my old post."

Brim's eyes opened wider and his jaw dropped.

"I told him that was my wish."

"Minister of Agriculture? . . . For the entire Syrian province?"

"Was that not my post?" Abdullah asked. "A new broom sweeps well the house. But be forewarned—you must still report to this vexing old man."

"Vexing? No sir. You have always been fair with me." Brim flashed to a realization he'd had recently—during his two years working for Abdullah, he found him to fill a longed-for role of mentor, that which had been lost to him with the death of Malcolm of Basingstoke.

The Egyptian shrugged his shoulders.

"But, sir . . . wouldn't my being a foreigner cause issues with such a high post?"

Abdullah shook his head. "His Excellency believes in enticing talent and knowledge from neighboring lands for what he calls the upcoming prosperity of Syria."

"But what of my age?" Brim asked.

"If the beard were all, the goat might preach. No, I shall present you at court the day before the viceroy departs."

NORTHERN TORTOSA

For the last week, the Tortosa festivities—planned to coincide with the visit of Viceroy Tankiz, his officials, and their families—had swelled the population. Arriving the day before, the only lodgings Cibalik Darcan, his three mamluk commanders, and their five men had been able to acquire was at a run-down boardinghouse in one of northern Tortosa's poorest neighborhoods.

Two of Darcan's commanders, sent out to request he be granted an audience with Tankiz, had already returned with denials from court officials; they claimed the court's agenda for the final four days in Tortosa had been filled. Disgusted by their failures, he sent them back to try again with other officials. While awaiting results from his third commander, he paced the room and thrust his dagger into its dilapidated furniture.

The opportunity presented by the viceroy's visit to Tortosa had justified their exhausting 150-mile ride up the coast during the last five days. If he could convince Tankiz of threats to Syria, he could possibly attain unrestricted access to the province. Such freedom would quicken their task and allow them to depart before any reports of their actions in Acre—as necessary as they'd been—reached Tortosa.

From what it had taken to extract the required information from Carlo Petri and his three junior scribes five days before, the risk of leaving any at Acre's Ancona chancery alive was too high. Petri's report of Tortosa's Genoese chancery being Ancona's intended destination for any response from Orsini made perfect sense—he knew his five mamluk mercenaries would still be monitoring the structure for any sign of Hastings. What still puzzled him, however, was Petri's claim that the boy somehow impersonated a minister of the Mamluk Sultanate.

He was still pondering this when he heard a soft knocking at his chamber door, in the correct syncopation they'd prearranged.

His third commander entered. "I spoke with three officials outside the old Frankish structure. Not only do they refuse to add to the viceroy's docket, they claim they must remove several double-bookings."

He plunged his dagger deep into a seat back. "I must gain audience with Tankiz!"

"I don't know what more—"

"You will revisit those officials," said Darcan. "You will tell them it is imperative I be allowed to inform the viceroy of grave threats to both Armenian Cilicia and the Syrian province. These threats come, not only from Mongol forces but also from rogue members of Christian military orders intent on wreaking havoc in the months to come."

CHAPTER 46

JULY 28, 6:07 P.M. GST

ARWAD

Sean Duffy applied half of the five-pound double-action trigger pull required of his M1911, floating its hammer back slightly, then froze. He did not expect the expression he saw beyond his weapon's front sight.

Instead of a surprised look on the young man's face, he conveyed contempt. Then, amazingly, he thrust his head deeper inside the hole.

What kind of brass balls does this guy have?

Only when the young operator cupped his hands around his eyes and over his forehead did Sean remember his inability to see the bottom from above. He lay in a deep shadow, hidden from any eyes accustomed to the daylight above.

That's what the major's nod had meant—you're invisible.

Seemingly satisfied, the young man pulled his head out of the well head. Sean kept his attention upward, half expecting a brick to be thrown down the hole for good measure.

He heard the distant sound of an engine starting, then felt the ground shake—the operator continued work with the jackhammer on the west wall.

6:30 P.M. GST

QOM, IRAN

In 1989, during a brief ceremony before the Supreme Council of the Cultural Revolution, he and others had been recognized for their contributions to Iran during its war against Saddam Hussein. He would never forget the pride he felt accepting the gratitude of his country's greatest clerics. Such memories would only intensify his disgust today.

Leaving his bodyguards in the hallway, Jahangir Nasser Rudahmi strode into the council chamber at the appointed time. He positioned himself on the carpet at the room's center. A minister droning on about infrastructure repair stopped speaking and glared as if insulted by the intrusion. The President of Iran, serving as chairman of the council, also seemed perturbed, but soon recovered. "Welcome, Imam Rudahmi."

He nodded toward the president, then turned to scan the room. The furnishings looked more luxurious than before. The four long tables, forming the square surrounding him, now appeared to be made of carved hardwood. Of the forty seated around him, he counted only six wearing the traditional robes and turbans of clerics. The others wore the suits of politicians. Two *women* even sat, side by side, at the end of one table.

Suppressing his anger at how secular the council had become, he turned back to the president. "Thank you for granting me this time to address the council."

The president nodded.

"I wish to speak of Christianity." He noticed puzzled looks.

The president frowned. "Not a common topic in this chamber."

Rudahmi heard a couple of men snickering behind him. By the time he turned, all appeared serious. He scowled at those near the source of the insulting chortle, then turned back to face the president. "The truth of Islam has eroded the Christian myths surrounding the Prophet Jesus. We know this. Yet they still believe the falsehoods. The reason is clear—despite its ridiculous dogmas, the Roman Catholic Church is remarkable for its organization and the resulting ability to propagate its lies. Today, I ask the council to join me in opposition."

The room fell silent for several seconds, until one of the six clerics spoke. "How so?"

He locked eyes with the man. "On Arwad Island, off the coast of Tartus, is proof of Christianity's greatest lie. What is needed—"

"Arwad?" asked the man who'd been speaking when he arrived, probably the Minister of Strategic Planning and Budget. "Arwad is now the nexus of Syria's civil war."

Rudahmi said nothing in response to the minister, instead turning to address the president. "Damascus has announced an ultimatum—if control of both Arwad and their Project 159 frigate blocking the ferry lanes are not returned, a bombing campaign may begin as early as tomorrow. Air cover will therefore be needed—perhaps MiG-29s from Tactical Air Bases Mehrabad and Shiraz . . ."

Heated questions came from all four sides.

The president held up both hands and waited for silence before speaking. "Imam Rudahmi, why should our air forces risk war with Syria to protect their rebels?"

"They are not Syrian rebels."

The room stayed quiet, allowing the president to ask the obvious question: "If not rebels, then who?"

He straightened his posture and lifted his chin. "The Faregh Alethesalan. The Holy Warriors of Gomrok."

Most in the room stood as confused shouts erupted all around him.

A suited man pointed at him, faced the president, and tried to shout above the clamor. "We have called for reviews of Gomrok's curriculum for years, always to be refused access!" The Minister of Education, Rudahmi assumed.

Another suit pointed. "He should be detained!" Probably the Minister of Justice.

Despite the president standing with raised hands, it took a full minute for the cacophony to diminish. "Imam Rudahmi, your service to our country is why you were granted the opportunity to address this council. It is also the reason you will not be detained."

A few ministers began protesting.

The president held up a hand to silence them before continuing. "If there truly are graduates from the Gomrok madrasa on Syrian soil, I order you to recall them immediately."

Rudahmi released his rage. "You do not understand!" Walking in a circle, he addressed the others. "None of you understand!" He marched toward the exit. "You're all fools! I must be allowed an audience with the Grand Ayatollah . . ."

10:48 A.M. EDT
FOGGY BOTTOM

"It's official," Gerald Burggraf said, after James Dougherty picked up his phone. "The DNI just gave Arwad top billing on the PDB. That's the—"

"I know—the President's Daily Brief."

"Yep. Did you see the tug footage from a half hour ago?"

"I did," Dougherty confirmed. "What *was* that?"

"We think an RGB-10 Smerch-3 anti-submarine rocket. They're standard equipment on Petya-class ships."

Dougherty recalled the horrifying footage. "It *obliterated* that tug."

"Yeah, like using a sledge hammer to swat a fly. The RGB-10 is meant for much tougher ships. Interesting that they waited until they were almost inside the blast radius. They may have even taken out some of their own on deck. This tells me they're unfamiliar with such weapon systems."

"That follows," Dougherty said. "We're hearing new details from Damascus."

"Tell me."

"Shortly after the tug was destroyed, they issued an ultimatum—if the terrorists do not leave Arwad and release the frigate, bombing will commence as early as tomorrow."

The line went silent for a moment before Burggraf responded. "Over five thousand of their own civilians populate Arwad."

"No one's been able to establish communication with anyone on the island, including me with any of Lambert's team's sat phones. Damascus is claiming most on the island are already dead."

"The Alumni probably cut the undersea landlines and activated a grid of signal jammers."

"That's our guess," Dougherty said. "In any case, the UN is holding emergency meetings and urging Damascus to delay any aggressive actions."

"I can see how they're frustrated."

"How's that?"

"They've cried wolf too often," Burggraf explained. "Damascus has referred to its own rebels as terrorists so many times that no one's hearing their claim of *external* terrorism."

CHAPTER 47

SEPTEMBER 20, 1312

WESTERN TORTOSA

After a rosy-fingered dawn, preparations began for the final day of Tankiz an-Nasiri's court in Tortosa before his planned departure for Tripoli forty miles to the south. Viceroy officials led those who'd spend the day in court to their preassigned seats in what had been the transept of Our Lady of Tortosa. Others having only temporary business with Tankiz sat further back in the former cathedral's nave.

Although only men would take part, Abdullah had arranged for Shayla to join other minister's wives in viewing proceedings through a finely latticed wooden wall erected at the end of the southern transept. Peeking through gaps in diagonal wood strips, she saw her husband escorted to a front row seat to Abdullah's right, south of the main aisle leading up the nave. After all had been positioned, sultanate officials began appearing from behind the ambulatory, prompting all to stand. At the end of the procession strode the viceroy himself. The officials filed past, and Tankiz stood in front of a raised chair placed at the center of the chancel.

Shayla leaned closer to the partition. The first thing she noticed about Tankiz, besides a bearded face younger than she'd expected, was the modest attire he wore relative to the elaborate robes and headdress choices seemingly favored by most of his ministers. His small white turban was wrapped tightly around his head, its end coiled loosely around his neck. His heavy red tunic displayed few embellishments, and his footwear appeared to be nothing more than felt slippers. The only indication of his lofty station were the four huge Sultanate Guards standing in pairs at his right and left, their large halberds bladed with the distinctive flow patterns of Damascus steel.

After the viceroy raised his right hand, she heard both a hush come over those assembled and a second indication of his authority—a booming voice that filled every corner of the structure. "Let us again thank Allah for the growing prosperity of Syria, brought about by the wisdom of His Grace, Sultan an-Nasir Muhammad."

Shayla heard the audience and several of the women around her voice in unison, "Thanks be to Allah."

Tankiz nodded and continued. "Before the court scribe reviews open issues from days past, and the agenda for today, let me personally thank the people of this region for their hospitality on this final day of my visit." He then bowed, a gracious and humble gesture she'd also not expected.

Those in attendance seemed to make a concerted effort to bow deeper.

After the viceroy sat, all others in the nave did as well, and a uniformed scribe began announcing administrative protocols. Not surprisingly, those assembled began whispering among themselves.

"Do you travel with the viceroy's caravan to Tripoli tomorrow?"

Shayla turned to see the woman to her left with the veiled hair now facing her. "No. Tomorrow my husband and I travel to the Bekaa Valley."

The woman cocked her head for a moment, reminding Shayla her Arabic, while improving, still retained a Greek accent. Then the woman's eyes widened and a smile appeared. "Are you, perhaps, the wife of the Cypriot *Breemlay?*"

"I am. He is to be made Abdullah al-Rasheed's successor as Minister of Agriculture today."

"Congratulations."

Shayla nodded. "My thanks to you."

The woman turned back to peer through the partition. "I hear today's first order of business is dispensing with a recent nuisance to nearly all the viceroy's officials."

Shayla frowned. "Nuisance?"

"If what my husband says is true, he's a vile, little man, who wouldn't stop pestering court officials for an audience."

"A disgruntled citizen?"

"No. Some emissary from the North. If the viceroy's officials are correct, he'll quickly wear out his welcome."

"Mongol?" asked Shayla.

"No. Some other ruffian. From the Kingdom of Cilicia, I believe."

AVIGNON

Nogaret trudged up the steps to Cardinal Orsini's chambers with two curia guards. He wondered if the old man would speak with more reason than he'd conveyed in recent letters.

"Guillaume de Nogaret to see Your Eminence," said the first guard at the open doorway.

Orsini waved to a chair fronting the massive desk he sat behind and addressed the guards. "Leave us. Close the door behind you."

The Italian cardinal's lavish chambers put his prior space in Poitiers to shame. Nogaret perused the paintings, sculptures, and tapestries as he sauntered forward.

"No Royal Guards?" asked Orsini.

"No need." Nogaret raised his hands in mock exultation. "I am once again blessed and protected by the church."

Orsini frowned at his false piety, or perhaps the knowledge of his excommunication being absolved by Pope Clement V the year before. "Curiosity compelled me to agree to your visit. Were my written responses to your queries unclear?"

"Much remains unclear regarding this summer's papal bulls. His Grace has concerns."

"Is that so?" asked Orsini, seemingly concerned.

Nogaret pulled a rough piece of vellum from a shoulder satchel and unrolled it on the desk. "From my copy of *To Foresee*, I read—"

"*Ad Providam*," corrected Orsini.

Nogaret relished translating lofty papal bull titles out of Latin, knowing how much was lost in translation. "Yes, of course . . ." He placed a ringed index finger on a sentence very near the top. "*He can tear out the thistles of vice from the field of the Lord . . .*" He looked up at Orsini with an amused grin. "Am I such a thistle?"

The cardinal said nothing, seemingly waiting for his next question.

"Of the Hospitallers . . ." He slid his index finger down the scroll while keeping a ringed pinky finger pointed at Orsini. "*As fearless warriors of Christ, they are ardent in their efforts to recover the Holy Land . . .*" He slapped the parchment as he looked up at Orsini, without the grin he wore just moments before.

"Yes?" asked the old Italian. "You wish to play *Advocatus Diaboli?*"

Nogaret smirked, slipped another small scroll from his shoulder pack, and unrolled it over the first. "And later, from *Recently in the Council*, the words—"

"*Nuper in Concilio!*" shouted the cardinal.

"Yes, of course . . ." This time he did not take his eyes off Orsini, seeing the old man approaching the verge of an outburst. ". . . *more useful for the aid of the Holy Land . . .*"

"What is your confusion?"

"Should this not refer to their Isle of Rhodes?"

Orsini's eyes grew large before he bellowed his response. "Recovery of the Holy Land is paramount!"

Nogaret sat back and straightened his lace collar while rolling his eyes. "You could now occupy Jerusalem no more than you could occupy the moon . . ."

The elderly cardinal stood with surprising speed. "The Holy See can call for cleansing the Holy Land as has recently been done with the Languedoc region."

Nogaret recognized the accusation, yet remained calm while looking up at Orsini. "It is true—the church killed my parents in the Albigensian purge after accusing them of Catharism. Yet their son is the man you see before you." He slowly stood while speaking. "Would the man I see before me be in such a position without being the nephew of Giovanni Gaetano Orsini . . . excuse me—Pope Nicholas III?"

Francesco Orsini appeared on the verge of physical violence, an act Nogaret knew he could use to great advantage. Instead, the cardinal slowly regained his composure and pointed to his chamber door. "Leave my sight."

"Very well." Nogaret began walking away, turning his head to one side. "I shall report on no addendums to the papal bulls, and begin drawing up the remuneration documents."

"The . . . what documents?" asked the cardinal.

Nogaret turned and stood by the small conference table near the center of the room. "The fees, of course . . . for the cost of imprisonments and trials. Surely you could not have thought that bringing five thousand heretics to justice would be cheap?"

"The king singularly decided on the mass arrests." Orsini pointed a finger. "I assume he left the details to you?"

"Well . . ." Nogaret tugged on the lace at his wrists to straighten his sleeves. "His duty as a defender of Catholicism did indeed compel His Grace to correct your negligence. In time, you may be forgiven."

Orsini seemed to ignore the insult. "To what amount would such fees reach?"

"I would guess a very high figure and growing as we speak." Nogaret shook his head with a look of forced concern. "When all is tallied, it would not surprise if the amount equaled the value of the order's lands and possessions in France . . ."

CHAPTER 48

JULY 28, 7:09 P.M. GST

ARWAD

Rick Lambert watched the tracked jackhammer operator, who was pulverizing what remained of the west parapet. Careful they weren't being observed, he led Danny and Pat to the courtyard's well head from the east entrance. They knelt behind the ring of bricks.

Pat stood, peering into the blackness. "Wakey, wakey, hands off snakey . . ."

"Wanker!" Sean echoed from below. "Get that damned rope back down here."

Lambert, also staring down the shaft, saw the white spot from a penlight being turned on. "Did you find anything?"

"Yes, Major. Pretty sure I found *it*."

Pat fed rope into the cistern. Lambert knew Sean would tie it directly to the carabiner on his Swiss Seat. All three men above stared into the abyss.

"Okay, ready," Sean said.

Each man glanced around, making sure no eyes were upon them, then grasped the rope and shuffled backward toward the courtyard's northeast corner.

After ten seconds, Sean's torso appeared. The three held firm until Sean rolled over the well head and crouched beside it, removing his Swiss Seat.

"Sorry we couldn't get back sooner," Lambert said. "They watched us every minute."

"No problem, sir." Sean handed him a one-gallon Ziploc bag containing a dark leather fragment. "It was pressed between two blank tiles, sealed together with tar just like at Kolossi." He pointed to a jagged edge. "This profile looks like it would fit well with the top half's bottom edge."

Danny had his nose inches from the bag. "Awesome!"

Pat nodded. "Not bad . . . but you're still a plonker."

Lambert ignored the sibling jealously. "How long did it take to find?"

"Not even twenty minutes. I just kept tapping tiles until I found some unsupported ones. A small fissure extended behind them. Reminded me of a safe deposit box."

"Let's start a pool for who the second apostle is," Pat said. "Twenty bucks gets you in."

Lambert chuckled.

ARWAD HARBOR

Maria Anna Belloci stood beside Omar Volkan on his vessel's bridge as he searched in vain for an unjammed radio frequency. As planned, she monitored the roof of the safe house using the captain's Steiner M2080 binoculars. She could not, however, resist periodically shifting her gaze up the slope to the fortress. A slight breeze had begun, pushing the cloud of smoke and dust away from the activity creating it.

Then she saw him. "*Bastardo!* I can see Ahmed Makarem . . ."

Makarem stood at the outer wall of the eastern parapet. He looked out over the slope to the harbor, occasionally shouting into a bullhorn aimed in various directions below. Whenever he turned to his right, she could just make out the hideous hole in his left cheek.

"Where?" Volkan asked.

"On the fortress wall." She handed him his 20x80 binoculars and recalled her sniper training in Italy. "I wish we had a way to take him out from here."

The Turk handed back the Steiner. "I will be back."

Maria spent three minutes alternating between watching the safe house and scowling with disgust at her former captor. She heard the captain climbing the steps back to his bridge, his breathing labored.

She turned when she heard him drop something and curse in Turkish. Three boxes lay below her, the label of each indicating they contained twenty rounds of 7.62x54mmR cartridges. She then saw Volkan gently place a weapon on the deck she'd only read about in her *Alpini* marksmanship courses—a Dragunov SVD semiautomatic sniper rifle.

She turned to him. "Captain, I think I could fall in love with you right now."

Volkan smiled and returned to his hopeless task at the communications console.

She cleared the rifle's chamber, then put the safe house in the crosshairs of the PSO-1 Optical Sniper Sight. She swung the long barrel toward the fortress just in time to see Makarem move toward the parapet's inner wall, out of view.

ARWAD

Ahmed Makarem wasn't sure what he'd seen. Looking down onto the courtyard, he'd watched three locals apparently try to bring water up from a cistern that hadn't been used in centuries. *The fools.* He'd brought the bullhorn to his lips, but then froze.

Another local had pulled himself out of the shaft and rolled onto the courtyard cobblestones beside it. When the first three joined the one from below, all knelt to the south of the well head. They began a discussion while huddled around something being held by the tallest of the four.

Makarem paced along the east parapet trying to get a line of sight on whatever they poked and prodded. He turned the corner onto the south parapet and approached closer. Their tight shoulder-to-shoulder semicircle behind the bricks of the well head provided no gaps.

Behind the bricks—are they hiding from my jackhammer operator?

He squeezed the push-to-talk trigger and shouted into the bullhorn in Arabic: "Who sent you men to the courtyard?"

All four flinched, then instinctually stood, turned, and looked up.

From twenty feet above, Makarem scanned faces, beginning with the tall man holding the object. His surprise at seeing that Major Richard

Lambert had survived the car bomb in eastern Limassol quickly gave way to a grudging acknowledgement of the agent's resourcefulness. To the right of Lambert stood his brain trust—Professor Dicarpio. On the far right stood the younger one who'd been photographed outside Kolossi.

He crossed his gaze over to the figure on the far left, expecting to see the Italian woman. For the second time in as many minutes, he was unsure what he was seeing.

How had the young man from Kolossi slipped around from right to left?

He jerked his head to again peer at the figure on the far right. He again saw the unidentified man from Kolossi.

The major mumbled something. All four sprinted for the entrance to the east wing.

Makarem reached for his SIG Sauer PC-9 ZOAF in the holster on his right hip and raced around the corner, then along the inner edge of the east parapet. The first of them had already entered the fortress. By the time he stopped and steadied himself, the second had as well. The third was nearly there. He focused on the fourth but, due to his heavy breathing, saw both 9mm rounds kick up courtyard dust as the last man disappeared. He let loose two more rounds in frustration before rushing to the outer wall and scanning above his iron sights. He saw none of the four emerge from the east gate.

They are not fools. They will navigate the interior of what remains and make me guess their point of exit.

He raced north.

The youngest man—correction: men—from the Kolossi photos are twins. If one had been in the Land Rover with Lambert and the academic, then the other must have been in Northern Limassol.

After he saw no trace of the men to the north, he turned and sprinted south.

What had I seen with peripheral vision as I'd scanned Lambert's face? He held something white—correction: clear—with a dark-brown rectangular center. A piece of leather in a plastic bag—one of the twins had found the scroll in the cistern!

At the corner of the south and east parapets, he scanned further south—nothing.

Makarem considered the time it would take to organize a search without using the radio clipped to his belt. He felt for the computer tablet in the large left pocket of his cargo pants. He was tempted to send the signal—over an obscure microwave frequency slightly above the radio frequencies being jammed—to deactivate the array of portable signal jammers. He could then issue orders to all via radio, but only after sacrificing the entire island's communications blackout. Orders from Gomrok demanded radio silence until end-of-mission.

He chewed at the ragged flesh inside his left cheek and tasted blood.

CHAPTER 49

SEPTEMBER 20, 1312

WESTERN TORTOSA

The court scribe continued his procedural pronouncements. Shayla yearned to break through the partition and warn her husband of Cibalik Darcan's upcoming audience with the viceroy. She knew, however, even quietly approaching him would draw unwanted attention.

She pressed her face against the wooden lattice only to discover that her view was limited to only a few rows down the nave. She saw Brim chatting with Abdullah, but no sign of the ambassador.

The scribe finally finished his administrations, cleared his throat, and lifted what must have been an agenda for Viceroy Tankiz an-Nasiri's last day in Tortosa. "Emissary Cibalik Darcan from the Armenian Kingdom of Cilicia."

Shayla saw Brim stiffen and jerk his head left to look down the aisle. She heard the crowd stir as a delegation approached. Darcan came into view, followed by three mamluks.

The mercenaries appeared as she remembered, but Darcan wore a formal red robe with a thick white stripe down the center, consistent with the colors of the crowned lion on the flag of Cilicia. On his head sat a reddened leather fez with white cloth trim at its bottom edge. Noticeably absent—politically wise, Shayla thought—was any indication of his country's Eastern Orthodox Christianity.

"What a strange outfit for court," said the woman to her left with the veiled hair.

Shayla nodded nervously. "Indeed."

Darcan stopped a respectful distance away, his three mercenary commanders took places behind him, and all four men bowed.

Shayla realized the purpose for the raised chair—it put the seated viceroy at eye level with those standing before him.

The viceroy raised a hand, quieting those in attendance. "Welcome to Syria, Emissary Darcan. What may we do for Cilicia?"

"Excellency, I come with warnings of an alliance threatening both Armenian Cilicia and the Syrian province."

"I have heard of your claim," began Tankiz, "but we share peace with the Ilkhanate as Mahmud Ghazan's conversion to Islam spreads. We talk peace with Oljaitu Khan and hope such negotiations lead to increased trade between our peoples. My ambassadors believe the era of the East plotting with the West is finished. Perhaps Cilicia should act in a similar manner?"

Shayla could hear muffled laughter coming from the nave.

Darcan seemed to ignore the hint at conversion. "Excellency, I speak not only of Mongols but of rogue members of Christian military orders already in Syria, preparing to reap havoc in the months to come."

"I have heard this claim as well but am told all surviving Christian knights from these lands are imprisoned in Cairo. Do you have proof to the contrary?"

"Several from the abolished Order of the Temple have evaded capture by fleeing east, Excellency. I hear of one, Brimley Hastings, who has even attempted impersonating the Syrian province Deputy Minister of Agriculture."

The viceroy let out a chuckle. "*Breemlay*? The Cypriot?" He turned to his left. "Abdullah al-Rasheed, do you recognize your deputy?"

"Yes, Excellency. The emissary from Cilicia is mistaken."

Shayla placed her hands on the lattice above her head, each fingertip wedged into gaps between wood strips. The next several seconds ground to a crawl. While a second round of stifled chortles emanated from the nave, Darcan and his three commanders strained their necks to turn their heads to the right, in the direction of Abdullah's voice, while being careful not to turn their backs to the viceroy.

Brim and Abdullah sat facing away from her position behind the partition, but the four men in front of the viceroy appeared to be looking directly at her. She knew they instead studied Abdullah and those around him.

For a moment, Shayla had a sliver of hope that the Armenian wouldn't recognize her husband. The two hadn't been in contact since the surrender of Kolossi nearly four years before. For the Muslim mercenaries, it had been five years since the raid on the Larnaca campground. Both times, Brim had short hair and a thin, sparse beard. He now wore his longer hair in a tight turban and oiled his dark beard to a point, in the local style.

Their stares continued. The brows of all four men were crimped above angry eyes scanning in minute angles to either side of Abdullah.

The muffled snickers from the nave gave way to a hush. Those in attendance seemed to sense something was amiss.

During the awkward silence, Abdullah turned to his right to glance at Brim—Shayla could see his puzzled expression—then looked back to the four men standing at the structure's cruciform center.

She knew Abdullah's unintentional betrayal was all they needed.

Strangely, the mamluk commander farthest away reacted first. His eyebrows shot upward, his eyes widened, and his mouth opened. He then seemed to forget all court protocol, turned to his right, pointed at Brim, and said something unintelligible to his colleagues. A moment later, all three mercenaries faced Brim, pointing.

Shayla saw Cibalik Darcan blinking and nodding in response to the words being uttered by the three behind him. Still, his torso faced the viceroy while his neck strained to continue directing his eyes right. It appeared he could not, *would* not, see past the turban, robes, and oiled beard to recognize the man he'd apparently been pursuing these last five years.

She watched Darcan's expression and could also see Brim in the foreground, sitting up straight, his head held high. His attitude seemed clear—their time running from this man would now end. She thought of their history together over the years: their first meeting as youngsters during his first trip to Cyprus, their reunion at the ill-fated Larnaca campsite three years later, their flight together east, their secret marriage on Ruad, the birth of their son, and finally their decision to stay in Syria and make the best life possible for their family. She continued her gaze at her husband's posture, decided she'd never been more proud of him than she was at this very moment, and adopted the same attitude he seemed to convey—their time running had finished.

The hush of the court's audience further gave way to absolute silence. No one moved, lest the very rustling of garments preclude their hearing of what would come.

Finally, Darcan's eyes widened, his body twisted to the right, and his head jutted forward. "Holy Jesus Christ . . ."

CHAPTER 50

JULY 28, 7:46 P.M. GST

ARWAD

Rick Lambert had just voiced his appreciation for Pat Duffy's quick thinking. He felt like doing so again.

Pat had been the first to dash from the courtyard into the east wing of the fortress, continuing to the open gate at the outer wall and pointing out the shadow of crenellated wall upon the dilapidated buildings of the eastern slope. Lambert had seen a figure's shadow—undoubtedly Makarem's—fill one of the gaps. Within seconds, the shadow began appearing and disappearing in the succession of crenellations leading north. The four therefore fled through the south gate and circled around through alleys back to the safe house.

He and the twins climbed the ladder from the tiny balcony to the roof, leaving Danny, eager to begin cleaning the scroll fragment, seated at the kitchen table. To the south, sounds of the fortress's destruction had ceased. To the east, the harbor was also quiet, Volkan's boat still at anchor.

Two boys with slung HK33s ran north, through the east alley, until they had a view of the rocky beach and mud marsh just beyond. After scanning the area for a few seconds, they reversed their course through the alley.

Lambert checked his sat phone. Signals still appeared jammed. He turned to the twins and rubbed his chin. "Leaving's only going to get harder. I'll be right back."

Inside, he retrieved a thick black felt pen and two pieces of paper from a desk drawer in one of the bedrooms, then sat at the kitchen table. Danny's eyes strayed from his work for a moment. "What's up?"

"Signaling Maria." In less than a minute he had thick eight-inch-tall letters on both pages. The first read *DOCK ON*, the second *CAUSEWAY*.

He held the paper between his lips and scaled the ladder, noting Sean with miniature binoculars aimed at Volkan's boat. "Can you see them?"

"Not the captain, sir," Sean said, laughing, "but Maria's looking at us through the scope of one big-ass gun."

"Huh, I wonder what other goodies Volkan has hidden away." He held up the two pages. "We're getting out of here before they start house-to-house searches."

Pat nodded. "Sounds good, sir. I'm cut to the onions with this nuthouse."

"She just turned left," Sean said. "She's talking . . . now she's looking through the scope again." A minute passed. "Okay, I see Volkan. He's on the stern deck. He's raising anchor."

Lambert waited until he could detect the vessel creeping toward the bridged causeway to the north breakwater. He understood—the captain tried attracting as little attention as possible. Even at such a slow speed, Volkan would get there first. "Let's go."

He followed the twins down the ladder. Back inside, they noticed Danny at the table—he stared at the scroll fragment with the same expression of shock he'd had after translating the top half in Limassol.

"The Professor's got something," Sean said. "Who's the second apostle?"

"My money's on Simon," Pat quipped.

The historian remained silent.

Lambert sat across from Danny. "Buddy?"

"It names no apostle . . ."

"But the second group?" Lambert frowned. "It names no leader of the second group?"

"It does . . ." Danny looked up. "It names the reason there *were* apostles . . . it names Jesus of Nazareth."

All paused, until Pat asked, "How long would this have been before His crucifixion?"

Danny shook his head. "That's just it—this journey east would not have taken place before then."

"Hold on . . ." Lambert gestured *time out* with his hands. "The Swoon Hypothesis? The Crucifixion Survival myth? The Nasranis don't believe that, do they?"

"The Nasrani Christians don't, but the Ahmadiyya Muslims do."

"Who?" Pat and Sean asked, in near unison.

"The Ahmadis believe Jesus survived His crucifixion and fled east in search of the lost tribes of Israel. They claim He died in what is now Kashmir after one hundred and twenty years of life."

All four were again silent for several seconds.

Danny let his hands float above the leather. "In the wrong hands, this could radicalize Islam against Christianity on a massive scale . . . launch Islamic crusades . . . ignite a holy world war . . ."

"Should we destroy it now?" Lambert asked, mostly to halt Danny's growing hysteria.

"No! This needs to be studied, radiocarbon dated, and—"

More shouts and footfalls from the alley silenced Danny's tirade.

"Then bag it and hide it," Lambert said. "The boat should be nearing the causeway by now. We need to get to it before Alumni barge through that door, or Syrian bombs slam through the roof." From under his thawb, he removed a folded one-gallon Ziploc bag.

"What's that?" Danny asked.

"A piece of Volkan's welding apron."

"Another decoy, sir?" Pat asked.

Lambert shrugged. "Worth a shot." He pointed at each twin. "Get Danny to the boat. Use the narrowest alleys—they'll be darkest."

"And you, sir?" Sean asked.

"I'll swing around north."

"I think we should stay together, sir," Pat said.

Lambert shook his head. "This is how it's going to go. Get Danny and that fragment to the boat. I'll join you there soon. That's an order." He poked his head out the door, scanned to his left and right, then looked back over his left shoulder before descending the outside stairs. "Remember Pac-Man?"

The three men behind him glanced at one another with puzzled expressions, then nodded.

"Good. Stay away from those ghosts . . ."

CHAPTER 51

SEPTEMBER 20, 1312

WESTERN TORTOSA

A collective gasp from all who'd heard Cibalik Darcan's words filled the nave.

Shayla then saw the Armenian, eyes wide with malice, turn his back to the viceroy and march several steps toward her husband. His actions prompted the two Sultanate Guards to the viceroy's left to quickly intercept and block his path to Abdullah—the highest-ranking minister in the direction he was advancing—with crossed halberds. Two additional guards rushed out from the ambulatory and took the vacated posts to the viceroy's left.

Darcan froze.

The viceroy leaned forward in his raised chair. "What were your words, Emissary Darcan?"

The Armenian, now pointing in the direction of Brim and Abdullah, switched his gaze between them and the viceroy. "You . . . He . . ." He breathed deep and collected his thoughts. "Excellency, this boy . . . this Brimley Hastings, is an outlaw from the Order of the Temple of Solomon!"

The nave erupted in jeers, with too many voices overlapping to discern individual sentiments.

Tankiz an-Nasiri raised a hand. When the clatter did not diminish, he stood. The nave again fell into silence. He scanned over those in attendance, clearly disappointed with such an outburst, before returning to his chair and turning to the Armenian. "A bold accusation."

Emissary Darcan, now facing the viceroy, bowed and waved a hand to his side toward Brim. "Excellency, I await his denial."

The viceroy turned toward Brim and Abdullah and made a parting gesture with both hands. The two guards uncrossed their halberds and stepped aside. "*Breemlay*, you may speak."

All in the nave looked to Brim. He stood, took a step forward, bowed, then paused for a moment. "Excellency, before fleeing to these lands, I was among the brethren of the Order of the Temple."

More gasps filled the structure. Looking past Brim, Shayla could see a line of elder mamluk warriors—possibly veterans of battles with Christian military orders at Acre and Ruad—seated in positions of honor at the northern transept. Each wore an expression of disgust.

"But your young age . . ." said Tankiz. "You joined their ranks on Cyprus before the arrests?"

"No, Excellency. They took me into the London preceptory at age nine, following the death of my mother."

"Age nine?" Tankiz asked, incredulously. "What of your father?"

"Conscripted into the army of King Edward I, he fell fighting Scots at the Battle of Stirling Bridge when I was seven."

Abdullah, who'd been staring at the floor, now joined all others looking up at Brim. Shayla saw his look of puzzlement replaced by an expression of wonder.

"So . . ." The viceroy moved his right hand in a circular motion. "A matter of survival." He looked to Brim with raised eyebrows, as if trying to extract confirmation.

"Yes, Excellency . . . but . . ."

The viceroy had begun to turn toward Cibalik Darcan, but looked back to Brim upon hearing his hesitation. "But . . . ?"

Shayla understood. The order had been such a dominant influence on her husband's life, he could not, *would* not, depict it as merely a means of survival. The memory of his mentor, Malcolm of Basingstoke, demanded more.

"In the interests of full and honest disclosure, I must report to Your Excellency this: members of my family had served the order over several generations. Carrying on this tradition was the driving force of my life . . . until . . ."

Tankiz cocked his head. "Yes?"

Brim lowered his head slightly. "I've seen power drive some to ambitions inconsistent with the original goals of the order. It's motivated me to question the role of such an order, and if there even is one anymore."

The viceroy seemed to ponder her husband's words. "I see." Tankiz then waved a hand toward Darcan. "And why does this man pursue you with such ferocity?"

Brim turned toward the Armenian. "Cibalik Darcan is the Cilician ambassador to Pope Clement V."

More noise from the nave prompted another raised hand from the viceroy before he turned to Darcan, eyebrows raised.

"Excellency, I . . . I serve the Kingdom of Cilicia in several roles. Those of his order have been arrested throughout Christendom. I'm tasked with taking him to Avignon for questioning."

"Emissary Darcan," countered Tankiz, "these lands have not been part of Christendom for many years."

Shayla heard hums of approval throughout the structure as the viceroy turned his head right and nodded.

At the northern transept, the line of elder mamluk warriors smiled at the recognition, returning nods of respect.

The ambassador seemed flustered. He glanced to the elder warriors, then back and forth between Brim and the viceroy. He pointed at Brim. "On Cyprus, his master killed one of your greatest warriors."

"In single combat—and your men killed him for it," said Brim. "As you killed my wife's father—in cold blood."

Darcan turned to the viceroy, shaking his head. "That was self-defense."

Brim now pointed at Darcan. "You killed him only after your men put him down with crossbow bolts to his legs." He faced the viceroy and bowed. "Excellency, I await *his* denial."

It seemed clear to all, from the erratic expressions from Darcan and his mercenaries, that Brim had spoken truth. The disgusted expressions from the elder mamluk warriors, focused on Brim just minutes ago, now faced Darcan as if appalled by a tale so bereft of honor.

"Enough of this." The viceroy held an open palm toward Brim. "The new issue of the Cypriot's identity will be dealt with in due course." He turned to Darcan. "I wish to return to the reason my court officials have organized your presence here today—were you and your men in Acre nine days ago?"

Darcan blinked several times as his commanders looked to him. "Yes, Excellency."

"At the Ancona chancery, perhaps?"

The ambassador waited a moment before answering. "Yes, Excellency."

"And your actions there?"

Darcan paused again.

The viceroy, apparently unwilling to wait for an answer, waved an arm over his head. "Bring them in."

From the ambulatory came five men in chains, each led to the viceroy's left by a pair of Sultanate Guards. Shayla tried to match the men's faces to those she remembered from Larnaca, but each was in a state of disarray. Three had blackened eyes, two dripped blood from their noses onto the floor tiles, and all five displayed the swollen bruising of prolonged beatings.

Upon seeing them, Darcan raised his hands and spoke over the increasing clamor from the nave. "Excellency, we harmed none from Syria . . ."

"That is why you and your men still possess your heads!" After glaring at the ambassador for a moment, Tankiz held up a hand for silence.

While the crowd quieted, Shayla noticed the reactions from Darcan's three commanders—with sadness in their eyes, they seemed to be making calming gestures with their hands and mouthing reassuring words. The men in chains responded with nods and slight smiles, revealing broken teeth. Such emotions seemed beyond military discipline and loyalty. She realized these men were family.

The viceroy seemed to make the same realization as he glanced between the five chained men and their commanders. He then turned to

Darcan. "Witnesses report four scribes from Ancona alive as you arrived, and none living upon your departure. Why did you kill them?"

Darcan slumped and said nothing.

"I see." The viceroy glanced to the five men in chains. "They also had no words." He turned back to Darcan. "I had intended sending you and your men to Ancona for trial, but since you act on behalf of the Roman Catholic Church, the traditional course of action is to offer a ransom."

Darcan seemed surprised and raised his gaze from the floor to the viceroy. "These men are veterans of the Mamluk Sultanate."

"Your *mercenaries* follow you, an ambassador to the pope. As such, these five will remain here while you, and the three beside you, sail west. Executions will take place in one year. You may return before that time to buy their freedom. Let us say fifty gold dinars each."

The court scribe cleared his throat, approached the viceroy, and whispered something.

Tankiz chortled. "Yes . . . of course . . . where would the pope find dinars? Let us instead say fifty gold *livres tournois* each."

"But, Excellency . . ."

The viceroy seemed to want no further dealings with Darcan and his men. "Deliver those four to the docks and deposit them on the first ship sailing west."

Eight more Sultanate Guards standing behind the viceroy escorted them toward the main aisle leading down the nave. The three mamluk commanders walked calmly with heads low.

Darcan, however, seemed to have no intention of leaving quietly. He turned his head left to glare at Brim. Something in his eyes told Shayla of his fear—that he would never again cross paths with Brimley Hastings. He struggled against the guards dragging him into the main aisle while keeping his eyes locked on Brim. "Tell me where it is! Tell me what you've done with it!"

Darcan passed beyond her view, still shouting demands while being dragged toward the narthex. Shayla looked at her husband, who stared silently down the length of the nave, a contented smile on his face.

CHAPTER 52
JULY 28, 8:02 P.M. GST
ARWAD

Ahmed Makarem recalled all forces back to the fortress. He ordered his eight seniors and four pilots to install the new explosive harnesses on the sixty-six juniors—eighteen from their Bekaa Valley reinforcement and forty-eight who'd fast-roped onto Arwad from the Mi-26s—before reissuing rifles.

All were now armed and standing outside the east gate, awaiting his orders.

From the parapet's northeast corner, he scanned the harbor from east to north through 10x25 compact binoculars. He clenched his teeth, knowing their target would most likely be within this ninety-degree arc. He saw no activity east, south of the refueling dock. The refueling dock itself, and the boardwalk north of it, also remained quiet. Only after directing his gaze to the northernmost edge of the harbor did he see it. Electricity seemed to flow through him as he realized it had not been there minutes before.

He held the bullhorn in his right hand and aimed it at those below while pointing with his left. "Converge on the fishing trawler with its bow run aground at the bridged causeway to the north breakwater! Seniors and pilots from the right, juniors from the left! Retrieve the scroll!"

For nearly a minute, he relished the sight of his forces plunging into the narrow alleys descending to the sea, periodically glimpsing them in alleyways aligned with both the setting sun and his line of sight.

A bright light from the east distracted him. Just as he realized it emanated from the Project 159 frigate a mile offshore, he heard the explosion.

Syria is willing to sink its own warship?

Makarem scanned the sky for Syrian Su-22 fighter-bombers. He saw none.

More blasts ravaged the deck and hull of the frigate. Astonishingly, some explosions seemed to be below the waterline.

A submarine? Aren't Syria's two Project 633 submarines inactive?

He lowered his gaze to the harbor, excited to see his seniors and pilots appearing on the boardwalk, southeast of causeway. Shifting his gaze north, he saw his juniors nearing the mud marsh, west of the causeway.

Glancing east, he saw the frigate now hidden by the smoke of burning diesel fuel.

Again looking toward the causeway, he expected to see his seniors and pilots.

They should be there by now.

Turning slightly right for a view of the boardwalk, he saw rotor blades turning atop one of the three operational Mi-8s.

Makarem felt an eruption of hatred. "Cowards! Traitors! Allah will make you pay for your betrayal!" Despite the bullhorn's volume set to maximum, he knew they could not hear him.

He dropped the bullhorn and retrieved the control tablet from the crenellation in front of him. Its screen displayed the option of deactivating the signal jammers, his first step in arming the harnesses.

Gomrok's youngest will be remembered for their sacrifice . . .

8:17 P.M.

ARWAD HARBOR

The setting sun's angle neared that of the eastern slope, making it painful to glance up at the fortress. Maria instead scanned the waterline to the south from the bridge's open port-side window. Through the Dragunov's optics, she was surprised to see one of the Mi-8s on the boardwalk about to lift off.

Pat, Sean, and Danny had arrived just minutes before. Volkan had given each an auto-loading 12-gauge shotgun with which to defend his vessel. All four men watched the entrance to the causeway and the waterline to the west of it from the starboard side of the pilothouse.

"There he is!" Sean said, pointing over the causeway to the beach. "He's really moving!"

Maria felt a rush of adrenaline and swung the rifle upward. "Make a hole."

The men parted, allowing her to rest the barrel on the starboard sill. From her perch, she could see Rick sprinting into the shallows of the mud marsh, surrounded by splashes from gunfire. She could hear the shots, but the gunmen had yet to emerge from the alleys between the beachfront apartment buildings. She turned back to Rick in time to see him fall forward, his face contorted.

"He's hit!" Pat shouted.

Maria was devastated. In an instant, every possible future she could have had with Rick had been erased forever. She slammed in the magazine of 7.62x54mmR and chambered a round.

The gunmen swarmed north but, since Rick had fallen below the water's surface, soon turned and darted east toward the causeway entrance.

"Here they come . . ." Sean said.

The gunmen turned onto the causeway and Maria got her first good look at them through the Dragunov's scope. They slowed to a walk, worried looks on their faces. She realized they'd gotten their first view of the Petya-class frigate's destruction. Many looked up the slope to the fortress. They seemed to regain their motive and moved in single file down the south side of the causeway. She could hear the shots and see HK33 muzzle flashes.

"Take them out, Maria," Pat said.

She took aim but was shocked by what appeared in the rifle's optics. "But they are . . . they are children."

A volley of 5.56mm rounds punched through the bridge.

"They're trying to kill us," Sean added. "Take them out."

Through the scope, she saw them pause and look to the southern sky. She heard the lone Mi-8 pass overhead and continue north. The collective nervousness of the child soldiers seemed to return as their apparent abandonment sank in. The sound of the rotors faded and she could hear Makarem's shouts in Farsi through the bullhorn. Glancing out the port-side window, she noticed the sun had just dropped behind a building north of the fortress.

To the voiced dismay of the men beside her, she repositioned at the port-side sill. She estimated the range to Makarem at about 250 meters. Normally an easy shot, but she hadn't had the opportunity to sight-in the weapon. She considered the semiautomatic nature of the Dragunov and decided to simply walk the impacts up the side of the fortress wall and work out the difference between point of aim and point of impact in real time.

The child soldiers responded to Makarem's commands by putting more rounds through the bridge. She heard one of the twins yell behind her and turned to see Pat clutching his right shoulder.

Volkan spoke. "You must take him off wall. Do it now."

She returned to peering at Makarem through the PSO-1 scope. The sun setting behind the fortress turned him into a featureless black silhouette. She lowered the reticle down the wall.

"Going hot!" she warned, before squeezing the trigger. The bullet impacted two bricks right and three up. While unsure of the size of the bricks, she continued walking rounds up the wall. Only when Makarem appeared at the top of the scope, his left hand gripping a flagpole for support as he leaned over the wall, did she get a feel for the scale of the misalignment.

She placed the PSO-1 center reticle two feet left and three feet below Makarem's center of mass and squeezed the trigger. His right side jerked violently backward, his back slammed against the flagpole, then his limp body tumbled through a crenellation to the stones twenty feet below.

"Damn . . ." Danny had crouched beside her.

The firing from the causeway stopped. Maria returned the Dragunov's barrel to the starboard sill and observed the child soldiers through the scope. Their twitching stares alternated between the fortress's vacant parapet, the now-listing frigate a mile offshore, and the Mi-8 disappearing to the north. Like a flock of birds, they all turned together and darted back toward the causeway entrance. In seconds they disappeared into the closest alleyway.

Volkan stopped the bleeding from Pat's shoulder with the application of coagulant powder and constant pressure. Sean retrieved gauze and a compression bandage from Volkan's first aid kit and wrapped his brother's shoulder.

Since the arrival of the child soldiers on the causeway, chatter had been heard from the radio console. Volkan began checking frequencies.

Maria heard a loud bang from the stern. From the bridge's aft window, she and Volkan watched a diving cylinder roll across the deck.

Volkan pointed at Danny and Pat. "You two stay here." He then looked at Maria and Sean. "You two with me." They rushed down the stairs, across the deck, leaned over the transom, and aimed three shotgun barrels at the stern's platform.

Rick Lambert looked up at them. "A little help here?"

Maria was shocked. "How can this be? I saw you shot."

"Shot? No, I heard some rounds come close but I wasn't hit."

"But in the mud marsh, through the scope, I saw you go down."

"Oh . . ." Rick took his left fin off, then held up his ankle to show several punctures. He looked at Sean. "Those damn crabs again . . ."

CHAPTER 53

OCTOBER 28, 1312

WESTERN TORTOSA

"I've seen many dramas unfold at court, especially with Mongol delegations," said Abdullah al-Rasheed with a twinkle in his eye. "But you upstaged them all, young *Breemlay*."

The Cypriot—correction: the Englishman—pursed his lips and shook his head at yet another reminder.

Several meetings had taken place between the two since the clash with Cibalik Darcan five weeks before. Each time, the conversation had become easier for Abdullah.

Upon the viceroy's departure for Tripoli, he'd taken over the chambers within the Frankish cathedral. He missed the smell of pitas from his old post at the adjacent bakery but enjoyed the natural light of the morning sun through the structure's eastern windows.

Brimley's face flushed red. "Please let me tell you again how troubling it's been, for both Shayla and me, hiding our past from you these last two years . . ."

"Like the Nile, you had concealed your sources well." Abdullah waved his hand. "But this we have discussed. You were protecting your family, and that is the end of it."

Brimley leaned forward in his seat and nodded. "You are exceedingly gracious, as always."

Abdullah shook his head and frowned, still amazed at how much respect he had for the young man before him. "It is unfortunate you cannot serve as a sultanate official here. If the decision was mine alone, you would. But there are too many warriors from my generation who've lost too much to the Christian military orders . . ."

"I understand, as does Shayla."

"The marksman hits the mark by pulling and letting go. So . . ." Abdullah slapped his thighs. "You and Shayla accept the mission east?"

"We do. In fact, Shayla had fewer concerns than I, probably because she sees the situation here more clearly."

"Excellent! The sultan has desired such an expedition for many years, the agricultural practices of India and China long being a fascination of his. But the right man to lead it has been forever absent, until now. You will have one of the largest and most secure caravans ever assembled, with safe passage documents signed by Sultan an-Nasir Muhammed himself, as well as Viceroy Tankiz an-Nasiri and Oljaitu Khan. Shayla will travel as a sultana, little Malcolm as a prince."

"We are grateful for such an opportunity," said Brim, nodding his appreciation. "I shall dispatch to you a constant stream of reports, explaining as many mysteries of the East as I'm able to decipher."

"I look forward to such readings."

"May we sail to our former island home tomorrow and bid our farewells?"

A frowning Abdullah crossed his arms and leaned forward onto his desk. "On one condition . . ."

"Sir?"

He held his arms apart and smiled. "That Abdullah is the last to hug little Malcolm before you depart!"

AVIGNON

It did not surprise Cardinal Francesco Orsini that Clement had assigned him the drafting of a response to the latest from the exiled Florentine Dante Alighieri. To the French pope, all from the Italian Peninsula were of the same mind. The countless reports of papal support by prominent Black Guelphs against emperor-loving White Guelphs were all for naught.

In his new treatise, *De Monarchia*, White Guelph Alighieri directly confronted Pope Boniface VIII's papal bull *Unam Sanctam*, challenging the secular authority of pope over emperor. The weakness of the current pontiff had naturally spawned such writings. When the curia moved back to Rome and someone competent became Vicar of Christ, such works would be banned. It would not surprise him if the whole of Florence received excommunication.

Orsini felt grateful for any excuse to set aside the debate with the poetic radical. The surprise notification of Cibalik Darcan's arrival in Avignon the night before, and his urgent request for a meeting at first light, certainly qualified.

The last dispatch from Darcan had arrived from Acre only a week ago. In it he'd named the destination to be used by Ancona for the presumptive reply to the letter from the boy Hastings—the Genoese chancery in Tortosa. The ambassador also communicated his desire to arrive in Tortosa in time to make his case, to the visiting Viceroy Tankiz an-Nasiri, for unrestricted access to the Syrian province. Because of this, Orsini assumed he'd hear nothing further for several weeks. Not being able to sleep, he spent the night under candlelight reviewing dispatches sent by the ambassador over the years.

The window of his high-towered chamber received the first eastern light of morning. With it, he hoped success from the East would follow, to replace the long series of preceding failures. He did not have to wait long for the guard's double knock on his open door.

"Ambassador Cibalik Darcan to see Your Eminence."

"Show him in, and close—" The sight of the Armenian shocked him into silence.

It had been nearly five years since Orsini sent Darcan to Nicosia with Hayton of Corycus. Since then, while reading the ambassador's monthly reports of flushing the brethren out of hiding on Cyprus, he'd pictured the man as he remembered him. Nothing could have been further from the truth. The thick black hair common to men of Asia Minor had been replaced by thin gray wisps unable to hide a mottled scalp. The fit and confident statesman from Cilicia now appeared gaunt and timid.

Darcan, seemingly puzzled by the sudden hush, bowed. "Your Eminence?"

"Ambassador, please sit," said Orsini, waving to the chair fronting his desk. Orsini remembered Darcan's purposeful, arrogant stride from five years ago. The man before him instead approached with a bent tentative shuffle, his head lowered. It seemed clear the ambassador would not be delivering positive information. Considering the man's service and the toll it had taken on him, Orsini decided to show mercy, regardless of what he had to say.

The frail Armenian lowered himself into the chair and looked forward, not with the firm stare of years past but rather with the tired, sunken eyes of an old man.

"You nearly overtook your latest dispatch." Orsini chuckled, trying to lighten the mood. "You must be tired from such a swift journey. May I provide wine or water?" He gestured to a small table to his right.

The haggard Armenian did not glance at the carafes. "No, thank you, Eminence."

After an awkward silence, Orsini spoke. "You journeyed from Acre to Tortosa?"

"I did . . ." Darcan appeared on the verge of breakdown. "And there I failed you . . ."

"Be calm, my friend." Orsini leaned forward and slid his hands across his desk in an effort to comfort the man, only to see him sulk back like a frightened animal. "You are safe here."

The ambassador nodded.

"So, you've learned nothing of the Roman scroll?"

"Nothing, Eminence."

Orsini had long entertained the wishful thought of the *Vectis Templi* being destroyed and the boy's offer being a ruse. "I suppose the scroll could have been consumed in the fires of Larnaca."

"Yes . . . possible . . . but his eyes told nothing when I demanded answers."

"His eyes? Hastings? Where did you see him?"

"At the court of Viceroy Tankiz."

Orsini's brow furrowed. "How could that be?"

"I . . . I have trouble understanding what I've seen with my own eyes—Hastings had been serving the Syrian province as Deputy Minister of Agriculture."

"My friend," began Orsini, seeing more evidence indicating the ambassador had lost much of his mental aptitude. "I'm sure the minister bore a striking resemblance to young Hastings. I was sure I'd seen Grand Master Jacques de Molay in a crowd just the other—"

"No!" The Armenian's resolve of years past returned for a moment, then dissolved. "I exposed his identity to the viceroy, after which he explained his service to the order in England and on Cyprus."

Orsini felt his smile vanish. "And the viceroy's response?"

Darcan's head lowered. "I was . . . escorted away before learning the fate of Hastings."

"You were not rewarded for pointing out the serpent in his garden?"

Nervous, seemingly involuntary laughter sprang from the ambassador. "No, Eminence."

After another uncomfortable pause, Orsini rolled his eyes and took a deep breath, feeling his patience falter. "Tell me what took place."

"To find Hastings we were . . . forced to take action while in Acre. Those of the Anconian chancery did not survive. I was granted an audience only after reports of such actions had reached the viceroy."

"You know this how?"

"He had five of my men brought out in irons."

This time, the pause came from Orsini. "What of the others?"

"They accompanied me in the hours leading up to my audience."

"Well, the five are surely dead by now, knowing how the—"

"No, Eminence," said the ambassador, still seemingly unwilling to raise his head. "Tankiz allowed me and my three commanders to depart with a message . . ."

Orsini ducked his head to the side, trying to look into the Armenian's eyes.

Darcan glanced to his right at the chest beside the desk. "After Hastings divulged my post as an ambassador to His Holiness, the viceroy suggested ransom."

Silence enveloped his chambers, and Orsini felt all sympathy for the man before him recede. But his rage at the incredibly dangerous position he'd been thrust into gradually gave way to contemplation. With how Darcan had described events in Tortosa unfolding, it was difficult to find fault—each adversary would naturally identify the other if it promised advantage. He concentrated on remaining calm. "Who else knows of this?"

"None. Only I and the three mamluk commanders."

"Who are where?"

"Just outside Avignon, but—"

Orsini slammed his fists on his desktop. "You bring Saracens to Christian shores *again*? You taint Avignon as you had Poitiers years ago."

The Armenian cowered deep into his chair. His lowered head began shaking from side to side. "It . . . could not have been otherwise."

"What is your meaning?"

"I have lost my . . . they now follow orders only when it suits them."

Orsini smirked. "And what suits them?"

"Fifty gold pieces for each of their five men," said Darcan, his gaze shifting again to the chest beside the desk.

Orsini raised his fists above his head but after forcing himself to relax during a long pause lowered them and placed his palms on his desktop. "Ambassador, you must understand—there shall never be such a ransom paid, just as there shall never be an acknowledgement of a papal representative at the court of Viceroy Tankiz an-Nasiri."

"But . . . the three await my—"

"You will go to them, release them from your service, and ensure they depart Christian lands."

The shaking of the ambassador's head intensified. "I . . . I cannot."

"You will comply with . . ." Orsini paused, finally understanding. He softened his tone. "I see . . . they now give *you* orders . . ."

The Armenian continued staring down at his hands in silence.

"How could this have come to pass?"

Darcan raised his head. "Ghazi's men . . . they're more than just mercenaries. They're tighter than any tribe or clan. They're all brothers, half-brothers, or cousins. They're all *family*."

He saw the fear in Darcan's eyes before the Armenian's head again sagged. He also understood the bonds of family loyalty—the feud between the Orsini and Colonna families had caused open warfare in the streets of Rome, a turmoil used by Clement and his French cardinals to justify relocating the Roman Curia first to Poitiers, then to Avignon. But unlike the killing of Christians by Christians in Rome, this would be different. These were enemies of Christ.

Taking his time, Orsini slid a small piece of vellum from a desk drawer and dipped a quill into an inkwell. "Tell me the exact location of these three."

Darcan did so.

"Tonight their exploitation ends."

Darcan's relieved breathing showed his understanding.

Orsini stood and strolled around his desk, prompting Darcan to rise. He took the emotionally drained ambassador by the arm and led him toward his chamber door. "Tell them their gold is being readied for your receipt tomorrow morning. Make sure all three are there just after sunset."

Darcan nodded.

"Cibalik, my friend—when God's work begins, step to the nearest corner, out of harm's way. You will then be relieved of your burden."

"Your Eminence." The ambassador bowed, then turned to begin his descent of the tower steps.

Orsini watched the Armenian disappear around the bend of the stone spiral, then strolled back to his desk. He already knew the men he needed—they would ensure the four just outside Avignon took all knowledge of events from Tortosa to their graves.

CHAPTER 54

AUGUST 4, 10:00 A.M. EDT

FOGGY BOTTOM

Rick Lambert had mixed feelings about being back in the US. He and Maria had just picked up the twins an hour before, after Pat's checkup at George Washington University Hospital. Maria had been kept there two nights prior, for observation after the extraction of the Alumni beacon implanted below her cerebellum. The four settled into chairs around the conference room table at INR HQ.

Ever punctual, James Dougherty entered. "Good morning. Professor Dicarpio will be along shortly."

All four stood.

Dougherty strode to Maria and took her right hand in his. "Good to finally meet you, Lieutenant Belloci. Recovering well?"

"Yes. Thank you, sir. And it is Maria, please."

"You must be Sergeant Pat Duffy." Dougherty extended his left hand due to Pat's right arm being in a sling. "How's the shoulder?"

"Still a little stiff, sir."

"And Sergeant Sean Duffy," said the INR department head, switching back to shaking hands with his right.

Sean nodded. "Sir."

Dougherty approached Lambert. "How long since you've been stateside?"

"Nearly ten years, sir. Too long . . ."

The two men shook hands warmly.

"Quite a team you have here."

"They did great," Lambert confirmed, pointing to Pat. "And with that sling, I can finally tell which twin is which."

"What happens when Pat's arm gets better?" Maria asked.

"Then I'm in trouble."

She rolled her eyes. "Okay, guys, give the major a *Charlie's Angels* pose."

They pouted for a moment, then acquiesced, both making finger guns and turning back to back.

"I don't get it. Besides the sling, they're mirror images of . . ."

"I think he has it now," Maria guessed.

Lambert hung his head in mock shame for a few seconds, then began nodding. "Pat's left-handed. Sean's right-handed."

Dougherty chuckled, then thumbed toward the door. "Your old friend, Professor Dicarpio—he's sure a bundle of energy."

Lambert nodded. *If you only knew the half of it.* "Danny's always been that."

Dougherty sat at the head of the table, prompting the others to sit also. "I brought him up to speed while he worked on the scroll fragments. I'd like to debrief you four also." He rolled his eyes and shook his head. "Where to begin . . . ?"

Maria raised her hand.

"Maria?"

"What of the child soldiers?"

"Ah . . . every time we think we have them all, someone on Arwad finds another. They found numbers sixty and sixty-one hiding in a bait shop storeroom yesterday."

"What becomes of them?" she asked.

"After Italian UN forces remove their harnesses, they're flown 250 miles south to Amman in the *Iwo Jima*'s CH-46s. Jordan's looking into their return to Iran. It's going to be a long road to normalcy for those kids, so they're taking it slow."

"I should hope so," Lambert said. "Please tell me the Italian blue helmets found Ahmed Makarem's dead body."

"They did. His back folded over a stone wall just east of the fortress, his right arm nearly blown off. They also found a smashed computer tablet near him."

"It's a start," Lambert said.

Dougherty scoffed. "Stay tuned. The Muslim world is furious with Iran. Jahangir Nasser Rudahmi has disappeared. The Supreme Council have denied responsibility, saying Rudahmi acted alone. The Supreme Leader has yet to publicly address the issue, but the entire Gomrok complex has been demolished down to its concrete foundations."

"Sounds like what Pakistan did with Bin Laden's place in Abbottabad," Sean said.

"Nothing to see here, folks . . ." Pat added.

"Exactly," Dougherty confirmed.

Lambert raised a hand. "What about that shallow-water frigate blocking the ferry lanes?"

"We got lucky there. Damascus formally asked the UN for help neutralizing that Petya after it destroyed their tug. We feared the Syrian crew had been locked belowdecks and would drown if the ship sank. Turns out the Alumni took over the vessel the day before, while it docked at Tripoli thirty miles south. At the time, most of her crew were on shore leave."

Lambert's frown persisted. "Omar Volkan said it was attacked with bombs and torpedoes, but he saw no fighter-bombers, no torpedo-bombers, and the water near Arwad is too shallow for submarines."

"He's right—MQ-9 Reapers are hard to see . . . and quiet."

"Drones?" Sean asked.

"Remotely piloted vehicles," Dougherty corrected. "The MQ-9s have carried GBU-12 general-purpose bombs for some time, the GBU-36 JDAMs being deployed only recently."

"But torpedoes?" Lambert asked.

"Yes, that's something new. US Air Force teams on British Sovereign Base Areas Akrotiri and Dhekelia have been secretly testing MQ-9s with Raytheon's latest Mark 54 lightweight torpedo variant. Prior to last week, they've only done dummy test drops. Launching from both bases allowed them to try it with live fish, and most hit their target."

Danny rushed into the room. "Hey . . . sorry I'm late." He inserted an HDMI cable into his tablet computer and grabbed the remote to turn on the ceiling-mounted projector. The screen opposite Dougherty soon began glowing with text. "I repeated the last line from the top half."

All read the translation of the text from the bottom scroll fragment in silence.

SECOND GROUP

APPROXIMATELY 20 FUGITIVES

LED BY JESUS OF NAZARETH

DISPATCH REPORT OF PROGRESS EASTWARD ONCE PER

MONTH

Below the text were enhanced photos of the faded ink-pressed seals Lambert remembered seeing on the original, perhaps from the office of Pontius Pilate's Magistrate of Judea.

Shortly after returning to Volkan's trawler, Lambert had told Maria of Danny finding the name of Jesus on the scroll fragment while in the safe house. He now saw her same worried look as she prepared to speak.

"So, this changes two thousand years of history?" she asked.

Lambert noticed Dougherty leaning back in his chair, crossing his arms and smiling in anticipation.

"Perhaps not," Danny said. "If authenticated, this could be an incredible find, but *'led by'* Thomas, or Jesus, could have meant *'led by their teachings'* . . ."

Lambert shook his head. "Come on, Danny. We know Thomas the Apostle was alive many years after the crucifixion. Why would the same phraseology be used for Jesus if—"

"That's the beauty of it!" Danny said, touching his temples with his index fingers. "Imagine you're a magistrate for Judea. Days after the crucifixion, the body of Jesus disappears. Weeks after, word spreads of His followers seeing Him alive. Later, His disciples begin leaving to spread His word. The Romans are left trying to keep Judea in one piece while fearing a Jewish revolt due to the chance they come to believe His death sentence had not been carried out. What do you do?" Danny raised his right index finger. "Keep in mind the state of Judea at the time—the seeds were being planted for the First Jewish-Roman War and the Roman Siege of Jerusalem only a few decades later."

With Danny in full professor mode, Lambert just sat back. "Okay, Danny. What do I do?"

"Think like a Roman. You write the order in language vague enough to cover all your bases."

"Meaning?" Lambert asked.

"The scroll commands Praximus to return the followers of Thomas and Jesus to Judea, to get to the bottom of things. If their leaders are still with them, so much the better. You used to like *Occam's razor*—I think this is the answer."

"Whose razor?" Sean asked.

"William of Ockham," answered Danny. "A philosopher and theologian. His idea was that the simplest answer is usually correct."

"So you say the scroll proves nothing?" Maria asked.

"Proof? No, there is no proof," Danny replied. "Only interpretation."

"Nevertheless," Dougherty said, turning to Maria, "There've been high level, secure talks with Vatican officials these last few days—they want it bad. Cardinal Dominic Batista is especially upset."

Maria lowered her head, then turned to Lambert. "Good."

He smiled, then turned to Dougherty. "Where are the two scroll fragments now?"

"Bits from the edges are being radiocarbon dated, then they'll be hermetically sealed. They'll make it to Vatican City eventually, but we have some security issues to work out first."

All nodded.

Dougherty continued. "Except for Cardinal Batista, most at the Vatican are pleased with the outcome. So much so they wish for this team to stay together and investigate other cases they deem important. It would allow them to keep their distance from controversial issues."

Lambert watched Danny nodding for a few seconds, then turned back to Dougherty. "How would that work?"

"You'd all be temporarily assigned here, INR would run operations using other Intelligence Community assets as needed, and the

Congregation for the Doctrine of the Faith would fund it covertly. The CDF even proposed a name—*Castellum One*."

Lambert frowned. "Watchtower One?"

"Hey, you got one!" Danny blurted.

After the laughter subsided, Lambert turned back to Dougherty. "Your bosses are okay with this?"

"Vatican City has contacts around the world we've dreamed of getting access to for decades." Dougherty shrugged. "This may all dry up after they get the scroll fragments."

Lambert nodded. "Sir, I'd like to request some time off first—Maria and I have planned a short vacation."

"Skiing the Julian Alps?" Pat guessed.

Lambert shook his head. "Kashmir."

Danny jerked his head toward him. "Roza Bal?"

"Yep."

CHAPTER 55

OCTOBER 29, 1312

AVIGNON

Cibalik Darcan watched in fascination as the first mamluk commander tossed the cloth-wrapped grappling hook over the northern crenellated wall, then climbed the knotted rope to the parapet. After wrapping the rope more securely around a merlon, the second ascended as the third tied the rope's end to his makeshift rope harness.

He cringed as the harness dug into his emaciated hamstrings. His back rubbed against wet stone as the two above tugged him higher. He looked out over the rain-swept Rhône as he rose. With dawn still hours away, all appeared nearly black. When they all arrived atop the walkway, he'd make one final plea for restraint before their final surge up the steps to Orsini's chambers. He had, after all, pointed out Orsini's exact location in the Fortress of the Wizards—their name for the Papal Palace.

He knew his mistake had been describing the chest by Orsini's desk, the same lockbox used to store hundreds of gold pieces years before in Poitiers. When he returned empty-handed from his meeting with the cardinal, however, he needed some way to assuage their rage and give credence to his story of them receiving the ransom amount the next morning. They either refused to believe him or thought an earlier, unexpected withdrawal would be safer. An afternoon had thus been spent searching for a grappling hook among the blacksmiths of the western quarter and procuring rope from the Rhône waterfront, followed by an extensive reconnoiter outside the palace.

Darcan glanced at the cobblestones thirty feet below before being dragged through a crenellation and dropped onto the parapet. The rope was removed from his harness and tossed back over the wall. The third

Muslim warrior appeared on the walkway mere seconds after he'd removed his harness.

The four men crept toward the so-called Tower of the Bells at the northwestern corner of the complex.

Darcan whispered from the rear in Arabic. "Let our actions be restrained."

The mamluk ahead of him glanced back. "Be silent."

When he'd climbed the steps to Orsini's chambers the morning before, the door to the fourth floor landing had been unlocked. He noticed this when the two papal guards from below walked out upon the parapet after handing him off to two others. The expectation of the unlocked door, as well as the pair of papal guards within, had been conveyed to the three in front of him, who now stood silent.

He took a step to his right and saw the lead Muslim with an ear against the heavy wooden door. The man nodded back at the other two, who each unsheathed a narrow scimitar.

The lead mercenary swung open the door as quickly as its weight would allow.

For a split second, Darcan saw two papal guards warming their hands near a wall-mounted torch. Both received curved blades through their necks before their hands reached the hilts of their ceremonial curtanas. Their knees buckled, and the two mamluks lowered them to the stone floor before extracting their blades.

Several seconds passed as each man listened for echoes of footsteps from below.

Darcan heard none, and broke the relative silence. "No more killing. I carry lengths of twine so we may tie up any—"

"Be silent," repeated the nearest mamluk, this time pointing a bloody-tipped scimitar.

He followed the three up the remaining five flights of steps. He hoped for the cardinal's absence, which would allow for a stealthy removal of his lockbox. Such hope vanished when, upon reaching the top landing, he heard several voices behind Orsini's door.

The cardinal generally keeps his door unlocked so papal guards can deliver correspondence. Was it locked now that some meeting was taking place?

The lead commander gestured for him to come to the front. He understood—assuming an unlocked door, he'd lead them in single file, so only a familiar face would be seen at first.

The mamluk behind him put a hand on his shoulder, pushed him forward, and whispered in Arabic. "Go."

The latch engaged, the door swung inward, and he was marched into the room.

At the head of his small conference table sat Cardinal Orsini, farthest away, facing the door. On each side of the table sat two figures, all four facing Orsini. Perhaps because of the darkness by the door, the cardinal did not seem to notice the intrusion.

Orsini looked up at the sound of the door being slammed shut and locked by the last mamluk. "Who is there?"

He was pushed into the light at the foot of the table. He bowed. "Apologies, Your Eminence."

"Ambassador Darcan? What are—?"

Orsini became silent as the lead mercenary strode behind the figures sitting to the cardinal's left, assumedly toward the chest by Orsini's desk. The two others took positions at Darcan's sides, scimitars raised.

The cardinal shifted his chair back, preparing to stand.

A command in Arabic came from his right: "Tell them to remain seated."

Darcan did so.

The mercenary behind Orsini threw open the lid to the chest, then turned and nodded to the two others beside him.

In the seconds of shocked silence that followed, he glanced at the two sitting to his left.

Impossible!

He'd kept up with curia politics while in the East, especially with news of the creation and deaths of cardinals. Despite seeing multiple reports of his death in Tuscany the year before, beside him sat the senile Cardinal Leonardo Patrasso. To Patrasso's left sat Cardinal Giovanni da

Morrovalle, an irritable little man he'd known in Poitiers who'd reportedly died earlier in the year.

He swept his gaze across Orsini to the two sitting on the right. Farthest from him sat the politically astute Cardinal Landolfo Brancaccio, who'd been seen with Orsini often while in Poitiers. To Brancaccio's left sat Cardinal Gentile Portino da Montefiore, a quiet man who had supposedly traveled to Lucca, dispatched there after Patrasso's death.

In a flash, he understood. He'd learned of the increasing use of traveling look-alikes during the escalation of street warfare on the Italian Peninsula between Orsini and Colonna family factions, allowing actual cardinals to remain safe behind their walls. The man in Lucca now must be Montefiore's surrogate. And it must have been Patrasso's and Morrovalle's surrogates who had perished, requiring the true cardinals to remain hidden away somewhere within the palace from then on.

Orsini ended the short pause. "You bring unbelievers into a house of God!"

"These are his mamluk dogs?" asked a furious Morrovalle, pointing at each.

"What do they say?" asked the mercenary to Darcan's left, in Arabic.

"Use not that vile tongue in this house!" demanded Orsini.

All three mamluks hurled Arabic curses at the cardinals, pointing their blades at any who appeared ready to stand. Three cardinals shouted back—only Patrasso and Montefiore remained silent, looks of fear on their faces. Darcan realized only he understood all voices and that a violent outcome had become inevitable.

A strange comment from the mamluk to his left made him turn his head in that direction. The Muslim had his blade planted in the middle of a painting, a depiction of two archangels spreading their wings while wearing Byzantine military attire.

"Please, you cannot," said Darcan in Arabic, suddenly understanding.

The addition of his voice caused a momentary pause in the shouting.

The mamluk repeated his comment in Arabic: "Yes, I think they wish to be like the bird men they so admire . . ."

All three mercenaries wore devious smiles as two sheathed their scimitars, positioned themselves behind Patrasso and Morrovalle, then pulled them up to a standing position.

"Ambassador," said Orsini. "What did he say? What are they doing? Tell them to unhand the cardinals!"

"Please, do not," asked Darcan again in Arabic.

Neither cardinal being ushered knew what was happening. The senile Patrasso even had a smile on his face, earning him an amused smile from his escort.

With Morrovalle five feet away from the window to the left of Orsini's desk—a large opening filled with translucent linen supported by thin strips of lead—his forced march accelerated into a forced run, with Patrasso and his escort close behind. The mamluk behind placed his right hand in the small of Morrovalle's back to propel him up and over the three-foot-high sill and into the center of the window covering. The sudden fracture of the lead strips easily ripped out the linen, allowing Morrovalle to pass through, Patrasso a moment after.

Wind permeated the chamber, further contributing to the shocked expressions from the three remaining cardinals. The clatter of rain masked any sound of impacts on the cobblestone courtyard nine stories below.

One mamluk stood behind Orsini and Brancaccio, placing his scimitar's blade on a shoulder of whoever appeared more likely to stand. The two others took a screaming Cardinal Montefiore by the arms, dragged him around the table, and sent him through the taters of linen and lead strips.

Cardinal Brancaccio was the next to be sent into the rain above the courtyard. Thereafter, all three mercenaries locked eyes on Orsini.

"Cardinal Orsini must remain alive," pleaded Darcan in Arabic.

"For what reason?" asked the closest mamluk.

Orsini is the prime curia advocate for financial support of Cilicia's resistance to Mongol advances westward. Without him, papal funds would, at best, diminish, and at worst, cease. Would these men care? No.

The three again turned toward Orsini.

"He is our source of support in the East."

Another Muslim spoke. "Our missions for this man are done. You have said this yourself. All that remains is the ransom."

To his credit, Orsini appeared stoic. "Ambassador, what do they say?"

He ignored the question, responding instead to the mamluks. "Take the gold from this chamber, but let him live." He nodded toward Orsini. "I will convince him paying the ransom is just. More gold will then find its way to you in the future."

"We shall indeed take this gold," said the mercenary closest to the chest, "to free our brothers-in-arms put in danger by his missions . . ."

Another finished the thought. ". . . but leaving him alive is too much of a risk, regardless of future potential."

With these final words, they set themselves into motion dragging Orsini to the window.

Orsini put up much more of a fight. He planted his left foot on the sill and his right on the window frame. He kicked back far enough to turn and face his killers, but his knees soon buckled.

The instant before Orsini disappeared through the flapping strips of linen, Darcan saw something he found amazing—the cardinal grasped at the closest wrist and curled his fingers inside the leather vambrace surrounding it. Orsini's momentum forced the wearer of the leather wrist guard to follow him out the opening. The two remaining grabbed at any loose bit of clothing, desperately keeping their comrade from following Orsini to the cobblestones below.

Each had a precarious hold on a leather trouser leg, their bodies anchored against the sill. Darcan could only see the boots of the third mamluk. By his struggle, it seemed clear Orsini still had a grip on the vambrace. Through the sounds of wind and rain, he could hear muffled screams as the third mamluk's boots moved from side to side.

Finally, the kicking stopped. Both men inside peeked over the sill while maintaining their holds. Satisfied, they stood and pulled their comrade back inside.

He observed the third mamluk's broken nose, undoubtedly caused by slamming into the exterior stone below the window, and pondered a future without Cardinal Francesco Orsini. The defense of Armenian Cilicia against the Ilkhanate would be significantly weakened without the mercenaries funded by papal treasure. When Mongol leaders—men who had been slowly converting to Islam—realized this, Oljaitu Khan would undoubtedly take advantage. The Ilkhanate would expand into the kingdom, and Muslim rule would result. Any Christian left standing would blame his family, their unstable hold on power lost. His family would blame him—the ambassador to the pope who allowed papal support of the Armenian Kingdom of Cilicia to end.

CHAPTER 56

AUGUST 8, 4:55 P.M. GST

SRINAGAR, KASHMIR

They'd become lost in the sprawling streets of the old Khanyaar quarter, and Rick Lambert's patience neared its upper limit. "We've been here before."

"No . . . I see it ahead. Very small, just like the photos."

He followed Maria's gaze. She was right. They finally found the Roza Bal shrine, less than five minutes before its closing time, and their arranged meeting time with Raja Kichlu, a young English-speaking Sunni cleric.

He saw the fronting billboard, just like he'd seen online, announcing the ancient sage Yuz Asaf buried beside the Muslim holy man Mir Sayyid Naseeruddin.

At the small entrance stood a man in a tight white turban and gray robe.

"Imam Kichlu?" Lambert asked.

The young man nodded.

"I'm Richard Lambert. This is Maria Belloci." He began extending his hand. "Thank you for—"

The young Kashmiri cleric held up both his hands. "No need to thank me. I must follow orders from the Grand Imam."

For the next fifteen minutes, the reluctant curator explained the history of Roza Bal—its place in *The Story of Kashmir* published in 1747, the 1770 court case entitling its custodian to receive offerings, and the attempted desecrations during the Indo-Pakistani War of 1965.

Lambert couldn't help noticing a group of Ahmadis in the northwest corner during the young cleric's pontifications. They wore large, distinctive turbans and spoke among themselves.

He noticed Kichlu's silence the same instant he felt Maria touch his arm. Both stared at him.

"I asked if you had any questions thus far."

"What can you tell me about those who believe Jesus is buried here?"

The Imam sighed. "Being curator of the shrine requires my learning of Ahmadiyya Islam, but I am generally not comfortable describing the Ahmadi belief that Yuz Asaf is actually Jesus, Son of Mary. I will, however, make an exception since, being Westerners, you may be unaware that the theory of the Penultimate Prophet being buried anywhere on earth is blasphemous to Islam since He, like the Final Prophet Muhammad, ascended into heaven alive and remains alive there."

Lambert continued to ignore the young cleric's arrogance. "Thanks for exempting us."

He noticed Maria turn toward one of the tomb's pink window frames to hide a smile.

After another nod, the curator described the Ahmadiyya Muslim Community with even less exuberance—the foundation of the movement in Punjab near the end of the nineteenth century, the Sunni tolerance afforded them in the interests of peaceful coexistence, and the small pedestal they'd maintained in the northwest corner of the shrine.

Lambert again found himself distracted by the Ahmadis, this time with good reason—all had their eyes fixed on him. An elderly man with severe cataracts broke from their ranks and shuffled forward. Maria seemed to notice him when he was ten feet behind Kichlu. Only when the man stood directly beside Kichlu did the young cleric stop his English monologue and address the Ahmadi elder in Kashmiri.

The old Ahmadi entered into a conversation with Kichlu, his milky stare never leaving Lambert. After a few verbal exchanges, the Sunni curator checked his watch, then gestured the other Ahmadis toward the door. "They know the rules—they are not allowed after hours. They will be the first back when doors open."

Two other Ahmadis gently guided their elder to the door, his cloudy eyes settling on Lambert two more times before exiting.

Maria pointed to the door. "Who was he?"

"They call him their seer," Kichlu replied. "On certain days, they say he has a gift for looking *through* those reincarnated, seeing them in their former lives."

"Does this happen often?" Lambert asked.

The young cleric nodded. "From time to time."

He felt relieved, until he saw the thoughtful frown on Kichlu's face. "What?"

"What is strange . . . oh, never you mind."

"Please continue," Maria said.

"It is just . . . well, he normally confronts people with descriptions of quite ordinary lives: farmers, storekeepers, fishermen . . . normal people. I have never heard him describe anyone important: no kings, no queens, certainly not the founder of his sect . . ."

"Founder?" Lambert asked.

"Yes, quite strange . . ."

"I read that Mirza Ghulam Ahmad died in 1908, and I was born in 1976, so that doesn't really work out."

"As I understand reincarnation theory, the soul, once separated from the body, spends an *indeterminate* amount of time in what they call 'formland' before transmigration."

"Formland?" Lambert asked. "Sounds like the Limbo or Purgatory of Catholicism."

The Sunni shrugged. "In any case, you would have had to spend much more time there, since he did not refer to Mirza Ghulam Ahmad."

"But he founded of the Ahmadiyya Muslim Community, true?" Maria asked.

The Imam wobbled. "Yes, but the elder Ahmadis claim the original idea of Jesus traveling east with the so-called Saint Thomas Christians was brought to these lands during medieval times."

"Brought by whom?" Maria asked.

"Their tale describes a Templar escaping the persecution of his order."

Lambert found the Ahmadis unsettling to begin with, but now his skin crawled. He shared a glance with Maria.

She broke the short silence. "What is the pedestal you spoke of earlier?"

Kichlu swung his arm around toward the northwest corner and began a stroll in that direction. "Over a century ago, the Ahmadiyya requested a space here to display a symbol of their faith. Those before me were initially apprehensive, fearing they planned some elaborate shrine-within-a-shrine, something in conflict with Sunni Islam. But they desired only this."

The three stood before what appeared to be little more than a broom closet. Within the three-foot-wide by two-foot-deep alcove stood what appeared to be a miniature wooden lectern, its top surface tilted toward them, with a small rectangular indentation at its center.

Kichlu pointed at the notch. "A Roman gaming stone of some kind was stolen by a young Vatican researcher in the 1960s, after the fools spent weeks helping him with research."

"Why do the Ahmadis value the stone?" Maria asked.

The cleric shrugged. "They say it was from the time of Jesus, and was somehow related to their belief that He traveled here."

"How'd it get here?" Lambert asked.

"They claim it belonged to the exiled Templar who thought he had followed Jesus to Kashmir."

Lambert frowned. "If the stone was stolen over fifty years ago, why is the display pedestal still here?"

The young Sunni smiled. "The Ahmadis requested this pedestal remain, as a reminder of Christianity's duplicity. My predecessors shared their sentiment, so the space was allocated to them in perpetuity."

They looked down in silence. Lambert slowly lowered a hand into his pocket. He felt for what had become his good luck charm these last few weeks, knowing he would not retain it.

Kichlu took two steps back, prompting Lambert and Maria to turn and face him. "Do you have any further questions before I secure the shrine?"

Indeed, but not for you . . . Lambert shook his head. "No, but thanks for the tour."

The young cleric nodded, turned, and began sauntering toward the exit, droning on about other important Sunni shrines in the area.

Lambert stood shoulder to shoulder with Maria, their backs to the pedestal. He slid the Sorvacore domino from his pocket and into the notch behind him. He heard the telltale click of a perfect fit, then glanced to his side to see Maria smiling; she didn't need to look either.

Empty-handed, the two strode arm in arm toward Kichlu. Lambert leaned toward Maria. "I think we need a Kashmiri translator, and a few more days in Srinagar."

"Absolutely."

CHAPTER 57

OCTOBER 29, 1312

RUAD

"So, you grew up in a castle?" asked Rifat Kanaan incredulously.

Brim shook his head. "We called them preceptories."

Rifat had been pouting most of the afternoon. Brim understood he'd been hurt the month before by the knowledge that so much had been concealed from him. Brim and Shayla planned to sail back to Tortosa with little Malcolm before sunset. They strolled down the path to the repaired staging dock as the time of their departure neared. Rifat was starting to open up, helped along by the stern lecture Amira had given him earlier.

"I suppose you wore a white robe and swung a broadsword?"

Brim shook his head again. "Sergeants wore black. On Cyprus, I preferred a shorter Roman gladius when outside Kolossi grounds."

Rifat smirked, apparently unimpressed at Brim's attempt at humility.

"During most of my years at the London preceptory, I wore the simple brown cassock of a novice monk. I worked in the scriptorium translating Arabic and Greek documents into French and Latin."

Rifat turned his palms upward. "But your Arabic—you speak as if born to a learned Syrian family . . ."

"I was trained in the spoken language by elderly knights who'd lived most of their years in these lands."

His friend abruptly changed the subject. "After the viceroy's departure, how went your first meeting with Abdullah?"

Brim flinched. "Awkward, until he asked if I'd concealed my past to protect my family."

Rifat raised an eyebrow, waiting for more.

"I told him truthfully that was indeed the case." Earlier, in the garrison courtyard, Brim had described Abdullah's plans for the expedition to discover agricultural practices of India and China. "Shayla and I have spoken at length about Abdullah's offer—we have an opportunity to see the wonders described by Marco Polo."

"Who?" asked Rifat.

"A Venetian merchant who cowrote a travelogue of his journeys east while imprisoned in Genoa. I translated his book from French to Latin before leaving England."

"He is still a prisoner there?"

"No. The last I heard he'd returned home to Venice."

His friend looked to the sky for a moment. "Why could you never tell me of such things? You and your family had nothing to fear from me. Why not tell me the truth?"

"The truth is all I ever told you, my friend. But knowledge of Shayla's and my past, prior to fleeing Cyprus, would have served no purpose."

Rifat did not look convinced but changed the subject again. "All those years with the Order of the Temple of Solomon . . . how is it you had not become fanatical, like the others?"

While he'd known having to speak of such things was a key factor in deciding to censor his past, Brim felt no harm could come from answering his friend now, on the eve of traveling east. "I have learned of things that have shattered my faith in large-scale organized religion."

"What things?"

"You understand the Christian belief in Jesus? His death on the cross for the sins of mankind, His resurrection, and His ascension into heaven?"

"Of course," said Rifat. "Such was the reason the Christians brought their war here two centuries ago—to somehow save the Holy Land of Jesus from Islam."

Brim nodded. "In those early years, while excavating the Second Temple of Solomon under the Temple Mount, the order found a Roman scroll they soon began referring to as the Praximus Command. In it were commands for the pursuit, capture, and return of Jesus to Jerusalem, after his crucifixion survival and escape east."

After two or three seconds of thought, Rifat's eyes became wide and his mouth gaped. "Could this be true?"

"It matches the format of command scrolls uncovered elsewhere. The possibility of its authenticity formed the basis for the order's two-hundred-year leverage over the Roman Catholic Church, even prompting those in Rome to label it *Vectis Templi*—the Lever of the Temple."

"You have read this yourself?"

"I have."

"Where is it now?"

"Hidden from all other eyes."

"And now *you* travel east . . ."

Brim looked deep into his friend's eyes. "Accepting this mission east, we also have the chance to walk the path of the Saint Thomas Christians, possibly in the footsteps of Jesus Himself. We're not sure what, if anything, we can learn from such a journey, but we have agreed—we shall not waste such an opportunity."

They arrived at their boat. A crew rigged sail for their return to Tortosa. Brim watched Amira embrace Rifat. Shayla's left arm wrapped around him while she held little Malcolm with her right. All looked east in silence.

Of the oaths sworn to his wife, Brim Hastings knew it would be his unconditional love that would be tested during their journey. In this, he knew, he would find no difficulty.

ACKNOWLEDGMENTS

A debt of gratitude to Katherine Anderson, for taking a chance on a debut novelist, and to the Dark Ink Press team, especially eagle-eyed editor Emily Hakkinen, talented cover designer Melissa Volker, and innovative marketing director Sheena Macleod, for their tireless work bringing this book to life.

To Professor Malcolm Barber, the world's leading living expert on the Knights Templar. This book would not have been possible without the research encapsulated into his masterpiece *The Trial of the Templars* and his willingness to answer my follow-on questions.

To C.S. Lakin, whose editorial prowess and willingness to listen to my whining without rolling her eyes has made this book much sharper.

To critique partner Keith Fisher, who will never let me forget my potentially disastrous wrong-word error of "cleaver" instead of "clever."

To Robert W. Cabell and the Renton Writers Salon (especially Frank and Jo Adamson, Maggie Alva, John Criner, Lesley Hatch, India Susanne Holden, John Lovett, Dan Post, J. Nia Watson, and Rose Christine Yzaguirre) for their years of patience.

To James "Jimmy Jo" Allen and the Squak Valley Writers Group (especially Chris Coleman, Susannah Howell Coleman, Grant Hetherington, and Jenny Rackley) for their willingness to struggle through my early drafts.

Thanks for reading. If you enjoyed this book, please consider leaving an honest review.

DARK INK PRESS

Printed in Great Britain
by Amazon